PRAISE FOR JOY CASTRO

"Joy Castro's writing is like watching an Acapulco cliff diver. It takes my breath away every time."

—Sandra Cisneros, author of *The House on Mango Street*

"Funny, sexy, and transfixing, Joy Castro's *Flight Risk* is a meditation on love, marriage, art, family, womanhood—and therefore, life itself. Castro skillfully builds tension, and the slow intensity with which the plot's arc forms gives the novel its exquisite and powerful impact."

—Chigozie Obioma, author of the Booker-short-listed novel *An Orchestra of Minorities*

"Completely captivating. Part Patricia Highsmith, part *Mexican Gothic*, part Daphne du Maurier, Joy Castro's *Flight Risk* is my favorite kind of story: one in which an outsider, dodging and weaving among insiders, stirs up tension, intrigue, and suspicion. With raw energy and sharp storytelling, *Flight Risk* is a novel about light and shadow, and I found myself craving its every twist."

—Timothy Schaffert, author of *The Perfume Thief*

"From the stunning opening lines of Joy Castro's *Flight Risk*, we know we're in the hands of a master storyteller, and it held me captive until the final page. With writing so evocative I could taste her words, Castro has wrought a sharply observed love story with a social conscience—an investigation of class, family, and the many ways we get each other wrong."

—Jennifer Steil, author of *Exile Music*

Flight
Risk

ALSO BY JOY CASTRO

The Truth Book: A Memoir

Hell or High Water

Island of Bones: Essays

Nearer Home

How Winter Began

Flight Risk

A Novel

Joy Castro

LAKE UNION
PUBLISHING

Text copyright © 2021 by Joy Castro
All rights reserved.

Published by Lake Union Publishing, Seattle

www.apub.com

Amazon, the Amazon logo, and Lake Union Publishing are trademarks of Amazon.com, Inc., or its affiliates.

ISBN-13: 9781542031929
ISBN-10: 1542031923

Cover design by Micaela Alcaino

Printed in the United States of America

Darling

"And, if anyone tells you that you know nothing, and you are not nettled at it, then you may be sure that you have begun your business."

—Epictetus

HAPPILY EVER AFTER

In the Beginning

Pregnancy makes you tired, they say. It's the effort of making all those new cells, I suppose—those tiny, translucent organs—that consumes your energy at a bone-deep level. Every moment seems like a good time for a nap. Sofas beckon.

I've seen other women's sonograms: the small twin lungs, the dark heart beating. At night, I close my eyes and see them, those hummingbird hearts. A few breaths later, I'm dreaming: open grassland, oceans softly rocking.

Nothing we can manufacture with our hands or our brains is so delicate and intricate, yet it all unfolds without our thought or will. Week seven: a beating heart. Week nine: nipples, elbows. Week twenty-two: eyelashes. Your body, doing all that.

Whether you want it to or not.

They say exhaustion hovers just above you like a blanket, ready to drop, ready to smother all those things you thought were so important: your career, your household chores, your circle of friends, the yoga class that seemed so crucial at the time . . . Everything melts away. You're an incubator, nothing but, your body a traitor to all your old causes. Equal pay for equal work, environmental justice, safety on the streets: very nice, but all you really crave is sleep—endless, luxuriant bouts of afternoon sleep, stretched out on the bed in a long rhombus of warm sun.

You arrange your limbs for comfort. Slumber closes down over you like a drug. You dream of a baby gazing up from your arms, curls shining, eyes radiant with love.

Then you wake, gasping for breath.

The List

The legacy from my mother is seventeen things.

1. A small white house in the hills of West Virginia. The paint, fading even in my childhood, surely curls back now, peeling away in long crumbling strips, exposing bare wood to the elements. Home. The nest. The scene of the crime. No one lives there now except the wild things.

2. A craving for nicotine. I chew gum, fiddle with paper clips, gnaw ends of yellow pencils.

3. A thirst for hard liquor.

4. A taste for rough men. Hers were bikers and truckers. Mine were attorneys, surgeons, sons of wealthy families, boxers, men who owned boats. All self-declared masters of their various universes. They seemed powerful, bold, magnetic. Control is sexy, until it's not. Married now two years to Jon—a Darcy, a Knightley, a truly good man—I like to think I have outgrown this particular inheritance.

5. A hunger to run.

6. A taste for cheap food. Hamburger Helper. Kool-Aid. Oscar Mayer. Uniform slices of rubbery pink bologna, red-rimmed, smeared with mayonnaise, squashed between spongy white slices of bread. Tuna casserole made with cream of mushroom soup and gray canned peas, with potato chips crumbled on top. Heinz ketchup squeezed onto Kraft macaroni and cheese and stirred with a fork until orange.

In Jon's circle, such things aren't eaten. They're punch lines, the stuff of aghast remarks. I cook them alone in the kitchen at night, after he's fallen asleep, and eat standing up at the counter, staring out over the black lake.

7. A suspicion of the state and its services. Social workers. Police. Anyone who wants to help us.

8. Silence. What you don't say can't haunt you. Plead the Fifth.

9. A love of dark licorice, sweet like danger. In my childhood, it was an exotic treat, rare and expensive—a delicacy, a thing that miraculously appeared at Christmas and birthdays or in the pockets of the men my mother saw. I'm told the taste for licorice is hereditary. You like it or you don't.

10. My long-boned, capable hands. They can change a tire, build a table, twist stuck lids off jars. Break a limb.

11. A belief in ghosts.

12. A jumpy metabolism. Skittish. My friends here in Chicago often ask what diet I'm on (or, more quietly, which pill I take—and where can they get some?).

13. A fear of incarceration, whether by reason of insanity or crime.

14. A love of fairy tales. She used to read them to me at bedtime. I would touch the illustrations with my finger while her scratchy voice unspooled the tale.

15. A fear of children. Their messes. Their perpetual demands. Their softness. The terrible fragility of their bodies.

16. A tiredness, bedded down deep in my bones. Even before I was old enough to drink, I woke in the mornings exhausted, worn and bleak, thinking, *Another day?* An old woman inside a young girl. And in my mother's eyes: that same look.

17. Grief. Like an ocean. Like madness.

The Dinner Party

I'd said I would buy the flowers myself, but that's not how it worked out. The two phone calls waylaid me. After cooking all day and making the whole condo immaculate (napkins ironed, wine glasses polished), I had only half an hour left to shower and dress for dinner, so I called Jon and asked him to stop by the florist on his way home.

I didn't mention that I'd gotten a call from the prison warden back in West Virginia, a state I hadn't seen since I boarded a Greyhound at twenty-two. I didn't say my knees had buckled when I learned my mother had died in her cell, that I'd clutched the back of a sofa to stay upright. I didn't mention Aunt Della.

I just asked him to buy the flowers for me.

———

In the shower, I stood with my eyes closed and my hand on the gray Italian marble, hot water streaming down, replaying again the second phone call. I'd been standing in my studio, still numb from the warden's news, staring blankly at Lake Michigan. When my cell phone rang, I didn't recognize the number, but the area code was 304.

There was no hello.

"You heard about your momma, then." Aunt Della's voice, warm as weed killer. I sank into the rocking chair. We hadn't spoken in twenty years.

"Yes."

"You coming home for the funeral?"

Home. I looked down at my lap, where my hand twitched like a separate animal.

"You don't got to, Bel. We'll get her in the ground. We got our preacher coming to do the service. It's the decent thing."

"Decent."

"We got it all took care of. You don't got to worry."

"Thank you." A sense of relief stole through me. Then guilt. "It's really kind of you."

"It ain't *kind*, girl. It's family." A long silence hung over us. "You gonna stay up there where you're at?"

"I don't know yet."

"You don't know." I saw her hand fly to her ample hip, as I'd seen it do so many times in childhood. "Well, you ain't got much time to figure it out." The sour music of her voice. "Funeral's in five days."

"Five?" I thought of planes, renting a car, trying to explain it all to Jon.

"Just stay up there in your big city. We're getting it all took care of. You don't got to lift a finger."

"I just don't know yet. I'm not sure."

"Well, you need to get sure," she said. "You need to—"

Abruptly, I pulled the phone away from my face. I hung up and turned the ringer off.

Her number flashed again and again.

———

I was still damp, dressed in only a black lace bra and half slip, my toweled hair a pile of dark ringlets, when Jon arrived with his arms full of white peonies and cabbage roses—soft, white, curling petals on the verge of a blush, fodder for still lifes by Dutch masters.

"Oh, darling!" I threw my arms around his neck. "They're perfect."

But instead of laughing and tossing the flowers aside and kissing me in the old way, Jon drew back, stiff, and held out the bouquets. I took them, trying not to deflate as he glanced around, his expression flat. On the long mahogany table, our silver gleamed. The wedding china shone. The whole condo was sluiced with aromas on which I'd worked all day: slow-roasted pork with lime and garlic, yellow saffron rice, black beans with bay leaves. Creamy flan had been setting all night in the fridge. When the guests arrived, I'd fry up the bollos and sweet gold maduros—Magda's recipes.

Jon's gaze flicked over me. In his eyes, something warmed, and I felt shy and hopeful, standing there in lingerie.

He turned away. "You'd better do something with your hair," he said, his tone neutral, objective—the tone he'd use to pronounce a verdict on an ultrasound image or inferior wine. He left to go change.

I carried the armful of flowers to the kitchen. Over the sink, I clipped the green stems with a quick, angled efficiency. In the various porcelain pitchers I'd collected over the two years we'd been married—Rörstrand, Wedgwood, Rosenthal—I bunched the blossoms into low, fat arrangements.

But in my hand, the scissors shook.

———

Marrying rich isn't all it's cracked up to be. There are, shall we say, strains.

Rich people fetishize everything. They fetishize their food; they fetishize their drinks. They fetishize their clothes and cars and jewelry and where they go on vacation. Everything has to have a story—from their oak-aged single malt whiskey to the burled walnut on the dashboards of their cars to their signed and numbered turquoise bracelets made on real reservations by genuine certified Native Americans. At dinner parties, they sit around telling each other stories of their expensive shit.

They even have a word for it: *provenance*. Where did my lovely object come from? Is it pedigreed?

Where I grew up in West Virginia, no one could afford such concerns. The food came from the Kroger. When you were lucky, you got to take home big plain white boxes with black words in block letters— **CORN FLAKES**. Plain white cans: **KIDNEY BEANS**. Sacks of rice. Brand-name food was a rarity, fancy sugared cereal an indulgence. You were glad things existed in the cupboard, and you cooked them, and when your mother said, "Shut up and eat already, for Chrissakes," you did.

Folks ate what they could get: squirrel, groundhog, deer, ramps, morels, blackberries—anything they could shoot or trap or farm or forage or buy in bulk. Heating up a store-bought frozen pizza, we felt like kings.

Jon knows none of this. I've become a person my mother would not recognize, a person she would loathe. I've become this person who, after a day in my studio, whips up halibut fillets and haricots verts and roasted shallots, a person who knows which cult Italian sauvignon to pair them with, a person who can operate her husband's four-thousand-dollar espresso machine. (My crema's like silk.) A person who shops at Marlowe, where lovely chic women crouch at my feet in the fitting room, pinning every hem to perfection, and a wide drawer holds a file folder full of notes on my likes and dislikes and measurements, in case Jon wants to surprise me at Thanksgiving with a cashmere coat the color of oxblood. My underwear comes not in a three-pack from Walgreens, but in discreet little silk bags from Boston with handwritten notes on the boutique's stationery from a salesgirl named Justine.

Rich people fetishize even what they eschew, the food they cannot eat: it makes them special. Here in Chicago, having people over for dinner is a logistical feat. Some of our friends are gluten-free by choice, while others decline all refined sugar on principle; some are vegan and some merely ovo-lacto vegetarian; some won't consume palm oil because of the rainforests and tiger habitats. Some are on that paleo diet, while others are merely lactose intolerant. It takes a spreadsheet.

At breakfast, listening to me fret about the evening's menu, Jon lifted his glass of skim milk.

"Dairy deserves better," he said, mock-somber. "Acceptance, not tolerance."

I laughed agreeably.

It's the kind of joke he can—in every way—afford.

———

I fixed my hair, got dressed, slid lipstick on, and practiced my smile in the mirror. When the mantel clock chimed six, our guests arrived, and the concierge let everyone up. We greeted them in the foyer, a little clot of festivity, and chatted, making introductions: a surgeon and his tanned, blonde wife—Jon's contributions to the dinner party. Mine were Manhattan gallery owner Lark Svenson, rail-thin and pale as a cave fish, and her husband, a gently balding antiques appraiser. Smooth, short sheets of steel-colored silk poured from Lark's scalp, and her shoes looked like torture fetishes. I wanted her to carry my work.

More than anything, I wanted the pressure a deadline would bring if Lark scheduled an exhibition. What Jon didn't know—what no one knew—was that for months I'd produced nothing. I stayed up late at night alone in the studio, yes, but really just to curl in my rocking chair rereading Duras, Rhys, Colette, the only writers I could bear anymore, their prose heavy, lush, as if read through a dense fog. Life-battered women who drank too much and risked more. Their language fragmented. Abrupt cuts. Things left unsaid. In college, all the budding feminists in seminar cried, *Woolf, Woolf,* and I liked Woolf just fine, but there was a cushioned, forced-air feeling in her sentences that my ear couldn't stop detecting, an upholstered leisureliness in all her artfully veering clauses and qualifiers, the sheer length of them, their padded quality—precisely the kind of leisureliness I, too, had now, and felt sickened by, standing in my studio, staring at all the odd objects I'd magpied from the streets of Chicago (the sun-bleached spines of pigeons, small rusted springs, a torn strip of satin-backed mink) and chastising myself for the way I was stuck, frozen, unable to move, to *make*. I stood in my studio, waiting, holding objects up next to each other, waiting for a whisper or hum, waiting for my hands to tingle and itch in the old way. But no euphoric vision came.

Booking a gallery show in New York would, I hoped, scare me into work again, force my hands to twitch with the old electricity, make me lose track of time until a piece was finished. I needed a deadline—urgency, anxiety, desperation: all the familiar feelings that stability had dulled—and this dinner was my opportunity to woo Lark Svenson into giving me one. The brutal blades of her cheekbones: you could whet knives on them. My own cheeks had the soft curves of fruit, which gave me a sweet, nonthreatening prettiness entirely out of keeping with my inner world.

I detached myself from the doctor and his wife and followed Lark and her husband through the living room, dining room, library, trying not to hover.

Before a shadow box on the wall, they paused. Its frame was made from old barnwood hammered together with rusted nails. Inside, inches behind a sheet of plexiglass, hung the facsimile of an official-looking document, all Gothic script and signatures, the text nearly entirely obscured by a black fall of crushed anthracite that looked as if it had dropped from the ceiling of the box. At the bottom of the frame, half buried, lay two faded blue tickets to a county fair and a scrap of white tulle.

I felt slightly embarrassed: the piece seemed obvious, reductive. But I wanted to show Lark everything, anything that might possibly pique her interest.

The balding antiques appraiser leaned close, adjusting his glasses. "What's the paper?" he asked. "Some kind of proclamation?"

"A marriage certificate."

Lark turned to me. "And this is coal, I presume?"

I nodded, trying to recall the wording I'd used in my artist's statement. "The piece protests fossil-fuel extraction industries," I said, "and the way they destroy human connection." I didn't say my mother's husband, her girlhood love, had died in a mining explosion. That I'd gotten only what was left of her.

"Hmm," said Lark, tapping her fingers on the edge of an ebony console. "Provocative."

Slowly they drifted from piece to piece, perusing all my old tableaux, murmuring things to each other that I couldn't quite hear.

For long minutes, they bent over the sculpture of a labyrinth: the tiny living bonsai hedges I'd shaved into a maze; curled sawdust paths; a minuscule ball of thread, held by no one, wending its way toward the center, where a small square photograph, black and white, of a very young and very beautiful woman—smiling, blonde, vivid—was affixed under a thin layer of smoked glass.

The antiques appraiser craned over it. "You can't really make out her features."

Lark's gray eyes wandered over the ceiling. "The Minotaur, yes?" She turned and looked speculatively at me.

I nodded.

"But is she truly monstrous?" She looked back at the ceiling. "Or just trapped?" The left corner of her upper lip twitched.

With a rush of relief, I realized it was a smile.

———

"And you made all this yourself?" our guests exclaimed at dinner, raving over the food, but Jon didn't glow with pride the way he used to, and he didn't glance appreciatively at my dark-red dress, all lace and bro-cade, tailored to fit my form like a glove. The other husbands glanced, though. I counted the minutes until someone used the word *exotic* to compliment me. (It was a little game I liked to play, like waiting for women to say, "I do Zumba!" as if that made us sisters. People liked to ask where I was from, and the answer, West Virginia, always took them aback. "No, I mean—" *Yes, I know what you mean.*) "Delicious!" the surgeon's wife kept exclaiming, shaking her pretty blonde head.

Cooking everything myself was a point of pride—like doing my own flowers, polishing my own silver, and pressing crisp creases into the napkins, instead of just hiring one of Chicago's many upscale caterers to "handle it," as Helene, Jon's mother, liked to say. She'd urged me to use her own favorite caterer ("so elegant, so discreet") when I'd first moved to Chicago, freshly wedded, and begun entertaining on Jon's behalf. "You're a lovely girl," she said, taking my hand in both of hers and exuding a professional warmth, "and your cooking's very nice. Very nice, indeed." She smiled, but her eyes flicked up and down me like a feather duster. "Jon's set, though, dear. Our set. What can I say?" She shrugged prettily. "Not Jon, of course. Not me, not the family. But some of our acquaintances are—well, just used to different things."

Politely and repeatedly, I'd declined professional help. I liked having my hands in the muck of it, liked to lick sauces from the spoon, and in the beginning, Jon had never seemed to mind the mess, thumbing away the white smudge of flour from my cheekbone and kissing my mouth. He seemed to love it all: the bright colors, the messy kitchen, the Tito Puente and Celia Cruz played loud on the stereo after dinner, so that sometimes a guest would push back his chair and hold out a hand to his wife, and suddenly we'd all be up and dancing in the warm glow of the fireplace, laughing, the rug rolled back, the vast blackness outside and the tiny lights of boats dotting Lake Michigan a dark backdrop we'd only notice when the music stopped.

Our dinner parties were so different from the starched occasions we attended at the homes of Jon's society friends: classical music (or—for the daring—smooth jazz), conversation at subdued volumes about noncontroversial topics, black-frocked servers gliding in with pretty plates that left you hungry.

I remember one dinner party we threw early on, when we were still close. It was late. Our guests had gone.

"I don't know how you do it," he said, collapsing into an armchair by the fire, his forelock sweaty, his collar undone, his tie wrenched askew. His smile was open and free, like the smile of a boy. He pulled me down onto his lap and slid his hand up my leg.

I leaned into his kiss. "Do what?" The fire crackled, and the room was dark and warm around us.

He drew away and took my face in both his hands.

"You bring everyone back to life."

The breath slipped from my mouth. The room began to spin, and I felt my cheeks go cold. I blinked hard and tried not to sway.

"What?" Concern fresh in his eyes. "Baby, what is it?"

"Nothing." Smiled. Smiled smiled smiled, as brightly as I could. "Nothing." Kissed him hard to stop the buzzing of a thousand wasps.

———

I'd learned silence early.

"I know, baby. I know," Momma said, rocking me on her lap. I was in kindergarten. "You just got to keep drinking water. The pain'll pass."

My arms were wrapped around my middle.

"I know, baby," she kept saying. "I'm hungry, too."

This was before my mother realized the economic value of boyfriends. Later, she wised up, and things got, in a manner of speaking, better.

But in kindergarten, cramps bent me in half.

"Don't you tell Gran, you hear?" She rocked me back and forth. "And not your aunt Della, neither. I don't need no more of her bullshit. Okay?"

I nodded.

"You promise? You swear? Say it out loud."

"I swear," I whispered.

"Good girl." She stroked my hair.

Secrets were a thing I learned to keep. A thing entwined with hunger.

———

But it wasn't only prohibitions that kept me quiet. From an early age, I possessed the capacity to harbor a variety of observations and opinions without ever giving them voice. Indeed, uttering them led to two unpleasant consequences: a commotion in the outer world among adults or other children, to whose views my own seldom conformed, or a strange diminishment in the intensity of my thoughts once I'd spoken them aloud, as if the very act of verbalizing had watered them down somehow. I preferred my perceptions keen and mine. A self-sufficient silence became my code.

Besides, in my experience, much of what the talkative classes uttered was surprisingly vapid, given the advantages they enjoyed. I always tried to listen politely, but I was thinking, *You've gotten here. You have all this, yet these anecdotes are all you have to offer? These litanies of complaints, these tales of low-stakes woe?* Even their voices tended to sound flat and bored as they delivered staccato catalogs of mild travails. I've smiled and nodded a great deal now. Conversation among the well heeled was a highly overrated sport.

Jon and the other doctor were talking about investments. I poured more San Pellegrino.

———

There were days, even after I met Jon and fell so starrily in love, when it got hard and I'd feel the sinking.

I'd make the bed, take a shower, pick out a pretty dress, and put on lipstick. Do my hair. But all the brisk little feminine rituals of saying yes to life would fail, and I'd feel the riptide sucking me down. I'd think *Uh-oh*, and check the day of the month, and usually my period lurked about four days away, like an evil aunt casting her spell—a pall, a gray gloom that hung over everything. And I'd brew mug after mug of Saint-John's-wort, and work out more, and try to avoid Jon so I could avert his kind-eyed questions about whether or not I was okay.

But once in a while, it wouldn't be PMS, and I'd have to think through anniversaries—so many, they dot the calendar like land mines, waiting for an errant foot to fall.

Once I'd realized which one it was, I'd walk out into the streets of Chicago. I'd walk hard and blind as far as I could. If I cried, no one stopped me. They didn't even look at my face. I'd walk past huge stone buildings until my feet hurt and my mind was numb and I was so far away from home that the thought of walking back daunted me, and then I'd stop and sit down and put my face in my hands.

I'd sit there until I was empty. It was all I could do.

Then I'd call a cab.

———

Once in a very great while on the wide sidewalks of Chicago, I'd find two severed pigeon wings lying side by side. Gray and white, with blood-tinged feathers. As if a very small angel had shed them and walked on.

Hawks, a friend told me, were the culprits. Cooper's hawks, red-tailed hawks. Ruthless, practical beasts, they ate only the pigeons' bodies—the soft, tasty, fleshy parts—and dropped the wings to rot.

———

Dinner was going well. Lark was making a to-do about how *fasc*inating the work of surgeons was, asking Jon and his surgeon friend for gory details about retractors and scalpels. She turned to me. "Oh, you must do something with this! Just imagine, having such resources so close." She laid a hand on Jon's arm. "What about a series with surgical instruments? The body." She sipped her tempranillo. "By the way, what are you working on now?"

I gave the elevator speech—something quick and false and fashionable about the intersectionality of identity and resisting neoliberal capitalism. (*Nothing, nothing, nothing,* drummed my mind. *That's what I'm working on. Forgetting those phone calls. Keeping this smile on my face.*) Desperate to change the subject, I turned to Blonde Golf Wife and pulled out my best hostessy question, my dinner party standby for those moments when the conversation flags or grows uncomfortable.

"How did you two meet?"

Posed brightly across a table full of couples, it never fails. Inevitably, one member says, *Oh, you tell it,* but then interrupts to contradict or add details to the story they've told before, a performance piece, a polished thing shaped to reveal something endearing or clever that displays their good taste or the tumultuous passion of youth. Sometimes the story runs long, full of tedious details, and they break in to correct each other about things that don't matter, and you keep nodding and smiling, thinking, *Jesus, enough already,* which was the case with Blonde Golf Wife and her surgeon's love-tale about a holiday party at Lake Geneva.

When she, in turn, asked Jon and me for our origin story, we kept it short, as we always do. We looked at each other and smiled, but his smile was vacant, perfunctory, and his eyes looked just to the left of mine. I laid my hand on his with excessive gentleness, and he said, "We met at a wedding."

The blonde wife broke in then to say something about how perfectly romantic that was, and the balding antiques appraiser hinted something sly about the aphrodisiacal power of other people's nuptials, and we nodded and smiled and agreed, and that was it. Done and dusted. A hollow, public version.

———

The particular wedding where we met three years ago was held on an estate not far from Madison, Connecticut. It belonged to the bride's uncle, who had no children of his own and thus doted on his only niece. His estate had lakes, oaks, a gazebo, and large stables. Hacking paths ran through his woods.

The ceremony was held in the great hall of the mansion, its stone fireplace mantel higher than people's heads. I didn't know the bride. Mark, the groom, had been a friend from NYU. Long ago, when we'd been grad students, he'd asked me out, but when he kissed me good night on the stoop of my apartment, his lips conveyed nothing but an eager athleticism, and mine, I'm sure, quickly telegraphed boredom. We both knew better than to pursue it. But it was a shame: we liked the same movies and books, the same people, the same cheap Indian restaurants. So we stayed friends.

Eventually tiring of the city (and of trying to survive on the sales of his quirky woodblock prints), he entered law school at Yale, where he met Jessica, who worked in the library and had a trust fund, which seemed exotic to me, but not half as exotic as the smoked salmon and duck and bottomless champagne her uncle served at their reception, or the paintings—a Chagall, a Klee, a Miró—that hung casually on the walls of his mansion, where I very clearly did not belong. The powder room, where I lingered nervously alone to apply and blot lipstick, was a marvelous vast vault of gray marble and gilt-framed mirrors. On the counter sat stacked small, thick towels that you tossed into a basket when you were done.

All that wealth, all that warmth, all those families and couples and love only highlighted, as in a Cornell shadow box, the fact of my own loneliness. I was there, after all, by myself. My boyfriend of the moment, who did something vague on Wall Street and liked unconvincing light bondage and expensive Bordeaux, had a meeting in Frankfurt on the weekend of the wedding, or so he claimed. I'd begun to wonder about his weekends away, but without much interest. Fairly expert in bed—as any forty-year-old, good-looking, wealthy bachelor is obliged to be—he was fairly dull outside it, and our dates consisted of my nodding politely six hundred times while waiting to go back to my little apartment and fuck, where my dachshund, Button, would whine anxiously from the corner until we were done. I didn't like going to his apartment; it was too perfect, like a design-magazine layout. It made me nervous. I was afraid I'd break or spill something. At mine, he'd glanced around and laughed. "Like camping out," he'd said.

I hadn't minded when he'd said he'd miss the wedding. But once there, surrounded by all the giddy warmth and prosperity, I oscillated between feeling generously caught up in Mark's visible joy and wishing (with all the self-absorption of the sad) that I'd brought someone—anyone—to stand at my side so that I could appear, at least, less lonely than I felt. It sharpened into a familiar pain.

When the vows were finished, all the guests flowed out to the broad stone-paved veranda, where a band was warming up, and a few of us trickled down the steps to the lawn. I tried to move slowly, but my legs itched to run. As soon as it was socially acceptable—and I'm lenient with myself on this score—I began to drift across the grass. I looked back; no one seemed to notice my escape. My pace quickened, and I headed for the trees. Behind me, strains of "A String of Pearls" wafted across the meadow.

At the forest's edge, I found a companionable-looking oak and slipped out of my sandals, cool grass flattening under my feet. I wondered if I could still climb—*Settle down, Isabel; you're thirty-seven, after all*—but reaching for the lowest limbs, I felt my muscle memory click in and swung upward, grabbling at the bark with bare feet, levering my weight, pushing up over branches, pulling myself higher and higher into the cool evening air, away from the hot, thick atmosphere that had unsettled me, that quilt of love and ease and security that weren't mine.

At last, high up, I wedged myself into a solid crotch of wood, my knees to my chin, the hem of my floral dress a little torn.

Up there, a soft breeze blew, birds sang, and the air was fresh and leafy. I looked down. It was a manageable tableau: the veranda was only a faraway toy, the mansion a dollhouse, the people just tiny bright figurines. Wind rustled the leaves around me, and my breathing slowed. I closed my eyes. The important thing was not to cry.

———

I'd always needed to climb. From my earliest sojourns in the forest as a child, I searched out trees whose tempting boughs swung low, whose rough trunks had knobs and whorls my hands and feet could grip. Because I started so young, I was fearless, a monkey made of rubber. I fell, bounced, and jumped up to climb again.

A kind of urgency propelled me upward. A need to see, to hold the world at bay. Perilous height was a thing I craved: that moment when I'd pause, panting, where the branches' thinness finally would no longer bear my weight, and peer down through the green layers laced loosely like an afghan's crocheted yarn.

Up there, the wind was cooler, the leaf-smell fresher. Wedged in the arms of a massive maple or Canadian hemlock, I could see across whole Appalachian valleys. Birds swooped close, and hawks' cries pierced the air nearby.

In elementary school, before teachers yelled and paddled it out of me, I would climb onto desks, tables. I would stand up there and look down. It just felt more comfortable. To sit in a desk, confined to its low vantage point, made me restless and twitchy like the boys. I wanted to climb, to see.

Later, in high school, kids used the word *high* to describe the giddy, light feeling of freedom that pills or pot or huffed paint brought. I knew why. Perched high in a tree, lit by the fine thrill of danger and pride, I could see everything, but nothing could touch me. The world and its troubles were small, far away, intriguing yet drained of impact, like a script played on a distant stage. High in a tree, I was all-seeing, yet safe.

If that was the feeling the drugs brought, then even my mother made sense.

———

"Hallo!" came a voice from down on the grass of the grand Connecticut estate. I startled against the trunk. Far below stood a man, handsome and well built, with tousled chestnut curls. "Hallo!" he called up again. His voice was deep and cheerful. "I've come to fetch stray maidens! There's cake to be eaten. Champagne to be drunk."

I shook my head and tucked myself more firmly into the tree's broad branches.

"Dances to dance," he called, an invitational lilt in his voice. "Songs to be sung."

I stayed motionless, frowning down, willing him to leave.

———

A few weeks later, over morning coffee, my hand in his, I learned that Jon had first spotted me in the great hall during the ceremony as the Episcopalian priest droned on about fidelity and God. Moving through the receiving line, he'd been three people behind me, shaking hands and hugging the wedding party, trying to hurry. He'd been only an arm's length away on the veranda when a college friend had collared him. He'd kept his pleasantries perfunctory, but when he looked up, I'd disappeared. Ah, there, that flare in the distance: my floral dress.

Grabbing two glasses of champagne, he took off in pursuit, gulping Dutch courage. Nothing I could have said or done, he claimed, would have made him leave that tree without me.

"You're a bit of a romantic," I said.

I'd come out in my robe to the balcony of the hotel suite he'd taken in New York to be near me. The coffee sat in a silver pot on a silver tray, gleaming in the sun. Jon was sitting there in his pale-blue Egyptian-cotton boxers, smiling in the late-morning light, pouring cream. On his thighs, the curling hairs shone gold. I thought I'd never seen anyone so beautiful.

I sat down, reaching across the little wrought-iron table to lay my hand on his. His skin was smooth, the large, steady bones of his hand like stones under the warm skin of the earth.

"Last night," I said, looking down. I hesitated. Smiled. Shy. There was no way to describe it. "That was exceptionally nice." I didn't say it was the best I'd ever had, or the wildest, or the tenderest. The way he'd touched my face. Looked in my eyes. Made me gasp again and again, helpless with pleasure.

His hand swiveled under mine and caught my fingertips, raised them to his lips. Looking into my eyes, he nodded.

And that was it, really: the only explicit acknowledgment, ever, of the extraordinary luck and ease we'd stumbled upon.

———

I spent two nights in a row in his hotel bed, dashing back to my small apartment in East Harlem only to feed and walk Button. On the third day, I let Jon come with me, and he lifted her into his arms, where she wriggled with delight. He scratched her head, her ears, the base of her spine.

"You know dogs," I said. He smiled.

On the third night, I didn't want to leave him. I fell asleep with my head on his chest, nestled into the hollow of his body, his arm around me. His heart thudded under my ear. Inside me, something new began: a deep, safe hum. Our chests rose and fell together in the dark.

"Isabel." His voice was low, almost inaudible. "This feels—different."

Breath eased out of me in a long, slow release.

———

On that first morning, on the balcony, when I accused him of being a romantic, he nodded.

"A bit," he agreed. His blue eyes were so dark and warm I had to look away.

"What a view," I said, pretending to care about Central Park.

———

Jon remained a good and generous lover. While other women my age got hot and bothered over twinkling stalker-vampires and mommy porn, I preferred Jon's brand of sexiness, steady and true—the sort I liked to imagine animated the postnuptial nights of Jane Austen's decorous heroines: couples who behaved like responsible adults in public but privately indulged in secret ecstasies that stayed unmentioned. Her discreet puns: Knightley. Nightly.

That's how it was between us: a pleasure that spilled into genuine kindness. Could he fill my car with gas? Was there anything at the store I could pick up for him? A hand on a shoulder, a hand on a waist, a long look. Dusk. Dinner. Then bed again.

It built up layer after layer around us, like a thick, springy cushion that couldn't be pierced by the slings and arrows of anything.

Or so I'd thought.

———

I couldn't have known all that when I peered down through the oak branches at him, my throat still aching from staved-off tears of loneliness. I didn't know he was a doctor—*Killer catch!* as my college roommates would have said—or loved to read, or owned a rescue greyhound named Tilly who padded silently around his apartment after him and curled up on the floor where he settled. I didn't know that watching him toss his sisters' children in the air in Santa Monica and Portland would one day make me sob alone into hotel pillows in both cities. I didn't know he'd propose to me in the quietest of ways, with no audience and no ring, in his parked car in the rain, laying a hand on mine and saying, "Marry me."

At the edge of the forest of the grand Connecticut estate, I just saw a handsome stranger, bending to untie his shoes and roll off his socks. He pulled himself up to the first big limb and found his footing. Steady and sure. He reached for another branch. He was coming for me.

A tremor convulsed my hands into sudden fists, and a chill swept up my neck. It wasn't fear, or the intimation of sex—I knew what those felt like. Too well. This was new, something different, something bigger, like knowledge or fate or doom. Like faith. Like the Red Sea parting, and you're supposed to step out onto the still-damp sand on the promise that those walls of water won't collapse and drown you.

Like trust.

Not my strongest suit.

———

At dinner with Lark Svenson and her balding husband and the surgeon and his bright, blonde wife, no one asked us anything further about the wedding where we met, and the chat turned to golf and art as it grew late, and what a single-payer system would mean for physicians' incomes—and did you know there's a show online where you can watch real people at Walmart wearing clothes so terrible it's hilarious? I tried not to visibly flinch.

———

Already it has become difficult to recall that, once upon a time, we grew up severed from the broad world and its knowledge, restricted to our local sources: town newspapers, an hour of television news in the evening, the books in the local library, the things our teachers taught us. Now children leap onto the internet before they can even read, and politically tailored news runs on multiple stations twenty-four hours a day. We carry devices that let us check our symptoms with the Mayo Clinic and find the best restaurants within a ten-mile radius.

At dinner parties now, if someone asks the name of the impoverished young shooter who triggered World War I, people dip for their cell phones. It's a ripple around the table, like fans doing the wave in an arena. No one needs to go into another room for an encyclopedia, much less rely on mere memory.

"I think it was a Bosnian," said the surgeon.

"No, a Serb," said Lark, still rummaging in her handbag.

"Gavrilo Princip!" cried the antiques appraiser, triumphant, holding his phone aloft. "And he was a Bosnian Serb, so you're both right." And then everyone got back to the discussion of poverty and terrorism, having neatly nailed down that fact.

We can do that now, about anything. Our curiosity crosses time and space. Our thumbs open epochs.

But in the West Virginia of my childhood, knowledge was a limited thing, scarce, like groceries or gas money, which made it—for me—a commodity to covet and crave. I became a good student as the years went by.

Unfortunately, the kind of information I needed was not available in the libraries of any of the schools I attended. The topic was taboo.

Clinical studies of mothers like mine did not abound, at least not at the YA level.

The university library—when I finally got to Morgantown—seemed vast, unimaginable, its rows of stacks a labyrinth. Even so, the relevant books filled only one small section of a shelf. Perhaps it was a topic few scholars wanted to research.

What I learned in those books consoled and confused me. My mother, according to the psychologists, was not a monster. Or at least, not a monster born, but a monster made, warped by poverty, isolation, economic hopelessness, the tragic patterns of her childhood, et cetera . . . and alcohol, addiction, the way men treated her and taught her to see herself.

It didn't quite add up. We'd been poor, yes, and my grandmother was a brusque woman, but not unkind. I hadn't known my grandfather; perhaps he was worse. But if so, my mother kept that secret well. Yes, she'd lacked an education, and she'd suffered the early loss of her husband, but she had friends from the factory floor—raw-boned, raucous women who sometimes sat at our yellow kitchen table pouring whiskey into their coffee, their lashes spiked with black, their laughter graveled by a thousand cigarettes, cackling uproariously at the bold, rude things that came out of their mouths. My mother didn't quite fit the profile of social isolation. And her boyfriends—well, there were many, true, and I knew some of them cheated. But I didn't recall them beating her or hurting her, and those would have been hard secrets to keep in a house as small as ours.

At the sparkling dinner table, talk had turned to my work again.

"The timing couldn't be more fortuitous, you know," said the antiques appraiser, smiling at me. "Lark's been looking for some outsider artists."

Lark coughed discreetly. "Darling," she said. "We use the term *outlier* now."

"Oh, yes? Well, outlier, outsider, what have you . . ." He raised his finger and took a sip of wine. "It's an interesting thing, don't you know. Most of the brilliant outsider artists of Latin America and Europe were mentally ill. They drew fantastical things on paper to while away their days in institutions. But here in America, outsider artists have usually been poor rural whites or people of color who can't afford to leave their communities. They've often made things out of junk. Bottle caps. Car parts. That kind of thing."

"They can certainly be eccentric," Lark agreed. "And it's not at all a well-heeled crowd."

Well-heeled, well-heeled. I hated that phrase. Like *down at heel,* which I first tripped over in college—a course on Dickens, I think— as if everyone grew up automatically knowing that their shoes, of all things, would be used to judge their true character and worth—or as if, even knowing that such an absurd ranking system existed, all people would have the time and resources to respond, assiduously polishing away all evidence of labor, wear, and the outdoors.

"But what does that mean, technically?" asked the surgeon. "Outsider? I mean, aren't all artists kind of . . . I don't know"—he chuckled—"outside? In some fundamental way? Absinthe, suicide, cutting off their ears and all that." His wife tittered obligingly. "Outside ordinary society, outside the mainstream, outside ordinary norms."

I wondered if I should go actually, literally, outside, so they could talk more freely.

"Historically," said Lark, "outlier artists have simply had no exposure to the artistic tradition. They haven't had access to a proper education, art school, the art world."

I thought back to NYU. Art school had been a misery: well-meaning white professors asking if I knew the work of Mexican artist Frida Kahlo and suggesting that perhaps I should try producing something like it—whatever that meant. Portraits of myself, resolute and furious, next to a sad monkey? Paint wasn't even my medium.

"I prefer the term *outlaw*," I said.

For a moment, silence reigned over the table, and then Jon's brow rose, and he smiled. The surgeon and the balding antiques appraiser threw back their heads and roared with laughter. The other guests laughed, too.

Jon had always liked this me, the brash one who talked back. Why couldn't I conjure her up more often? His cold moods silenced me, shook my confidence, drove me inward, underground. Silence, exile, a cave of one's own.

Lark pursed her lips and squinted. "There's something so haunting about your pieces—beautifully wrought, yet macabre. Almost frightening. Like that mobile, which recalls Calder—but so small, so light, so fragile."

Chewing, her husband nodded. A scraggle of dark hairs on his Adam's apple bobbed when he swallowed. "The opposite of massive," he agreed.

Lark turned to me. "Those bleached pieces of a skeleton—what was that?"

"The bones of a dove," I said.

"Ah, yes. I see." She smiled. "Counterbalanced by those pink plastic barrettes, the kind a child would choose. All pink and white, delicate, floating—"

"But so disturbing, that juxtaposition," said her husband. "Childlike innocence and death. A kind of fairy-tale hideousness."

In the corner of my eye, Jon sat silently, watching them.

"Yet aesthetically so perfect," said Lark. "So deceptively lovely. There's such a visual glossiness to it all, such a polish—"

"A high sheen," her husband put in.

"Yes. Just so," she said. "It feels accessible, inviting, crafted for the pleasure of the viewer. You keep looking, drawn in by the beauty, thinking you'll understand." Her eyes roved over me, appraising, approving. "But you don't. Not quite."

"Or at all." Jon shoved a gold slice of plantain around with his fork.

"Well, well!" Lark swiveled toward him, her thin brows aloft.

Jon's eyes lifted from his plate, and he wore his public face once more. He smiled his social smile. "I have a brilliant wife."

Our guests murmured polite assent, and talk turned, blessedly, away from my work and on to some impending Sotheby's event, but I thought Jon's locution odd. Not *Her work is brilliant*, or even—if he felt compelled to stake a claim of ownership—*My wife is brilliant*, but rather a doubled kind of containment: *I have a brilliant wife*. Static, as if I were just his object, his possession—as if obtaining me were something he'd accomplished, something that reflected on him.

Quit being so goddamn sensitive: my mother's voice, echoing in my head. It was true. I scrutinized everything, chewed on each detail. I was lucky to love a man who called my work brilliant. How many husbands did that?

I rose, folding and smoothing my napkin onto my chair. "Who'd like dessert?"

———

Once the plates and spoons had been distributed, the espressos had been made, the first bites had been taken, and the exclamations over the flan's perfect smooth dense sweetness had died down, the antiques appraiser turned my way again.

"I mean, that Minotaur piece—truly striking."

Beside him, Lark nodded. "Devastating."

"But isn't it a bit odd, though," he pressed, "for you, as a Latin, to allude to Greek myth in your work, rather than drawing upon something more—I don't know—culturally authentic? Something Aztec, perhaps? Incan or Mayan or something?"

I could feel the tiniest twitching of muscles above my left eye. *As a Latin*. I made myself blink the slow blink of calm.

"Oh, I don't know." I tried to keep my shrug and tone light. *Isabel Morales, you want that show.* I wanted a regular gallery in New York. "My whole education insisted that your stories *were* my stories. That Greek and Roman and European and English and white American narratives were the only ones that mattered. The only ones at all, really." I made myself smile, and I made it look genuine. "So I feel no compunction about stealing them now."

I rose and moved toward the stereo, glancing at Jon, hoping he'd smile again, hoping he'd give a nod and there would be dancing, but he frowned and gave his head a little shake and said something apologetic to the table about an unfortunate early meeting at the clinic the next day.

Everyone gradually left, murmuring good-guest effusions about the food and the view. Jon flicked the stereo off, and then it was just the two of us alone in the dark. There was no sitting by the fire. No being pulled down onto Jon's lap. He cleared the table with me and then stood by the windows, staring out at the dark lake.

I didn't say that I was lonely, or that his distance hurt. I didn't say a word. Jon went off silently to bed, and I made no move to speak or stop him. In the dim-lit kitchen, I rinsed off uneaten morsels and smears of sauce and loaded the dishwasher alone.

Correspondence

The next morning found me in the bathroom, retching. The gray marble was cool under my hand as the room heaved around me.

Jon knocked. "Isabel?" His worried voice. "Everything all right?"

"I'm fine." Gripping the windowsill, I focused on the flat horizon of the lake and willed the bathroom to hold still.

By the time I came out—teeth brushed, curls tamped down with a wet hand, robe pulled tightly around me—his concern had faded, and he was lacing his running shoes. His cool, analytical gaze was back, and he looked up skeptically.

"Did you drink too much last night?"

I looked at him, my lashes still damp from the sheer force of vomiting. I hadn't drunk anything but water with dinner. He hadn't noticed.

"Maybe," I said.

He left for his run.

———

When Jon first started to talk seriously about having a child, a month or so after we married, I thought laughter would bark out of me, short and sharp. I thought my lips would tuck and curl with scorn.

Instead a softness started low in my belly and spread. Molten. Gold. Like the crack-an-egg thing kids do on your head.

When I could finally speak, my voice was husky, strange to me. I tried to sound wry. "You're aware I'm past my prime for that kind of thing." I patted my abdomen, thinking of my age, of all the viscera inside slowly winding down.

He shook his head. "Thirty-eight? You've got plenty of time." He grinned, his unspoken cliché hanging in the air between us: *Trust me, I'm a doctor.* His eyes grew serious, and he took my hands in both of his. "But we should try. Soon."

Jon didn't know my background. He didn't know what he was asking. He'd just made the reasonable assumption that, like most women, I wanted a child.

His face was open, full of hope and love.

My eyes grew hot and watery, and I nodded.

Only later did I start to feel afraid.

———

Alone in the condo, I made coffee and thought about phoning Saqlain. I hadn't seen him since well before my wedding, but there had been a time—in my twenties, when I'd been entirely alone in the world—when Saqlain had guided almost my every move. His advice, though brutal, had always been sound—a harbor, if not exactly safe. I curled with my warm mug in a chair by the bedroom window, wrapped in my bathrobe, watching the bright, chilly sky lighten over the lake, the washes of austere blue.

What does Jon say? Saqlain would ask, his voice the same as ever—a deep, rough timbre, clipped prep-school syllables.

He wants one. I took a sip of coffee and stared out at Lake Michigan. *But he doesn't know. I haven't said anything. I haven't even done a home test yet.*

Saqlain would chuckle. He'd always enjoyed a good deception. When we'd met, I'd been a despairing art-school dropout, but he'd already been the chief risk officer of a bank with branches in Beijing and Dubai. Now, a steady string of successes later, running his own consulting firm, he discreetly declined to name the multinational banks that were his clients.

A baby will ruin your art, he'd say. He'd said it before. *Trust me, Isabel. I've seen it again and again. Bright, talented women. They have their first child, and that's it. They start going to baby exercise classes and putting organic vegetables in the blender. C'est ridicule. Oh, there are exceptions. A few continue to work, to make their art, to thrive. But do you think you're one of them? Do you really think you're that strong?*

I didn't know how strong I was. He didn't actually know French.

I could imagine what he'd say. *A beautiful woman with a beautiful body. Why would you want to destroy that? For what? A mewling, puking little monster? God, what they do to the tits.*

Outside, snow began to fall. Once, long ago, I had taken Saqlain seriously. He was older; he knew the world. I had trusted him precisely because he never pulled a punch—like a Neil LaBute play, a cruel glimpse behind the curtain of how men really see women, which everyone pretended wasn't there. I'd been relieved to hear the merciless truth.

And children ruin marriages, let's not forget. You were so happy to find that husband of yours, what's his name, Jon, the doctor. Will you be happy in a house full of brats in the suburbs?

I imagined him rambling on.

With Jon and his family, with my art-world connections, I performed only the self I'd selected and polished, the self I wanted to be: Fake it till you make it. And I kept waiting to make it, and it kept not happening. (Success, renown: They would have happened by now, wouldn't they? If they were going to happen?) But Saqlain knew me. He'd mentored me, bossed me, rescued me, ruined me. *Bad idea, bad idea,* I told myself, my finger hovering over his number—and I didn't dial. But I wanted the sound of his voice so badly, telling me what to do—like a child craving her security blanket, a junkie needing her fix.

Think of the political angle, he'd say. *You're always going on about the environment, no? Well, it's a warming planet. An overpopulated planet. A violent planet.*

I knew all that. I thought about it every day.

And why so urgent? His voice would take on that pseudo-avuncular tone, the one that had lured me once upon a time when I was young, a country mouse in a metropolis. *You have everything you need, everything you want. Why wreck it all? Why now?*

I stood up, restless, haunted by the warden's phone call, the image of my mother's body in her cell.

You wanted to make art? Well. Now you do. But I wasn't producing. *You wanted to marry the doctor? You married him.* But now he was distant, withdrawn. *Why risk your whole life for a baby?*

I knew what Saqlain would say. He analyzed risk for a living. His wallet held credit cards made of palladium, of gold. *Don't do it. Don't have the child. Don't even think about it. Do the math, Isabel. It's the most fundamental investment strategy of all—*

I placed my hand on the flat of my belly and stared at the snow falling into the lake. The front door of the condo opened and shut: Jon, home from his workout.

"I know, I know," I muttered aloud. Saqlain had lectured me so often, I knew the punch line by heart: "Never risk what you can't afford to lose."

Jon walked into the bedroom, pulling off his sweatshirt. He paused on his way to the shower and turned to look at me. I still held the phone in my hand.

"Someone interesting?"

No one. Myself. A ghost. I cleared my throat. "Lark. We were talking about dates."

"Lark?"

"Svenson. From last night. The one who owns the gallery. She might want to show my work."

"Oh. Great." His smile looked vague. An effort.

"I guess so."

Impatience tapped the corner of his mouth. "That's why you invited her, isn't it? That's what you wanted, right?"

I didn't know what I wanted.

"Yes," I said, so he'd stop asking.

———

I'd never been one to hanker for a child. *Hanker*: a good West Virginian word, an old-woman word, the kind my aunt and grandmother used. *Hanker. Reckon. Holler* as a noun (a valley, the hollow between hills). *I reckon I'll head down the holler; I've got a hankering for some ramps.* (Wild onions dug from the forest floor, crusted with dark dirt.) When a child behaved in ways too big for her britches, they'd say she'd gotten "a mite osterpatious," a word I carefully memorized that never showed up on the SAT.

Anyway, I never hankered for a child, much less reckoned on having one.

One of my earliest shows, in fact, featured my preference. A beautiful old-fashioned pram, lush with linens, had no baby nestled inside. Instead, I'd tucked between the hand-embroidered sheets a lovely old leather-bound book, its spine embossed, its pages edged with gilt. The symbolism was clear: stories, not babies, would be my offspring. Art. A collector snapped it up.

It was a beautiful show: *Nature v. Culture*, that old dichotomous formula I'd learned in college, agonistic, like male v. female, or Art v. Life, always two boxers squaring off for a fight. But inside the little *v* for *versus*, I'd bedded moss and twigs, filling in the space until it looked like a green heart beating. Nature [Heart icon TK] Culture.

In addition to baby buggies full of books, the show included antique oak bureaus, their drawers standing open, spilling thyme and ivy, green leaves tumbling over tarnished brass pulls. One huge book—an atlas I'd found at an antiquarian bookshop—stood up, open, its innards carved away. Inside, I'd built a miniature forest out of real twigs, tiny leaves (glossed green forever with fixative), and backdrops of painted, layered tissue that deepened into darkness.

A forest inside a book. A book inside a baby carriage.

A mound of dirt at the bottom of a claw-foot tub.

It began as just a habit of mine in college, making things with my hands when I was jittery, when I couldn't settle, when memories stalked me like a hound. I prowled estate sales and Goodwills for objects that evoked some murmur inside me—that made me want to put my hands on them, like a man you've just met but know you must touch. I'd buy them cheap and take them home and look at them awhile. Did they need refinishing? Stripping? A pattern of black lace inked up their tan legs? Once the decision was made, then the slow, patient labor—the silence and solitude, my hands moving with their own quiet purpose—is what let the peace come back, the way animals slip out from between the trees when everything falls quiet.

The finished pieces stood around my various apartments until friends admired them and I gave them away. To me, they were just a way to coax myself through bouts of nerves in college and art school, where such things weren't taken seriously. Then I dropped out and got the job in the gallery, and Saqlain came along, with all his contacts and worldly knowledge. Our arrangement lasted for seven years, during which I was left to develop my skills and vision as I pleased, working in utter isolation, informed only by my solo trips to museums and the heavy coffee-table books full of color plates I checked out of the public library. I poured out my exquisite, ruined soul—as I thought of it in my twenties, as one does—into objects no one wanted. Unsatisfied, I hauled them down to the dumpsters. And I grew. After Saqlain, slowly, my work began to take off, and eventually I did well—hardly a darling of the New York art world, but eking out a living no more or less precarious than most. I didn't have to wait tables anymore, or do any other kind of paid labor; I was independent, a working artist. I lived in a two-hundred-square-foot studio with Button and felt lucky.

Everything changes when you marry a doctor who comes from money. Sometimes you have to entertain, and the people you entertain are rich. Sometimes their spouses are serious collectors. They make admiring noises about the odd objects tucked in nooks around your home, and one thing leads to another.

Life astonishes me.

When I was a girl at college in Morgantown, I read the used copies of *Vogue* other girls left in the dorm lounge. I mean really *read* them, the way I studied my textbooks—especially the profiles of clothing designers, jewelry designers, and interior decorators. The workers. The makers. Though the photographs of their work sometimes seemed oddly underwhelming, I was awed by the trajectories. I knew what it would have taken, for example, for my second cousin Elsie, who hand-stitched custom-fit clothes for herself and her friends, to suddenly open her own boutique in Paris: a miracle. So I assumed those elegant women in *Vogue* had talent far beyond the people I knew back home, and that they had worked terribly hard, day and night, to succeed. I admired them and their textiles brought back from Morocco. I would think of the extraordinary, mysterious difficulties of planning such a trip. (You would need a passport, for one thing. How did one procure a passport? I had no idea. No one I knew had one. Several adults I knew back home didn't have driver's licenses.) It would be years yet before I met people who jetted in and out of countries with less trepidation than I'd felt boarding the subway for the first time.

It was only much later that those country-girl scales fell from my eyes. At NYU, I began to edge into a world where people were children of the rich and well connected, where young people could afford to take unpaid internships at museums and design firms because their parents bankrolled them, where daddies cut their daughters hundred-thousand-dollar checks for start-up funds. (And when that idea failed, another check.) What shocked me was the ease of it—bright, pretty, rich people being excited about each other's projects.

Now that I'm on the other side, I see how simple it all is: wealthy friends murmur some enthusiastic words to each other, and suddenly events are born. Two weeks ago, Jon and I sat at a sparkling table—him in a tux and sapphire cuff links, me in a backless blue silk gown—and listened to a speech about spina bifida while we ate roast duck with caramelized mango and small purple potatoes. Five thousand dollars a plate, it cost. Then everyone stood around chatting, glowing with this wonderful thing we'd done.

I knew better than to say anything about it to Jon in the car on the way home. That's his world. He comes from it. Its assumptions are his, and I've got no more right to criticize his people than he would have to mock mine if he knew them. I tell myself this, again and again. If Jon's doctor friends want to compare notes on Scottish golf courses, it's none of my affair.

The upshot of it all? I learned that breaking into a scene (art, music, publishing, film) wasn't really all that difficult for the rich and well connected. And now I had the benefit of being both.

For my shows, which took place in a nice little Chicago gallery on West 35th, I priced the pieces this way: I took the cost of all the materials (I kept a ledger) and added it to my hourly wage (I kept a log). Then I multiplied the total. By ten.

And collectors do not even blink. It is the grandest joke. A twenty-piece show, even after the gallery takes its cut, leaves me with enough money to live (frugally) for a year.

Jon used to be proud of me, intrigued, fascinated by each piece, its intricacy and mystery. He would ask me questions—smart, genuine questions—and listen to my halting answers as I groped for words to describe what came to me in dreams.

But that was before.

"Pin money," he laughs now, his eyes the cool faraway blue of glaciers.

———

While Jon showered, I pulled Aunt Della's most recent letter from the locked wooden box in the drawer of my nightstand: spiral notebook paper, torn like confetti down the left side, creased hard and stuffed in a white business envelope.

Our dear Bel, it began, in firm pencil, the sharp slopes of her cursive denting the page. *Wondering how you been doing, we all hope you are well. You could write more often, that would be nice. Not much going on here. Billy is fine, his kids still growing like weeds. Social security don't go far so Billy helps us out. Not that you'd care about that, living your fine life up there in the city. Your uncle Frank is fine, too, just sits around watching TV now with his leg so bad and of course still the black lung. Team's not doing so good this year so he's not happy.* She meant football at the local high school.

Aunt Della's clockwork letters arrived once a month. I should have felt grateful, but I always slid a nervous finger under the flap. Usually it was banal, benign: who got married, who had kids. Sometimes it was sad but remote: an accident down the mine that killed three boys I'd gone to school with (but couldn't really recall), another local store that folded, a mining spill in one of the rivers.

Take care now.

I refolded the letter and slid it back into its paper sheath, into the box.

I pulled out an older letter in a different hand, frail and crinkled with years. I held the envelope: thin, cheap paper, the blue ink faded. There at the center was my name above my aunt's address in Mercer, where I'd gone to live when the cops had come, and there in the upper corner was my mother's name, her assigned number, and the address of the West Virginia state penitentiary for women.

I slid the letter delicately from its envelope, holding it in my fingers, reading the paragraphs I knew by heart until I got to the last line's promise: *And all your troubles will be swept away.*

In prison, she'd gotten clean and immediately gotten Jesus, and the letter was full of exhortations to trust on the Lord. At fourteen, having been raised by my mother and her assortment of drive-by boyfriends, I had my doubts.

I folded her letter back up, sliding my finger along creases she pressed there decades ago.

———

Jon came out of the bathroom, toweling his hair. He dressed and left for work, each of us calling the half-hearted farewells that had, months ago, replaced our kiss good-bye. Alone, at loose ends, I wandered from room to room.

When our realtor first brought us to look at the condominium, just before we married, I'd stood dumbstruck, staring out at Lake Michigan from the thirtieth floor. Glass ran from our feet to the ceiling, spanning the wide living room.

Behind me, as if from a great distance, I heard the realtor say, "As you can see, it overlooks the shed."

I peered down. With this enormous view—blue lake, blue sky, vast—why would anyone care about a shed?

But then I realized. The Shedd Aquarium, she'd meant. Of course.

"And you can walk to shopping," she continued. "The Magnificent Mile."

Sure. Shopping. And I could walk to the Art Institute, or jog alongside the lake in the morning if I wanted. Didn't Oprah have a place around here? It was a cool glass aerie—the suite at the Plaza in *Gatsby*, the Drayton's roof in *Passing*, a beautiful sanctuary high above the sweat and toil of the madding crowd.

The realtor toured us through the building's amenities: the coffee shop/deli/wine bar, the eco-friendly dry cleaners, the fully equipped gym, the dog-run terrace on three, the indoor pool on five. The twenty-four-hour doorman-concierge.

Jon loved it. He asked when we could sign the papers.

Myself, I couldn't stop laughing. In wonderment. In disbelief.

———

As a child in West Virginia, I ran wild in the forested mountains. I left the house when I pleased and came back at dusk's dark tail.

My mother never asked what I did alone in the woods all day. Now, her behavior would be called neglect, but at the time, I relished the solitude and psychological privacy that her utter lack of curiosity afforded me. I never had to explain the games that might come to feel foolish in the telling: Narnia, voicing all the characters in turn; or fairy tales; or horse, galloping hard, tossing my mane from my eyes; or Indian scout, stepping silently, snapping no twigs.

Most often, I was just girl-in-the-woods, crouching, listening, sprinting sudden and hard. Black bears weren't unheard of in the region, so I was careful, but deer and squirrels were what I mostly saw. The occasional woodchuck. Rabbits now and then. A fox, stock-still, bright eyes glistening, red tail flung out and tipped with white. And the trees themselves. Oaks, maples. The way their leaves rustled. Pines, their beds of needles springy and thick under my rubber soles. Moss as green as emeralds. A whole world schoolbooks didn't care about.

It was as though a veil or screen hung at the forest's edge, and I could step through it into a secret, magical world of which grown-ups weren't aware and on which they had no purchase. My place. A place I could run to, where hot furious tears could stream down my face with no one to see or mock. The forest seemed so vast and strong, a green web. A refuge. My substitute for a playground, for friends, for a father—

Sometimes, lying on my back on a bed of moss or pine needles, gazing up at the jagged patch of blue between treetops far above, I felt strange explosions of joy in my chest, as if my very rib cage had opened to the sky and sunlight could flow down into my heart. Eyes closed, I'd watch red flicker against black as branches moved against the sunlight.

So the forest was my church, too. My cathedral. My magic cinema.

Behind our house, dark woods quilted the ravine and then rose steeply into the high hills. Only a small backyard, a swathe of patchy grass, lay between the woods and our glassed-in back porch. Sometimes in cold weather, sitting on the enclosed porch at dusk, doing my math by the whir of the electric space heater, I'd glance up and see three deer nuzzling the grass, or a doe ambling delicately with her fawn—and once, a twelve-point buck, who lifted his head and stared back at me for long seconds until he turned and stalked into the trees.

We lived in hunting country. It would have been dead easy to place a brown salt block in the yard or scatter feed corn every evening. Get them used to coming. And then, when deer season opened, just raise one window and prop a rifle on the sill. Free, good meat for the taking.

Momma's boyfriends, watching TV and drinking cans of beer in the front room, would have loved it. Be the big man. They all had guns.

So I never spoke of it.

Deer came and went, silent, lovely in the fading light, for all the years I did my schoolwork at that table.

———

In the condo, I had a little wing of my own, a studio where I constructed my odd objects, and Jon had an open-plan alcove office, where he worked when he was on call.

Some evenings, I'd walk in and place a mug of coffee beside him, rub his shoulders as he peered at his screen, where gray, ghostly parts of children's bodies hovered: a rib cage, a cranium, a leg. He read the images. A pediatric radiologist, he got paid almost a thousand dollars an hour to look inside children's bodies and report what resided there: a fracture, a tumor, a hematoma, a clean bill of health. He wrote back with his report bearing the life-or-death news.

Sometimes, in cases of possible abuse or wrongful death, he sat in court and testified, and sometimes his testimony sent parents to prison. Sometimes, at home, he'd mutter angrily about people who shouldn't be allowed to have children. I'd be carefully silent then. I'd rub his shoulders, thinking, *I have married a great and compassionate and brilliant man.*

Every couple of months, he flew to Haiti with a team of doctors and nurses. He'd stay a week or two, donating his time and skills to a hospital in a small mountain village fifty miles up the coast from Port-au-Prince. He'd sweat all day and sleep in a building like a barracks. He saved people. He told women their children would not live, gripping their hands as they sobbed.

At night he sat on a rooftop with the team and the local doctors and nurses, eating plantains and mangoes and pork and goat. A warm wind blew. Dried brown palm fronds clacked against each other in the dark, and stars sprinkled the black sky overhead. The doctors and nurses talked and drank rum.

Lily, an obstetrician, was someone he mentioned a lot. Or perhaps he didn't mention her more often than the other staff, but hers was the name I remembered. Was the lilt in his voice only my imagination?

A great and compassionate and brilliant man, I made myself think. *A good man. The kind you can trust.*

Clothes

My small silver suitcase lay open on the bed, empty, waiting. I stood staring down into its cream-colored satin lining. Nothing in my closet seemed particularly suited for a funeral in rural Appalachia.

Over the years in New York and Chicago, my wardrobe had evolved. Around the house, Jon liked me in sleek yoga clothes, and now I had plenty of money for two-hundred-dollar pants, eighty-dollar tanks, cashmere hoodies, all of it soft as whispers, made from ethical fibers in the muted hues I preferred: bark, moss, dove, slate, river—colors whose names reminded me of the forest, which was ironic, given that I wore them indoors, high over a city, in a cube of glass and steel. I bought the clothes Jon expected to see me in.

I do have jeans, but instead of the sturdy, cheap, secondhand Wranglers I wore in West Virginia, they're three-hundred-dollar affairs with strategic whiskering and artfully placed pockets, designed to make my backside still look fetching.

For my rare meetings with a collector or anyone else I need to impress, I have suits—structured, sleek things from Prada and Armani in colors like charcoal and sand—and then dresses for social occasions with Jon: beautiful, swirling, floor-length gowns in heavy silk the color of jewels. A few floral tea dresses. Lace bustiers made in Italy. Three all-purpose little black dresses with sleeves of differing lengths. Soft little shrugs for my shoulders.

But it's all camouflage. Mirrors and smoke.

I pulled a black dress from its hanger, folded it into the suitcase, and stood there, looking down.

———

Sometimes my mother would make me a jelly sandwich to take along into the forest, and I'd wander up and down hills with the brown wax paper stuffed in my pocket until I got hungry, the bent white bread soggy and stained purple. I drank from the little creeks; it didn't occur to me not to.

I wore denim overalls over a plain white T-shirt in summer, and a flannel shirt in fall and spring. Tennis shoes were fine until winter, when she'd grumble because last year's boots were too small and she'd have to spend more money. In town, where we went to the thrift shop, I learned to head straight for the boys' aisle. Boys' boots were hardier, with thicker, grippier soles. Their jeans had reinforced knees.

In spring, I took the small spade and sack my mother gave me, and I'd watch for ramps as I walked. When I got home, she'd wash and chop them and throw them in the skillet with butter, and the house would fill with their oniony smell. I knew how to find molly moochers and distinguish them from the false, poisonous mushrooms. As an adult, I've seen morels (as I learned to call them) served in fine restaurants, a delicacy, but when I was a child, they were mountain food, spring miracles that kept hunger from the door, a chewy, tasty substitute for meat we couldn't afford. Momma sizzled them in lard or threw them in the skillet with eggs.

Every three years or so, I got a dress, and I wore it only to church with my grandmother. (My mother never went. "No way, sister. God's got enough to do.") My lone dress hung on a wooden peg, waiting for Sunday. In the first year, it would fit too long and loose, its cuffs dangling to my fingers, my slight frame swimming in its bodice. The third year, it would squeeze like a vise and be embarrassingly, hem-tuggingly short when I sat in the pew. The middle, just-right year was all I knew of grace. When my grandmother died, I didn't go to church anymore, and I didn't wear a dress again until the funeral, when I wore an old black one of Della's, cinched with one of Billy's belts.

My mother might have enjoyed a girlier daughter, a sweet, giggling little gossip in pink. But perhaps not. Such a child would have begged for dance lessons and gymnastics, and sparkly barrettes and nail polish, and long sessions of hair brushing and curling, and my mother always seemed too tired and broke for any of that.

The forest made me cheap, undemanding—even useful. A provider. Easy to ignore. And she seemed to like me that way.

———

I crouched by my bedside table and spun the combination lock of the jewelry safe Jon had given me. ("Why," I'd asked, "when this whole building is Fort Knox?" He'd frowned and replied, "Why not protect valuable things?")

The small steel door swung open. One by one, I lifted Jon's gifts to me from their little velvet cases and packed them into my jewelry roll along with a crisp stack of bills, not thinking much about why I'd choose to take my small fortune along. I tucked and locked everything into the base of my vintage black Bolide.

———

If I had any real style at all, I owed it to my sister-in-law Sophia.

Jon's mother had named her two daughters after screen stars. Unfortunately, like all parents, she'd had to name them far too soon, as babies, before they bloomed into the women they'd become. Consequently, Audrey was the one with auburn hair, a showgirl figure, and poochy pink lips (which, now that she was "aging," as she said—thirty—she regularly re-poofed with tasteful jolts of Restylane), while Sophia, the middle child and closer to my age, was small and slim, hard as a bone of soap.

It was Sophia who'd taken to me. Pity, I guess—at least at first: a sort of neutral but intense kindness, like pressing coins into a beggar's hand and meeting his eyes and saying, *God be with you*, earnest as church. But then she really did warm up. By the second year of my marriage to Jon, we'd become friends. She was imaginative and effusive and warm, and my silence was a thing she didn't mind.

She liked to visit Chicago every couple of months from her boisterous home in Portland, leaving the children there with the nanny and her husband and jetting in for long weekends to shop. She stayed in her mother's big house in Lake Forest but often ditched Helene to lunch downtown. We'd stroll for hours along the Magnificent Mile.

"Portland's a dream," she'd say, letting a scarf slide through her fingers at Hermès, "but, Cookie, there's nothing like this."

I had to agree. Jon and I had visited her in Portland—which I liked: it had roses and rain and was very green. Like England, without the history.

I liked shopping with Sophia. She knew what suited her, and she knew what suited me. "No, no, no," she'd say, snatching away some snug chiffon frivolity I'd held up to my chin, the kind of thing Saqlain had once liked me in. "Now *this*, on the other hand . . . ," replacing it with a simply cut jacket, navy blue and soft as butter. And she was always right. She knew her way around the haughty saleswomen, too, with their long legs thin as chopsticks. They didn't intimidate her.

If I managed to appear stylish, it was due to Sophia's offhand tutelage. I used to confuse Roberto Cavalli with Italo Calvino; when I saw **D&G**, I thought of Deleuze and Guattari. Sophia put a stop to that.

After a shopping session, we'd plunk down exhausted at one fey little joint or another that a friend of a friend had insisted she simply must try—and inevitably, a place of which I'd never heard, though I lived mere blocks away. Sophia wasn't shy about ordering cocktails at midday. While we waited for our salads to arrive, she'd sip a sidecar and sift through her trove of purchases, pulling one bijou after another from bright bags clustered at her feet. She'd ooh and aah like fireworks, thrilled all over again.

"I'm mad for Argentina," she announced one day, apropos of nothing, at one of our après-shop luncheons. It was early May, and we'd just beaten the rain indoors. On the windows, fat silver beads swarmed, gathering mass and then tumbling down in rivulets. "Everything Argentinean. Tango. The Pampas. Old Nazis. I've never been. Have you?"

I had not.

"I might just have to leave Michael, you know." She stared off dreamily, her cheek couched in her palm, her elbow propped on the white damask. Michael was a day trader. They'd been married twelve years. She met my eyes and nodded earnestly. "Oh, yes. Just leave him behind and take up with a handsome tango teacher with smoldering eyes. And a thin pencil mustache, perhaps." She considered. "But only a very thin one."

I smiled. "What would the children do without you?"

"Turn feral," she said, not hesitating. "They'd become a little band of savages, wilding through the hills of Portland, wearing coyote skins. Michael would toss raw meat into the backyard in the evenings and urge them to say their prayers, and they'd run off howling and screaming, their jowls flecked with blood."

Our salads came. She picked the onions off and laid them to the side.

"Well," she went on, "a girl can fantasize. Marriage is hard, you know. Well, of course you do. You're married. To my brother, of all unlikely people. No one—but no one—expected that, let me tell you. Why buy the cow and all. We thought he'd stay Chicago's most eligible bachelor forever." She forked up some wild spring greens and chewed, delicate as a fawn. "But I see it. Absolutely. I completely see why he went for you. I mean"—she waved her hand—"aside from the obvious ornamental value."

Once the dust of our whirlwind courtship had settled and I'd found myself ensconced in Jon's context, surrounded by his history and his peers, I'd puzzled over the question myself. Chicago's star bachelor—and me, a thinly made-over refugee from *Deliverance*. I took a slow sip of my dirty martini, and then, in a tone most casual, asked, "What do you mean?"

She nodded, warming to her task. "Those other girls—Mother was always parading the pick of the litter under his nose. Perfect pedigrees, excellent families, the *veddy* best educations—and of course, my God, miraculous genes. Like a chorus line of Carolyn Bessette clones, rest her soul. I could hardly tell them apart.

"He'd take them out, of course, to humor Mother and be polite—and I'm not saying he didn't have his fun: sometimes he'd take them to Saint John or Banff or wherever, so it's not as though he didn't have a nice time, too." She dropped a light palm on my arm for a moment and let it flutter away. "Oh, don't be jealous. He didn't love any of them." She swallowed down a gulp of her sidecar. "He was bored. Utterly bored. You could tell. Audrey and I always said so.

"But you—you, he couldn't stop mentioning. Just saying your name. Isabel this, Isabel that. Isabel thinks such and such. Isabel wants to go to Rome. We couldn't believe it. Finally!

"And then we met you, and it all made perfect sense. I mean, Jon's a romantic—*obviously*—but he's also smart. A one-note pony won't hold his interest. All those girls were open books—*wide* open, if you know what I mean. No, to be serious, they might as well have just walked up wearing their résumés. All their wares right out there for the taking. Everything plain as day. Like those old-time theater gals with their strap-on boxes, 'Cigars! Cigarettes!' What were they called? Usherettes. My God, don't you wish they'd let you smoke in here?"

I nodded. The occasional smoke on the sly was something Sophia and I stole in common.

"But now you, Cookie—if you're a book, you're a closed one. Closed and locked, like one of those diaries they used to make. Do they still make those? I had one, as a girl. Blue leatherette, with the most cunning little gold lock. Mother found the key and read the whole thing, the bitch." She wagged a finger. "Don't trust that woman! But you don't. Of course not. Why would you? You're smart, too. Smart and different—West Virginia! Who ever comes out of West Virginia? I didn't even know they were allowed to leave. I thought guards stood at the borders, propped on their muskets. Hatfields and McCoys.

"And you're quiet. Full of secrets. Pandora's box. What could be more of a challenge to a man like Jon? Think about it." She waved her fork around like a cheroot or magic wand. "Think what he does for a living. X-rays, ultrasounds . . . He *sees through* people. He reads their insides."

I pushed lettuce across my plate with the knife.

Laughing, she reached over with one finger and tucked a lock of hair behind my ear.

"Someone who won't play show-and-tell? You're catnip, Cookie. Sheer catnip."

———

That was early on. I wasn't catnip to Jon anymore.

Three months ago, I'd gone secretly, alone, in a kind of fugue state of ambivalence, to have my IUD removed, propelled by a curious mixture of motives pure and less so—a genuine desire to "move forward," as people say, with our lives (as if a child, which Jon wanted so badly, was the inevitable end to every love affair), but yes, okay: to try, to hope, to take the risk . . . Fear of losing him was a bad reason to do anything; I knew that. But rarely have I enjoyed the luxury of unmixed motives. I got myself up on the table, put my feet in the cold steel stirrups, and let the doctor do it. And nature seemed to have taken its course. But Jon's coldness . . . I hadn't been able to tell him. Wasn't even sure myself. Couldn't bear to take the home test, to know for sure one way or the other . . .

I didn't have to go to West Virginia. I could handle everything over the phone from the safety of my studio, faxing signed documents if necessary. I didn't need to drive through those dark hills, hold my mother's dead hand, exchange platitudes with blood relatives who'd never called. I lifted the black dress from the suitcase, shook out the folds, and hung it back up in our closet again.

I stood at the window, arms crossed, facing the horizon. Distant storms hung over the lake—high, dark banks of clouds. No boats were out. The sky looked cold, metallic.

Sometimes, over the years, it had felt simpler to act as if I had no kin at all. I'd carried my longing with me to New York, sure. But now I was grown, I was firm, I was clear in my mind. I had my carefully constructed life. I had Jon (more or less), our friends, our glassy condo, our sturdy bank accounts. If this baby thing would just happen, it could all work out.

There was no need to muddy things up, said wide Lake Michigan. I nodded back at its steely surface.

I turned and stared again into the creamy lining of my suitcase. My hands were on its hard shell, ready to fold shut its emptiness and stow it back in the closet.

And then the landline rang.

The Inheritance

"This is Conrad Kniseley, from the firm of Johnson, Kniseley, and Cerullo," said the voice. He asked for Isabella Martin, a name I hadn't used since my junior year of college, when I'd carried the petition and other legal forms down to the court clerk and paid the fees to change my name forever—done with being Stella Martin's daughter, with being a bastard, a foster child, a criminal's girl, a joke.

"Isabel Morales. But yes, that's me."

"I'm calling in regard to your mother's estate."

I sat down on the bed. Year after year, I'd paid the cheap taxes on my mother's land, like paying a peculiar kind of tithe. Blood money. From the one who got away.

"Ms. Martin, we'd like to assist you in the matter of disposing of your mother's estate. As you may know, estates can be quite complicated. Paperwork and so on. Legal matters. In your mother's case, there's substantial property. A house, acreage, furniture, personal belongings . . ."

I laughed, imagining shaking a gasoline can over our shitty old furniture.

"Ma'am?"

"Nothing." I closed my eyes and saw the house go up in flames.

"Now, I see that you currently make your residence in Chicago."

"Yes." I sat there with my eyes shut as the little white house burned and burned. Dark smoke, thick and choking, rose above the trees.

"Very nice place, I hear. Chicago."

My eyes opened. "We like it." I heard myself employ the *we*, as if girding myself—the royal *we*, the marital *we*, the social cocoon of being wanted—as if stating clearly, for the record, *I am not all alone in this world.*

"Never been there, myself. I get up to Pittsburgh sometimes for a Steelers game. Take the wife shopping."

With my free hand, I clicked the metal clasp of my suitcase. Back and forth, back and forth. Click. Click. Click.

"So anyway, I don't know if you're inclined to return for the funeral . . ." He left a leading pause.

I looked out at Lake Michigan.

"But if not, the firm of Johnson, Kniseley, and Cerullo would be more than happy to handle all the necessary arrangements."

My voice came slow. "What kinds of arrangements?"

"Well, for example, the disposal of personal belongings. Our firm works with a reputable local company. This company assesses salable items and offers them to the public in an estate sale—or auction, if the client prefers. We also contract with house cleaners, property stagers, and local realtors to arrange for the sale of your house and land. Many heirs find it more efficient than handling things on their own. You yourself, for example, could just stay right there in Chicago, and we'd take care of every detail."

Heirs. I made a noncommittal sound.

"What's more, in your case, we've already received two inquiries, so you're in a fortunate position."

"Inquiries," I repeated.

"Elaine Carter at Capston Brothers Real Estate called. She's prepared to put your property on the market for one nineteen nine. A fair market price, given area comps, she tells me."

"I thought the land was worthless," I said slowly. That's what my aunt Della and uncle Frank had repeatedly told me—in person, when I lived with them, and later in the handwritten letters Aunt Della sent. *Just a bunch of dirt and squirrels and a falling-down house don't nobody want.*

"Oh, not worthless," Kniseley said. "No. We're talking forty-five acres of mature hardwoods. You've got a creek and river frontage. The land backs up to a protected state wildlife management area. All that adds up."

"One nineteen nine," I said. In Chicago, that bought you a studio apartment in a sketchy neighborhood—maybe. In West Virginia, it bought you a forest.

"Plus, you've got a couple of acres of arable land right around the house, and Elaine says someone's been farming it, so that's an asset, too, depending on what your buyer's after."

I sat straighter. Someone was farming our land?

"But what's really going to make your day, now, is this second offer." Conrad Kniseley cleared his throat and paused, as if for drama. "A private concern has contacted me, and they are prepared to make a bid . . ." He paused again. "Of more than double that amount. Three hundred thousand dollars."

I sipped quick air. Accustomed as I'd become to money, this was still a windfall of a different order. So much, so unexpectedly.

I rubbed my foot back and forth on the thick taupe carpet. "What kind of private concern?"

A long pause fell on the line.

"Well, I'll be candid," he finally said. "The other party wishes to remain anonymous at this time—though of course if we progress to contract, the identities of all parties will be disclosed."

"And how quickly could that happen?"

His voice brightened. "If all parties agree to terms, we could courier the paperwork to you in Chicago by next week. That is, if you're satisfied with the offer. Any negotiations, of course, would prolong the process."

Three hundred thousand dollars was a fortune in West Virginian terms. Kniseley's assumption that such a sum would sway me was reasonable. If I were really pregnant, and if things with Jon were falling apart in an irreparable way, three hundred thousand dollars would make for a very soft landing.

I entered the closet, slid my black dress off its hanger, and opened the suitcase again.

"I'll be back in Mercer for the funeral, Mr. Kniseley," I said. "I look forward to meeting you."

———

Courtesy of Helene's insistence, Jon and I had a strict prenup. After dinner one night at the Turner mansion, she'd pulled out the legal document drawn up by the family's attorney, about which Jon had warned me apologetically in advance.

"It's nothing personal, dear, you understand," Helene said, sliding the sheaf of paper across the burled mahogany. Shafts of light from the chandelier shifted across the dark blur of print. "It's exactly the same one that Michael and Joseph signed when they married my daughters."

I glanced at Jon. His face looked awkward, pained, as he stared out at the dark garden.

Helene tapped the document to draw my attention back. Her mouth lifted in a bright little semblance of a smile. "It's just to protect everyone concerned," she said. "You know how protective a mother can be."

"Yes, of course," I lied, smiling back. *What would a rich fiancée do?* So I read and signed it without flinching, the heavy silver pen cold in my grip. I'd be damned if I let her slip Jon even a glimmer of doubt as to my motives. I was marrying him for love and love alone, and if it didn't work out, I'd pack my two suitcases and go. I knew how to travel light and leave a place fast.

Meeting Helene's glittering gaze, I pushed the prenup back across the table.

———

To my surprise, the landline rang again. I set down the rolled socks I'd been tucking into the corners of my suitcase.

"Hello?"

"Isabel Morales?" A man's deep voice, low and warm.

I hesitated. "Yes?"

"Ms. Morales, you probably won't remember me, but my name's Nic Folio. We went to high school together."

I sat down on the edge of the bed.

Everyone had known the Folio brothers: star running backs, three in a row. They broke records. Heroes. Local gods. Talk of the county. Rocky, Tino, and Nic, who'd been a senior when I was a freshman. Lingering at my locker at my new school, I'd watched, shy, as he passed in the hall.

"We called you Bel Martin back then."

Brawlers, too. *Short fuse on them Folio boys,* people said. Clean fighters, though, if I remembered right. Never pulled a knife. They'd just beat the cuss out of someone and leave him bleeding on the ground.

"Why are you calling me?"

"Ms. Morales, I work for a security company named Liberty Protection. The attorney Conrad Kniseley contracts with our firm to provide security for certain clients. He told me you were coming to town."

I plucked at the sleek black fabric of my leggings. "I'm not his client."

"Mr. Kniseley asked me to put myself at your disposal, ma'am, during your visit to Mercer. I can drive you, escort you, whatever you need."

"I don't need anything. And why would Conrad Kniseley think I want a security detail?"

"Maybe you won't, Ms. Morales. Maybe you won't. But—"

"I know how to drive. And I know Mercer."

"Ma'am, be that as it may—"

"Really. Thank you. I won't be needing your services."

"Listen, Bel, I'm sorry about your mother."

I felt slapped. "What?"

"I'm sorry about your mom, Bel."

"Isabel." My hands shook. "My name's Isabel."

"I remember what happened. We all felt bad for—"

I slammed the receiver onto the cradle.

The phone rang.

I let it ring.

———

"Come here, sugar shoe," my mother used to say when I was little, pulling me close against her ribs. "String bean," she'd call me, nuzzling my hair, her breath hot on my scalp. "Baby duck."

I'd thought for sure there was love there, the kind a body could trust.

I thought of these things as I set my packed suitcase and Bolide bag by the door. As I plumped the pillows on our bed. As I looked out at the darkening lake, sipping hot chamomile tea.

Jon would be home soon. He'd change clothes and glance through the notes for his speech. We'd drive to the gala. I'd have to tell him.

I looked down. My hand on the cup trembled, my mother's long-boned fingers echoing in my own.

The Gala

That night, Jon drove. He looked dashing in his tuxedo, and I'd worn his favorite gown, a long one backed with a sheer sweep of black georgette that dipped to my tailbone. He'd always preferred mesh or lace to bare skin: to see, but not quite. Something elusive. From the demure keyhole closure at the nape of my neck to the small of my back, my flesh was clad in shadow. Seducing him later was my last-ditch plan to reconnect before I left.

But when I'd walked into the living room with my hair pinned up, a few locks drifting dark around my face, my makeup soft and glowing, he'd made no comment, no gesture of appreciation, and disappointment settled in my chest. In the elevator heading down, he didn't take my hand, and I couldn't bring myself to reach for his.

Bright shop windows blurred past as we drove through the dark city, and I fingered the jeweled minaudière in my lap. Jon tuned the Sirius to some sultry music, faux Latin, slow and cool, old-school; every song sounded like "The Girl from Ipanema." He said a few things about his keynote, about Haiti, about the fundraising goals for the evening. We made stiff small talk until I couldn't anymore.

"I need to go away for a few days," I said.

"Away?"

"To West Virginia."

A crease appeared between his brows. He knew West Virginia meant home, a place I didn't go.

"It's fine," I said. "I just need to take care of a few things."

"What kinds of things?"

"I leave on Thursday."

An eyebrow rose, and his head turned briefly. "Tomorrow?"

"I'll fly there and rent a car. I'll be back in a few days. A week, maybe."

"A week." Furrows multiplied like a primitive irrigation system across his handsome forehead. "What kinds of things?" he said again.

"It's fine," I said. "It's nothing. It won't take long." I looked away.

A block went by. Two.

"Isabel?" He reached out across the seat and enclosed my hand under his. His warm skin against my skin. It had been so long. Tears pricked hot in the corners of my eyes.

I took a deep breath. "My mother died. I'm going to her funeral. I have to take care of her estate."

Even as I spoke the words, I knew *estate* sounded far more glamorous than the mildewed litter that would greet me, but *shit* would have been crude.

I couldn't say what Jon looked like, what his eyes held, because I couldn't look at him.

But a tremor ran through his hand, a convulsion he stopped before it became a squeeze.

In Jon's hands, tremors mattered. Though he ultimately chose radiology, he cross-trained in surgery, like all medical students. He had stitched people closed; he had pushed scalpels through live flesh. He knew, more than most people, how to keep emotion from his hands.

His voice, when he spoke at last, was lower and stranger than I'd ever heard it.

"You told me you were an orphan."

———

I did tell him that. At the time, over two years ago, I tried to think of it as a sin of omission. Better a mysterious blank, I told myself, than the rotten truth.

I do respect the clarity of the word *lie* and the difficult valor of never telling one, but it doesn't leave much room for nuance or dire straits, and my history was nothing but gray area. Respectful, Jon had asked only once about the absence of a family tree, of relatives I needed to visit at holidays or send birthday cards to. *Orphan* was enough of an explanation for him.

It's not that a curious light didn't filter into his eyes; it did. It's just that he didn't press me. I don't know if that's some upper-class reticence thing or what. The rich, in my limited experience, don't talk openly, preferring to express affection by dispensing stock tips and thin smiles. I was grateful for his don't-ask-don't-tell policy.

His mother, Helene, was less trusting, even after I'd signed the prenup, but my name, carefully and legally changed, thwarted her efforts when she raced, before our wedding, to have my background checked.

I'd known nothing of it at the time, but according to the report—which I found on Jon's desk later, just after our move into the condo together—I'd sprung fully formed, an Appalachian Athena, from the brow of a WVU dormitory at the age of twenty-one. Thanks to West Virginian efficiency and shoddy record-keeping before the days of computerized everything, the trail ended there.

Unpacked boxes still cluttered the living room. Jon was chopping red and green peppers. The pasta I'd learned to make by hand was drying on little wooden racks. Shaking, I dropped the file on our granite counter. "What's this?"

He stopped cutting and squinted at the lavender folder.

"Oh, right." He laughed. "My mother. Don't be mad. You know how she is." Shrug. "She hired some guy to check you out."

I forced a smile. "And I passed inspection, apparently?"

He laughed again. "I don't know. I never read it. She gave it to me, and I stuck it in a drawer."

I looked at him. "You're serious," I said. What mortal could have so little curiosity? After stumbling across the report, I'd crouched in his alcove office, panicked, reading every page, along with the handwritten note on lilac-scented card stock that Helene had tucked inside: *Are you sure you want to move forward with this, darling? Lots of unanswered questions here.* I pushed his arm. "You can't tell me you never even looked at it."

He rinsed his hands and wiped them on a cotton towel. He took my shoulders and looked into my eyes.

"That's my mother, Isabel. Not me. Okay? Not me."

He picked up the file and led me by the hand to his alcove office. Leaning down, he flipped a switch, and his industrial-strength shredder, designed to chew whole medical files, began to grind. I stood in silence as he fed Helene's suspicions into its metal maw.

He switched it off. "Okay?" His palm cupped my cheek, and his blue eyes were dark and warm. "I'm not my mother. I don't care where you came from, or whether your grandfather went to Harvard or Yale. I love you now."

I nodded.

"I love you now," he said again, his voice soft. And then his hands were in my hair, and my hands were on his face, and we didn't eat our pasta until very late that night.

———

Helene probably couldn't help her tendency toward suspicion any more than I could, albeit for different reasons. As a child, she'd been trained by her mother to evaluate (covertly) the quality of a porcelain tea service (when visiting society friends) by holding up a teacup to see how much light passed through its thin walls. One could thus unobtrusively sum up the taste and wealth of one's hostess.

I came to learn this very early in my relationship with Jon, when Helene held up a cup at the top-floor restaurant at the Art Institute of Chicago, gazing at it absently. I asked, and she explained.

Then her speculative gaze turned to me. She squinted. "You're a sharp-eyed little thing, aren't you?"

I'm taller than you, I did not say.

Perhaps that was the very moment when Helene's suspicions of me began—that abrupt tilt of the universe when the observer learns she's the observed. Or perhaps they'd lain dormant already, and that moment just blew their embers to hot life.

When she'd invited me—just me, alone, a month before the wedding—to lunch, I felt touched, welcomed. I thought she wanted to get to know me, that she wanted us to be friends. Only her well-honed social skills enabled my misimpression to persist until the main course, but as one gracious question followed another, I began to feel lifted and held to the light myself.

"West Virginia University?" Thin eyebrows arched toward her hairline. Her smile was like something cracking. NYU had passed with a nod of approval, but WVU was different.

"I'm from West Virginia originally," I said, hoping my own smile looked more natural than hers. "It's a beautiful state."

"My goodness. I'm sure it is." Her laugh: champagne flutes dropped from a great height. "And is there running water?"

In the air, something shifted. A whiff of sulfur.

I loved Jon. I wanted his mother to like me.

I smiled along gamely, pretending it was a harmless little joke we were both in on. "They've even got electricity," I said.

They've. A little chip fell from my soul, as surely as if I'd taken a chisel and hammer and struck the blow myself. It's just that easy to sell yourself out. Your family. Your past. Your home. To chip away at the truth of yourself until you've sculpted some strange new being who stands in your place.

Self-invention, they'd called it admiringly in my twentieth-century-novels class. It permitted mobility. The American way. Gatsby and all that.

But what if you got to the new place, your goal, only to find yourself new and strange and somehow gone?

Sitting in that chair of soft leather in the restaurant of the Art Institute, I remembered the outhouse in my grandmother's backyard. When I was a child, I was scared to go out there alone at night. Gran would walk beside me, holding my hand. While I peed, she'd stand just outside in the dark, whistling, so I'd know she was still there.

In her kitchen, she'd pour boiling water from the woodstove into a galvanized metal tub, mixing it into cold water with her arm until it was just right for my bath. "Try it now, sister," she'd say. Too hot. She'd add more, stir again. "Okay. Now." Finally, she'd sigh with exasperation. "Okay, you ain't no princess. Get on in there." But she'd ruffle my hair and kiss me on the forehead as I stepped into the water.

When we met, Helene was older than my grandmother had been the last time I'd seen her alive, but two women couldn't have been more different. Helene was sleek and groomed, soigné, her peeled face fresh and nearly lineless, her carefully edited figure clad in slim dresses. Her bobbed lemonade hair shone and swung when she moved, and her feet were smooth as silicone in their sandals, her toes tipped with small shields of dark garnet. So diligently had she protected herself over the years, like a fine animal or piece of bone china, that her arms, lean and firm from tennis, were unfreckled. Her wedding ring—and her husband's; she cultivated the role of rich widow—rotated loosely on her finger, silently telling the story that she was even slimmer now than in her blooming youth.

My grandmother's body, back home in West Virginia, had told a different tale, a story of hard use and depletion, of Cheetos and defeat.

Her white hair wisped close to her visible scalp, her face and throat and arms and chest were blotched with brown, and when she pulled off her four-dollar tennis shoes with slow moans of an evening, her fat, flattened feet looked like they'd been hammer-smashed. Everything hurt. That was the lesson of her life: aching feet and arthritic wrists and a prolapsed uterus. ("My womb done fell.") Life used you up and hurt you, leaving you alive and in pain for a few decades of loneliness until Death came to collect you and cart you off to heaven or hell. There were reasons people prayed so hard and sang so loud with their eyes clenched shut in the little white church on the hill. My grandmother walked like a damaged robot.

But her hands were kind, even when her voice said rough things. Her touch was honest. It spelled love against my skin, and I trusted her. ("Because she's too worn out to beat you," Aunt Della would snort.) She melted sugar into caramel on the woodstove and dipped apples into it. Handed me a warm, sweet, dripping globe.

A small, forgettable woman in a holler in the hills. She couldn't wear her wedding band, or even her husband's after he passed; her fingers, she said, "got old and fat," and anyway, she said, "Marriage is a young gal's game. Don't nobody care if I'm a widow or an old maid. Ain't nobody going to be knocking on my porch come sundown. I'm past all that, and a good thing, too." She'd chuckle. "Got enough problems. Don't need no man."

In Lake Forest, Jon's mother—to quell the exhortations of her well-meaning friends—listed her profile with an exclusive matchmaking service, but she refused to go on a first date with anyone whose net worth was under ten million.

There in the restaurant at the Art Institute, listening to Helene's calculated lilt, I felt a trickle of hatred, and I pressed my lips together. I looked down at my duck confit to mask my eyes.

But it was myself I hated.

———

At the Turners' stately home in Lake Forest, where Jon and his sisters grew up among marble fireplaces and topiary, his father's study still stood pristine, preserved, a shrine: all the law books on shelves, ceiling to floor, with one of those ladders that roll around the edges of the room. Leather club chairs by the fireplace. An antique globe aged brown and long unspun. All of it, like in a movie.

The remains of the great man himself sat on the mantelpiece, his ashes and chips of unburnt bone cradled in an urn of bronze.

When Helene introduced us on my inaugural visit there, I was "Jon's new friend."

The urn was "Harold." The urn was "one of the most esteemed circuit court judges in the history of Chicago." It was "advisor to three mayors," and there were framed photographs on the wall to prove it: men in suits shaking hands, their smiles turned to the camera.

"I should really put him in the family mausoleum," she said, gesturing toward the little urn. "But I just can't bear . . ." Her fingers plucked at the diamond at her throat.

"It's so small." Feeling sad for her, I blurted what I thought. "A whole person. A whole life."

"Yes." Her voice was soft, her gaze absent.

"So little, really. Even if we're esteemed. Respected. It doesn't matter. In the end, we're really all just the same."

Helene frowned. When she turned to me, her lips were pursed, and her eyes glittered. "Well, hardly the same," she said. "But how would—"

"Come on," interrupted Jon, entering the room, his smile broad. He slipped his arm around my shoulders. "I'm famished, and our reservations are for eight. You can give Isabel the nickel tour another time."

Instantly, smoothly, the offended look slid from his mother's face. She smiled. "Of course, darling," she said. She laid a hand on his free arm and steered him away. With his arm gone, my shoulders felt a sudden chill.

———

The first couple of times Jon went down to Haiti after we married, he asked me to go with him. "You have to," he said. "You'll love it, Isabel. And it means so much to me."

I couldn't. I'd seen on television the squalor, the tents, the cholera, the bare dirt, the suffering, the salted mud cakes baked in the sun to assuage people's chronic hunger. I knew the role I was supposed to play: visiting princess, gracious and infinitely kind but aloof by virtue of my very loveliness and wealth, a pristine bird released from her golden cage for a benevolent little sojourn in the real world.

I was afraid my façade would slip, that I'd start shaking, crying, that I'd betray some too-intense kinship with the poor, that I'd be unable to let go of some bereaved mother's hand, that something I saw—some wounded child, some unfixable awfulness—would tip me into a panic attack: the chest flutter, the dust-mouth, the inability to catch sufficient breath. *Getting triggered*, we call it, but it's not much like a trigger, really: more like a trip wire I stumble over, and everything explodes, and even I don't know, for a few moments, what's happening. Standing there numb and shaking, my mouth open, my hands clutching each other, twisting—oh, I know what it looks like from the outside. I've been told. By employers, mainly, and a few erstwhile boyfriends. *What the fuck is wrong with you?*—a shattering line I couldn't bear to hear from Jon. I wanted him to think of me as strong, clear, sound, and as effortlessly buoyant as the girls he grew up with, those equestrians and debutantes who became socialites or international human rights lawyers. Not some broken bargain-table thing.

Haiti, I feared, would overwhelm me. The truth would show: my long familiarity with mess and filth, with hopelessness, with grief, with the abject. And Jon—clever, watchful Jon, who saw through people—would detect the true citizenship of my soul. He would guess everything, and I would be undone.

At another of those early interrogation lunches with Helene, my eyes wandered from the fat square-cut diamonds at her ears (three carats?) to the teardrop diamond pendant that hung at her chest, to the several diamonds and emeralds that flashed on her fingers. Her hands, for a woman of her age, were still surprisingly smooth and unspotted. (I would later learn that she got weekly hand facials along with her manicures.)

In all, counting the bracelets and her watch, she wore perhaps two dozen gems, a parade of subtle, costly light. Her every gesture sparkled.

I wore, as usual, only a smooth silver locket that hung on a silver chain at my throat. Inside it, I'd wedged a tiny photograph.

When, at fourteen, I'd had to pack in such a hurry, I grabbed the snapshot of Charlie off the refrigerator. I carried it with me for years, tucked inside my wallet.

When I sold my first major piece, I cashed my check, walked into Tiffany—if it was good enough for Holly Golightly, it was good enough for me—and bought the locket. I clipped the tiny face from the snapshot and pressed it carefully inside.

When Jon and I got engaged, I asked for a silver ring so it wouldn't clash with the locket, which I wore every day. He laughed and got platinum, and the same for our wedding bands.

He never asked what was inside the locket. Perhaps he didn't even realize the little silver oval was hollow, that it had a tiny clasp you could open.

But Helene's gaze fell upon it again and again.

———

We kept our wedding simple, to Helene's express dismay, so that Jon's side of a church, packed with friends and relations and Chicago's fine old-society families, wouldn't put my own bare pews to shame. Instead we stood before a justice of the peace, me in a dress of dove-gray silk and clutching a small bouquet of poppies, Jon grinning like a madman, and then took a taxi to O'Hare. Jon had always wanted a honeymoon in Paris.

When we returned two weeks later—plumped up by French food and wine and too many trips to Ladurée, thinned down again by long walks through the city and long nights in our suite above the Seine—Helene's fury had diminished to a simmer, but she was still tight-lipped when we met. I'd robbed her of the showpiece wedding of her only son.

"Give her time," Jon said. "Let her stew. She'll get over it."

But she didn't. Jon, she rapidly forgave. But I remained a pariah, a thief, and her suspicions of me grew.

Her manners were so impeccable that I, coming from a brusquer world, often failed to sense her hostility. At the society functions she threw, I sometimes felt like a character in a Henry James novel, the naïve and bumbling young American amidst the worldly old-money Europeans with titles and references I couldn't descry—though I wasn't hunting a husband, and no one was actually European. I hated those awkward evenings. But Helene was perfectly polite. Strategic, too. To Jon, she said only innocuous things about me or complimented some bland achievement, easy to praise—my career, some art piece, a casserole I'd labored over—so that when I came to him, worried about this or that slight, a double-edged comment, he could say, quite honestly and innocently, "She really likes you, Isabel. She really liked that wine you gave her. Really, sweetheart. You need to relax. It's all in your head."

I stopped asking Jon about it, and Helene and I drifted along in an uneasy truce. *She's Jon's family,* I told myself sternly. *My family now. And sacrifices are what you make for family.* So I brought casseroles. I sat at the Turner family table with Audrey and Sophia and their families at holidays, and I laughed lightly to deflect questions about when we were going to have children of our own. At Christmas and Mother's Day and her birthday, I brought Helene exquisite and tasteful little gifts. But I began to make excuses not to see her. On nights when Jon was slated to take her to the opera, I'd develop a convenient headache or exhibition deadline. Months slipped by.

He was a good son, and she was a widow: I had no desire to come between them. But over time, it became clear that she planned to give me no similar wide berth.

———

About six months ago, when Jon was prepping for one of his trips to Haiti, Helene invited me to accompany her on her weekly spa day.

"See? She likes you," said Jon. "She's making an overture."

She picked me up outside our building in her black Mercedes, her ringed hands on the leather-wrapped wheel.

I bent to get in, my smile hesitant. "This is so nice of you," I said.

"Think nothing of it." She waved a hand. "I go all the time." I pulled the car door shut; it closed with a satisfying thunk. Heavy. Well made. Secure. We pulled into traffic. At the first red light, Helene swiveled and let her eyes trickle over me. "And besides, why shouldn't you enjoy some decent grooming once in a while?"

I rode along, feeling unkempt, fingering my wedding band, thinking, *Jon likes the way I look.* Thinking, *Men's heads turn when I pass.* Finally thinking, *You're just jealous, and alone, and growing old.* But none of it felt good.

At the spa, the two of us were manicured, pedicured, and massaged side by side. Women smeared mud on our skin while Helene kept up an irregular stream of commentary about tennis, foreign films, and the various arts organizations, boards, women's clubs, and charity groups to which she belonged. Our brows were waxed, and Helene had her lip and chin waxed, too. I was grateful she suggested nothing more intimate.

After our facials and sauna, we headed into the long, hushed swimming hall. The blue pool threw flashes of light on the walls and ceiling.

Marble columns bordered the water, and women lay in various stages of languor. Relieved to be rid of Helene's monologue, I dropped my terry-cloth robe on one of the chaise longues and headed for the pool.

I swam lap after lap, relishing the cool, wet silence, practicing the rotary breathing I'd learned in a college PE class. (In the ponds and creeks of childhood, I'd taught myself an awkward crawl, my head always stiffly held just above the water.) The day had been, after all, benign, Helene's running commentary friendly enough. Perhaps this was how she'd bonded with her own two daughters: the quick shiv of critique couched in genteel language, followed by shared details of their social circle. Perhaps this was what all rich mothers did.

I pulled myself out, dripping. Blinking away water, I walked to where Helene lounged. As I approached, her smile seemed unnaturally broad. I reached for the towel to blot my eyes, still blurred from chlorine.

I saw then what she held.

My locket. Open in her hand. She'd pulled it from the pocket of my robe.

Her smile, for once, had spread to her eyes. There was no disguising the pleasure in her voice. Like drips of acid. Like a snake's ecstatic hiss.

"Who's the pretty baby?"

———

Without thinking, I snatched the locket from her fingers, turned, and half ran back to the locker room, where my clothes seemed to slide onto my body with a crackle of electricity. At the reception desk, I slapped my credit card down. While the lineless yoga-Barbie ran my charges, I called a taxi.

Even once I'd locked myself into our clean condo, the pulse thudded in my ears. I paced along the windows, back and forth, imagining what Helene would do with the information she'd gleaned. How she would ruminate upon it, making up various scenarios.

How she'd pour it, like poison, into Jon's ear.

———

"Very nice," I replied that evening at dinner, when Jon asked how our spa day had been.

I'd spent the late afternoon making dinner, lighting candles, setting the table with our best silver and china, and decanting a bottle of excellent malbec. Insurance.

"Very well," I replied, when he asked how my interactions with his mother had gone. His brow was unclouded, and we made love twice that night.

———

But the next evening, when we met for dinner at Francesca's, after the glasses of cold prosecco arrived, his troubled gaze kept flicking to my throat. Helene had called him.

"You can tell me anything, you know." His voice was kind, searching. "I mean it. Anything."

"I know."

"Really," he said. "Anything at all."

I turned my heavy silver fork over and over on the tablecloth.

"You can trust me," he said. "I love you."

"I know."

The waiter came with hot bread, and I felt grateful for the little speech he gave about the evening's specials.

When he left with his tray, I asked quickly, "When does your flight leave?"

"Eight thirty," said Jon. "But listen, if there's anything—"

"Can I give you a ride to O'Hare?"

"No, thanks. I'm set. But—"

"You'll be back Saturday? In time for dinner?"

"Yes." He took my hand. "Look, I know deflection when I see it."

I said nothing. *What about subterfuge?* I thought. *Do you know subterfuge when you see it?* His mother had twittered away all day, lowering my guard. Her fingers had dug into the pocket of my robe.

"Listen," he said impulsively, squeezing my hand. "Why don't you come with me? Don't say no. Just come."

My laugh was short and sharp. "No." I didn't want to be just one more do-good project. Pitiable. Pretty wife as disaster island.

Mouth tight, Jon looked away. He released my hand. Drained his glass.

I broke off a small piece of bread and drizzled it with oil, relieved to chew in silence, relieved when the appetizers came, relieved when Jon, ever immaculately gracious, began to talk about the cases awaiting him in Haiti. But as he talked, I began to think of warm winds, of kindness in the midst of suffering. Of exhaustion at the end of long days, of the adrenaline high after a successful surgery. The camaraderie of the team. Rum on a rooftop, the warm wind blowing. The need for comfort and release. The delicious lure of the forbidden.

I imagined Lily's lashes, long and curling like a giraffe's, softly whisking her smooth cheeks. I imagined the way she'd lower and lift them, glancing up at Jon in the starry darkness, her eyes glinting with light and promise. I imagined her hands moving, graceful as birds in the air between his body and her own, shaping all the possibilities of touch.

Distant was not how I wanted Jon to feel when he jetted off to Port-au-Prince.

"It's me," I said. "The baby's me."

Jon's eyes flew to my face. He set down his fork.

I reached behind my neck and unclasped the chain. I held the locket over the table between us and tried to still the tremor in my hands. My fingernail slid between the slender silver bars that held the locket shut. I flicked it open.

"The children's home didn't take many pictures," I said, "so this one is special."

Jon nodded, glancing back and forth from the small photo to my face.

Trembling, I waited for him to call me out. To call me a liar. To say how hair so golden could never turn as dark as mine. To say simply, *That's a boy.*

"I see it," he said at last. He looked up at me and nodded, smiled. "The eyes."

That's what trust looks like.

My throat clenched hot with love and guilt.

But then, just for a moment, fast as the flick of a whip, a corner of his mouth quivered. Doubt. He didn't trust me; he was *trying* to trust me.

A different thing altogether.

———

The following morning after Jon left for the airport with a distant kiss, I undid the clasp of my locket and wrapped it in a silk handkerchief. I cleared a space at the bottom of my desk's lowest, deepest drawer and nested it into the back corner, burying it with old sketchbooks that would never see the light of day. I shut the drawer and locked it.

Since then, each day before starting work, I touched the drawer's handle like a talisman. I closed my eyes and saw him laughing, tossed high in sunlight.

Charlie.

———

At the bank building on Michigan Avenue, Jon and I took the elevator to the highest floor and threaded our way through a swarm of Chicago's nouveau and not-so-nouveau riche to find our place cards perched on a round table sparkling with china, silver, and glass.

Helene swooped down upon us just before the lights dimmed. "Darling," she said, looking only at Jon, "I took a cab into the city." He hadn't told me she'd be there. "I didn't feel like driving this evening. I don't suppose you'd mind giving me a lift home?" She waved her glittering hands and laughed as if she'd said something delightful.

I stared at her. Depending on traffic, it could take us a good hour to drive her back to Lake Forest after dinner.

She glanced at me, then looked away. In Jon's favorite dress, I suddenly felt vulgar—too much, too exposed. One couldn't very well seduce a man with his mother in the room, much less while driving her home at night.

Jon glanced at me, hesitated.

"I'm thinking of making a gift of my own," Helene continued quickly. "To your cause. To Haiti. But I'd like to know a little more about the hospital. We could talk in the car."

Jon paused, then nodded. "Of course," he said. "It's no problem." He moved off toward the lectern, drawing his note cards from his breast pocket. I tried not to see Helene's quick triumphant glance.

———

To be suspected is a terrible thing. It makes you nervous, jumpy, as if perhaps you might really be guilty after all. You doubt yourself. Your calm hands start to tremble, committing small clumsy mistakes; you apologize for nothing, for everything, and he looks at you in confusion—or irritation: you can't tell. You grow more nervous still.

That first summer when we moved in together, it had been heaven: to take our coffee on the balcony on bright mornings, the soft sounds of birdsong and traffic drifting up from far below. Making dinner together late at night, passing cooking tools back and forth as if by intuition, laughing, as the lake faded from gold to black. An ease and pleasure that infused everything.

But those sweet times between us had almost come to feel like a soft, faraway dream. I didn't know what had caused the rupture or how to win him back. The memory of the times I'd tried still scalded.

I couldn't say when things began to go awry, but it seemed to happen all at once, in a tumble, a tangle: Helene's suspicion, Jon's desire to start a family, his invitations to Haiti, his growing distance, and then his trips down to Pierre Payen, when he'd be gone for a whole week every month or two. I began to pick small, stupid fights before he'd leave, hoping for some sign of affection, and greet him grimly upon his return, with a false casualness, as if I didn't care, hadn't much missed him, hadn't lain awake nights in the wide bed wondering if he'd been in someone else's arms.

———

Elegant in his tuxedo, Jon stood on a dais in the reception hall, all eyes locked upon him.

"Almost ten million people live in Haiti," he said, laser pointer in hand. "About the same population of the Chicago metropolitan area." Scenes flashed on the large screen behind him: turquoise water, palm trees, beautiful resorts that had once been plantations. A collective sigh rose from the audience, who knew Chicago's bitter chill awaited us outside.

"But almost sixty percent live in poverty, and nearly a quarter live in what the United Nations defines as 'extreme' poverty." Behind him: thin-limbed children with weary eyes, elderly men with tumors that bulged like knees, mud cakes to dull hunger baking in the sun.

I sipped my wine. On my gilt-edged plate, fat prawns curled.

"Since staging its successful slave revolution—the only country in the Western Hemisphere to have done so—Haiti has suffered dozens of coups, decades of internal corruption, pyramid schemes, and political intervention and military occupation by other nations, including the United States." Around me, the well-heeled wealthy rustled. Silver clinked against china. I scanned the crowd. There were only four other people of color. Onscreen, dark faces flashed: mostly young children, smiling wildly at the pencils and soap in their hands. I wondered at what age a person stopped being sympathetic enough to generate charity—what the sell-by date for a Good Object was. "Then, as you know, the earthquake hit in 2010, followed by the cholera outbreak . . . Haiti's list of tragedies, preventable and otherwise, goes on."

Outside, the lights of Chicago glittered in the blue-black night.

"Yet the Haitian people remain vibrant, resilient, and smart." In the flashing slides, water towers perched like cubistic bugs on top of cement-block medical buildings, their bright paint peeling under the relentless scorching light. Patients sat in the hospital's open-air waiting room, fanning themselves, palm fronds and breadfruit hanging green above them. Fierce sunlight splashed everything.

On a dusty road, motorcycles laden with three passengers each—no helmets—whizzed past tap-taps, the small local buses crammed with workmen, schoolgirls in uniform, women with baskets on their heads. Even goats perched atop the tap-taps, which were wildly, intricately ornamented with swirling daubs of paint and bits of broken mirror, each with a hand-painted name: **MERCI JESUS**, **REAL MEN**, **DIVINE OPTION**. Someone in the audience giggled.

"The Haitian people long for economic independence, and they're working for it. Our team's medical efforts contribute to the foundation of health they're already building." Jon smoothly and modestly described the work there: the clean new latrines, the rows of neatly planted crops, the newly trained midwives who walked through the mountains from village to village with medical instruments tied in scarves on their backs. How the Haitian doctors and nurses were eager to train on medical equipment they'd only heard described on the phone by their relatives in Miami. The dire need for vaccinations, the high and bloody rate of vehicular accidents, the cruel new practice the gangs in Port-au-Prince called quadding: shooting a rival in the neck—not to kill, but to paralyze for life, imposing the burden of his care on an already struggling family (if he had a family at all). Around me, people gasped softly, shaking their heads.

He talked about the grassroots peace-building, the sustainable farms, the way local collectives, run by Haitians, were weaning themselves from the largesse of NGOs.

He talked about what ten dollars could do, ten thousand, a hundred thousand, and as he spoke, a heady sense of pity swelled in the room. Checkbooks splashed open on the tables. The thrill of noblesse oblige, high on its own fumes.

A hand gripped my arm: Helene, leaning across. "Isn't he just marvelous?" Her whisper plump with pride.

It was everything I could do not to shake her hand off. I knew my smile was too tight, too stiff, but I couldn't soften it. Everyone—you could tell from the little flushed nods of approval—felt the same way about Jon. Such terrible conditions, so safely far away—and Jon, the rich and gallant hero, leaving luxury behind to sleep on an air mattress in an uncooled room, to eat stringy goat meat cooked in a filthy kitchen (we'd seen the slide) and brush his teeth with bottled water, the only kind that was safe. To examine patients in stifling, windowless cement rooms, wearing a headlamp for those inevitable moments when the power failed. To use a clunky old C-arm X-ray machine from the 1950s—it appeared on screen, provoking startled laughter from the doctors—when his practice in Chicago had the sleekest new equipment dollars could buy. And then to come, cuff links twinkling, to this high floor of a beautiful old building to tell the tale.

But for him, it was a choice; it had always been a choice. He spoke from a position of supreme security, luxury. It's easy to play the hero when you've always had it all.

I sat at the round table in the dark, surrounded by sparkling society people, listening to Jon lecture about faraway suffering. His chair sat empty between his mother and me.

"In closing," he said, "let me just note that it's important to approach this situation with great care. In showing you what our team is doing, I'm sensitive to the charge of having a white, upper-class, American savior complex. I do recognize those pitfalls." He clicked a new slide into place: a dozen Haitian nurses and doctors regarded us from the steps of the clinic. "So we try to enter the situation with respect, curiosity, and the willingness to listen and learn. To be wrong. To start over. To serve. To respect not only the autonomy of the patients but also the authority of the Haitian specialists who're on the ground, day in, day out—who don't get to jet away after a week or two to plentiful clean tap water and a functioning postal service, feeling like noble do-gooders."

Inside my dress, my shoulders straightened. A noble do-gooder was exactly how I'd always imagined Jon saw himself. This was new.

"We know we'll make gaffes. Cultural errors. We know we'll tread on toes and have to apologize and make amends. But the alternative is to do nothing. The alternative is to turn a blind eye, a deaf ear." He loosened his tie, ran a hand through his brown curls. "Look. Our country, afraid of a slave revolt here, punished Haiti. For decades. And every white person in this room has benefited, directly or indirectly, from Haitian suffering. When people are traumatized, immiserated, and underresourced—in part due to long-held policies by our own country—turning away is not something I can do." He paused. "And neither should you."

I gazed at him. A softness stole over me, and I felt myself smile. From the stage, Jon caught my eye and smiled back. A real smile.

"Let me introduce to you the members of our team," he said. The slides ended, the lights came up, and doctors and nurses began trooping onto the stage. Their smiles were solemn and sweet, their suits more or less tailored, their dresses more or less chic. They stood on the stage more or less awkwardly as Jon announced their names and told an anecdote about each one: the young surgeon who always brought fancy French soaps and nail polish for the cooks; the audiologist who'd been stung three times by jellyfish but wouldn't stop night-swimming in the sea; the head nurse, in whose refrigerator large brown bottles of Prestige, the local beer, seemed to mysteriously multiply (the team laughed); and then Lily, an obstetrician who—

I stopped hearing. Lily was tall and slender, with smooth gold hair that fell past her shoulders. Her wide, pretty smile was sincere, and her hand glided onto Jon's arm, lingering, as he shifted to stand beside her.

I sat very still, my heart reeling like a drunk in free fall, and tried to recall if Jon had ever mentioned that Lily lived in Chicago. Knowing he hadn't.

I stared at him, realizing fully for the first time how easy it would be for a wealthy, clever man to conduct a discreet affair. I stared, willing him to look at me, willing his handsome face to turn and shoot me some quick glance of reassurance, but his eyes were alight with good deeds and laughter. Lily's lips were at the height of his throat. She shone with the groomed and coddled glow that came only from a lifetime of love and wealth. Beneath the table, I dug my nails into the fleshy part of my palm.

It was the kind, easy way she smiled and moved that scared me, the warmth. The grace. The confidence, as though she knew she belonged up there, belonged next to him. I remembered those rare times when I'd had to speak on stage, the struggle that it was, the way I'd fought to keep my hands from visibly shaking.

Helene's ringed finger tapped my wrist. She leaned in. "Isn't that one lovely?" she whispered, her breath hot and shrimpy. "The one in the light-blue dress."

I nodded, my smile a tiny tightness, remembering well Sophia's description of the Carolyn Bessette clones that Helene had paraded past Jon, hoping for a match.

Up there on stage under the lights, Lily stood, pleased and calm as royalty. Holding the microphone off to the side, Jon glanced down and murmured something. Her answering laugh was full. Their eyes locked and held.

"Where are you going?" Helene clawed the air for my arm, but I was on my feet and stumbling for the exit.

I spent the last half hour in the ladies' room, throwing up.

———

I could have taken a cab home, could have let myself into the quiet condo, grabbed my packed suitcase, and spent my last night in a hotel.

But I didn't want the drama, didn't want to make a scene, didn't want the questions that would inevitably come later. Didn't want to concede—so publicly, with Helene watching—defeat.

When all the clapping had ended, I rejoined Jon and Helene in the foyer at the wall of elevators and slipped with them inside those golden doors, the floor rushing away beneath us. We stepped out together into the cold night and waited, Helene's visible breath steaming in clouds of praise for her son's fine performance, while the valet brought the car down.

Helene turned to me. "Would you mind if I sat in front with Jon, dear, so we can talk about the hospital?"

I glanced at Jon, waiting for his protest: *No, that's Isabel's place. My wife sits up front with me.* But his gaze was trained on the building's grand entryway, as if waiting for someone particular to come out.

I shrugged at Helene. "Go ahead."

She slid in with a frosty smile.

The valet opened the back door for me, and I got in. We sped through the black night.

———

In the front seat, Helene questioned Jon about Pierre Payen, the clinic, its financial structure, its needs . . . I sat in the back like an exiled child, my coat folded on my lap, feeling a strange exhaustion weight my limbs. My head thrown back against the dark, soft leather, I watched the shimmering film of lights rush overhead in the back windshield. The voices blurred. I let my eyes slide shut.

They opened when I heard my name.

I leaned forward. "Sorry, what?"

Jon's profile tilted an inch in my direction. "I was just saying you might want to talk with David Enderby at some point."

"Your money guy?"

"The family's wealth manager, dear," said Helene.

"Why would I want that?"

"If you'd like," Jon said, "he can advise you about the savings you have now. How to maximize your investments."

Helene gave a half turn and a stiff little smile. "The money from your art and so on."

"Thank you." My tone was careful. I had so little put away. Why did they suddenly care what I did with it? I stroked my coat as if it were a puppy. "I'm fine. Really."

"Money can get complicated," Jon said.

"I'll be fine."

"Investments are complex," said Helene. "One never knows."

"Oh, I'm pretty sure," I said.

"I just think it might be good," said Jon. "It might be wise to have an expert weigh in."

I leaned back. The seat had already cooled, and it chilled my back's bare skin.

"Thank you," I repeated, agreeing to nothing, and let the silence fall.

———

Arriving at the mansion in Lake Forest, the three of us headed not for Judge Turner's oak-lined library but into Helene's "little refuge," as she called it. It wasn't little, and it was full of white-and-gold Louis-the-Something furniture and pale-blue damask drapes that fell to the floor and pooled in picturesque crumples that the maid shook out and rearranged each week. A refuge from what, I couldn't say.

Helene made a great production out of finding her checkbook in the drawer of the frail antique desk, and then selecting just the right pen. "Just make sure it all goes to that good work down there with those poor suffering people," she said, signing with a flourish.

Jon swirled whiskey in the bottom of a Russian cut-crystal glass that had once been held by his grandfather. He stared out at the dark lawn, where the fountain had been stilled for the night.

"Of course," he said, and moved to take the check.

But she pulled it away, fanning it back and forth, as if Montblanc ink dried so much more slowly than other sorts. "I'm quite proud of the work you do, darling."

"Yes. Thank you, Mother."

She relinquished it into his outstretched hand.

Jon looked down at the amount. His left eyebrow rose. "That's generous."

"Well, of course, dear. You do seem," she said with a thin smile, "to enjoy helping the needy."

———

In the car on the way home, I asked Jon nothing. Inside our dark condo, I changed into shapeless pajamas and got silently into bed beside him. We didn't speak. I didn't ask about Lily, or if he was having an affair, or why he'd never happened to mention that she lived in Chicago.

My flight would leave in the morning.

My period hadn't arrived.

There was only so much I could afford to know.

LINES OF FLIGHT

United Airlines #483

No one has ever accused me of being a morning person.

In line for security at O'Hare at four a.m., I shuffled, groggy as a zombie, and held my passport out upside down to the TSA guy. When I entered the view-you-naked booth, I didn't even bother to stand up straight. At the gate, I sat in a stupor, staring down at the locket with Charlie's photograph, flicking the little clasp open and shut. There he was. Then gone. Then there again, looking as if he were alive. I sat mindlessly clicking it until the woman next to me gave me a glare like Aunt Della's.

But once aboard the plane, where the cabin smelled like jet fuel and strong cheap coffee and the flight attendant was chipper to the point of mania, her breath a cloud in the freezing air, I began to wake up. I belted myself into a window seat and glanced around to note the location of the exit nearest me.

Outside, it was still dark, but the runway lights twinkled, and a tangerine streak of promise lit the horizon. If I hadn't known better, it would have felt like an adventure.

————

Once upon a time in my twenties, the rituals of flight terrified me: the squeezing in, the buckling, the flight attendant's recitation of what we should do if various things went horribly wrong, and the bleak knowledge that such information was unlikely to save us. *In the event of . . .* Such placid words for a nightmare.

At the gate, I'd swallow Dramamine half an hour before takeoff and then buy whatever alcohol was offered as soon as the cart rolled down the aisle, hunching with the huddled masses, their elbows crushed against my ribs, cringing at each stranger's wet cough. I'd arrive in a strange city, dehydrated and buzzed, and sleep in cheap hotels with my arms locked around a pillow.

Later, all that changed. First class made a difference.

In first class, before the plane has even taken off—while the other passengers are still boarding, back there in the hinterlands, struggling to cram their objects into overhead compartments and wedge their bodies into cramped seats—flight attendants come and ask if you'd like anything to drink. Anything: wine or sparkling water or vodka rocks. If you choose wine, they keep coming by to refill your glass. They bring you a hot washcloth to wipe your hands.

In first class, they bring you—my favorite thing—a little ceramic cup full of warm nuts. The first time, I was surprised. "From now on, I want someone to *always* warm my nuts!" I said, delighted, to Jon, who laughed and kept repeating it. In first class, you eat hot steak with peppercorn sauce and drink all the wine and whiskey you want, while people in the back pay eight dollars for a box of pickles and crackers.

In first class, they call you by your name. *Ms. Morales*, they say, smiling. They make you feel like a person.

Respect, it turns out—or the semblance thereof—is just another thing you can buy.

Magda

Jon loves the Cuban food I cook, never questioning its origins. I don't know where he thinks I learned to make it.

Surely not through endless trial and error in my tiny New York kitchenette, my Spanish-English dictionary propped open on the counter, Magda's handwritten pages gradually darkening with smudges of olive oil from my fingers.

———

In New York, I'd become curious about what it meant to be Latina.

Back in West Virginia, where the Latino population was minuscule—.03 percent, the census said—wondering had gotten me nowhere. But New York featured Latinos of all ethnicities and nationalities: Colombians, Dominicans, Cubans, Puerto Ricans, and more—along with the Mexicans of which I probably, according to my mother, might be one.

Taking classes at NYU, I ate lunch from food carts on the street: cornmeal tamales filled with torn pork; hot and garlicky bollos pulled from vats of bubbling peanut oil and dropped in a paper cone; slices of mango that flopped like goldfish; fried bacalao; black beans and saffron rice. Burritos, enchiladas, flautas. Though the feminists of color I was reading in grad school explicitly forbade me to "eat the other," my hunger led me from street to street, my tongue enchanted.

What is culture when it tastes so sweet and strange? Half my blood was Latina, of some sort, but I knew no Spanish, danced no salsa, had never pounded a molcajete. I was afraid I would forever be a tourist in my own life.

One cart owner seemed friendlier than most: Magda, a tiny, elderly Cuban woman with black eyes that snapped with light, a downward-turning pink mouth, and dark wiry hair wound in a knot at her nape. I kept coming back to her cart for plátanos maduros: thick gold slices of ripe, sweet plantains, cut on the diagonal and fried in pure Spanish olive oil, lunch and dessert all in one. I came back so often that she began to tempt me with other dishes. "Try," she would say, and drop a pinch of this or that into a paper bowl: papas rellenas stuffed with red peppers and ground beef, or ropa vieja, or bits of fried and salted squid. I pushed extra dollars into her tip jar.

One day she handed me a little lidded plastic dish, brought cold from home. I opened it. "Flan," she said, handing me a plastic spoon. "Try."

I spooned its firm, cold custard into my mouth, the almost-burnt dark caramel sounding like a bass note beneath its thick sweet cream. My face must have shown something, because she laughed her crackling laugh.

"¿Cómo?" I asked. I'd learned that much.

She shook her head. "Solo comparto esta receta con mi familia," she said, smiling. She said it again, slowly, so I could understand.

And I did. I wasn't part of anyone's family.

At home, I looked up recipes on the internet and in the Cuban cookbooks I checked out from the library. In my tiny kitchenette, I tried one after another—and they were tasty. Both Button and I plumped up a bit, which was probably a good thing. But nothing tasted like Magda's flan.

———

West Virginia. Playground. Second grade. I swooped down the metal slide and staggered a few steps forward in the gravel, catching my balance—and there before me, all staring and giggling, stood the girls who ran our classroom: Missy Robinson with her hand on her hip, her pink jeans color coordinated with her striped T-shirt; Tina Nicoletti, with dark, smooth hair that fell to her waist and swished when she tossed it; Anna Tucker, with her pale-blonde bangs and slow-moving blue eyes, her moony face and new Levi's (still dark with dye, which meant her family was rich); and a few other girls who held sway. All giggling and whispering.

Anna Tucker got pushed forward.

"Hey, Bel," she said. She flipped the long curtain of blonde hair behind her. "Are you part nigger?"

I looked at them all, the blood hot in my ears.

I knew from TV and teachers that the proper word was *Black*, and I knew the three Black kids in our school: two sixth-grade boys and a quiet fifth-grade girl named Sondra. They seemed nice. They sat at a lunch table by themselves, with plenty of space all around them.

I took quick inventory. My skin was tan all year, and my dark hair was thick and crinkled. I knew from the mirror that my lips were fuller than my friends'.

"I don't know," I said. "I can ask my mom."

A giggle rippled over them like a wave.

"She don't know," they said. "She don't know her own daddy."

"With her momma, it could be anyone."

"My daddy said Stella Martin'd fuck a horse if it stood still."

Delighted gasps, a whirl, a scatter of gravel, and they melted off under the monkey bars.

I stood, hot and confused. Wondering. Shamed.

My mother worked the late shift for the next few nights, so I was home alone with time to ponder the question. When I woke up on Saturday, she was gone—buying groceries, maybe, or off to see a boyfriend. I made myself a bologna sandwich, wrapped it in wax paper, and headed into the trees.

When I got home from the forest, it was dusk, and my mother sat on the couch watching TV, eating McDonald's out of a white paper sack.

"Hey, baby," she said without looking up. "Where you been?" She held out the fries.

I took one and chewed, standing before her. I must have radiated some strange, nervous energy, because she glanced up, and then she muted the television.

"What's the matter, sugar?"

I couldn't remember ever having been so anxious. My breath came hard.

"Momma, am I part Black?"

"What?" The fries fell in her lap. "Oh my God, no." Her laughter sounded angry, and her mouth twisted as if she'd sucked something sour. "My God, baby. No. Give your momma a little credit."

I don't know what happened on my face then that softened her—what look of fear or sadness—but her eyes grew kind. "Hey now, Bel," she said, reaching up to pull me down beside her. "Now you come here." She took my face in her hands. She smelled like salt. Her eyes bored into mine. I squirmed next to her on the couch. "Now listen. You're a Hispanic. Your daddy was Hispanic. I don't know; Mexican or something. His last name was Morales. He was a trucker. I only knew him a little while, baby."

I reached over and scooped the fries up, dropping them back in the paper bag. "What was he like?"

She stared into the TV as if she were staring past the screen and its pictures and a hundred miles more.

I tapped her hand. Softly. "Momma."

She turned to me, her eyes refocusing. "How's this even crossing your mind, peppercorn? Are kids at school talking shit to you?" She squinted. "Calling you names?"

I nodded.

She took my shoulders in her hands, gripping tight. "Well, listen here, and listen close. Okay?" She looked fierce and shook me a little when she spoke. "You are a Martin. Half Hispanic from your daddy, but one hundred percent mine. You hear?"

I nodded again.

"You're mine. I made you. You grew inside me, and you're part of me forever." She held her hand up next to mine. Larger and paler, it did look otherwise identical. Mine was a little replica. "Forever. You understand me?"

"Yeah," I said, confused and warmed.

She put her arms around me and squeezed tight. "And you ain't no Black. You're beautiful, you hear me? The most beautiful girl in the world. Don't you ever forget that."

I was seven years old. She had said nothing like that to me ever before, about being beautiful. A glow spread through me like relief.

"You tell those little brats to fuck off. They call you names again, hit them hard."

———

It happened in the lunchroom.

Teachers on lunch duty stood against the wall in the corners, too far away to hear us over the clatter of trays and the chatter of children. I was walking with my melamine tray full of food, eager for the one full meal I'd have that day, when Tina Nicoletti said loudly, "Too bad Bel's part nigger." Her dark hair swung.

I stopped and took a breath. My own voice was just as loud.

"No, I'm not. I'm Hispanic." I tossed my own hair. "You know. Like a Mexican." I made it sound special, superior.

A silence fell. There were so few Latinos in West Virginia that the girls didn't know any new slurs or stereotypes to wield.

Suddenly I looked over at the Black kids' table. Sondra's eyes were on me, and she'd stopped chewing. A bit of air went out of me.

But I walked on to my own table, where my friends waited, and sat down with a little flounce like I'd seen the cool girls do.

———

The following week, I carried my tray to the table where Sondra sat.

"Do you want to come sit with us?" I said.

She glanced at the two boys at her table. Met my eyes. Shook her head.

I scuffed my tennis shoes together.

"Is it okay if I sit here?"

She looked at me in silence. Shrugged. Nodded.

I put my tray down and sat.

Eating, I glanced over at her. Her shy smile, her kind eyes. As our halting conversation picked up speed, we began to laugh together. Watching Sondra, I saw how wrong my mother was about who could and could not be beautiful.

We never got close. Too much divided us.

But we talked to each other in a friendly way, and sometimes after school, waiting outside for the bus, we'd leave our book bags nestled side by side on the cement steps and play on the spoil heaps. We'd climb their sliding slopes, laughing as our feet slipped away under us with each step, our tennis shoes coated with coal dust. The creek, crusted with foam, ran yellow in the valley below. We didn't know the very air we breathed was laced with particles of soot.

From time to time, I'd sit at Sondra's table, and once in a while she sat at mine. We stayed friendly until my mother got arrested and I had to go.

———

Thinking back now, I understand that the sofa of my childhood was a cheap, ugly sofa. Green-and-brown plaid, it was a hand-me-down many times over, lumpy and stained. Our TV, too, was already old, outdated, its screen bulging from the big wooden cube of its cabinet.

I see that my mother, who was kind to me that evening long ago, was ignorant, a racist, a damaged, uncritical product of her time and a perpetuator of its cruelty.

I know this is how we learn prejudice: twisted in with love and our own eagerness to belong, like a braid that's hard to unravel.

But it was a Saturday night, and my mother was at home with me. I had her all to myself. She thought I was beautiful. The lamplight shone around us. We sat on that sofa for hours, watching show after show, until even *The Love Boat* and *Fantasy Island* came on, and she did not make me go to bed. I didn't understand the jokes, but I laughed when my mother laughed, and when we leaned against each other and ate our apple turnovers, they were still warm.

———

In New York during the winter, I stopped frequenting the Latino food carts and ate indoors more often. Weeks passed. It was a cold spring, and it was easier to stay inside my apartment in sweatpants, eating ramen and microwaved meals, than go out into the streets.

But eventually the weather changed and grew hot. One cabin-fevered, early-summer's day, struck by the desire for sweet plantains, I went out for a walk. I headed down the long, sun-soaked blocks in the direction of the Cuban food cart, and when I spotted its red umbrella from a distance, my steps quickened.

But behind the cart, wearing an apron, was a teenager. He smiled and asked in easy English what I wanted.

"Where's Magda?" I asked.

His black eyes clouded. His grandmother, he explained, had had a stroke, and then a heart attack. In the hospital, she had died.

My legs turned to water, and I slid onto a bench. The first tears leaked hot down my cheeks. Then, uncontrollably, I began to sob.

The boy leaned down, a puzzle in his eyes. "Wait," he said. He patted my shoulder awkwardly. "Are you the girl that eats flan?"

I nodded, hiccupping.

"Ah. Okay, okay." He held up a hand. "My grandmother, she left something for you."

He went back to the cart and pulled open one of its stainless-steel drawers. Rummaged inside. Held aloft a thick square of folded paper.

The boy came and sat on the bench at my side, and he patted my shoulder again. "Don't be sad," he said. He opened the folded pages. "She wrote this down for you."

I took it from his fingers and willed my wet eyes to focus. In a halting hand, in Spanish, she had written down her recipes: for papas rellenas, for plátanos, for bollos, for roast pork. And for her inimitable flan. *Vaya con Dios, mi'ja,* she had written at the bottom, with a small inked heart.

My daughter.

I put my hands over my face, swamped by guilt.

"The girl that eats flan," her grandson had called me.

I had never told her my name.

———

Is culture a taste you can acquire? A mother who finally feeds you?

In our glass kitchen high above Lake Michigan, I cooked Jon and our guests elaborate Cuban dinners, salted with the hot, bright noon of loss.

———

West Virginia. A warm, sunny day in September. Ten years old, sitting cross-legged under the yellow table, watching.

My mother sat in one of the vinyl chairs, her legs jutting out defiantly, her arms crossed over her chest. The kitchen smelled of bacon and molasses and the buckwheat cakes she'd made for us that morning. When Aunt Della had shown up unannounced with her bucket and bleach, my mother and I had still been sprawled in front of the TV, a little giddy from sugar, watching cartoons and singing along to the K-tel commercials.

Now Della stood at the oven. "You got grease all over this here stove top," she said, scrubbing, the loose flesh of her upper arm juddering back and forth. "Begging for a house fire, crudding it all up like that." Her iron-gray curls shook with each stroke.

My mother's pretty lips pressed against each other in a flat line. Her eyes were narrowed at Della's broad back.

"Not fit for man nor beast," Aunt Della said. "How you think you're fit to raise another one, I do not know. Don't ask me. What was going through your head, I cannot say. Lord help us all. Another mouth to feed."

My mother's hands went to her waist. "I can't say my head was particularly involved," she said. "Anyways, you won't be feeding it."

"No, by God, I won't, and from the looks of that one there"— she jerked the green sponge toward me—"neither will you. Skinny as string."

"Bel's going through a growth spurt. She's getting her height." My mother's skin was dull, her hair already losing its luster.

"Getting her height, is she? She been getting height her whole life?"

My mother smoothed her hands over her rounding belly. "How about this for a notion? I'll take care of mine, and you take care of yours. Seems like you got your hands plenty full back over to the house."

Della spun. "Leave Billy out of it. You gonna watch me clean your kitchen, then tell me to mind my own business? You got another think coming. What would Momma say about this mess if she were living?"

"Living or dead, Momma can kiss my ass."

Della stilled, a kind of violence clouding her blue eyes, the sponge in her hand like a missile poised to launch. "Listen at you," she said. "No respect."

"Leastaways I never beat my girl. More than Momma could say."

"And look at her." The sponge jerked my way again. "Running wild like a little monkey. Just look at that hair."

I reached a tentative hand up to touch it. It hadn't been brushed since the previous morning, before school. My toes were rimed with dirt from playing barefoot outside.

My mother recrossed her arms. "I don't remember signing her up for no beauty pageant."

Aunt Della snorted. "And not likely to, neither, what with her running wild as a little Indian."

"There's things better than pageants and worse than Indians."

"I reckon so. Still, that girl could use some civilizing."

My mother tilted her chair back on its two hind legs, the way teachers wouldn't let us in school, and stared Aunt Della down. "You want to come over here and clean? Come on in, you got a key. You want to preach? Go ahead, you got a mouth. But you think I'm going to change jack-shit about my life, you just keep dreaming, Della Dunn. We're fine like we are."

"You might be a lot of things, sister, but one thing you ain't is fine." Aunt Della sighed, and the blue flames in her eyes died down. She gave a heavy nod of finality that included us both. Turning back to the stove, she muttered, "Lord tells us look after widows and orphans." Her shoulders shook as she scrubbed. "And sure but He don't ask a lot."

My mother glared at Aunt Della's back for a long moment. Then she looked down at me. The skin around her mouth softened, and she winked.

———

Jumping class means agreeing to believe that there's something gross about the body, something filthy about its messes and flows, its grime and smears, the whorls of clutter it leaves in its wake. In adulthood, I learned that whole strata of people feel disturbed by the greasy smudges fingers leave, the slick smear of a mouth on the rim of a glass, a pile of laundry left to wrinkle on a bed.

Growing up half-feral with my mother, I didn't know about disgust, and I was happy.

———

"A late-life baby," my mother liked to say of Charlie, though she was only twenty-eight when he was born. "A surprise," she said.

An easy child, she called me. "Oh, you were always an easy child," she'd say later, explaining away my survival, when I visited the penitentiary. "So quiet."

It was true: I entertained myself, watching the world. I lived in books and the dense woods that cloaked the mountains around our little house. I preferred doing my homework on the glassed-in back porch with the little whirring space heater to watching the blaring TV in the front room, one of her men-friends' feet up on our furniture, and my mother nestling under his big arm or jumping up to get him a beer even when it wasn't a commercial.

When Charlie got big enough to crawl and toddle and then properly walk and run, he was not an easy child. His hands were in everything, plastic sacks of peat torn open by his stubborn fingers, its brown crumbs sticking everywhere, sprinkled across the engine of a car whose hood stood open. A toaster oven turned upside down and taken apart so completely that no grown-up could put it together again.

His experiments on the world weren't the half of it. He wanted attention, interaction. For Charlie, it wasn't enough to dig in the mud with a stick: he wanted you to watch him dig while telling him a story about a magical boy who dug mud. He loved stories, and I was the one who told them, who tucked him in at night, smoothing the light curls back from his forehead, the one who carried him around the woods on my too-small girl's hip, pointing at cardinals and teaching him how to tell the brown woman-birds from the bright-red men. In the mornings, I was the one who dressed him and tied his shoes and made sure he ate his oatmeal. In the evenings, I lured him to his bath with stories of whales and octopi and coaxed him back out when his little fingertips wrinkled like peach pits.

All those things were my job. Momma was too busy with her men. Besides, she would say, Charlie behaved better with me.

———

Perhaps it is impossible for people who don't have younger siblings—or, to be more precise, people never charged in childhood with complete responsibility for their younger siblings—to imagine the huge and tender hollow that such caretaking carves out in a child.

As a wealthy society, we can agree that five or eight or even ten is too young an age to begin caring for others, to put someone else at the center of our attention and concern, to engage in the actual daily activities of ensuring a more helpless child's survival in the world, the endless little labors: the constant watchful eye, the quick swoop of the protective save from electrical outlets, rocky creek beds, the bottle of pills your mother left spilled across the coffee table. But it happens nonetheless. This way of moving in the world: it becomes habitual. It leaves marks. It leaves an emptiness.

When photographs hit the news of Latin American children kept in cages by our government, good progressive middle-class Americans were outraged (but not enough) by the image of girls as young as seven or eight—kind-eyed little girls, sweetly smiling—with toddlers on their hips. Good US citizens were outraged (but not enough) to learn of the rations in the camps: cheap, unfresh, unvaried food packets of questionable nutritional value.

Standing around after yoga class, raking my hair loose from its knot, chatting with the other elegant, aghast, well-to-do women—many of them svelte young mothers—about the news, I did not say, *That was my childhood.*

———

Charlie clung to my mother in a way her men-friends couldn't countenance. "You raising some kind of sissy?" they'd bark, when he was affectionate with Momma, hugging her knees, leaning against her shins as she sat on the couch. A golden, shining boy always clamoring for attention, he'd play with his Matchbox cars on the braided rag rug, pushing the little wheels up and over the woven bumps, driving them onto her feet. Sometimes he'd block the boyfriend's view of the TV, and there'd be yelling.

I tried to get Charlie to come to the back porch with me, but the TV pulled him like a magnet. My mother complained to me about it.

"So don't watch *Dukes of Hazzard*," I said one day in the kitchen. "Watch the news or something." A box of Hamburger Helper stood on the counter, its fat little white glove smiling jovially. "Charlie'll get bored and leave."

She guffawed, turning a package of ground chuck upside down over the skillet. "You think Pete's gonna watch the news?"

The difficult thing about men-friends, it seemed to me, was that they wanted all of a woman's attention for themselves. They liked *making* babies well enough, but they didn't care much for the final product.

———

The forest was my place, but sometimes as he grew older, I took Charlie. He'd run ahead of me on his little legs, or I'd carry him on my back up to the old stone trapper's cabin, which stood high on a hillside, hidden among thickset maple trees on a bluff. I loved the cabin: its dark, snug secrecy. Green moss crept to the edge of its fieldstone porch. I'd asked Momma about it—who had lived there, when it got built—but she didn't know. "Afore my time," she said.

The sturdy cabin's single room had a stone chimney and floor. There was an old wooden bedstead (the mattress long since hauled or rotted away), a bureau (its drawers crooked and empty), and a table with a lone chair. The only door had been well made, tightly fitted to its frame, and the cabin had no windows, so lumbering creatures had been unable to make their dens inside, but birds and bats had come in through the chimney. Their droppings dotted the stone hearth. Mice had built nests in the bureau's drawers.

Sometimes I imagined the fur trapper who'd lived there. I pictured him sitting before the fire on a cold night, eating hot venison alone, smoking his pipe. Playing his fiddle, perhaps, or whittling. Outside, the cabin's stone porch was sheltered by an overhanging roof. The porch had a good view of the valley. If you stood on tiptoe, you could see the creek far below, winding like a silver snake.

That cabin was our hideaway, our playhouse. Birdcalls spliced the air, and wind rushed through leaves; green-filtered sunlight dappled the moss. If we lay still and quiet long enough, all manner of creatures would shuffle past. Woodchucks, deer, rabbits. Once a red fox, the white tip of its tail swirling out like a flag. (Charlie breathless with thrill.) Raccoons at dusk.

Sometimes in summer, Charlie and I sat there on the porch in the rain, watching a storm blow through. I'd lean against the logs, he'd crawl into my lap, and I'd tell him stories until he fell asleep, his thumb lodged in his little pink bud-mouth.

He liked my versions of the fairy tales Momma had once read to me (before she lost interest in things like reading). With Charlie in my lap, his dense weight rising and falling with each breath, I'd close my eyes and see the bright pictures from the Grimms' book, the castles and princesses and boys who turned into birds. (The cruel parents—the ones who turned their children out of doors, or poisoned them—were seldom illustrated.)

I'd tell Charlie the stories to the best of my recollection, and he was a tough customer, jerking unexpectedly upright if I left out some detail. I'd soften my voice, lower and lower, until he began to twitch like the paws of a sleeping puppy.

On the porch of the cabin, I'd wrap my arms around him and let him doze until the rain stopped. It gave me something, that holding. That peace, the warmth and small weight of him against me. Carefully, gently, I'd push to my feet, staggering a little, and carry him, still sleeping, down the hill toward home.

I came to love abandoned places, derelict, unconsidered, no longer molded by human purpose. There was a wild, untrammeled feeling in them, free from humans with their rages and needs.

Even in adulthood, in New York and Chicago, construction made me wilt. I knew it was a failure of my civic enthusiasm, but it all seemed like so much noise. The silence of ruins felt more like home. When humans stopped caring about what they'd made, Nature stepped in, wreathing old walls and roofs with vines, pulling whole buildings down into a green embrace.

———

"The Six Swans" was Charlie's favorite fairy tale, and it began with a king's inexplicable cruelty to his sons. *If our next child be a girl,* the king told his wife, *our six sons shall be put to death, that she may inherit all my kingdom.* The king had six coffins built and hidden away in a macabre death hall, awaiting his sons' little corpses.

The queen, heartbroken, told her youngest son, Benjamin (shades of the Bible, of Israel's twelve tribes—there are twelve birds in some variants of the tale), who led his brothers into the forest for safety. If the newborn child turned out to be a boy, then the queen would fly a white flag of safety from the castle's tower, and they could all come home again. If it was a girl, she'd fly a red flag, for blood, for warning.

A red flag flew, and the brothers knew they could not return. They traveled deep into the forest and found a little cabin, where Benjamin kept house and the older ones hunted—for years. Exiled in the woods, outraged at the whole fairer sex, the older brothers made a pact to kill any maiden they met.

Meanwhile, the princess grew up in the castle.

What is the age of curiosity? How old is a young girl when she begins to question all the practices of the adults around her, cloaked so long in normalcy? When does she ask why things must be the way they are? (What does this torn photograph mean, this bottle of pills in the medicine cabinet? Who was my father? Why are some people rich while others go hungry? Why are some mothers clean and calm, picking their children up from school in washed cars, while mine lies on the couch, asleep, a brown trail of dried vomit on her cheek?)

The young princess, investigating the castle, discovered the room full of coffins. In another version, she found little white shirts in the laundry. She asked her mother, who disclosed all. Heartbroken and guilty for the crime she'd unknowingly committed against her brothers by the mere fact of her existence, the princess trekked out to the woodland hideaway, where she met Benjamin (falling upon each other's necks in a tearful embrace, et cetera), who then convinced his rougher brothers not to slaughter her.

The princess, overjoyed, agreed to clean their cottage, cook their meals, and tend their garden, gladly trading the privileges of royal life for the chance to be her brothers' loving maid. Happily ever after.

But not quite, not at all. Because the poor princess, unused to gardening, clipped six lilies—whereupon an old wise woman, who happened to be standing nearby, cried out in sorrow and informed her that those lilies were *actually her brothers*, who were now turned into swans (or ravens, in the variant).

Sudden rush of wings and feathers. The brothers swirled up like a storm and were gone.

The princess sobbed, contrite, until the old woman said yes, all right, perhaps there was one remedy—but it was far too taxing for a princess. *Tell me,* the girl said. *I'll do anything. Anything, to get my brothers back.*

If you are silent for seven years, said the old woman, *neither smiling nor laughing, and you weave by hand new shirts for your brothers* (from blossoms, in one version; from stinging nettles, in another), *then you can turn them back into men.*

It goes on. It's a long, strange, convoluted story. Silent yet still lovely, the princess marries a king. As a new queen, she bears children and is accused by the bitter old dowager queen of eating them (the old queen steals the infants away and daubs blood around her daughter-in-law's mouth). Due to her vow of silence, the young queen can't utter a word in her own defense.

Finally, the king, despite his love for her, must sentence her to death. In the very last minute, she's bound at the stake, waiting for flames, still sewing the very last sleeve of the very last shirt, when the seventh year ticks to its close, and the six swans swoop down in a cyclone of wings.

The queen tosses the shirts upon their backs, and they turn miraculously into men. (In one version, the unfinished sleeve lands on Benjamin's arm, and he turns into a man with one white wing. I have always felt tender toward Benjamin, caught between worlds, the brother who kept house, who kept faith.) The young queen's years of silence end. She tells her husband all. They retrieve their children and banish the wicked mother-in-law.

The End.

It's a twisting tale, and I made the mistake of telling it to Charlie once. He took to it immediately, begging for it time after time. Boys who could turn into birds enchanted him. In early childhood, the notion of slipping easily into another creature's skin seems so natural and right. Sometimes Charlie would gaze out over a field, his eyes as ruminative as any old man's, and begin, "When I was a crow . . ." He'd chatter on, embroidering a nonsense tale with complete certainty and a serious expression.

When I learned about reincarnation, I wondered about Charlie and his crow stories. I wondered if his soul could have chosen his short, truncated life for some spiritual purpose of its own. Wasn't it pretty to think so?

As a little boy, excited by the fairy tale, he liked to run in circles and flap his arms, cawing, until I threw a T-shirt at him. As the fabric fell upon his shoulders, he'd straighten up and drop his arms.

He'd turn to me, his eyes wide. "And now I am a human boy," he'd say somberly. "A prince."

"Yes," I'd say, gathering him in my arms, trying not to squeeze too hard. "Yes, you are."

———

My own favorite fairy tale, of course, had been "Cinderella," as it was so many girls': Who doesn't love a sweet innocent who can do the dishes, do the mopping, as the Disney mice sang, but then transform in a twinkling and enchant a prince? Well, that Charles Perrault had a lot to answer for, slapping a happily-ever-after on the end of things, as if Cinderella just U-Hauled her stuff to the castle and never looked back—as if she never wandered alone at night down the dark vaulted hallways, unable to sleep, wondering what the hell she was doing in such an impossibly grand place, the small soft scrapes of her footsteps on stone echoing in the eerie chill. Knowing that going back to her stepmother's house was unthinkable, but hardly feeling at home with the liveried servants and cut crystal and her new husband, who wore all the correct kingly behaviors like an effortless garment, never stumbling over what to do or say or wear. As if Cinderella never stood in front of her own closet, panicking, or fell into sinking silence at royal cocktail parties, wishing to God she were anywhere else. How horribly ill at ease I felt most of the time. Once I lay on the yoga mat in a particularly wrenching twist, and the thought came to my mind, simple and unbidden, detonating against the quiet hush of Sanskrit chants and flute music: *Why does it have to hurt so much?*

Quick liquid trickled down my face as I lay there in the half light and palo santo smoke among two dozen other twisted bodies and realized I hadn't meant only yoga and wondered what the hell was wrong with me and if it would ever get better.

Washington Dulles International Airport

At 8:38 a.m. precisely, our wheels touched the runway, our bodies sucked simultaneously forward as the pilots braked. Out the window, the November sky rang its bright blue like a bell.

I turned on my cell phone and sent Jon a quick text. All around me, people were doing the same thing.

Sometimes I think of us all, temporarily inhabiting the same vehicles, the same streets, but with our networks of love overlapping, like layers upon layers of spiderwebs until the whole thing is a dense, silver mesh so strong that no one can pull it apart. Envisioning this thick, tenacious web of love helps me feel less irritable when people are hopelessly slow or bump me with their baggage. I think, *We don't know each other, but you love someone as much as I do, and somewhere there's a person waiting for you who'd be wrecked if you didn't come home.* That awareness of love—all around, all the time, flowing—somehow buoys me up, makes me tender and patient, when I'm in public, where it seems we become so easily exasperated with each other.

Whenever I reviewed the mental highlight reel of my honeymoon with Jon in Paris, there were of course the standards (the wonderful things one tells one's friends: the candlelight cruise on the Seine, the Monets, the Rodins, the out-of-the-way bistros—and, even more, the wonderful things one doesn't), but what seemed most vivid were the moments of stillness within movement, the little interstitial bouts of bliss: standing close in front of him on the Metro, swaying, his warmth pressed against my back, his arm around me, his lips pressed to my hair, and every now and then a kiss dropped upon my fontanel. My eyes would close. The noise continued—the clacking on the tracks, the blurred roar of the engine—and the swaying kept on, but everything would feel perfectly still and quiet. No time. Only a kind of radiance. His nearness. The soft electricity between us.

Those ordinary moments, saying nothing in the gray flickering light of the subway between sights we intended to see, stayed more real to me than any arches of triumph.

———

At Dulles, I had a layover of almost four hours. Numb and aimless, I wandered in and out of shops full of luxuries, fingering men's cashmere sweaters and squirting so many expensive perfumes on myself that eventually I had to go to the bathroom and scrub my wrists clean.

At the Massage Bar, I lowered my face gingerly into the chair's padded face-hole, wondering about flu epidemics, while a Ukrainian woman whose name badge said Tammi attempted to cleave my torso in two. After half an hour, I stood up, dazed with release, inordinately fatigued, wanting only a place to lie down and nap.

The gate for my flight to Morgantown was a small, cramped ghetto on the bottom level of the airport. The chairs, of which there were too few, bore the marks of long battering, and middle-aged businessmen stood around, talking loudly into their cell phones, their polyester suits shining with hard use.

———

Jon doesn't know about the anxiety: to do, to make, to keep busy, to keep from thinking, remembering. People imagine that because I smile and rarely speak, I'm calm, but it's just a placid act. Art—making new shapes from old things—was the only way I'd ever found to turn the panic into joy. Straw into gold. But it wasn't working anymore.

To while away the time, I took out my embroidery, a design I'd borrowed from a dust jacket by Vanessa Bell. Stitching was a habit I'd developed to give the illusion of productivity, keep my restless hands busy.

In college, we studied Virginia Woolf, but I was more drawn to Vanessa Bell, the silent sister who painted, the one who designed the covers for Virginia's self-published books. (Hogarth Press, their enterprise was called, named after the Woolfs' home in Richmond—Hogarth House, from the days when houses had names. The press was a project, Leonard wrote, to keep Virginia's hands busy, distract her from her madness.) Virginia and Leonard had no children—only each other and their books—and during World War II, Virginia drowned herself in the River Ouse, her pockets full of stones. Vanessa had her paintings, her artist husband, her lovers, and her three children. Redolent with life, she endured a dozen heartbreaks and two world wars.

I fell quietly in love with Vanessa's ugly paintings, her faceless, muddy figures in unattractive rooms, sympathizing with the way she groped to find a style—imitating now Picasso, now Matisse, searching out a vision that could be her own. That humble lostness endeared her to me. Her graphic designs for Virginia's dust jackets seemed deliberately clumsy—her rough, repeated shapes, the uneven lettering—especially when viewed next to the stylized curls of Art Nouveau or sleek angles of Art Deco. *A person made this,* the book covers seemed to cry—a person raw, imperfect, shaken by the world's violence, and struggling to see. Stubborn. Sensuous. Something sullen. A silence that speaks. *You think you know beauty? I will make a beauty unlike anything your eye can comprehend.*

110

A year ago, on those long, dark Chicago evenings when Jon was at the clinic or down in Pierre Payen, I began to play with Vanessa Bell's designs. With my legs folded under me on the couch, I sketched her Hogarth Press dust jacket designs onto panels of canvas with colored pencils. Then I embroidered them, satin-stitching to fill in areas of color. It was hard to find floss to match Bell's palette; she viewed the world through a grayed scrim.

When I finished the first one—a facsimile of the cover of *Jacob's Room*, brown and black on mottled cream—I fashioned it into a handbag, a clutch, lined with a scrap of gold Sevillian silk, and sent it to Sophia for Christmas. After New Year's, when I turned my computer back on, there were requests for six more handbags from her Portland socialite friends.

I stitched during the *PBS NewsHour*. Sometimes, listening to stories of violence and disaster, I glanced up to see bodies and blood. Sobbing parents carried children, small bodies limp, limbs dangling. I took deep breaths as my hand picked and lifted its way across the canvas.

If you find the interstices where threads cross, you can slip the needle in, effortless. Down through, back up, stitch after stitch. A picture emerges. You've broken nothing, but everything is changed. The strange idea possessed me, as I was sewing, that I was somehow stitching Vanessa Bell into myself, grafting her vision onto my own flesh: her silence, her patience, her maternal desire. The ability to look, to change.

She designed a dozen dust jackets for Virginia's books, and I've embroidered eleven. Eleven elegant women in Portland and Chicago carry the handbags I've made. I was on the twelfth, *A Writer's Diary*, black and a strange tomato orange on a beige background, published after Woolf had drowned herself. Days after she'd walked into the river, they found her body and dragged it out. A young man who'd pumped petrol for the Woolfs was there when she washed up, sodden and swollen. "A horrible thing," he recalled in old age, shaking his head, his pale-blue eyes leaking. "A horrible thing. And her such a lady, too.

Always wandering up and down Rodmell with her pretty dress trailing the ground." He closed his eyes and smiled. "Eccentric, she was." He shook his head again, as if shaking off the vision of her bloated corpse.

When I met him, I was in England on a two-week study trip I'd won. To this day, I'm not sure what studying abroad accomplished. It's hard to say what our experiences do for us, even those we carefully choose and pursue. I just know I saw with my own eyes the smoky inglenook at Rooks Nest (the boyhood country home of E. M. Forster), and Henry James's Lamb House in Rye, and a dozen other places that amply demonstrated, discouragingly, what all those writers I loved so much had in common: They were rich. They came from money. They felt the luxury and freedom to innovate, to experiment, to write weird things only the avant-garde would read. When traditional publishing houses wouldn't take their work, they could afford to buy a press, as the Woolfs did, as Gertrude Stein and Alice Toklas did, or pay the vanity fees. Today, they're canonical. A tricky thing, reception. An unpredictable thing.

Afraid and marginal and poor, I paid attention. My English trip gave me a bit of cachet I stashed away. Now and again I'd pull it out at a dinner party, no doubt gauche as Gatsby with his brief stint at Oxford—but, like Gatsby's, my stories all were true: I'd gotten sloshed at the Bird and Baby, punted on the River Cam. I'd sat in Henry James's walled garden and pretended it was mine. I'd walked through English fog, tiny pearls beading my eyelashes. I'd been to Brighton but couldn't recall why—I remember only rocks crunching under my feet as I walked the beach alone, wind whipping my eyes as I stared out across the Channel, wishing for a mackinaw.

It was the only time I ever went abroad alone, and it was such a timid place to choose, England: nothing too foreign or frightening. You see this tendency in poor people, country people—the timidity, the fear of travel, of the unknown, of being lost and alone in a strange place with no money and no one to call for help.

Lucy. That's the name I liked for a girl—from Forster's Lucy Honeychurch. A British name, but easy to twirl toward Spanish: Lucia, Luz. For boys, I was less sure. Jon liked good old solid names, names out of history or Shakespeare or the Bible: Henry, Samuel, Thomas, Luke.

Fine, I'd say, fobbing him off. *That's fine.*

As long as he didn't say Charles.

Aunt Della's

At fourteen, after my mother's arrest, I went to live with Aunt Della, and I transferred to the town school, where we were learning about Hiroshima and Nagasaki. No matter how many American lives our US history teacher kept telling us were saved by the *Enola Gay*, my young heart was outraged.

"But was it worth it?" I said in class, almost in tears, pointing to the fact that little kids got killed. At least in regular wars, mostly soldiers died. They'd signed up, or at least knew what they were in for. "Our government killed *children*," I kept saying, my voice getting louder and louder.

Later, I said it to the principal, and then I said it to him again, in front of Aunt Della, who'd been summoned from the factory early, and I could tell from the way she sat, heavy and stiff in the chair, not looking at me, that she wasn't pleased.

"Mrs. Miller doesn't understand why she became so agitated," the principal said. He was a bald man who kept pinching the bridge of his nose and saying *disruptive* and *excessive*. My aunt nodded, staring down at the pocketbook grasped on her lap.

But when he explained that our teacher had shown slides of the white outlined forms of schoolchildren who'd been instantly vaporized by the bombs, Aunt Della closed her eyes and held up her hand to interrupt him.

"Just let me take her home," she said.

Aunt Della's hand lay on my shoulder all the way out to the truck. She came to the passenger side with me and opened my door.

"It's okay to be upset." She stared out across the sun-spangled roofs of the cars. "It's okay."

Breath rushed into my mouth. Dizzy with relief, I floated up out of my body and hovered above, staring down where the two of us stood in the parking lot.

I'd been afraid she'd yell at me that I was crazy, like my mother did when she was high.

———

My mother wrote each week from the penitentiary, her letters a maudlin mix of promises, Jesus, and self-pity. I wrote back short, obligatory notes in blue ink that said Aunt Della and Uncle Frank were treating me well (true), I was doing well in school (true enough), and I was making new friends (false). In the hallways, kids veered around me. Clustered at their open lockers, girls glanced over at me, whispering to each other behind their hands.

But Aunt Della did treat me well, and Uncle Frank mostly kept to himself. He often pulled extra shifts at the mine, "for extra cashola," he said cheerfully, which he spent on lottery tickets and cigarettes and cases of Pabst. His regular paycheck went straight to bills and groceries; Aunt Della saw to that. Hers did, too, and anything left over went into savings. "He wants to carouse around like a teenager, he can work for it," she said, all stern.

But once when he won fifty dollars from the scratch-off, he bought her a new bathrobe, a pink tube of rose-scented cream for her hands, and a necklace with a rhinestone set in a little gold heart. When she opened everything up, she flung her arms around him. The crinkles fanned out from the corners of his closed eyes as he hugged her. "You make me feel like a girl," she said.

I couldn't help starting to love them a little bit.

———

Aunt Della was heavy where my mother was thin, stern where my mother was lackadaisical. Where my mother was careless, Della was neat as a pin.

Aunt Della's forearms were thick with muscle from working with her hands her whole life: at home, cleaning and chopping and hauling, and on the line at the factory. But above the elbow, she bloomed into soft fat, and she stayed fat the rest of the way down: a thick torso, a lumpy rump that wobbled, ankles sloping with wads of extra flesh, mottled purple by all the tiny blood vessels that had given up.

Even in the few black-and-white family photos from their youth that remain, Della stares wearily at the camera, heavyset, her features already tilted with worry, her hair cropped close to her skull, practical, while my mother is airy and fey, glancing off, her limbs tossed casually around, as if even the photographer hadn't been able to pin her, for a moment, to stillness.

My mother married for love at sixteen and became a widow the following year when her thirty-year-old husband died in a mine explosion. She inherited the house and acres he'd bought with his coal-mining paychecks; his life insurance paid everything off, but Stella Martin did not wear her grief with dignity or her widowhood with discretion. Her pattern of brief and stormy liaisons was well established by the time I was conceived with a long-haul trucker. During all the years I lived in that little white house at the forest's edge, a panoply of men paraded through. After me, she mastered birth control. Except for one lapse.

"God, no," I heard her say once to a friend when she was pregnant with Charlie. "On purpose? Why would I? One's bad enough."

———

"How's school going?"

"Okay."

This was my daily uninspired exchange with Aunt Della. She didn't seem particularly interested, nor had she dealt with the Mercer Independent School District since her son had dropped out five years before as a seventeen-year-old sophomore whose favorite pastimes were baseball and shooting potato guns. Billy hadn't seen the point of school.

But he was beautiful. All the girls thought so. Now twenty-two, he came by the house sometimes, lean-hipped in his low-slung jeans, his dirty blond hair falling into his eyes.

"Hey, little cousin," he'd say. His gaze would slide from my feet to my eyes and then back down again. "Growing up, huh?"

A pulse of electricity would run through me, and I'd stare past his shoulder, ignoring him, my whole body tense like a deer's. The dark tang of his sweat haunted me.

He'd laugh and wander to the fridge, grab a Mountain Dew or one of Uncle Frank's beers, hassle his parents for money. He lived in a trailer with friends a couple of hollers away, and they all worked on cars. People who couldn't afford a proper mechanic would tow their cars out to Billy's, where they'd sit in the yard until one of the guys could get them running again. I'd never been there; I wasn't allowed.

Billy wore T-shirts with the sleeves rolled up, and his arms were muscled and sleek. When he asked for money, Uncle Frank would utter disgusted epithets. Only after he'd left the room, shaking his head, would Aunt Della dig into her pocketbook. When Billy came over for the evening, she'd bustle around to cook chicken cacciatore or turkey tetrazzini, his favorites, but if it was just Uncle Frank and me, we got fish fingers from the freezer and baked beans from a can.

Before he left, Billy would let Aunt Della hug him. She'd squeeze him tight and close her eyes. "My Elvis," she'd say. "My king." His green eyes stayed open, staring off, as he submitted to the embrace.

That's how it had always been with Aunt Della and Billy. After he was born, my mother said, Aunt Della needed an operation that took out her womb, so Billy was the end for her in the baby-making department. She'd always clung to him.

Uncle Frank was less enamored. "That boy needs to get a job," he'd say. "Fixing them cars is fine, but he needs a regular job with a paycheck and insurance." Word at school was that Billy and his friends' real income came from a whiskey still they ran in the woods behind their trailer, and they'd sell to kids if you had enough money. Billy cut a glamorous figure, and some of that glamour trickled down to me.

I was grateful to have it. During that period of my life, I was shell-shocked, my little brother dead, my mother freshly sent to prison. My hands shook. Aunt Della and Uncle Frank lived in Mercer, a little coal town with grim two-story houses wedged next to each other on steep streets, so the forest was far away from me. I had nowhere to hide and no one to hold. I felt alone in the world and hungry to focus on ordinary things, to look like a normal girl. Homework. Being popular. Everyday wants and worries.

———

One afternoon, I was sitting at the kitchen table, doing my math.

"You know you're welcome to stay here with us as long as you need," Aunt Della said.

I looked up. She was putting away the dishes I'd washed when I'd come home from school.

"Thank you," I said carefully. Something was at stake. I didn't know what.

"You're family." She glanced over her shoulder at me.

I nodded.

"And family looks out for their own."

"Oh, really?" Aunt Della snapped. "You want to tell me what is?" She turned to look at me, a dishrag in her hand, and then mashed her lips tightly together, as if to stop more words from spilling out.

———

After the premature demise of my cheerleading career, I borrowed a yoga videotape from the high school library. I don't know where I'd heard of yoga—on TV, probably—but I was curious.

Aunt Della had agreed to switch shifts at the factory with a friend for a couple of weeks, though she was much put out, since she hated evening shifts. They threw off her biorhythms, she said.

With Aunt Della gone in the evenings, Uncle Frank and I had fallen into the easy pattern of TV dinners during the six o'clock news, and then he'd get a beer and the *Reader's Digest* and settle into his recliner while I did homework or watched some sitcom on TV. It was late spring and growing warm, and the house had no air conditioning. We kept the windows open, and I changed into shorts and tank tops as soon as I got home from school.

One night I fired up the VCR. When the yoga tape started, Uncle Frank said from his recliner, "What's that now?"

"Just exercise."

"Reverend Jonas spoke out against the yoga." He coughed his usual miserable hack, suffering already with what we'd later learn was black lung, and sat there wheezing, catching his breath.

"I think this is secular yoga," I said, guessing that he wouldn't know the word and would therefore drop the subject. "Not the Hindu kind."

He drank his beer and watched the screen for a minute. "Huh," he finally said. "Well, you won't catch me getting all bent up like no pretzel. But don't look like it could do you no harm." He heaved himself to his feet. "You go on ahead. Think I'm going to turn in early." He headed down the hall.

I didn't have a mat like the people on TV, so I did my best on the carpet. It was an hour-long workout, and when it ended, I was sweating hard. Red dents welted my elbows and knees.

The next night, I did the yoga workout again, and the next. Uncle Frank headed off to bed early each time. I began to wobble less in the triangle pose, and my shifts from the plank to the cobra grew smooth. Maybe I'd never be a cheerleader. Fine. But I'd have this other, esoteric fitness thing that my classmates couldn't do.

One night, I was about three-quarters of my way through the video, bent in a downward dog pose, my head toward the floor, when a voice came through the screen door behind me.

"Nice view."

I scrambled to my feet and spun around. Billy let himself in.

"It's yoga." I wiped the sweat from my upper lip.

He let his gaze roam up and down me. "It's something, all right. Don't let me stop you."

"No, it's okay. I'm finished." I pushed rewind and turned the television off.

Billy headed for the fridge and stood there with it open, its white light gilding his muscles, his messy hair. "Any leftovers?" He cracked open one of Uncle Frank's beers and looked at me, his green eyes sleepy like a cat's.

I couldn't think.

He opened a cupboard and pulled out a bag of potato chips, unpinching the clothespin and leaving it on the counter.

"Where's everybody at?"

"Your mom's working second shift. Your dad went to bed already."

"Christ Jesus, they got you living like a senior citizen," he said, settling onto the couch. He took a long swig of the beer. "Can't raise a girl like you without some fun once in a while." He sprawled back, an arm behind his head, and patted the cushion next to him. "Come on over here."

I hesitated, rubbing my foot along my bare shin.

"Come on now, little cousin. Keep me company. Help me eat these chips."

I crossed the living room and perched on the edge of the couch. My breath came fast and shallow. All I wanted to do was swivel toward him and look at his eyes, his mouth, his carved cheekbones, his tousled gold hair.

I locked my eyes on the blank gray TV screen instead. His beer can zoomed into view. His large hand, its browned knuckles, the tendons under the skin. The can tilted toward me.

"I don't drink."

Laughter. "Sure, you don't."

"I don't."

"Yeah, okay. Whatever you say, little cousin." The beer can went away again.

We sat there quietly. I thought he'd want to turn the TV on, as he usually did, but he made no move to reach for the remote. The silence swelled tight around us.

Slowly, I reached for the can. I took a small sip, gave it back. Squished the unfamiliar sourness around in my mouth, swallowed. Reached for it again.

"Atta girl." The room was quiet. "You smoke?"

"No."

"Weed?"

"No."

"What *do* you do?"

I tried a tiny smile and risked turning to glance at him. "Homework."

His green eyes were soft. "Girl, you gonna waste yourself on homework every night?"

"I have to. I want to be a doctor." The first and last time I ever said it.

And he didn't laugh. His voice turned sweet and serious, and he put down his beer. "Really?"

I felt shyer than before. I nodded. "A pediatrician."

We looked at each other. He put his hand on my arm, and his touch was soft. "You miss him pretty bad?"

I couldn't speak. The whole room got hot and watery, and the house seemed to expand and swim around us. A loud, strange vibration filled my ears, a hum that rose and fell like the throb of cicadas. The edges of the room started to go black, and the blackness crept toward the center of my vision, as if it would engulf everything.

"Hey," he said, leaning toward me. He touched my face with his finger, pushed back a lock of my dark and sweaty hair. "Hey now." His face slowly grew larger, his eyes softer, his lips gentle as we kissed.

Then, from the porch, we heard a strange noise. Click. Click. Click. I lifted my head and looked through the screen into the dark. Billy turned.

Outside under the porch light stood Aunt Della, staring at us. Her fingers snapped the metal clasp of her pocketbook open and shut, open and shut.

———

When the school bus dropped me off the next day, I had almost forgotten the awkward, sad loveliness of the previous night and the brisk way Aunt Della had hustled Billy out the door and me off to my shower. Seven classes and a hundred small social encounters in the halls and lunchroom of East Mercer High had driven my encounter with Billy to the corner of my mind reserved for uncomfortable moments, things about which I could do nothing and that were therefore best to ignore.

When I got to the house, Aunt Della was standing on the porch staring out at the street, her gaze cold. Next to her sat two bulging garbage bags, dark green.

My things.

"No!" I cried, dropping my book bag and running up the steps to her. "No!" I threw my arms around her, tears springing thick and fast in my eyes. "No," I cried. "Oh no, please. Please, no."

But she wouldn't look at me, and she jerked out of my grip. She just grabbed a bag and started dragging it.

"No," I cried. "Please. I'll do anything. I'm sorry." I was sobbing by then, collapsing on the steps, my legs buckling.

She stopped and turned back to me. "Oh, yes? What are you sorry for, then? Huh, girl?"

What could I have said? Sorry for being female, fourteen? For feeling lonely and sad?

Aunt Della turned away. "Slut like your mother," she muttered, dragging the bag across the grass.

"Don't do this," I cried.

"She wouldn't have been at that truck stop, you wouldn't have even been born. Like a stray dog, she was. No one's going to ruin my boy's life."

She heaved the bag into the pickup's bed.

———

It did something to me, Aunt Della's curt rejection. The world came a little more untethered during that brusque and silent drive to Social Services.

Sometimes, even now, things move in my peripheral vision. A clock, a sofa, a parked car. They shift, jerk. I look up, and there they'll be, inert.

Sometimes when Jon's not home, I'll walk past the doorway of a darkened room in our condominium and have to stop. I back up, my hand against the wall, to make sure the figure I saw standing there isn't real, that it's only a trick of the shadows.

Sometimes it's a man who turns out to be a bureau.

Sometimes it's a beckoning woman who turns out to be only a curtain, drifting in the fan's soft breeze.

Sometimes it's a child who turns out to be nothing. Nothing at all.

Miss Marie's

After Aunt Della threw me out, I spent a week in the county facility, sleeping on a bunk bed, avoiding the other girls. Then the social worker, a thin older woman with lacquered tan hair and a small, fussy smile slicked an unnatural pink, drove me through cold rain in her station wagon to my new home.

"Kids like Miss Marie. You'll like her," she said. It was more command than reassurance.

When we pulled up outside, Miss Marie's house seemed very modern. I was used to houses like my mother's and Aunt Della's: little wooden-frame structures, pier-and-beam, white (the cheapest paint color), with rickety front porches and unevenly lurching boards for stairs, or houses faced with tar paper, rough to the touch, their tan or gray bricks palpably false, with maybe a bony hound or two lounging in the dirt. But the house we pulled up to was a real brick ranch with a garage, set flush to the earth, surrounded by its fellows in the first suburb I had ever seen. Lawns and sidewalks and houses on both sides of a gently curving road—the kind of place I'd seen on *The Brady Bunch*.

We got out of the car, and I pulled my green garbage bags from the back seat. By the time we got to the small cement porch, the bags were spattered with large clear drops of rain. I shivered.

Miss Marie opened the door right away. She was a tall, ample woman with long arms and a large belly on which her breasts leaned.

Her hair was short and gray, her smile came easily, and her eyes were a vague and friendly blue. She wore lilac polyester shorts and orange flip-flops. She was an ungainly assortment of limbs that extended from a plump, wobbling center, which gave her the appearance of a benign spider. She held a toddler on her hip.

Miss Marie looked me up and down. I knew she'd been informed already about whose daughter I was, but there was no cold judgment in her eyes. She smiled a vague smile.

"Well, come on in," she said. She turned; contorted trails of purple knotted the backs of her legs. She led us past a kitchen, where boxes of Cap'n Crunch and Count Chocula stood open on the counter, and into a small living room where a game show was on, the volume loud. Miss Marie never reached to turn it down. Two young children sprawled on the carpet in front of the TV. They did not turn as we settled on the sofas.

Miss Marie asked me the usual questions—school, hobbies, boys. Rummaging in a brass bowl, she told me I'd have no curfew. She pulled out a house key attached to a large round puff of peach-colored fake fur. "Here you go," she said, putting it in my hand.

Then the social worker passed her a clipboard, and people on TV screamed and won appliances while Miss Marie flipped through form after form, initialing each page and signing her name. She shushed the toddler, who still clung to her side.

Only for a moment did her blue eyes sharpen. "When will I get the first check?"

"The initial disbursement should be mailed within the month, and then they'll arrive every two weeks as usual," the social worker said.

Miss Marie nodded and turned back to the stack of forms. Finally she passed the clipboard back and cantilevered herself to her feet. "Come see your room," she said, and I picked up my garbage bags and followed her.

"I'll wait up here," called the social worker.

We descended a narrow staircase, and I feared for a moment that I'd be living in the only kind of cellar I'd known: cold, dark, with seeping dampness and cobwebs. But Miss Marie's basement was carpeted and warm. A tall upright freezer hummed. She opened it, showing me shelf upon shelf full of ice cream of different flavors and boxed pizzas. "Help yourself," she said. "Anytime." I saw why kids liked her.

"Watch out," she said, as we navigated a maze of boxes piled as high as my chin. Several had never been opened, and they still had shipping labels on them from various mail-order companies.

She reached through a doorway and flipped on the light. "Bath." With its built-in stall shower and frosted-glass door, it was a cleaner, more modern bathroom than any I had ever used. The mirror was lit by overhead bulbs, like in a movie-star dressing room on TV, and a vase of brown and orange silk chrysanthemums sat on the counter. Brown towels hung neatly from brass bars.

"Who all shares this?" I said.

Her gray eyebrows lifted. "Just you, pet. I keep the little ones upstairs with me." The toddler on her hip had fallen asleep.

She led me into the room that would be mine, with its astonishing queen-sized bed. I had never seen one so large. It was cloaked in a green bedspread and stacked with a thicket of pillows. I set my trash bags down.

On the nightstand stood a ceramic sculpture of a Native maiden, her long swoosh of black hair swept back as if by wind, her beaded buckskin outfit as skimpy as a stripper's. She appeared to be looking longingly into the distance, and when I followed her gaze to the dresser across the room, I saw the object of her desire, a matching warrior, crow-haired and bronze, his torso direct from a late-night commercial for exercise machines. The wood-paneled walls also carried the Native motif: framed paintings of maidens and braves in forests, next to water-falls, paddling canoes across lakes—always just a man and a woman, as though indigenous people came only in pairs. In the corner on the floor, an ovoid metal trash can bore a similar prelapsarian scene.

My voice was shy. "Are you Indian?"

Miss Marie chuckled. "No, pet. I just collect them."

I nodded.

"Pretty, though, ain't they?"

I nodded again.

Suddenly a child's wail came from upstairs. The toddler startled awake on Miss Marie's hip and started to whimper.

"Well, get your stuff put away," she said, and padded out, the soles of her flip-flops flapping.

———

I stayed with Miss Marie for the remainder of high school, and my monthly visits to the penitentiary fell into this routine: my mother would start with a couple of general questions about how school was going, and then launch quickly into a defense, as if I were her accuser. Her confessor. As if I could proffer absolution. "You don't know. I'm clean now. I'd never do such a thing," she'd say. "It was the drugs." The kids who straddled their motorbikes at Mazza's during lunch sold crank and weed and mushrooms and acid, but I was afraid to try any of it. "You don't understand," she'd say. "But maybe you will one day." She'd go on, saying similar things in different words. I'd sit there, cold and silent, until our time was up.

Back at the brick ranch house, Miss Marie was easygoing, with her loose house rules and her kitchen cabinets full of sugar. She relied on the same cheap packaged foods my mother preferred: oily orange cheese slices you peeled away from their plastic sheaths, vegetables that slid wet and limp from an opened can. I never saw a head of lettuce in that house.

Miss Marie seemed to have gotten stuck in her own teenage years: her lax standards, her freezer full of pizza and ice cream, her occasional long bouts of giggling at sitcoms, her too-candid attempts at girl talk. She once informed me that, when women got old and couldn't catch a man anymore, not to worry, there were vibrators now. They came in all colors: purple, pink. Would I like to see one?

No, thank you, I said politely, taking a Dr. Pepper from the fridge, relieved when she dropped the subject.

The ceaseless flow of small children in and out of the house bothered me, so I retreated downstairs as often as possible, where kids under twelve were not allowed. It took me a while to realize that Miss Marie ran a drop-in day care as well as emergency foster housing; one crowded day, there were fourteen children in the house. I steered clear of the youngest ones, especially the ones who were old enough to talk. I tried not to befriend them. I couldn't bear the sound of their small, high voices calling my name.

————

Not all of my mother's letters from prison were about Jesus. She liked to write about how, as soon as she got out, she and I would run away to Atlantic City, which she envisioned as some kind of magical paradise, as a place where *even folks like us can catch a break, Sister.* She knew this for a fact, she wrote, because the women in the pen had told her so. *Johnna Rae made four hundred there in one single weekend,* she wrote, neglecting to include Johnna Rae's methods.

You and me, Sister, she would promise in her letters. *Just you and me.*

————

It wasn't Miss Marie herself but a college-educated friend of hers who decided to make me her special project. Her name was Edith Honeycutt, and she had a blonde beehive hairdo, coral frost lipstick, and long hard nails that tapped on the steering wheel as she drove.

She had taken to mentoring me once a week because she'd "heard your story" (hushed tone). She and Miss Marie had been friends since kindergarten, but after high school they'd "followed different paths." Edith Honeycutt picked me up each week in a long Lincoln Continental the color of straw, and we drove around aimlessly while she talked.

Edith Honeycutt loved her car. She had it washed and custom-detailed twice a month. The upholstery was the palest shade of cream, and it was smooth and squishy, like pantyhose stretched over a sponge. In her house, with its clean pastel walls and vases on glass tables, its lack of chaos and children and dirt, I moved carefully, afraid I might crack something or spill the foaming glass of pop she handed me. I preferred riding around so I could stare out the window and give my short, bland answers when she asked how school was going and if I was making friends and what I planned to do with the rest of my life. It's easier to lie when you're looking out the window. Whatever I answered, she'd say, "Oh, peachy! That's just peachy!"

Edith Honeycutt was freshly divorced and liked to talk about women's lib. She brought me her old copies of *New Woman* and *Ms.* "for inspiration," and she said not to worry too much about being a Hispanic, since things were changing for my people, too. She could have been thirty-five, or she could have been sixty; she just seemed old to me.

She would drive through the Wendy's. "What beverage would you like?" she'd ask, making clear the parameters of her generosity, and I'd order a Coke or a Frosty and then stare out at the trees and hills and little houses, sucking my straw, as she drove around saying encouraging things about how to thrive as a woman in a man's world. She told me about the organization NOW and how she was a member while I wondered how she got her cone of hair to stay aloft. She was a paralegal at the town's law firm. It sat in a brick building between an antique store and a shoe-repair shop that always looked dusty.

————

At home with her hands full, Miss Marie had little time to notice my doings, check my homework, or track my whereabouts. She had no rules. I came and went as I pleased. At the new high school, friends were easy to make. All you had to do was drink Schlitz with them in parked cars by the creek.

In the mornings, I caught rides to school with different people. In the afternoons, we'd go to the Dairy Queen and suck down cold shakes. We'd go to McDonald's and split one large order of fries among six girls, each of us competing to take the fewest. My new friends didn't really talk about much except the next drink or the latest coach or teacher who'd been a douchebag. I kept my mouth shut. If they'd heard about what my mother had done, they didn't ask questions—whether through kindness or apathy, I didn't know. But I was grateful. Their incuriosity let me drift along, unobtrusive and inconsequential, cloaked in a benign invisibility.

Things could be worse, I would tell myself, feeling strong and grown up. It was something I'd heard my mother's factory friends say to each other over beers at our kitchen table. Your man leaves? Your son gets killed? Your daughter's pregnant by her high school teacher, you can't make rent, you've got no money left for groceries this month? *Cheer up: things could be worse.* I'd comfort myself with that, thinking it made me tough like them.

On a bright, cool Tuesday I walked down the stone steps of the high school, my new friends around me, talking.

"Hey, Bel," a male voice called. I looked up.

A friend elbowed me in the side. "Oh my God!" she whisper-shrieked. "Who's that?"

My gaze followed hers, and I stopped where I stood. Across the street, leaning against his metallic blue Trans Am, stood my cousin Billy. His shining hair, his broad shoulders in their T-shirt. Muscled arms. Lean hips. That lazy grin.

I hadn't seen Billy since I'd moved to Miss Marie's. I hadn't seen anyone from my family. No one had even called.

"Hey, Bel," he said again. "You want a ride?"

My friends jostled against me, giggling. One girl whispered, "If you don't, I will."

I hoisted my book bag higher and made my voice as casual as I could. "Sure."

———

Eight hours, a bag of Wendy's, and a bottle of Jim Beam later, sitting in his Trans Am on a bluff overlooking the river, Billy kissed me.

He'd already asked me how school was, if I liked it at Miss Marie's, how I was doing, if I missed my mom. He'd listened intently, nodding, his warm eyes fastened on mine like a leopard's. For hours, we'd talked, and I'd basked in his attention, his earnest nods, the way he laughed when I tried to be funny.

It occurred to me suddenly that it was the longest anyone had talked with me in months. The weight of my loneliness slammed into me, like a bad storm's horizontal rain. I'd just begun to cry when he lifted my chin.

Slowly, softly, he kissed me on the mouth the way girls dream of being kissed. He stroked my hair. "You're so beautiful, Bel," he said. "I've missed you." He held me in his arms. The last time I'd been held was when my mother clung to me, screaming, and cops had to pry her away. Billy's arms felt warm and good.

When he reached for my jeans, I pushed him away. "Come on," he laughed. "You know you want it," he said, and definitions get slippery there. I wanted his arms around me, and the shivery chills of desire, and the feeling of being loved. I wish I could say I fought and bit, that I stabbed his eye with a ballpoint pen or cut him with an X-Acto knife from my book bag. But I didn't. I cried and pushed and said no, and then, when he wouldn't stop, I just went limp, the way a rabbit will. I turned my face away and wept. I felt dead—or not dead, because that would have been a relief, but as if I were dying, and as if every last thing around me were dying, including my romantic dream of Billy himself, and my world was just rubble around me.

———

Did I report Billy, a member of my family, the light of my aunt Della's life, the handsome older guy into whose cool car at least a dozen people had seen me willingly climb? Did I explain to state cops why I'd drunk a bottle of Jim Beam with him while parking for hours on the high bluff over the river—and then changed my mind about what, to them, would surely look like a foregone conclusion?

Of course I didn't. I felt as guilty as if it had all been my fault.

———

It's a joke people tell: West Virginians and their cousins. I've heard it often enough. I've even smiled patiently along with new acquaintances who, upon learning where I'm from, believe it's an amusing thing to say.

A joke was never what I wanted to be. I kept my mouth shut.

Pittsburgh

When my period failed to arrive for the second month, I told Miss Marie, and she stood right up from the couch. A toddler slid off her lap to the floor and began to wail.

"You watch the babies," she said. "I'm going down the drugstore and buy you a test." At the front door, keys in hand, she turned back with a grin and an exaggerated wink. "I won't say it's for you. Let 'em think ol' Miss Marie's got a little something going on."

Then she was gone. I righted the toddler, reached over to mute *Jeopardy*, and then just sat there, waiting, my hand on my belly, a new assortment of children crawling around me whose names I didn't know.

———

"Well, don't you worry," said Miss Marie, her arm around my shoulders as we looked down together at the little blue plus sign. "We'll call Edith."

"Edith Honeycutt?"

"She's taken girls up to Pittsburgh for me before."

My voice grew small. "What's in Pittsburgh?"

"It's where they take care of problems like the one you got." Miss Marie patted my arm. "Now don't you worry," she said. "They say it don't hardly hurt at all."

I closed my eyes. The room swayed.

———

"Hey now," Miss Marie was saying. "Hey there, now." I was lying on her couch without knowing how I'd gotten there.

Miss Marie nodded.

"You just hold on," she said, and she disappeared. When she came back, I was sitting up, and I drank the sips of water she urged on me. "It's going to be okay. It's all going to be just fine." Then her blue eyes shrank and she stared out the sliding glass doors to the deck. "You got any money saved up?"

———

"You don't have to thank me," said Edith Honeycutt, her hands on the wheel as we headed north on I-79. "Consider it a gift. Consider it my investment in your future." It was the third time she'd said it. Her voice brightened further. "Think of it as a loan you can pay forward to some other bright, deserving girl someday."

I already knew she was paying for the operation. Miss Marie had told me. I had already said thank you. I wished she would stop talking about it.

I let several miles go by without saying anything. When we were passing Morgantown, I craned to see if the university was visible from the interstate.

She said, "I know this is hard. Maybe it would help if you had something to look forward to." She glanced over at me. "Afterward, I mean."

I looked at her.

"What's your favorite restaurant?"

I thought about it. The obvious answer was that I didn't have a favorite, because I didn't go to restaurants—never had, aside from Wendy's and McDonald's and Dairy Queen.

But this was my chance. I thought of commercials I'd seen on TV. "Red Lobster."

"Oh, Red Lobster! I love Red Lobster. What a good choice! Well, after your procedure, Isabella, we'll go right to Red Lobster. We'll have a wonderful dinner."

Green mountains blurred by. I wasn't used to interstate highways, to the speed. I liked the way the edges of everything softened and smeared.

"Well?" Edith looked over at me again. "How does that sound?"

I turned and stared at her. "Peachy."

———

The room was pink and gray. The poster on the ceiling was of flowers in a hillside meadow, like *The Sound of Music* or a mountaintop that had been strip-mined long ago and grown back tame and pretty.

The nurse was kind, but when I asked if I could hold her hand while they did it, she pried my fingers away and wrapped them around the clear rubber gas mask they'd put on my face.

"Here," she said. "Hold that."

———

At Red Lobster, I ordered the popcorn shrimp platter. I had never eaten shrimp before.

Edith Honeycutt got us two virgin piña coladas.

When the waiter delivered them, she said, "To celebrate!"

I looked at her.

"Your freedom." She lowered her voice. "From the crushing burdens of premature motherhood." She clinked my glass where it sat on the table. The two little paper umbrellas jostled each other.

I ate everything on my plate and drank my piña colada.

"You don't have to thank me," she said, pulling out her wallet.

———

"Can you pull over?" My eyes were closed.

"I can't right now," said Edith Honeycutt. "We're in a tunnel."

"I'm going to be sick."

"Oh, Jesus God to hell. Well, hang on." We surged forward. "Don't you dare throw up in this car," she said.

I opened my eyes. Her hands gripped the steering wheel at nine and three, and the tunnel was a long dark tube that would never end. I leaned my head back, which made it worse. The lights flashed by overhead. I closed my eyes again. I imagined the whole mountain above and around us, its weight collapsing down to crush everything.

When the car slowed, my eyes opened. We were out of the tunnel, and it was dusk, and we were careening to a stop on the shoulder. As we braked, tiny rocks pinged inside the Lincoln's wheel wells.

"Okay," she said, before we'd even stopped moving. "Do it."

I unbuckled my seat belt, opened my door, and leaned out as far as I could. Traffic roared past on the left. My body bucked, and everything came out. My throat burned. My eyes were wet and hot.

Finished, I wiped the spit-strings from my mouth and stared down at the pile of little shrimps. Some were unchewed and still curled. They lay there, pink on the dark gravel, and I hung above them, staring. They had been alive in the sea, and then trapped, and then frozen, and then fried and inside me, and now here they were, beside a highway in Pennsylvania, and it was getting dark.

"I'm sorry," I whispered to the shrimp. Tears ran down my face. "I'm so sorry."

———

On my next visit to the penitentiary, my mother—due to her many months of good behavior—was allowed to hug me. Guards tensed, but no one interfered. I'd been searched.

We sat across the table from each other. I tried to make small talk.

"What is it, baby?" she kept saying. She peered at my face. Sober, she wasn't as easy to fool. "What is it?"

Finally I let it spill out—everything, except Billy's name. I let her think it was just some boy from school.

At some point—when I started to talk about Pittsburgh, I think—she got up and came around the table. She sat down next to me and pulled her chair close, and as I began to cry, she pulled my head onto her shoulder. She stroked my hair, her hand gentle.

It was good to tell someone, to accept her comfort. Contrary to what Miss Marie had promised, it *had* hurt. Worse, it had fallen like a curtain of secret sorrow over what remained of my life. Food didn't taste good. On the drive home through dark hills, Edith Honeycutt had told me a dozen times what a good decision I'd made, how prudent I'd been, how mature, how responsible—what a permanent burden I would have placed on myself and the taxpayers of West Virginia if I'd made any other choice. I'd stared at the window, at my own translucent features superimposed against the dark rushing night outside, as her voice went on and on, droning and chipper until all her words ran together in a blur like the high whine of machinery.

I wanted to believe that I'd done the right thing, but a sad guilt twisted me when I lay awake at night in Miss Marie's basement. Unsure, I'd lie there with all those Native figurines around me, wondering if I was a good person.

So it was a relief when my mother put her arms around me, and I began crying harder. The guards paid no particular attention.

"Baby," my mother kept saying, stroking my hair. I leaned against her, the pain slowly draining out of me, my sobs abating, my breath coming in slow draughts like drinking good water. I stayed like that for a long time, my eyes closed, my head rising and falling on her shoulder with each lift of her breath.

Then a sudden little rush of air came out of her. A laugh.

I sat up and turned. "What?"

"I can't believe it, sister." Her blue eyes were wide, her smile soft and bright with a kind of honest wonder. "You killed your baby. Now you're just like me."

———

That day, I left the prison for the last time, numb, as if a bleak white flash had simultaneously illuminated and annihilated everything inside me. My brother was gone; my mother was gone. And between the clambering, clinging toddlers at Miss Marie's and the shock of the Pittsburgh clinic, even my nascent dream of becoming a pediatrician had somehow melted away.

And I, too, in a sense more significant than I could understand at the time, was gone. What functioned mechanically in my place from then on was just the imprint emblazoned where I'd been, the dry and fragile hull, the deflated skin that's left when the snake slithers off.

United Airlines #4067

I'd almost finished embroidering the twelfth and final Vanessa Bell dust jacket, and though several people had requested more, I planned to stop. I didn't want to repeat, to manufacture. These little purses were their own odd project, a way to incorporate Bell's vision by stitching it into my memory, staring down at her patterns in my own lap, as if my needle could somehow cross time and space.

I felt a kind of greed: not either-or, but both. Not a dichotomy. Not only Virginia, verbal and brilliant and childless and self-destroying, or only Vanessa, maternal and mute and painting and surviving—but both, both worlds together: the brainy, skittering stream of language but also the loved, held child. I wanted to want that.

A Writer's Diary was almost done. I didn't know what I'd do with it. I carried the materials with me in a linen sack, a small and soothing portable chore. When I had a spare moment, I stitched.

I never sold the purses, never wanted to go through the hassle of obtaining permissions from the Woolf estate. I just gave them away. They were, after all, only the strange byproduct of the real work I wanted to do: to inhabit a vision, dwell inside it for a while, hold it inside me. To pay attention, like paying the tithe of your life.

———

It was late afternoon when Lark Svenson called. The phone to my cheek, I stared around at the other waiting passengers while she talked. Yes, she'd be interested in a small show. She had dates available—two full weeks—next July. Would that work? Yes. Could I also possibly fly in and give a gallery talk? She had a friend on the faculty at CUNY who worked on Latina outsider artists (*That's what I am, then?*) who could interview me. We'd sit in leather chairs on a little stage. Perhaps it would be livestreamed.

Yes, that would work. Yes, I could. Yes, I said, I was thrilled, though I wasn't, and I couldn't have explained why.

Yes, yes, yes. The wildly anticlimactic conversation took all of six minutes.

———

Sometimes I wondered if I was meant to be an artist at all, or to be in love with anyone at all—if I might have been better off in my small flat alone, making my strange objects at all hours of the night, speaking to no one, under no mother-in-law's surveillance, eating a handful of nuts or an apple when hunger struck, not cooking or smiling or whisking around to set a pretty table for two or pouring wine or making love. Just living simply on my own, doing my work, moving to my own rhythm, unobserved and unselfconscious. Perhaps it was upscale domesticity itself—that warm, close, magazine-lovely thing we've all been told we want—that was suffocating the art out of me. Installed in my so-called perfect life, with a plush and tidy little studio—the room of my own that Woolf touted (so the clutter of my tools and random objects wasn't scattered organically all over the kitchen and bed and floor, as it had been when I'd lived alone, but instead was cordoned safely off, unseen when guests arrived)—all the small domestic tensions had arisen to enclose me. Some days I sat in my studio, holding an object I'd found, waiting for some small flash of inspiration, some sense of what to do next, but my mind would circle like an anxious animal back to Jon—the small spat we'd had the night before, the armored glance he'd given me, the brusque way he'd swept past. *He's just busy,* I'd tell myself. *Preoccupied.* But my mind would chew on such moments with a sort of bewildered pain, wondering how, so quickly, we'd come to that. When I'd finally remember the object in my hand, I'd look down to see that my thumbs had been frantically rubbing it, like worry beads. And no art came.

Perhaps, long broken and bearing too many secrets, I was just no good at love.

———

When my flight was finally called, there was no comfortable Jetway to walk down. An orange-clad worker propped open a door, and we were herded out into the chilled, bright air, past jets, equipment, and fuel trucks. Our plane was a small silver tube, a little turboprop with its blades whirling, as if we were heading to the nether regions of some polar clime. We abandoned our carry-on luggage in a pile on the asphalt, climbed the metal stairs, and hunched to enter the small door.

I strapped myself in and looked around. Aside from two heavy-set women in matching pink tracksuits, everyone was a businessman. Everyone was white except me. The pilot's young voice told us our flying time was sixty-nine minutes.

The plane veered slowly out toward the runway, its engines churning so loud it felt as if we were sitting inside one large motor. Cleared for takeoff, the little plane gathered itself, and we charged down the runway at a high whine.

As we lifted from the ground—that breathless, buoyant, impossible moment—I thought, *This—all of this—is what it means to go home.*

New York

At twenty-two, freshly arrived in New York for graduate school, I felt lonely. My flannel shirts and fifteen-dollar haircuts didn't suit the sharp streets of Manhattan. In my studio critiques at NYU, the other students spoke a strange language, full of assumptions I couldn't track, their hands' bold gestures buoyed by something—a confidence, a sense of importance—my own had never known.

Back home in the forest, I'd learned to be still. Quiet. To listen and observe. If you were silent, small creatures would creep out from the underbrush. Birds would flutter down and land close by. If you listened to the footsteps of your mother's various men-friends, you could know exactly where they were in the house, which rooms to avoid. If you stayed quiet on the back porch, they forgot you existed.

In New York, everyone was loud. Talking, yelling, insisting, declaiming. I longed to be alone and under trees. Even Central Park seemed a poor excuse for nature after the wild woods I had known.

My apartment was a small white room with a sink in the corner, and my window faced a wall of brick. Down the hall were showers and toilets the residents had to share, and they weren't often clean. My folded clothes sat stacked in crates against the wall, and crates served as my bookshelves, too. Cockroaches were my only living company at first, until I bought a small ivy plant and put it on the windowsill. (Plants, it seemed, needed only light and water—not a view.) The plant seemed happy there, and I occasionally found myself talking to her. I named her, unimaginatively, Ivy.

I longed for something animate, though, something that responded. One day on the sidewalk, a man was selling long-haired dachshund puppies—unpedigreed, like me. Tiny and brown, they squirmed in his cardboard box. I knew it was a stupid idea: that I didn't have the space for a dog, or the time to walk one, or the money to spare for food and a leash and vet bills—much less the fifty dollars to give the man: the hundred-dollar bill in my wallet was for two weeks' worth of groceries. More significantly, I didn't have the time or energy to be responsible for anyone but myself. I was waiting tables at nights at an Italian restaurant where tips weren't great, and my days were consumed with reading assignments for school and painting and going to my studio classes on campus and to the library afterward to track down an allusion the professor had made—the sort of literary or theoretical reference (Gaston Bachelard, Hélène Cixous, Jacques Lacan—why were they all French?) that left me free-falling through the abyss of my own ignorance. There was far too much to do, to learn, to catch up on. I had no time for a dog.

She rode, warm and wriggling, inside my jacket pocket all the way home. I named her Button.

Button's company helped—got me out in the park, out on the streets, made children stoop to pet her when I assured them she was safe. In the apartment, she padded after me—not that there was much room to walk around. When I settled on the bed to read, she curled up next to me. When I washed my face at the sink, she sat on the rug, alert, staring up at me in fascination. And she was soft and sleek to stroke, a warm, living thing to pick up and hold as I stood at the window staring out at the grimy brick and mortar. A small, dense weight that felt good in my arms.

But human company I couldn't seem to find. I hadn't managed to make any friends during the heated arguments in my classes, where

I felt confused and intimidated, where the other students dressed either so elegantly they looked like Audrey Hepburn or in ways that could only be ironic, with their thick black-rimmed glasses and plaid polyester pants, which I couldn't understand—why spend so much money to be ugly? When I spoke, which was rare, the professor would often look at me for an extra beat, then carry on as if I hadn't said a word.

Nor had I bonded with the waitstaff at the restaurant. Everyone was busy and rushed, on their way home or to auditions or school. And the conversations with patrons at the tables were a mockery of human interaction. I began foolishly, with genuine friendliness and interest at each table, but soon realized that the entire endeavor was—as we'd say in a theory course—performative. My job was to manufacture smiles, anticipate the customers' wishes, and obey.

Both arenas were a little depressing.

Oppressed by the close darkness of cement, overwhelmed by the strangeness of new languages yelled in the street, the crush of people I'd never know, I retreated into the haven of my apartment, where I'd hung bright posters from the Met over the stains on the walls. Sometimes I'd sit cross-legged on the bed (which was also the couch), sketching on my lap-desk (which was also the cutting board). On the windowsill, which I'd named Windowsilly, Ivy would be flourishing, and Button would be curled like a comma next to me on the quilt. I'd say things like, "Now, this isn't half-bad!" and "Nice place you got here, Bel!" in the accents of my aunts and uncles, as if they'd suddenly swung by for a visit. "Sure do like your apartment!" They'd be impressed with the fact that I lived in a building with an elevator, and really my room was not so much smaller than some of their own living rooms back home.

And then I'd realize that I was talking to myself. That I was impersonating relatives who never wrote to me.

That I'd named not only my plant and dog, but an inanimate object, too.

———

In grad school, I struggled. The hardest part was feeling out of place among the young artists whose peer I was supposed to be. I could not love their clever explanations of their paintings, full of allusions to critics everyone else had read. Their cool, brainy work was so ambiguous that my critique was always, "But what does it *mean*?"—at which the other students laughed. Among them, I felt crude, simple, my need for coherence somehow gauche.

To my surprise, the course I loved was Critical Theory. I fell into it with relief. The distance on things, the objectivity, the pleasures of analysis were all so welcome: to be able to *see* a thing—like poverty—instead of just being immersed in it, to understand its interlocking parts and how they clicked together and moved, to re-see it all in new ways, from different angles. Theory promised that the world didn't have to be a thing that swallowed you whole: it could be held at arm's length, turned side to side, examined, explained. And then explained again another way. To be told by bona fide smart people that one could read the same situation in multiple ways was a kind of liberation that felt true. And to know that by shaping and delivering one's own vision so that it was legible to others (making art, reading radiology images, giving lectures about Haiti), one could influence how others read a situation and what they did about it—well, that was power.

Critical Theory I, II, and III—I dropped out before I made it to IV—turned me into a woman who knew why, as diligently as I might play Baroque concerti on my stereo (lending my tiny apartment the bright hopefulness of a Jane Austen film), I still craved the plaintive country-and-western songs of my childhood. Or how, when I was about to get my period and felt low, I longed only for Kraft macaroni and cheese poured rattling from the box—hot, tasty, coated in a slick of yellow paste—not the fancy New York versions with Gruyère and chunks of lobster.

Our taste, theorist Pierre Bourdieu would say—our literal tongue-taste most of all—is formed when we're children. It means home. It tastes right. People might polish their jagged edges away as they climb the socioeconomic ladder, but when we lick, our tongues don't lie.

Saqlain

In West Virginia, I was not considered beautiful—not in the hamlet of my childhood, or in Mercer, or at the new high school I attended after Charlie died, or at the university in Morgantown. US culture has now come to appreciate features that were not considered assets in the Appalachia of my youth, where blonde, blue-eyed models—minty cheerleaders, glinting in sunlight—still reigned as the ideal.

When I got to New York, my beauty crept up on me. I'd always been told big-city people were unfriendly, but men leaped to hail cabs for me, retrieve objects I dropped, buy my coffee, my meal, even my bags of groceries at the checkout counter. It took a while to realize that I'd stumbled into an ugly-duckling narrative. But harder still was to realize how little it assuaged the fundamental loneliness of my life, and beauty was a strange new power I didn't know how to wield, as if I'd been handed a sword too sharp and heavy for my own good. When I applied for work in restaurants, hoping to wait tables, the manager would shake his head. "Oh, no, no. We want you out front." As a hostess. But hostesses made less: no tips, just hourly. I took waitress jobs instead.

But tips weren't great, either, so I quit waitressing and became a Gallery Girl: one of that tribe of leggy, ornamental, preternaturally agreeable young women who greet rich art buyers, making them cappuccinos or pouring them unoaked chardonnay, praising their taste while they browse. The gallery job made sense for me. I loved art—provocative, haunting, mute—and I loved the gallery itself: the pale ash floors, the rush of AC on a hot summer day, the low, cultured voices in which everyone spoke, the refinement that felt like safety, the cool hush a respite from the blaring streets outside and the loud chaos of the world.

Over time, in my apartment, depressed by my many failures at NYU and inspired by the range of things I saw while working at the gallery—*That* could be art? It counted?—I began to make little objects of my own, carving with an X-Acto knife into the sides of the pages of free books left out in front of used bookstores. Just an idle pastime, girlish. Then I started picking up fallen branches in Central Park and smuggling them home, furtive, so I could whittle them into long shapes, sylvan abstracts in smooth wood. Good to hold. Eventually I began making more complicated things, assemblages of little objects I picked up on the street for no good reason. A lost earring. Pieces of a pocket watch. The small pelt of some soft dead animal. Making order out of abandoned things helped my hands stop trembling, helped me control the panic that flooded my apartment at night.

It seemed a strange, obsessive pursuit. I showed my creations to no one. The satisfaction they brought me felt altogether too strong to be safe.

At the gallery, behind the desk, I often read my way through slow hours, small, thick used paperbacks I'd buy at the Strand: *Madame Bovary, Anna Karenina, Sister Carrie*. I checked books out of the library about Cézanne's liberation of form from color, Joseph Cornell and his shadow boxes, Remedios Varo and her lacquered surreal visions. Sometimes I'd page shyly through them, wondering if I could ever make anything worthwhile.

———

Saqlain, a regular client—flat white, no sugar—was in his midforties and not bad-looking. Tall. Brusque. Wavy, thick black hair that shone. He came from a place called Riyadh but had gone to Cambridge, he said. With his Armani suits and silk pocket handkerchiefs and glossy black shoes, he looked like any of thousands of men on the streets of Manhattan, except for his darker skin. I felt for him. He chatted about Beijing and Dubai, which I had to look up in an atlas so I wouldn't feel stupid the next time he came in.

When Saqlain walked through to see what new pieces we'd gotten, he'd always pluck up whatever book I was reading and inspect it. "Ah, yes," he'd sometimes say. "A fine one."

Once he asked me what I really wanted to do with my life.

I felt shy. "Be an artist," I said, trying it aloud for the first time.

His smile was wan. "Of course you do," he said, and drifted away to inspect our latest offerings.

But after that, he seemed to take an interest. Sometimes, if it got to be dusk outside and the two of us were alone in the gallery, he'd ask offhandedly if I were going home to my family or out with a boyfriend. I had neither, I'd truthfully reply.

One evening in May, he arrived just before we closed. As I locked up, he said, "You're good at what you do, Miss Morales." He called me that. Very formal.

"Thank you, sir." I twisted my key in the lock, heard it click.

"You've clearly got professional potential. Organizational skills. Maybe we should have a little talk."

"Really?"

Saqlain nodded. Avuncular. "A conversation about your future."

I'd never considered a career in banking. For the first time, I wondered what bankers did all day. Saqlain drove a black Porsche—I'd carried wrapped, padded pieces worth thousands of dollars out to where it waited double-parked, lights flashing—and he wore all those suits, of course.

I couldn't afford any car at all, and just feeding Button strained my budget. "Okay," I said. "I'm here from noon to seven most days."

He squinted. "It's not a conversation for the gallery."

Perhaps I could work in a bank—not as a teller, but in one of the upstairs offices. I could earn a real living, plan for a future.

"Let's go to dinner," he said. "A business dinner. We can discuss it."

I hesitated. I'd checked my bank-account balance that morning. Rent was due.

"My treat, of course."

I nodded.

He asked my address, and I told him. He said Friday at eight o'clock. "Does that work?"

I nodded again.

"Don't you want to write it down?"

I smiled. "I'll remember."

It would be nice to talk with someone about my future. To believe that I had one.

———

When Friday arrived, I felt happy all day: on my subway commute and quick walk to NYU, in a dull lecture ("All Hands On Deck: Letting Metonymy Work for You") from a visiting artist who addressed his remarks to the middle distance and pushed his glasses up his nose four dozen times. Even in studio critiques that day, when I said I admired the realism of someone's painting and the boys in their beards and wing-collared plaid shirts rolled their eyes, I didn't mind. I had someone to see, someone who saw potential in me. A future.

I rode the subway home again so I could take Button out, and I could hear the note of hope in my voice as I chatted to her while we walked. It was a brisk, sunny day, with gusts of wind that pushed the last of the dried brown leaves into little rising swirls. The sky was cloudless and blue, which meant the night would be cold. We might even be able to see stars. Button's tail waved like a flag of silk as she rushed from one side of the sidewalk to the other, sniffing and curious.

I remember bending to ruffle her fur. "You dear, sweet little objective correlative," I said.

———

"My other car," said Saqlain, across the table from me at the sushi restaurant, "is a white Mercedes."

It sounded so much like a bumper sticker that I laughed—loudly, startling him. Startling myself. I wasn't much of a drinker, and he'd poured quite a bit of sake by that point.

"That sounds very nice," I quickly amended, trying to be polite. He'd picked me up in the black Porsche. "It's just—I don't have a car at all." A laugh burst out of me again. I thought, *You're drunk, Bel Martin. Drunk, drunk, drunk.*

He glanced around, but there was no one to hear. We had a private room. We sat on cushions on the floor, and the table was low, the room dark, lit only by candles that flickered in black stone jars. Almost everything was black—the walls, the rugs, the floor, the tablecloth and napkins. On the table, the white china seemed to glow and levitate, and a single orchid arched on its long stem as if weary of its own white grace. The silent waitress slipped into and out of the room in a kind of wooden trench, so that her hands were level with the tabletop and she could easily serve us our platters of sushi and hot sake and more sake. Saqlain had already eaten shark, and a kind of fish that could be poisonous, and other things he explained in great detail, but all the sake blotted it out as soon as he said it. The night had grown late and it felt like we'd been sitting there for hours, drinking and drinking until everything was funny. It was hard to sit cross-legged on a cushion in the knee-length dress I'd worn, but I'd gradually forgotten about it. The room felt very warm.

We were supposed to be discussing my future opportunities in the banking industry, but our talk had rambled instead to movies and books we'd read or wanted to read. He was nice, and wittier than I'd expected. Cambridge, I guess. Or perhaps it was just the glow wrought by my small white porcelain cup.

Saqlain had ordered for both of us. He hadn't even asked me what I wanted, but in truth I was relieved. Sushi wasn't a thing I'd tried before, and the thought of raw fish made me squeamish. I'd caught and cleaned enough creek trout to know that being cooked was their only redeeming virtue. When Saqlain had told me in the car where we'd be going, I'd imagined mauled chunks of flesh, bloody on the plate.

But what came out were elegant strips, clean, pale, arranged in shapes like roses and fans, decorated with slivered bits of green and orange vegetable. It didn't look like fish at all, really, but like some futuristic food from science fiction, made stranger still by the chopsticks I was supposed to use. Saqlain wielded his deftly, without a thought, but I kept dropping mine and laughing.

"You really are a little country mouse, aren't you?" He gazed indulgently at me.

When the waitress brought our bowls of miso soup, of which I'd never heard before, I said, "Oh, good! Miso hungry," as if no one had ever made that joke, and his smile curled.

Entering the restaurant, we'd had to remove our shoes and stack them in a wooden cabinet, then climb a small flight of stairs behind the hostess, who led us through a warren of rooms with closed doors.

"So this is weird," I'd said.

"It's very exclusive," Saqlain had murmured behind me, his hand on the small of my back. And then we'd sunk down to the cushions and begun the long evening of sake and laughing.

"I'd like to discuss your future," he finally said, and I straightened up on my cushion. At last: the reason we were here. I blinked, tried to feel sober. "Now, remind me," he said. "What is it you went to school to be?"

My heart sank. "An artist." The alcohol had diminished my usual shyness about claiming this, but it still depressed me. "I'm not doing very well, though. The professors keep saying I'm not fulfilling my potential." I hadn't told anyone. There wasn't anyone to tell.

Saqlain only nodded. He didn't even smile the patronizing smile that middle-aged people seemed so quick to deploy.

"I'd like to help you achieve your goal, and I think we can be mutually beneficial to one another. I'd like to propose an arrangement." As he spoke, he nodded frequently, as if agreeing with himself. "Your rent and other expenses will be covered, and we'll find you a very nice apartment in close proximity to my own. A *very* nice apartment, if you wish," he repeated. "Your wardrobe will be furnished. You'll have a generous allowance. You won't need to work. You'll simply be—" He broke off and stared down at his clean, shapely nails, his tanned hands. He cleared his throat and poured us both more sake. "Available. You'll simply be available to me when I visit."

"If I wish." The room was starting to tilt on its axis. I noticed, as if from a great distance, the way he used the future tense, *will*, rather than the conditional, as if it were all preordained, and he was just letting me know.

"It will only be a few hours a week," he said. "In the evenings." He smiled a bland, professional smile, the kind he probably used when telling strangers that his bank was going to take over theirs.

"Oh." My voice sounded odd. "Oh," I kept saying to everything he said. There would be no bank management opportunity. No latent executive talent of mine had been recognized. My eyes and cheeks stung hot.

I took deep breaths, pretending to have understood all along. Under the table, my hands twisted and wrung the black napkin. The waitress came in, smiling and pretty, and took the dirty plates away.

Saqlain sat silent until she left. "There are other desires I would be happy to fund," he said. "Are there any designers you like?"

I paused. "Architects?"

He laughed. Then frowned, when he saw I wasn't joking. "No. Fashion. Clothing."

I didn't know.

"Come on," he said. A coaxing smile. "Every girl likes pretty clothes. If you had all the money in the world, what would you like to have?"

It was an appealing thought. I sometimes window-shopped. Who didn't, in New York? I wandered through plush stores, fingering the soft hems of garments I couldn't imagine affording.

I named a couple of shops where I'd coveted cashmere sweaters, camel-hair coats, silk blouses whose sleeves I'd slid across my wrists.

"You could have them," he said. "You could have it all. Whatever you liked."

I hadn't, as a child, paid much attention in my gran's little white church, but suddenly I recalled the story of Jesus fasting in the desert for forty days and forty nights, and how Satan came to him when he was weak and hungry, offering him power over kingdoms and the riches of this world.

Yes, there were things I craved. There were art supply stores that I liked to browse, full of tubes of oil paints (cadmium yellow, Prussian blue, alizarin crimson), nine or twelve or sixteen dollars each. Fat tubes of titanium white. Thick sable brushes. There were stationery stores where I slid my hands across the velvety paper of bound blank books in colors like periwinkle and sage, with ribbons to mark your place and little discreet numbers already printed in the bottom corners of the pages. In the stationery stores, you could hold and test the glossy fountain pens, their beautiful weight balanced in your hand like the hand of a tango partner, their ink silking out smooth trails onto the paper—

When tempted in the desert, of course, Jesus had said no, as befits the Son of God.

"When I travel on business, you could come along," Saqlain continued, his gesture expansive as if he were proffering the very globe. "Rome," he said. "Shanghai. Paris."

Aside from my two-week trip to England and a brief road trip to Boston, I'd been only to West Virginia and New York (and glimpsed the states between them through the window of a Greyhound bus, though I wasn't sure that counted). Well, and Pittsburgh.

I hesitated.

"I'm clean," he said. "I've been tested. I'm attractive." He waved his hand across his chest as if displaying the dessert tray. "I'll take care of you. You'll have everything you need, everything you want."

Looking back across the years, I've sometimes wondered why Saqlain singled me out. I was pretty, but merely in the way a hundred thousand other girls are pretty in New York, and I felt awkward, gauche, untutored. I've since learned that men find young flesh itself a commodity, no matter what's going on inside it; the inner lives of young women are, for many men, irrelevant, or merely piquant. Maybe my very awkwardness itself, along with my bookish ways, bespoke a dewy kind of innocence.

I suppose, really, that my greatest allure stemmed from my simple availability. He'd already ascertained that I had no family to watch out for me, no boyfriend who'd protest, no trust fund to give me confidence while I pursued my impractical art. No one to watch over me. All alone in the world, I must have looked ripe for the plucking.

"But I have a dog," I said nonsensically, my throat suddenly tight at the thought of dragging sweet little Button into it.

"Your dog, too, of course," he said. "Bring it along. You would be free of the gallery, free of working. Just think of all the time you would have to make your art! You could make art all day."

The room tilted, began to slowly rotate around me. I looked down at my sake cup, the marks of my mouth littered scarlet all along its thin white porcelain rim. I thought of the invisible underpaid person bent over a sink in the back who would have to scrub my lip prints away.

There is always an underbelly to pleasure. There's always someone who cleans up the next morning, who strips the soiled sheets from the bed.

I had already been that person.

I nodded.

United Airlines #4068

The layover at the Morgantown Municipal Airport was a mere twenty minutes, for deplaning and boarding only. Those of us continuing on stayed in our seats while the plane idled.

Outside, passengers descended the staircase and milled about, waiting for their bags, already shouting into their cell phones over the engines' roar. The flight attendant walked through the cabin and asked us if we'd care for anything to drink. *Whiskey,* I wanted to say. *Make mine a double.*

"Just water, please."

I pulled out my phone. The urge to text Jon was already fading, as though I'd entered another realm, another dimension, where time and space weren't quite the same, where Jon himself was just a magical story I'd told myself in a faraway land—a prince, a mirage, a sweet fever dream. I slipped the phone back in my bag.

Soon the new passengers were boarding, and the little plane groaned its way up into the air once more. Our flight would be short, a mere hop, so our cruising altitude stayed low, hovering just above the mountains.

Below us unspooled fold after lovely fold of dark-green land, fertile and forested, occasionally gashed by a strip mine. Now and then, a runoff pond's waters glowed a sick opal.

———

After Charlie's death, I saw ghosts everywhere: on playgrounds, on the street, in schoolyards. Voices like Charlie's calling for their mommas. Little blond children of his height and build. I would find myself accelerating toward them, leaning down, looking in their faces.

Faces, unforgivably, not his.

Hallucinations haunted my peripheral vision: Charlie standing at my elbow when I was doing my homework. Charlie flickering on the edge of the woods as the school bus passed by. Eerily still in the corner of a dark room. Alive and laughing. Bruised and dead when I went in to take my bath.

I became a person who switched on all the lights in a house as soon as she walked in.

I became a person who courted darkness.

———

The engines' whine abruptly shifted, and our bodies tilted against our will. The final descent had begun.

It had taken me so long—so many years of unrelenting anxious labor of various kinds—to get from West Virginia to my glass apartment in Chicago, to a view of a lake that sparkled, to wide expanses of flat land where I could clearly see what lay around me. A bank account that made me feel safe. Work I could quietly love. A husband with an education, a profession, dignity. Who did not slap me or call me names or make me parade around a penthouse in thousand-dollar black bondage gear.

Years, it had taken. Month after lonely month of scrambling and confusion and labor and fear. Decades: to leave the past behind, put it tightly in a drawer, shove it shut, and turn the key.

And now, in a single day, I was back. Just like that.

Green ground hurtled up fast through the wispy clouds. The sky was the color of smoke.

ALMOST HEAVEN

Country Roads

At the airport, I picked up a small red rental car, threw my suitcase into its hatchback, and began to wind my way southeast, up into the mountains, afflicted with a strange blend of dread and anticipation. Forested slopes rose high around me.

In New York and Chicago, I'd gradually grown used to feeling neither small nor large: just one person doing her work in a city full of people, living her life among others. But driving back into West Virginia's steep, brooding hills, the metal shell of my car like a fragile capsule of protection, a kind of whistling in the dark, I began to remember what it was like to feel small, isolated, vulnerable, the only human in sight. Signs of civilization quickly dwindled, and trees bristled tall and dark on both sides of the narrow road. The engine whined as I curved and climbed on roads edged by abrupt drop-offs into thin air. White wooden crosses jutted up, festooned with fading plastic flowers, where drivers had careened over the brink.

For three hours I drove, twisting through hills that grew darker and higher, an occasional plume of pale smoke against the trees the only sign of human habitation. Country music flickered on and off as radio waves found and lost me between the mountains' dense mounds of earth, and bare black tree trunks climbed the hills like regiments. By the sides of the road, thick mats of brown leaves covered the soil, and torn trash bags spilled white diapers. In ditches, refrigerators yawned, waiting for a wandering child to climb inside. Rusted cars lay at the bottoms of ravines. Darkness lowered in the sky like a warning.

As the car rose and plummeted, its automatic transmission groaning on steep grades, I remembered the summer scent of the green-leafed canopy shifting softly in the sunlit wind, with shafts of gold striking the forest floor. I recalled the mapled mountainsides of autumn and the crisp air like cold buttermilk, and the thin tangle of spring, the hopeful shoots thrusting up through the thawed mat of leaves. The tang of raw ramps pulled from the earth. I remembered foxes and deer and lumbering black bears with their cubs, and raccoons rinsing small wild apples in the creek at dusk, and hawks aloft, silently hunting. I remembered the green curl of fern fronds and the emerald softness of moss dotted by tiny white blossoms on hair-thin stalks. Boulders spangled with green lichen. Cardinals and sparrows, black-capped chickadees flitting from twig to twig, chipmunks darting, squirrels scolding each other, rabbits freezing into statues at my approach and then loping away, pausing to nibble. The slow rise and fall of their tawny haunches. A dozen deer leaping in unison, their white tails lifted. I remembered climbing high into trees and welding my small body against their warm trunks, feeling alive and awake and a part of it all.

But now the trees' bark was black with cold rain, and the gray sky and sharp wind made everything feel like bitterness and death. No leaves were left to fall.

"If only you'd have been there," my mother liked to say when I visited her in prison. "If you'd just done like you were told, it never would have happened."

Deeper into the mountains I drove.

———

At last I turned from the numbered rural route onto Mercer Run, which hitched and looped its way down into a high-elevation wooded valley.

The road's shoulders broadened, and I began to see signs of human habitation: an AutoZone, a Dairy Queen, a yellow metal barn converted into an antiques mall. Soon the road emptied its sparse traffic into the tiny town of Mercer itself: nine square blocks of civilization, the county seat. Mercer, an odd-sounding name, the name of some early settler. As a child, a teenager, I took for granted its strange swirl of *mercy* and *murder*.

Slowing, I crossed Burke Street and passed the fire department and Ocheltree Theater with its single screen. Saint Mary's Catholic Church, a Mexican restaurant called Los Norteños, the police department, the county courthouse, Country Cookin' restaurant, Holy Lord Bible Church (**REPENT! NOW IS THE TIME!**), First National Bank, the Open Book (a Christian bookstore), the old gas station with a AAA sticker in its window, and Kerri's Antiques & Bead Shoppe.

At the corner of Jackson and Mercer, I slowed. There sat the Cracked Egg Café, the post office, the familiar brown brick Mercer & Sons Pharmacy (with *1932* carved in cream stone over the door), and Mercer Hotel, the old brick Victorian where I'd stay. I pulled into the gravel parking lot.

Mercer Hotel

When I cast my thoughts back to the past, like casting for fish in a stream, what I seem to pull up are the loneliest moments, those incidents when I felt most betrayed or bereft. Forlorn.

Yet my life has been filled with beauty, too—the beauty of the forest, of my own body and Jon's, glazed with sweat and moonlight. Button's copper tail swishing back and forth in the sun. I've sat in the soft jade jewel box of Ladurée on my honeymoon, high on sex and the loveliness of Paris, my lips closing on macarons delicate as air. The cunning bracelet Jon clasped around my wrist (not long after I'd lied to him about the picture of Charlie in my locket): curved wings that stretched around the circumference of my wrist bones, dozens of tiny feathers wrought in black rhodium. Sapphire eyes, a platinum beak. A hawk. Dazzled, I'd lifted my wrist to hold it to the light, tilting it to watch it sparkle. A strange and lovely piece, it felt elegant and outré back home in Chicago, a bauble that stood out at the various galas we attended . . .

But against the peeling laminate counter of the front desk in the lobby of the Mercer Hotel, it looked louche as a leopard on a leash. I unclasped it and dropped it in my handbag.

"Checking in," I said, and gave my name.

The youth behind the desk (I say *youth* advisedly, for he was neither boy nor man) was buttoned badly into a maroon blazer. Light hair fell over his forehead like hay, and his blue eyes appraised me. A small rectangle pinned to his chest said Tim.

"Yep, gotcha right here," he said, staring down at a computer well past its prime. He pushed a key across the counter. "Double bed, clean towels." The fact that he felt it necessary to mention the cleanliness of the towels depressed me, and fatigue swept over my shoulders. I thanked him, took the key, and turned. A small hotel bar glowed red with promise, but I crossed the lobby, pulling my roller bag. The elevator moaned and shuddered all the way up.

On the third and highest floor of the Mercer Hotel, the walls of my room were paneled with laminated dark wood, and a nubby white chenille spread failed to disguise the bed's central sag. All along the bedspread's hem, firm white balls of fluff hung suspended from little strings, giving the bed an air paradoxically both festive and austere, like a Puritan circus. I hadn't seen bedspreads fringed with white pompons since childhood, when I'd seen them all the time. The cheap furniture was overlain with pseudo-Victorian clutter: fringed and beaded lampshades, doilies limp on every surface.

But mercifully, there was no dust, and when I pulled the bedspread back, the sheets were so white and clean as to seem boiled. In the bathroom, no nest of tangled hairs lay in either drain, and no corpses of insects littered tiles the hue of old Band-Aids. I tore the paper wrapper from the thin white bar of soap and washed away the grime of travel. (I'd forgotten to pack a bar of Roger & Gallet's linden.)

It was an ugly room, but it was clean. It was warm. It would do.

I lifted my suitcase to the imitation Victorian desk and unfastened it. Inside lay the little soft objects of my life: the black dress ready to be shaken out and hung on a wire hanger in the narrow closet, the jeans and sweaters and T-shirts and underwear, the rolled socks wedged into the cups of my bras. The high-end barn coat, just in case. The travel set Jon had given me: a little cashmere-covered pillow, a cashmere throw.

From my handbag, I drew my jewelry roll, a soft sausage of beige velvet secured with rose-colored ribbons. I sat down at the tiny desk, slowly slid the bows apart, unfurled the rolled velvet, and shook out the queen's ransom that Jon had given me over the brief span of our marriage—a few sapphires (my favorites) and emeralds, but mostly diamonds and rubies. "I like red with your dark eyes," he'd said at a restaurant one night, reaching across the table to stroke my cheek.

I pushed the shimmering objects around on the desk: platinum chains slender as a filament, glittering tennis bracelets (though I didn't play), glinting rings—I could have worn one on each finger if I'd liked. Jon came from a family where women's worth was measured in carats. (Exhibit A: Helene.) Jewels functioned as proof. Curious, I'd discreetly had the pieces appraised. Easily a hundred thousand dollars lay scattered across the scarred wood.

I slid them around with my fingertip. They'd been pried from the ground by people whose working conditions were probably as bad or worse than those of the coal miners of Mercer.

Strange how things' origins can be cut and polished away.

Once upon a time, the jewels had made me feel real. Worthy. The kind of woman that men give diamonds to: delicate, beloved, desired. Someone whose husband didn't stop wooing and wanting her once she'd signed the papers. Every birthday, Christmas, New Year's, anniversary, like clockwork.

Even Mother's Day, last May. "For the future," Jon had said, clasping the chain at the nape of my neck, his lips and fingers light as a breeze. The fat pear-cut had fallen cold between my collarbones, and I'd shivered. I hadn't worn it since.

I drew a deep breath. Tied up the jewelry roll. Did not question why I'd brought my fortune with me.

I put all my things carefully, tidily away, and when I felt my stomach gurgle, I realized the sushi in the DC airport had been my last meal, hours ago. I pushed aside the lace curtains and the thick panels behind them. The sky had grown blue-black. Mercer's few blocks of lit signs and streetlamps glittered below, surrounded by a swallowing expanse of darkness.

I lifted the beige telephone receiver from its cradle and pushed zero. Tim's voice. "Front desk."

On the off chance, I asked, "Does the hotel have room service?"

Tim choked. "Lady," he said, "this ain't TV."

I hung up. Grabbed my purse and coat and headed down to the lobby.

"Okay," I said. "So where's the best place to get dinner?"

Tim's wide blue eyes locked on mine. "Los Norteños," he said. "That's Mexican." He smirked. "But I guess you know that." A beat while I said nothing. His eyes dropped. "If you like chicken-fried steak, biscuits and gravy, that kind of thing, then Country Cookin' for sure." He fiddled with a ballpoint pen, clicking its tip in and out. "For breakfast, Cracked Egg across the street."

"What about a good salad? And maybe fish?"

His eyes shot back up to my face. His smirk grew. "Didn't think you was from around here."

The night was blue and cold. Few cars passed me as I walked the block north to the river gorge. There was nothing romantic—nothing like Paris or Prague—about the iron bridge that linked the two halves of Mercer. Its metal sidewalks were narrow and slippery, and the railing was only a rusting waist-high grid. A pickup truck rumbled past, and the metal vibrated under my feet. I paused near the middle and looked down into the gorge. Far below, glossy with the sheen from a solitary streetlamp, water rushed cold and deep, the color of coal. I hurried on to Los Norteños.

Warm inside the little Mexican restaurant, crunching corn chips with good salsa, assailed by a peculiar brand of exhausted tension, I read the four texts on my phone: three messages from Jon, asking me to call, and a fourth from Sophia: Where've you run off to? Madagascar? Jon's frantic. Have you taken a lover at last? It'd serve him entirely right. Call me. I must know everything.

I flipped back to Jon's texts. Are you all right? Call me, darling. A tight vibration spiraled up my neck and scalp. His words hung on my screen, simple and clear, yet I strained to focus, as through a haze.

Finally I tapped a brief reply: All's well. Settled at hotel. Fine. I stared at it. Love you, I added, and hit send.

Sitting there, staring blankly at the screen of my phone, I remembered lying in bed with Jon: the strange limp bliss that drenched my limbs after sex, as if all my cells were breathing happiness. That extraordinary ease and ecstasy I'd found with him: nothing else had ever come close.

I wondered if Lily was finding it now. The delicate muscles at the base of my rib cage convulsed.

Sometimes when I thought of Jon, I'd find myself swamped by a sudden surge of irritation. His flawless manners and perpetual kindness were a smooth surface I couldn't ruffle, like the calm glass of a lake, while I was all prickly shards that never quite fit. Possessiveness. Fear. Improper hungers: for the harsh hot smoke of a cigarette, the solitude to sob aloud, a random man who passed on the street.

When my little lusts flared, I took precautions. Alone in the condo of an afternoon, I'd read erotica or watch porn on my laptop, pick up a new trick or two, and surprise Jon that night. He was appropriately grateful, and it worked: the sex stayed fresh, and I stayed loyal.

But I noticed we didn't kiss much, those nights.

Sometimes I thought about that swan story, the one Charlie liked. I thought of that young queen in love, her lips sealed by a vow, dutifully popping out one little heir after another, only to have them stolen away. I wondered if, when the king traveled, she ever fretted about the allure of faraway maidens, or hid in a larder to gobble royal éclairs, or eyed the brawny castle guards with desire. I thought of her sleeping unaware as her mother-in-law, the old dowager, smeared her mouth with blood, as if she'd devoured her own children, until even her husband suspected her and tied her at the stake to burn.

I guess I liked the story after all, convoluted as it was. It wasn't simple, didn't stop at happily-ever-after. It kept going past the pretty wedding, past the halcyon honeymoon where the young bride twirled, enchanted, through all the rooms of her new castle, past the salad days of love, and right into the bitter, sordid heart of marriage: suspicion.

Aside from college dorms and until I met Jon, I'd always lived alone, while all around me people navigated love, home, family. I knew other people had their struggles, but from the outside, they seemed to handle it all so easily, as if love and belonging were simply part of the natural order of things.

What my childhood taught me: love is a thing that stops.

So when Jon seemed to fall in love with me so simply, so deeply, and so fast, I felt skittish. If something sounded too good to be true—as Saqlain had taught me (painfully)—then it was. I scoured Jon's behavior for signs of betrayal. The other shoe—however well heeled—was sure to drop. Better to get the devastation over with.

The food came. Beans, rice, lettuce, guacamole (nice and fresh, with chopped tomato and a generous squeeze of lime). Forgoing the Negra Modelo I craved. Or something stronger. Even eating a meal had become strange now: wondering what I'd keep down. All around me breezed the sounds of Spanish from the waiters and busboys, and I felt a pang. There'd been no Mexican immigrants in Mercer during my childhood—no Latinos at all. I wasn't good at bearing loneliness.

Perhaps it would be best to end it all quickly. Better now, legally, than later, cruelly, and finish like my mother, rotting in some cell . . . I thought about Pittsburgh, the drive it would take to get there. Take care of everything on my own, spend a night to recover, fly out of the Pittsburgh airport. Jon would never need to know.

And if it were true—if Jon were having an affair with Lily? What then? I was—by all inward signs—pregnant. If I kept it, could I stay with a man who'd betrayed me, if it meant stability, comfort, even luxury for my child? Many women struck that bargain for the sake of their children and their own bottom lines. A two-parent home, ponies, private school. Travel, books, museums, and eventually the Ivy League. Making art out of lost objects wasn't the most secure career in the world, and when Latinas still made only fifty-four cents for each white male dollar, no one could blame me for knowing where my bread was buttered.

Or perhaps it would be best to take Conrad Kniseley's offer on the land. Take the money. With that, plus the jewelry, I'd be set for several years, whether I decided to have the baby or not. I could go home with money in the bank, figure out what to do about my marriage. About everything.

I chewed and swallowed, chewed and swallowed, staring at a string of red plastic lights shaped like chili peppers. The plaintive lyrics and polka thump of norteño music from the jukebox whined loud in my ears, and the tense threat of a headache lurked at the base of my skull.

Finished, I paid, tipped well (with the eternal survivor's guilt of a former waitress), and walked back in the dark, my soles sliding on the icy metal sidewalk of the bridge. In the hotel lobby, Tim and I ignored each other, and the elevator grumbled all the way up. I was glad to lock my door behind me, pull off my boots, and drop my clothes on the chair.

I pulled one of Jon's T-shirts over my head, wrapped the cashmere throw around my shoulders, and crawled into bed, curling on my side, tucking the cashmere pillow under my arm for comfort. But nothing warmed me.

It had been a long, strange day, a rocky odyssey from the smooth and lovely shell I wear—the carapace of the one-percenter—to the broken girl I used to be.

Between the crisp sheets, I lay cold, my hand on my belly, unable to sleep.

The Flood

Clutching my throat, I woke.

In the dream, a great flood had swept Charlie and me away from our little white house. Charlie clung hard to the top of a wooden fence post, looking back toward home, but surges of water kept pushing him under. He'd surface, gasping desperately, and then disappear beneath the waves again.

"Come on," said my fourteen-year-old self, calm yet urgent, the way one often is in dreams or terrible emergencies. I grabbed his arm. "If you want to live, you've got to let go."

Charlie opened his hands, trusting me, and we held each other tight as the current carried us, magically buoying us up, lifting us, cradling us, swirling us safely past barns and pickup trucks. We traveled a long way until nothing looked familiar. Eventually, the torrents calmed, and the floodwaters tamed into a smooth, placid glass we glided on. Floating on our backs, we held hands and drifted, languid.

At last, at the edge of a green forest, a soft wave deposited us on dry ground. We stood up. All the water drained away. A path ran up the hill between the trees, and on it stood a magnificent elk, massive and cocoa brown. He lowered his great antlered head down to us, and we reached to stroke his muzzle. His nose was dark velvet under our hands.

I crouched and put my arm around Charlie's thin shoulders. "See?" I said. "The important thing is to stay afloat. Where you end up doesn't matter."

———

Which is a lie, of course. The lie I told myself for so long.

I lay in the black room, staring toward a ceiling I couldn't see, until I fell asleep again.

The Cracked Egg

The next morning, I woke while it was still dark. Victorian kitsch heaved around me as I groped my way to the unfamiliar bathroom and lost what was left of my Mexican meal.

A shower as hot as I could bear. Jeans, sweater, boots, barn coat, bag. I opened the blinds to a cold gray dawn.

Down in the lobby, Tim was gone, replaced by a plump blonde woman talking on the phone. She flashed what passed for a smile as her eyes followed me to the door.

Outside the gelid air bit my skin and smelled faintly of woodsmoke as I crossed Jackson Street. When I opened the door to the Cracked Egg Café, its rush of warmth laced with all the hopeful smells of morning—eggs, coffee, toast—I began to cheer up. The diner was noisy with people and clattering silverware. Every booth was full.

But as I headed toward the counter, a hush fell gradually over the room—not a sudden silence, but a slow muting, as if someone were twisting the volume down. Faces swung toward me as people waylaid one conversation after another. They looked me up and down, then glanced across at each other, eyebrows raised. A crowd of them and only one of me: not just a stranger in city clothes but my skin a shade too dark for local. Fear swam through me, and my breath shallowed as I moved across the room as if underwater. Shoulders back (don't show fear) but head inclined (don't look for trouble), slight smile, quick glide of generalized eye contact. Not a threat, not a troublemaker. A home-girl, if only they knew it. This home that was never a home.

I sat on a stool at the counter, and a woman's pink bustline zoomed into view. Tina, the name tag read. "Coffee, hon?" she asked, brown pot already lifted. I turned over my cup. Tina poured and cracked her gum. Mint whiff. "What can I get you?"

"Two eggs over easy, please. Wheat toast." I studied the plastic menu. "Do you have grits?"

"'Course we got grits. Great grits, greasy grits, grits to beat the band."

"Grits, then, please."

She disappeared. Steam rose from my coffee, and I poured in cream, remembering the relief I'd felt years ago in New York when I learned that the fancy new food, polenta, that was suddenly popping up on every restaurant menu was merely a dressed-up version of the humble grits of my youth.

Conversation resumed around me, bustling, loud: men in work shirts, a deputy sheriff with his hat on the counter, women in plaid flannel for the farm or skirts for office jobs downtown. Grooved faces, brittle hair. People aged hard in the country. Bad food, manual labor, cigarettes. Worse.

Across the diner, too far away for me to hear their conversation over the general din, sat three white women and a man, all wearing matching black sweatshirts with large white letters. **NO SANCTUARY**, the sweatshirts read, and I felt a pang of fear—not on my own behalf (they could harass me if they chose, but I was, after all, a citizen, born and raised right here) but for the sake of the people I'd seen at the Mexican restaurant the night before, and for all their partners and parents and children at home. I wondered how many of them lacked papers, and how vulnerable they'd be if a community like Mercer decided to turn against them.

The No-Sanctuary people smiled and laughed as they bent over notepads and showed them to each other—they seemed to be making plans of some kind—and I wondered, not for the first time, how good it must feel to exclude and blame the powerless. Why the allure was so chronic. It was a thrill I'd never understood.

I pulled my phone out. There were two texts from Jon.

6:33 a.m. Doing okay?

7:16 a.m. Twelve minutes ago. Good time to talk?

Visitation at 6 this evening, I typed. Will call after.

A funeral wasn't enough, or so Mr. Bascum, the funeral director, had assured me on the phone. People apparently needed a further opportunity to look at the body and say sympathetic things to the mourning family, so visitations were generally held in the evenings, convenient for working people, while funerals were usually scheduled during the warmth and light of day, when the body could be gotten more easily into the ground.

Tina the waitress plunked my food down. In the white pile of grits, a pat of yellow butter was dissolving, and grill grease crisped the edges of my egg whites. Toast lay limp with heat and butter at the edge of the plate. My earlier nausea had passed, and I poked the yolks with my fork and sopped up their yellow sauce with toast. High in the corner of the room, a lone fly swooped and circled.

I chewed my breakfast, wondering idly if anyone from my past recognized me, if someone in the crowded diner was, even now, leaning over, hand cupped, to a companion, to say, *Look—over there. Isn't that—?* and then deciding no, it couldn't be, not after all these years.

Someone sat down on the stool next to me. Tina materialized.

"I'll have the special." His voice was rough and deep.

"You'll have whatever you want, sugar." She grinned and sashayed away.

I scanned him out of the corner of my eye. Big, tanned hands, muscular, veined. Working man's hands. Clean white nails. He flipped open the local paper, held his coffee like a doll's teacup.

He turned and caught my eyes on him.

He'd aged exceptionally well. Warm, brown eyes, surrounded by creases. Cheekbones: high. Curling black hair. Midforties. Italian, a descendant of the waves of immigrants who came to work the mines. A hard mouth, the kind I'd always liked.

"Bel Martin," he said. He folded his newspaper and laid it down.

I pressed my napkin to my lips. "Nic Folio."

"I wondered if you'd come." His eyes flicked up and down. "Been a long time."

I focused on the last of my grits while Tina refilled my coffee. She whisked away, hollering about eighty-sixing the waffles.

"How have you been?" I said, my voice low and reluctant.

"Good." He lifted his coffee to his lips, swallowed, and looked at me over the rim. "Good enough. Working security's a steady job. Two boys, hell-raisers. An ex-wife down in Bluefield. You?"

"I'm an artist. No children."

"Art," he said. "Cool. I'm not much into art, myself. I like hunting, fishing, and hockey"—he flashed the old charming, devilish grin that had melted girls in high school—"but I'm pretty sure long walks on the beach would be fine if that's what you're into."

I drew away, shaking my head. "Does that ever work?"

He laughed. "Sometimes."

"I'm married."

"I see that." He nodded toward my ring. "But funny thing. I don't see a husband. Just thought I'd get right to it. All due respect, Bel. I'm a busy man."

I rose and gathered my things. "People call me Isabel now."

"Whatever you say." He grinned and put out his hand.

It hung in the air between us for a long moment. My awkwardness grew, but he waited until I reached out. We shook. Warm, firm, calloused. His smile broadened.

I pulled my hand away. "I should go."

He nodded. "Fare thee well, then, Isabel. Hope to see you around here again. At seven thirty a.m. or so, Monday through Friday."

At the cash register, waiting for my change, I glanced over. He'd unfolded his newspaper again and was reading the business section, such as it was. Silver glinted in his black hair.

His legs were long and lean, his shoulders broad, his Levi's and work boots clean. His heavily muscled arms hadn't changed since his days of football glory.

I looked away.

Capston Brothers Real Estate

Outside, the sun was higher, but the wind blew cold. I headed north on Mercer toward the bridge.

My body: this thing I wore, this attraction machine, of which I could flash slices—a wink of knee or clavicle, a sliver of thigh, a plunge of back—and suddenly men who'd been strangers became quite interested in knowing me well. Saqlain had taught me the laws of supply and demand. For seven long years, he'd taught me, until his desire waned—whether due to my increasing age or increasing independence, I was never quite sure: I'd gained a small reputation as an artist and become impatient with Saqlain's control. Interesting men wanted to date me, and I no longer needed his support. We parted as friends. Still frequenting the restaurants and clubs where we'd gone together, I found myself sought by other powerful men. I knew how to flirt and how to hold myself aloof, how to pace desire. As a pastime, it was pleasant enough.

After Jon, all that stopped. My body became a private thing again. Real. Mine. And I was happy. Satisfied.

But sometimes I missed the game of lure and reveal, the body itself a kind of Scheherazade, telling its stories, slowly doling out mysteries.

When I thought about pregnancy, I worried. According to what women said, one's body becomes not one's own at all, and pregnancy wreaks sad havoc on the very bits of the body designed to entice, which become serviceable, utilitarian. Worn. At least, that's what I've been told by friends who are new mothers, their own breasts as romantic to them as gas pumps.

Oh, there's surgery. Lots of women do that. But even then, you become only a successful work of restoration, like a fresco newly brightened—not your own original, sublime self. The mark of use forever upon you.

Oh, love, I suppose—love for the baby, your precious, adorable little perfect child—makes the sacrifice worthwhile, just as you're making your permanent exit (make no mistake) from the truly serious sex market. For all intents and purposes, your career as a beauty is over.

Standing on the iron bridge, staring down into the watery cleft, my gloved hands gripping the railing, I felt my mother's ambivalence in my bones: her love for us (such as it was) poised against her need for attention, sex, exhilaration, for flirting over pool cues and cold beers, for dancing fast to loud music, for craving and being craved. Not the dispiriting trudge of feeding two children she couldn't afford.

It scared me, like a fist inside my forehead, that she made a kind of sense to me. Perhaps, like her, I would never be safe—a safe bet, a safe house, a shelter. Trustworthy. Perhaps I would always be high-risk, a gamble, a site where social workers' doubts would cluster.

How I wished there were a test, simple as a finger prick, a welling red pearl of blood to tell the certain truth about me. Could I be trusted? A child. Could I bear that burden, that strain?

———

Shivering, I left the bridge, crossed Main Street, and turned right toward Capston Brothers Real Estate. Icy wind filtered through my hair.

I'd found Elaine Carter online. *Are you looking for an experienced real estate agent that can lead you through a "stress-free" transaction? As a prospective home seller or buyer, I understand the importance of having a dedicated professional on your side.* In her website photo, she'd looked thirty, with sparkling green eyes and red hair that cascaded down in sharp waves; I didn't count her shiny white teeth, but someone could have.

When the doorbell jangled and she crossed the reception area and pumped my hand hard, I discovered that the real Elaine Carter was at least three decades older. But vigorous. Bright. Strong. The V-neck of her light-blue sweater framed deep, freckled cleavage.

"I am *so* glad to finally meet you, Ms. Morales," she said as my hand began to palsy in her grip. "That plot of land you got out there has a *lot* of potential," she said, leading me to her office, "and I mean a *lot* of potential." Her rear end belonged to a plumper woman than her top half, and beige polyester pants were doing her no favors. I rubbed life back into my knuckles.

"You just make yourself comfortable," she said, leaning, tapping vigorously away at her computer keyboard.

I sat. A small window looked out onto Turner Street. A coal truck rumbled past, its heaped load shining black.

"Here we go," she said, twisting her computer monitor to face me. "Now you just take a look at these comps." She ran her fingernail down the screen. "One thirty-nine nine. One nineteen nine. One forty-four nine . . ." She kept scrolling down. "We can make you some real fine cash off that land. Fast cash, too. I'm thinking it'll be a pretty quick turnaround. Quick for this market, I mean." She sat down. Shrugged. "I won't lie. I won't tell you it's not sluggish. Ever since '08, things have been a right mess, don't you know. For all of us. But it's picking up. We are definitely seeing movement."

"Good," I said.

She clicked her keyboard. "Now, let me just show you something to get you thinking. What we might do for an ad. I know you haven't signed anything, but I went ahead and did a mock-up." She smiled, tapping a key. "At Capston Brothers, we go the extra mile."

A photograph of my old house filled her screen.

My throat made a noise.

White. Little. Paint peeling. Surrounded by trees. Autumn leaves, brown and gold.

"Now this is just a preliminary shot, you understand. I was out there anyhow, and I had my camera, so I was like, *Why not?* It's just to show you what the listing could look like. We can take a better picture if you want."

"It looks fine."

"Oh, good," she said. Beamed. "Good. Wonderful. Now, just let me be real frank for a second, honey—what good is that land doing you? Just sitting out there, and you all the way out in . . . I forget. Conrad said you're living out west somewhere."

"Chicago."

"Right, exactly. Away to the city for years and years now, he said, and seems like maybe the nicest thing you could do for yourself would be to make the best of a bad situation. Cup half-full, you know. Clean break."

It was cliché hour, apparently.

"Take the money and run?"

Her eyes went all wide and concerned. "Oh, no, sugar," she said. "Not what I'm saying. Not what I'm saying at all. Look, I know you just lost your momma." She leaned across the desk and patted my hand. "Grief is a process. You take your time. Your emotions are probably all riled up right now. You take all the time you need. And when you're ready"—her business card flipped out like prestidigitation—"you just give me a call. We'll get you all taken care of."

I tucked the card into my bag. "I appreciate it. I do. I'm just considering . . . options."

Her bottom lip fell away from her top one, just for a moment. Then both her lips stretched broadly out, like rubber. All those teeth. Pink gloss coated her brown lipstick. "Options?" She spoke fast. "What options? Other realtors? Are you talking to Nicoletti and Sons? Because let me tell you something about Chuck Nicoletti—"

"What?" I frowned down at my knees. "No. I'm not talking with other realtors." I didn't mention the anonymous offer of three hundred thousand. "This is all just happening—my mother . . . I'm trying to figure out what to do."

Even as the words left my mouth, I felt their inadequacy, my stiffness, like I was speaking memorized dialogue, inevitable, like the script had long ago been written, the script of after-someone-dies, and I was helpless against its power, sleepwalking through the prescribed gestures, the ritual utterances. No one could choose any other words. I could no more name what I was actually feeling—the bleary confusion, the nausea, the sad longing, the lostness, the stray bursts of fury—than I could bring my mother back to life.

I looked up. Elaine Carter was saying something, looking at me with an expression that might have been sympathy. She was asking how long I would be staying in Mercer.

"I don't know," I said slowly. "A few days." I'd booked return flights, but they could be changed.

"There's no rush on any of this," she said. "If we don't sign anything just right yet, we can always handle it long-distance." She smiled. "Of course," she said. "You just take your time. Whatever you want to do. You *are* the client."

I'd failed to notice the moment I became one, but I said nothing.

"Just give it some thought. If you want to talk some more, I'll be seeing you at the funeral home tonight."

I blinked. "You knew my mother?"

"Why, we were in high school together, sugar. Before she dropped out to marry that Martin fella. Devoted to him, she was. All the boys at Mercer High chasing after her, and she just wanted that man twice her age. Good-looking fella, right enough, but none of us could figure it. Rest of us being cheerleaders, going to prom, having a life, and she just wants to move out to the mountains and cook and clean for some old man. Headstrong, Stella was." Her eyes grew distant. "She was always a wild one, for sure, but seems like she just went crazy after that mine exploded." She shook her head. "If you'll forgive my saying so. I shouldn't be sitting here talking about your momma to you."

"No, it's all right," I said. No one else ever had, except Aunt Della.

"But I'd be coming to the visitation tonight whether I knew your momma or not. In case I *do* end up representing your home and acreage—up to you, of course—I can start putting out some feelers for you. You never know. Could be some neighbors of your momma's there, looking to expand. You'd be surprised how many deals get started at funerals. Or weddings." Brash laugh. She pulled a pink plastic hairbrush out of a drawer, leaned back in her chair, and started pulling nested hairs from the bristles. "I mean, that's how I found out about that piece of land coming on the market any day now, too. At a funeral. Same kind of situation, death in the family. Old fella, natural causes. No house, just woods. Fifty acres or so. Backs up right next to your land. Shares a fence line, I think. They're going to be asking around a hundred, and I know it's going to move fast." She rolled the mat of red hair between her hands and dropped it into the trash. "Weddings and funerals, like I always tell the young folks just starting out in real estate. Got to maximize your contacts. Got to get you a nice outfit, because weddings and funerals are the lifeblood of the business. Leastaways around here."

I stood. Thanked her. Got out into the cold sunshine as fast as I could.

Johnson, Kniseley & Cerullo, Attorneys at Law

Flanking the broad stairs of an imposing stone building on Burke Street, two small cement lions reposed on their plinths. As a child, I'd stared up at them, wanting to climb on their backs just for a minute, to put my arms around them, to pretend they were mine and could bear me away. (Aunt Della, taking me with her to run errands while Momma slept one off: "Quit your lollygagging, girl.")

The building's wooden doors were twice my height and heavy, their brass handles cold even through my gloves, and they opened onto a lobby floored with flecked old granite. On the wall in a glass case, a black felt panel held little white changeable letters for offices that came and went. Next to it hung the large permanent brass plaque for the law firm of Johnson, Kniseley & Cerullo, which occupied, apparently, the whole third floor. If there was any money in Mercer, it lived here.

The elevator was much larger than the one in my hotel, its ride smoother and silent. In its mirrored walls, I looked gaunt, my shoulders hunched. I stood up straight and raked my fingers through my hair.

The elevator doors opened onto a lobby plushly carpeted in crimson. Behind a desk sat a woman my age, an overdone blonde-bombshell type.

"Hello," she said, looking up. "Welcome to Johnson, Kniseley, and—" Her hand went to her mouth. "Oh my God," she said. "If it isn't Bel Martin." She got to her feet.

I recognized the face. Her hair was still blonde, her eyes still blue and wide. But I couldn't place her.

"Don't you remember me?" she said. "Anna Shingleton? Anna Tucker, as was?"

One of the girls who had taunted me, so long ago in grade school. The dim one.

"My God," breathed Anna. "It's like seeing a ghost." She blinked fast. "But a real fancy ghost. You look so elegant and everything." She wore a pale-green sweater and skirt and pearl earrings too big to be real. She'd filled out well and kept her figure, but her face was still moony. "We always did wonder what happened to you."

I forced a smile. "Is Conrad Kniseley available?"

She sat down. "Let me check the book." She began sliding her fingernail down the pages of a heavy leather-bound calendar, flipping the pages in a slow, concentrated way, frowning down.

Finally she looked up. "He is," she said. "He is available." She stared up at me. "You want me to see if he's free right now?"

Anna seemed not to have grown brighter with the years. "If you would, please."

She picked up the phone, spoke, and hung up.

"Mr. Kniseley says to come right in." She rose, swiveled, and led me down a hallway into a small anteroom, her heavy floral perfume floating back to me, her steps small and halting like the steps of bound feet. On the frosted-glass panel of a wide wooden door, Conrad Kniseley's name was painted in gold letters.

Her knock was soft, his answer a growl. She announced me and stood aside.

"Ms. Martin!" Conrad Kniseley stood up, the picture of heartiness. His face was florid, his hair a flock of thinning sandy curls.

"Morales," I said. "Isabel Morales."

"Ah! Very good, very good." A starched white napkin cascaded from his shirt collar over an ample paunch. In the blond thicket of his beard and mustache, his lips were moist, fleshy, and bright pink, like the tip of a dog's penis. We shook hands. "You caught me at my lunch. Hearing set for noon thirty. What's a man to do? But sit down!"

He waved at two red leather chairs. I sank into one, its slick surface cool through my jeans.

"Now," said Conrad Kniseley, waving his hand with a benevolent flourish, "let us have conversation." He dug back in to the plate of chicken-fried steak and mashed potatoes. Chewed, swallowed, stabbed up another lump.

"This concern," I said. "The one that's so interested in my mother's property."

"Ah," he said, wiping his lips, his hands, on a second napkin. "Ah, yes."

"I take it that it's some kind of mining company."

"Ah," he said. "Ah. Well." He regarded me. "Well, I wouldn't feel comfortable saying that no, it's not a mining company. But then neither would I want to divulge anything about the other party that might indicate that yes, it definitely is a mining company—particularly since I've agreed to keep its identity confidential, unless there's evidence of real interest in moving an arrangement forward in a serious and committed fashion, with the sincere expectation of a positive resolution. You see how things are."

"Hmm," I said. "Of course, it's impossible for me to make a decision without a full understanding of the context."

Nodding, he drank brown liquid from a small glass, then opened his mouth to speak.

"For example," I continued, "let's say—just hypothetically—that my mother was opposed to coal mining on principle—politically—having lost her husband in a mining accident." She wasn't any such thing. Politics, she'd said more than once, was a game for rich people.

"Without knowing if the concern is a coal company, how could I make a decision about the disposal of her land?"

"Ah," said Conrad Kniseley, nodding, steepling his fingers. "Ah. Yes. I take your meaning." What impressed me about Mr. Conrad Kniseley, Esquire, was the imperturbable friendliness in his hazel eyes. He had a finely honed affability. He handled me in the deft, cheerful way a pizza chef handles dough. "And, if that were indeed the case—just hypothetically, of course—would there be any other objections to such a company's interest? Given, that is, that your mother herself has passed on?"

My fingers laced together in my lap. Other objections. Climate change? Uncle Frank's black lung? Ruined rivers? Children with cancer? Flooding, droughts, glaciers melting, sea levels rising, wildfires raging out of control, coral reefs dying while jellyfish swarmed—

But I wasn't an activist. I was a probably pregnant artist with a potentially crumbling marriage, trying to figure out how to afford my future.

"No," I said. "That's all."

"I see," said Conrad Kniseley. "Yes, yes. Well, that's a highly legitimate concern." He wiped his mouth. "I hear what you're saying," he said. "I do. Yet they're making great advances nowadays, you know. Great advances. Technology. Innovation. Surgical methods of extraction. Safety precautions. Which is just to say, if you think you could possibly be amenable to a sit-down, it could be that the other party—whose identity I am keeping completely confidential, you understand—might be entirely capable of allaying your very reasonable concerns. A sit-down, you know. A discussion. An exploratory conversation."

I studied my hands. "Let's just say—again, hypothetically—that I would be open to such a discussion, but that I remain quite attached to my mother's land. Very attached. For sentimental reasons. I grew up there, after all."

"Ah, yes. Yes, I see. Well, one does, doesn't one? Get attached."

I nodded soberly. "Given the situation, what might this anonymous other party be prepared to do? To help alleviate the emotional pain of my loss?"

His smile split his red cheeks into pleased round quadrants, as if I'd just displayed fluency in his native tongue. As if we'd begun to conspire. "Ah, yes," he said. "I see. Naturally. Alleviate." He nodded. "Yes. Well, it's my pleasure to inform you that I am authorized"—he whipped his napkin around in a little swirl of excitement—"that I am authorized to offer you"—he paused—"up to four hundred thousand dollars for the property."

I looked out the window. Across Kenton Street to the east, dark forested hills rose in waves. A slender gray plume of smoke hung among the distant trees. I remembered what Saqlain had taught me.

I sighed. "That's a little sad," I said. "Probably not as sad as I am. But sad." I gathered my things and made as if to rise.

"Five," he said quickly. "Five hundred thousand. But that's their maximum bid. That's the most I'm authorized to offer."

I turned and looked directly at him. "The very most?"

"Yes. Truly. The absolute very most." The crinkles on his forehead multiplied.

I let the warm look seep into my eyes, the gentle, grateful, surprised look that had always worked on boxers and bankers and men who owned yachts. I sat down again. "Well," I said. "Now then. Five is—generous."

"Ah!" he said, stretching his arms luxuriantly. The semblance of anxiety vanished. He wiped his lips with the second napkin and tossed it onto the desk with the satisfaction of a cat with cream; I half expected him to lick his whiskers. "There's nothing quite so"—he searched for the word—"*invigorating* as the gratitude of a pretty woman."

I let a little frown make my face seem stern. "I'll think about it. That's all I'm willing to say at this point. Please let your clients know that more evidence of the firm's concern could be . . . persuasive."

"Mm. Mm-hmm. Duly noted. Persuasive. Thinking about it. And that's really all one can be expected to do," said Conrad Kniseley, nodding, "in circumstances such as these—which, if I may say so, as a strictly objective observer, are very fortunate circumstances in which to find oneself." He glanced at his bulging gold watch. Then at my face. "Aside from the most regrettable passing of the loved one, of course," he amended. "And now, look at the time." He snatched the napkin from his shirtfront and got to his feet, stuffing sheaves of paper into a brown briefcase. He popped a round peppermint in his mouth and crunched. "Yes, you think about it, Ms. Morales. Think long and hard. There's an opportunity here, my dear, a very fine opportunity indeed. An opportunity for all of us—I'll be candid; I don't mind showing my cards to a lovely lady—to profit quite, quite handsomely."

I rose.

He gave my hand two hearty pumps and pressed the buzzer.

"Anna," he said, "see Ms. Morales out."

The Anteroom

But Anna didn't see me out. Leading me back down the hall, she turned and laid a light hand on my arm.

"Bel, do you have a second?"

Dazed, I nodded and followed her. My heartbeat slapped inside me. I'd just nearly doubled the offer. Half a million dollars. Independence and security I'd never dreamed of. Five hundred thousand meant a down payment on a place in a good, safe neighborhood in Chicago, savings, a couple of years of paid expenses without having to worry. Stability. Safety. Jon could do what he liked.

Anna ushered me into a sort of waiting lounge with brown velvet davenports and Thomas Kinkade paintings on the walls. A window overlooked Burke Street.

"Shh," she said, widening her blue eyes and placing a finger on her lips. "I'll be right back."

She pulled the door shut behind her. Through its frosted glass I could see vague blurs of blonde and green, and then she disappeared.

I sat there, fidgeting with my nails, longing for a cigarette or whiskey, listening to the bustle and fuss of Conrad Kniseley's departure from the office, looking at the warm little pricks of painted candlelight glowing in the windows of Thomas Kinkade's snowy cottages. Five hundred thousand. Hazy human shapes passed the door. Silence descended, broken by occasional muffled murmurs. The furnace kicked on. Just as

I began to wonder how long Anna would leave me there, she slipped in and closed the door.

"So." She sank into the opposite brown love seat and leaned toward me, her hands clasped together. "How *are* you?"

Sunlight fell from the window between us, and I began to see the small incursions time had made: creases at the well-creamed corners of her eyes; the crumbling erosion of her lip line under the careful application of rose lipstick; a barely perceptible rim of white hair at her scalp, like the thinnest of haloes, before yellow dye coated the strands; the soft spills of flesh under her arms at the edges of her bra. I wondered which signs of age she noted in me.

"Whatever happened to you?" she asked. "Where did you go?"

It was difficult to tell whether the curiosity in her wide blue eyes stemmed from warm human interest or the chillier hunger for gossip. I remembered childhood, the bland delight in her face as she and her alpha friends teased me.

I donned the bright, impervious smile I wore to medical fundraisers. "I live in Chicago now." Her eyes darted to my left hand, which I obligingly lifted. "I'm married."

"Me too," she said quickly, holding up her own sparkling bands. "Three kids. Girls. All teenagers. Driving me crazy. But all of them healthy, thank God." Quick laugh. "You got kids?"

My smile affixed itself to my lips. "No."

"Oh." She nodded, her eyebrows drawn together in sympathy. "Oh. So you work, then?"

"I'm an artist. My husband's a doctor." I ordered it that way for strangers, to ward off their speculation about my own financial success or lack thereof. Once they heard *doctor*, they didn't ask.

"Ooh," she said. "Nice. Tommy's still down in the mines."

"Ah."

"You don't remember Tommy? Tommy Shingleton?"

"Sorry."

"Well, you've been gone a long time." She sighed and leaned back in the love seat. Shook her head. "No one's going to believe this. No one. You being here and everything." She leaned forward again. "Why *are* you here? You moving back to town?"

A short laugh escaped me.

Quiet hurt flashed across her face. Then she smiled. "No, of course. Why would you? Living in a big city, with a doctor and all." She nodded. "So why *are* you here?"

I took a breath. "My mother's funeral."

"Your mother? The one who—" Silence dropped like a curtain. Her pale cheeks filled with blood. In the corner of the floor, forced air rushed from the vent.

"Yes," I said. "That one."

"Oh, I'm so sorry." She reached over and settled her hand on mine like a small cold pillow. "I didn't know she died."

"The funeral's soon," I said. "I just need to get a few things tied up."

"Oh! That's why you're talking to Mr. Kniseley?"

I smiled.

"Of course." She kept nodding, solemn now, and pulled her hand back. She tilted her head. "You know who's going to be really surprised to see you." She nodded, agreeing with herself. "Yes, he sure will. Billy Dunn is going to be wild."

"Pardon?"

"Billy Dunn. He carried a torch for you for years. You didn't know?"

I stared. Shook my head.

"Oh, totally. Spray-painted your name all over the eastbound bridge. Wrecked his truck and told everyone it was for the love of you."

A quiet numbness crept through my limbs. I'd always known that some fairly peculiar things went by the name of love, but this took whatever cake was left.

"I mean, for sure, all that was years ago now. But still, with Donna divorcing him and everything—I'm just saying, he's going to be pretty interested to hear you're back in town."

I stood up. "Just for a few days." I tapped my platinum rings with a fingernail and gave her a smile of finality. "And I'm married. Not to mention Billy's my cousin."

"I know," she breathed, pushing to her feet. "That's what makes it all so star-crossed and tragic, like Romeo and Juliet."

It was perhaps the strangest revisionist history I'd ever heard, but Anna's eyes were wide and cloudy, chocked with dreams. Perhaps, with three kids and Conrad Kniseley to manage, and Tommy coming back tired from the coalface each night, she needed all the illusions she could keep.

"I've really got to go," I said.

She opened the door. It took only a few steps to escape the hallway and cross the lobby. Behind me, Anna kept saying consolatory things about my mother being in a better place. Then the elevator doors were closing, and I was briefly alone, sinking in its box of blessed peace.

Bascum & Sons' Funeral Parlor

From his deep, cavernous voice on the phone—an underground sound of dripping stalactites and vast dangling colonies of bats shifting in gloom—I'd imagined the undertaker as a tall, cadaverous man, with pale waxy flesh and hair black as a moonless night. But when I got to Bascums' Funeral Parlor, Phinney Bascum turned out to be quite short, with a thatch of rusty hair, a face flushed as an overripe peach, and a warm, emphatic handshake. He smelled of fresh baked goods. He spoke artificially slowly, as if he'd been taught in some generic funeral school that the bereaved could bear nothing too rapid, even speech.

"You have my warmest wishes at this painful time," he said. "Here at Bascum and Sons, we shall do all we can to ensure the beautiful and peaceful rest of your loved one."

He paused between utterances, as if to give each phrase sufficient time to sink and sift through layers of stunned grief in the hearer's mind before finally settling on the sandy floor of comprehension, and he used no contractions, as if mourners might be insulted by the casualness of leaving letters out.

But his somnolent manner failed to soothe, and I found myself growing more impatient with each slow sentence he pronounced as he led me to his office. We sat. Phinney Bascum was dwarfed by his huge wing chair, and between us lay the polished, unnervingly empty slab of his desk. A gas fireplace put out no heat at all.

"Can I see my mother?"

"Of course," said Phinney Bascum. "Of course you wish to spend some precious moments with the beloved. So very natural." Pause. "But unfortunately, we suffered a staffing issue, and my assistant was unable to assist. You understand."

I didn't.

"The consequence being, I am afraid, that the beloved is not quite, quite ready yet. To be viewed, that is. A few finishing touches still left to do." Somber nod. Modest smile. "My own specialty."

Preferring not to envision the specific touches to which he referred, I stared at the selection of urns on the shelves above his head. The brushed-steel one looked chic, like something to put in a high-end kitchen.

"But if you would like to come a few minutes before the visitation this evening, perhaps, before the guests arrive, she will be available for viewing then." Long pause. "You can have some private moments."

I said that would be fine, signed the papers he put in front of me, and wrote a check. He delivered his thanks in a measured, grief-appropriate fashion.

Then he cleared his throat. "You do not remember me, I think. From school."

I blinked, squinted at him. Nothing flickered.

"I'm sorry," I said.

"It is understandable." His eyes fell. "You were—very pretty." His face lifted for a moment, then dropped again. "Are. Are very pretty. And I was—I was not a popular boy."

What I remembered about school was being poor and hungry and bullied, and trying to get through the day so I could get back home to the forest and Charlie. I strained to recall a younger version of Phinney Bascum—to recall even his name.

"Honestly, I don't remember most people," I said. "It's all kind of a blur to me now."

"Ah," he said. "I see. Well."

"Really," I said.

"It is," he said, "perhaps understandable, given—" He fiddled with his fingers. "Given everything that occurred. With your loved ones."

We sat there. The gas fire hissed.

"Well," I finally said, "I should go. Thank you for handling—all this." I gestured vaguely.

He nodded. "But wait," he said. "I do have something for you. Before you depart."

He slid out of his wing chair and stooped over something in the corner. *Depart* sounded more ominous, coming from him, and even his movements were unnaturally slow, orchestrated, as if choreographed—as if he often stood alone in this office and rehearsed how to bend and turn smoothly so as not to startle the bereaved. I felt sad for Phinney Bascum. It seemed like he could have been such a normal, cheerful man if he'd gotten some ordinary profession. I imagined him coaching a daughter's soccer team, his quick, spontaneous cheers full of slang.

He straightened and placed a medium-sized cardboard box on the desk. It was taped shut.

"The warden at the penitentiary gave me this. For you." Pause. "It contains the personal effects of the beloved. The items she was allowed to keep in her—her room." He gave the box a small, slow push in my direction. "They belong to you now. They are yours."

I stood and shook his hand again and thanked him. I picked up the box. It was surprisingly light. Inside the cardboard, its contents slid and rustled in my arms.

Phinney Bascum walked me to the door and opened it. Cold bright air blew in around us.

"Remember," he said. "Come early, if you would care to spend a few moments alone with your loved one."

"Thank you," I said again, and for the first time, I let myself look directly into his eyes. They were wide and sweet, the shocking blue of cornflowers, and for all the stiff and calculated polish of his manner, they were genuinely, almost unbearably kind.

The General Store

Back in the parking lot of the Mercer Hotel, I stowed the box of my mother's effects, unopened, in the hatchback of my red rental car. I flicked my phone on. Jon's text read, Isabel. Call me.

Later, I texted. I thumbed it away and dropped the phone in my purse.

In need of something warmer than the elegant silk jersey sweaters I'd packed, I walked to the general store. Among its wide, familiar aisles, its barrels of nails, its Proustian scents of sawdust and seed corn, I wandered between chainsaws, red nylon halters for horses, and toothed tools I didn't remember the names for, my feet traversing the old rough gray boards, splintered and bitten by boot heels. I found the shelves where men's flannel shirts were stacked and felt my way through them, choosing the softest ones I could find. With their thick polyester padding, they'd be warm. I bought two shirts of red plaid, took them back to my room, peeled off the price tags, and stacked them on the dresser.

I ate lunch alone at the Mexican restaurant, napped (a sudden plummet of exhaustion) in my hotel room, went running (with gloves and ear-warmers, my thighs throbbing at the unaccustomed hills), and showered in the small tub, the plastic shower curtain sticking cold to my wet hips.

I blew my hair dry and slipped into my black dress.

The Visitation

At a quarter till six in the evening, the sky already blue-black, I arrived at Bascums' Funeral Parlor and made my way down the corridor to the viewing hall marked *Martin*. The room stood empty and dim, filled with the residual death smell of lilies. Fuzzy flocked wallpaper: maroon velvet on dull gold. I stood in the doorway and flipped on more lights.

Padded chairs stood in rows. At the front of the room, yellow spotlights blazed down on the coffin and its few sprays of flowers.

I walked up the center aisle toward the casket. A fierce trembling was happening all over my body. I felt like throwing up. The last time I'd seen my mother, she'd been in prison. I'd been fifteen.

When I saw her, my breath stopped.

Small. Older. Thin in the box, eyes closed. Her hair gray, her skin pale from years of little sun. But the same. Everything so familiar, so known, except the small grooves cut in the flesh around her mouth, around her eyes—channels that must have worn into her skin gradually but looked stark and sudden to me. The still-beautiful bones of her face, my own architecture mirrored back.

In death, she wore a charcoal sweater, a strand of yellowing faux pearls, a navy skirt, and old-fashioned suntan hosiery that oranged her shins. Her outfit had been provided, Phinney Bascum had told me, by a local charity. Sensible gray pumps. She looked as though she'd come directly from a secretarial job at a failing concern.

"Momma." The sound was a whimper, not my grown voice. My voice at nine, at five. A child's voice, lost and losing. All the air rushed out of me in a sad sigh, like the wave that pushes you under for the last time.

In Chicago, I'd been sure I wouldn't want to see her, but now that I was here, so close to her small and harmless body, my hand reached out for hers. Her flesh was chilled and strange. Limp, stiff, weighted. Holding her hand, I felt—just for a moment—the strangest surety that she'd clasp my fingers and open her eyes.

Sister, I heard her say in the silence of the room. In my black heels, I swayed.

But the moment passed. Nothing happened. I stood there, her hand in mine, making myself breathe in and out. I rubbed my fingertips against hers, trying not to think of what they'd done.

———

In graduate school, I once road-tripped up to Boston with some fellow students to take a two-day master class with a famous painter from Nigeria. Two of the women in the car were African American, one was Vietnamese American, and then there was me, the sort-of Latina.

The famous Nigerian artist had done a lot of paintings about ghosts—ghosts and memory, ghosts and history. The two Black women were from Long Island and Jacksonville and knew his work from their undergraduate years. They started telling us about hauntings and visitations they had personally experienced. Chains rattling in an old house in Savannah. A suicide uncle in the stairwell at night, lit up, hanging from nothing.

Then the Vietnamese girl chimed in about her mother's ghosts, which she'd sometimes seen herself, hovering above thresholds in the wooden house in Nebraska where her parents had been settled as refugees in the '70s.

I sat quiet.

Someone said, "What about you, Isabel? You got any true-life ghost stories?"

I thought for a moment in the back seat. The motor's vibration shook my bones.

"No," I lied. "I've never seen a ghost."

A long silence followed.

"Ha," said one of the Black girls. "No surprise there."

The car rattled beneath me. Perhaps half a mile sped by.

"What do you mean?"

"I don't know." She shrugged. "You just don't seem *open* to the spirit world."

In years to come, I would be able to recall the famous painter in his bright dashiki and Vuarnet sunglasses. I would remember his broad gestures that swept the air around him. But I couldn't remember anything I learned about art that weekend.

What stuck with me was that moment when there wasn't really too much I could say about my purported lack of openness to the spirit world. I'd ridden in silence the rest of the drive north. How could I have explained to those cool and clever artist girls—girls I wanted to impress, girls with whom I wanted to belong—that it took all my strength to shut the ghosts away?

———

In the funeral home in Mercer, West Virginia, I turned my mother's left hand over and slid her sleeve up, just a little. Searching.

There, across her wrist, was a blur of blue-and-black ink—not the name I had expected, the tattoo in Gothic script she'd worn home the day that Charlie died . . .

I remembered the way she'd peeled back the dressing, proud, to show me. She'd come into the house giddy and laughing, a white bandage taped to her wrist.

"Momma?" I started to panic. "What did you do?" I was scared she'd injured herself on the line again. The factory wasn't a smart place to be high.

But she held her arm up proudly. "Looky here, baby. Look what your crazy momma done gone and did." She peeled back the tape. *Bull,* I read in crusting curlicue letters. Blood still oozed. "Gonna show that man my heart is true!" she sang, her eyes vacant.

I turned away in quick disgust.

Bull drove a Harley, and Bull drove a truck—an enormous red Dodge with oversized wheels, its chrome grille huge and looming. He sold drugs of all kinds: crank, pills, crack. Weed, too—if you were, in his words, pussy enough to want it. A tall, muscled man with a shaved head and a drooping mustache the color of mud, he lived on steroids, steak, Wild Turkey, and protein shakes whipped with raw eggs in the blender. To Bull, my mother was little more than a customer, a lay, someone who'd cook dinner for him and his boys if they dropped by unannounced with a Kroger bag full of cheap cuts of beef, and even I, at fourteen, could see that Bull didn't care whether my mother's heart was true or not.

His friends revolted me: loud, strung out, jittery—men with big muscles and big mouths. I kept to myself when they came by, hiding on the back porch with my homework or heading for the woods. I tried to take Charlie with me, because some of them thought it was fun to tease him, the way some adults find children's lack of comprehension amusing. It sickened me—their loud laughter, the confusion on Charlie's little brow—and I tried to scoop him away as soon as I heard the roar of their motors, the crunch of their tires on the road, but he liked to hang around the men, watching and imitating them, repeating words they said.

My mother's tattoo made me feel sick. Why should she pretend? Bull was just one more guy; he'd soon be gone. Why splash his name on her wrist for all to see?

Now his name was gone. In prison—sober and clean, with time on her hands—she'd sought to blot it out. Dark clouds of ink billowed across her skin.

I felt a small, cruel rush of vindication.

To touch clean skin, I pushed the sleeve a little farther up her forearm. It felt lewd, intrusive, but I couldn't help myself. I wanted to see some sign of innocence, pure skin before the fall.

But there, in blue ink, wavering and unsteady, sideways, in my mother's own hand, on the canvas of her flesh near the inner crook of her elbow, were two names. *Bel*, her arm read. *Charlie*. I closed my eyes. A dry sob washed out of me. I saw it like a vision: her lonely cell, the contraband needle, the ink tube (carefully cut open) from the ballpoint pen, the blood wiped repeatedly away with wetted tissue. The waiting and tending while it healed.

Charlie and I were the scars she'd finally worn.

And my grief felt as if something caught me behind the knees—a blow, slow but sharp—and I buckled and sank, and two men were catching me, saying, *Bel, Bel,* and they eased me toward the row of chairs.

——

That's where I was, breathing into my hands, with Billy Dunn and a well-meaning stranger leaning over me, when my aunt and uncle entered the room. I heard the timbre and drawl of their mingled voices, knew who they were before I stood and turned to greet them.

The sight was a shock. Middle-aged when I'd known them, Aunt Della and Uncle Frank were now old. In their faces, gaunt hollows alternated with pouches of gray flesh. Uncle Frank walked with a cane, his every breath an audible wheeze.

Aunt Della's eyes raked over me. "Well. My, my. Look at who's here." She drew close, lifting her arms for an embrace. I leaned in, still unsteady on my feet. She felt densely upholstered, a sofa too tightly stuffed. Her pats on my back were rapid, brisk. "Don't you look just fine." Uncle Frank hung back.

He held me at arm's length. "I wouldn't have recognized you, Bel," said Uncle Frank. "Looking so growed up and all."

"So rich, you mean," said my aunt.

"Now, Della—"

"Thank you, Uncle Frank." I gave him a quick hug. Over his shoulder, Aunt Della's eyes narrowed, as they'd narrowed each time I'd hugged him when I was a teenager. "It's good to see you."

"I would've." Billy's voice was husky. "I'd have known you anywhere."

I finally let myself look at him. Billy Dunn, love of my young life and a rapist, was now a shipwreck of a man, his eyes red-rimmed, his hands scarred and battered, his fingernails rimmed with the kind of black that doesn't scrub off, his blond hair brittle and badly cut, his shoulders held at a tense angle that belied some chronic pain. A whiff of stale whiskey hit me. I could barely make out the echoes of his youthful beauty. He blinked.

"Surprised you could make it back," said Della. "Been a long time. A real long time. Hear you're doing good." She nodded. "Real good. Got yourself married to a doctor and all. Must be nice. Nothing to do all day."

"I'm an artist."

Della barely contained her snort. "Like I said."

"What kind of a doctor is he?" asked Uncle Frank.

"A pediatric radiologist." They looked blank. "X-rays," I added. "Of children."

"Now ain't that wonderful," said Aunt Della. "You don't got any kids of your own, though, do you?"

I shook my head.

She planted a hand on her thick hip. "Well, Billy here's got three. Ain't that right, Billy?" She didn't pause or look at him. "Trisha's fifteen now, and them boys are getting big. Three mouths to feed, and Donna done hightailed it to Kentucky." Behind her, the room was filling up with people.

"Congratulations," I murmured. "About your children, I mean."

"Single man taking care of them all by himself. And he ain't no doctor."

"Della," said Uncle Frank.

A small commotion in the doorway made us all turn. Elaine Carter, the real estate agent, sailed in on a tide of strangers, talking loudly, her red hair swinging.

"Come on," hissed Della, batting Uncle Frank with a corner of her purse. "We got to make a line."

"What for?"

"What do you think, what for? To receive the sympathy, of course."

I got in line. For the better part of an hour, I shook hands with strangers, near-strangers, acquaintances, and distant relatives, shifting my weight from foot to foot, listening to Aunt Della say again and again, "She had her trials and troubles, Lord knows, but Stella was a good girl at heart."

"So sorry for your loss," murmured strangers. "She'll be missed," they said, pressing my hand between theirs. "Blessings on you, child," said elderly ladies with names like Luvina and Wylene and Wavie Lura, friends of my deceased grandmother who had seen the notice in the paper. Their heads quavered on their necks, and they smelled like lilac powder. They clutched my arm. Thin curls wisped white around their faces. "Peace be with you." They said it with such kindness, I began to cry.

Billy materialized at my shoulder, a clean tissue in his hand. "Here, Bel."

I took it. Pressed it to my tears.

"I'm sorry, Bel," he said. "Really sorry."

I turned to look at him.

"I'm really, really sorry." His eyes were the same lazy dark green that had made my belly flutter in high school, and they were serious now. The strange, sick trembling came back into my limbs. "I mean it, Bel," he said. He looked into my eyes and gripped my arms. "I'm really, really sorry."

The room fell away. He wasn't talking about my mother.

My heart skated fast in my chest, and I felt a wave of nausea. I tried to feel kind. Here he was, a middle-aged man, poor and country—the father of a teenaged daughter now. A man for whom something had finally clicked. He had become sorry. He was trying to make amends. He had waited more than twenty years for this moment.

I knew the forgiveness he wanted, the succor, the absolution—perhaps even a flicker of the shy adoration that once shone from my eyes when I glanced his way.

But it was all insufficient, too weird, and much, much too late. My forehead felt hot and woozy.

I did what I do at events with Jon's doctor colleagues when someone casually denigrates the poor or says something genteelly racist, and the glittering room reels for a moment: I paused, took a breath. Gathered myself. Smiled my charity-gala smile.

"Thank you for your kindness." My voice was robotic, bright, and in its mechanical cheer, it bore a kind of cruelty I didn't entirely mind, a kind of extremely polite *Fuck yourself* the alert ear can detect.

Billy heard it. His eyes dropped. I sidestepped out of his grasp, turning to the next person in line, and let a stranger press my hands and say how grieved she was for my loss. Billy slowly turned away and began to speak to someone else. Eventually he was out of arm's reach, and the visitation wound on, interminable. To distract myself, I focused with detached admiration upon the way Elaine Carter worked the room, her warmth and volume calibrated to the mood of the occasion. The crowd dwindled, and when at last she arrived next to us, it was as if a discreet piece of choreography had swept to its finale.

Her condolences were perfectly pitched, sincere, but they had a practiced feel. She shook hands with each of us, dwelling on my mother's passing for a sufficient number of sentences before gliding into a discussion of the land.

"It's a real opportunity," she said. "Of course, there's been someone farming there. We'll need to get that cleared up before we put it on the market."

Aunt Della's head snapped around. "Why, that's our Billy," she said. "My son. Ain't no harm in farming my own sister's land."

Billy stirred uneasily. In truth, I had no reason to mind, but I couldn't see why he was so keen to drive half an hour from town to farm it. Spare land wasn't that hard to come by.

"Well." Elaine's voice at my shoulder was bright and brisk. "Be that as it may. I can't wait to see what Isabel will decide to do with it. It's a very active market right now. Very active."

"Is that right?" Della's face swung toward me. "And what does Miss Isabel think she's going to decide?"

Her elbow nudged Billy's. He startled, then spoke.

"Farming those acres has been a help to me, Bel. A real big help in hard times."

"Exactly." Della nodded, her eyes sparking with hot life. "And what kind of woman would take a living away from her own kin?"

Billy's heavy-lidded eyes were on me, too, and Elaine Carter turned to see what I would say. Uncle Frank stood a little distance away, arms folded, yet perhaps because of his very stillness, or the way he stared so intently at an oversized vase stuffed with faux dogwood branches, I had the sense he was keenly listening.

I looked down at the beige carpet, at the black toes of my six-hundred-dollar shoes. I didn't know what to say. I honestly didn't know what I'd do with the land. What to do with myself.

"Billy's the one's been looking after it, checking up on things all these years. Making sure that house don't get broke into." Aunt Della sighed a martyr's sigh. "I reckon the most Christian thing would be to sign that land over to your cousin."

"The most Christian thing," I repeated softly. The walls wavered, and all the surrounding voices blurred and went dim. I touched the bare place at the base of my throat, the place where my locket had once rested, the place on my body that had been designated for so long for grief and silence. Everything felt numb and glassy and very distant. I wanted a drink.

"I believe we're here to mourn my mother," I said. "Not talk business."

Elaine Carter audibly exhaled.

"Bel's right," said Billy.

Della shook her head and clicked her tongue. "Always one to look out for yourself," she said. "Guess some things don't change."

Uncle Frank didn't move a muscle. He just kept staring at those fake dogwood branches like they were the most interesting things in the world.

The Bar

When the visitation ended, I declined Billy's offer of a ride, and everyone hurried through the cold to their cars. I walked back alone in the dark. My heels slipped and skidded as I crossed the ice-slick bridge. As a coal truck rumbled past, the metal walkway quaked, and I gripped the rail with my gloved hand. Near the middle of the bridge, I stopped and looked down. Below me coiled dark, viscous depths.

Soon, when temperatures dropped further, small crystals would form at the river's shallow edges. Thin white shelves of ice would protrude from the shores all winter, but the deep center channel wouldn't freeze. It ran too fast for that.

Reaching up, I slid a bobby pin from my hair, held it out over the water, and opened my fingers. Tiny and dark, falling, it turned invisible long before it hit. There was no splash.

I imagined it swirling away below the surface, sucked deeper and deeper by the current, battered against rocks and dragged downstream.

———

Tim gave me a quick up-nod from behind the counter when I got back, quaking with tension and cold, to the lobby of the Mercer Hotel, feeling louche and vulpine in my black garb and ruined eye makeup. All I wanted was a drink.

The hotel bar was laden with almost all the charms of Victorian brothels. The barstools, like the unfortunate drapes, were red velvet, and a fat pink lamp with a fringe of beads squatted on top of a battered old upright piano, its yellowed keys gathering dust.

Behind the mahogany bar bustled a woman who looked ready-made for the place. Middle-aged, pretty, ample of bosom, chestnut hair caught up and pinned Gibson-girl style, she polished glasses with swift vigor, like she expected a post-opera rush.

But the bar was quiet, with only three patrons: a man in a blue suit reading his iPad, a man in a gray suit reading his cell phone, and Nic Folio, who swiveled on his red velvet stool when I entered. His glance flicked up and down.

I walked over and shouldered off my coat.

"Hello again," I said.

"I was hoping you might show up."

I sat down. Nic Folio had always been astonishingly good to look at, like a model in a catalog for rugged outdoor gear (the lean and stubbled jaw, the dark-lashed eyes)—as if he should always pose against a backdrop of snowy peaks or fly-fish a Montana river or relax in a plaid bathrobe on the rustic porch of his cabin, a light wind perpetually raking the black locks back from his brow.

"How did you know I was staying here?"

"What are the options?" He smiled. "Not unless you want the Treetop Motel out on Route 6."

"Oh, I know that place." It had fascinated me as a child. Two long white arms of rooms sloping down a hillside. Little blue doors. Evergreen trees. A pink neon vacancy sign, always lit. I'd begged my mother to take us on a vacation there. It had a small cement pool.

"Yeah. You and every meth cooker in the county."

"Oh." My vision faded. "Too bad."

"Things change."

The energetic barmaid arrived before us, flicking the bar towel around. "What can I get you, love?"

Aberlour, neat. And make it a double. Nic already had something brown in a glass.

"Club soda with lime, please," I said. His brow rose, but he said nothing.

The barmaid shot soda from the gun, gave the lime a sharp twist, and had the virtue of disappearing once her duty was done. In the dark, quiet air of the bar, Nic Folio and I could have been alone. Our hands rested loosely around our glasses on the bar.

"So tell me about your children," I said.

"Good kids." He shrugged. "Twenty-one, eighteen years old. Football, baseball, the usual. Oldest one's up at Fairmont State."

I smiled. In Chicago, most of our friends had toddlers in Montessori. "You started early."

He shrugged, grinned. His dark eyes latched on mine. "When you know what you want, why wait?"

I tapped my nail on the glass rim of my tumbler. I thought of the short, shuddering elevator ride and the dim hallway that were all that lay between us and my chenille-covered bed.

"I remembered you," I said. "I mean, who you used to be. What people said about you. You and your brothers."

He took a long drink of his whiskey. "That a good thing?"

I tilted my gaze carefully away. "It's not bad." In the mottled silver mirror that hung behind the bar, we looked like what we were, a man and a woman, poised on the verge of something hazardous and alive. We sat in silence, drinking, and the room grew warmer with each swallow.

He took a long drink of his whiskey, and I wrapped both hands around my glass, its slick cold column sliding a little against my skin. My fingers tingled. His dark eyes met mine in the mirror. I watched us as if I were drugged.

On the bar, his little finger slowly extended away from his own glass and reached toward my hand. Gently, tentatively, it touched my knuckle. Stroked it very lightly, then held still against my skin.

I stared down at my drink. Tiny silver pearls of effervescence clustered on the wedge of green lime in the useless, harmless liquid that left me sober.

Slowly, I pulled away. Opened my purse, laid a five-dollar bill next to my glass. Stood up.

"Good night," I said.

Nic Folio's eyebrows lifted, but his chiseled face remained unperturbed.

He could take me or leave me. I remembered those rumors about the Folio boys, too.

———

Alone in my chilled room, I stood at the bathroom mirror. I looked gaunt, blasted. The glare of the overhead bulbs streaked me with shadows.

Shivering, I washed my black dress, its armpits acrid with nervous sweat, in the sink. I laid it on a clean towel on the floor and rolled it into a long terry-cloth tube, as my mother had shown me long ago during those times when the washer broke or the pipes froze or the electricity got cut off and we had to do all our laundry by hand. I walked back and forth on the towel's white tubular length, my weight squeezing out moisture, and then unrolled it, shook the dress out, and hung it in the cold little closet to dry.

Too tired to talk, I texted Jon. All's well. Will call tomorrow. I left the ringer off and plugged in the phone to charge, thinking of the way things used to be between us. Effortless, natural, the way rain fell. The way I'd wanted him, always, as soon as he wanted me, whenever he wanted me. *Besotted,* I used to think. *I am besotted.* The wild golden bliss that would suffuse me, the way my whole body seemed buoyed—

I wondered if Lily were experiencing it now, and all I wanted was for him to tell me it wasn't true, there was nothing to it, it was all just my feverish imagination conjuring shadows to torture me with because I couldn't believe a good man would love me—I couldn't *bear,* actually, for a good man to love me: Steady, reliable, interesting, sexually fulfilling, and faithful love from a good man? It conflicted too radically with what I'd seen and known, so it was impossible to trust. Yet I wanted it so badly, wanted him to reassure me, to soothe the doubts away, to swear that Lily was nothing but a colleague and friend—and not even, at that, a very good friend (with maybe, thrown in for good measure, a crack about some unattractive quality she had, something he could never desire in a woman)—just someone he'd worked with in Haiti who happened, by sheer chance, to also live in Chicago, but of course he'd never gotten together with her while at home, and he'd simply forgotten to mention the fact that she lived in our city and would be onstage with him at the gala that night because it was utterly immaterial, of no import whatsoever, because she didn't matter to him at all: that's how I wanted the phone call to go (his voice unhesitating and clear, untroubled, even surprised and a little amused, as if it were all the simplest misunderstanding)—or better still, the face-to-face conversation when I got home, after which he'd fold me in his arms and murmur sweet nothings about always loving only me, et cetera, and I'd cry a little in relief and feel becalmed, and then we'd make love that would start soft and tender, light as feathers, his eyes warm on mine, and then grow as fiery and animalistic as the wildest sex we'd ever had, blotting the thought of Lily permanently from my mind. And his.

That's how it would go. And then I'd get a test and tell him about the baby, and happily ever after is the way we'd all live.

I pulled out a fresh towel and turned the shower on hot, waiting until the bathroom filled with a cloud of steam that obscured my reflection. A dark ghost in the mirror, I stepped into the tub and let the water scald the day away.

———

Once, back in New York, I built a family of silhouettes from bent wood painted white. White for empty, white for death. Life-sized, human height, a foot deep. Three of them: a woman, a half-grown girl, and a little child. They were freestanding, and they stood in my apartment for months, pale ghosts punched into the air. Blank spaces where a family should have been: real and physical presences I had to step around, their bright-white paint a shock to the eye.

After the paint dried down, I asked the Central Park groundskeepers if I could have the saplings they were clearing out, the thin little scrub trees. I hauled them home in bundles, wiped them clean with a soft cloth, and spent days holding them up to the silhouette frames, choosing and arranging. Then I sawed them to size and affixed them inside.

Three white silhouettes, filled with forest.

"So," said a new short-term boyfriend. "That's a little disturbing."

"Hmm," I murmured. I privately disagreed. *Disturbing* was what other people had: boisterous voices at holidays, a home to go home to, cozy cardigans their dads used to wear, golden retrievers and fat sofas and the warm aromas of pot roast in a cheerful Mission-style bungalow on Butternut Drive. Their parents paying for things—clothes, college, cars, travel, down payments—long after they'd reached adulthood. Parents who cared about their lives, their work, their friends. Storybook lives of safety and ease.

What I had were Button, and Ivy (who'd traded up to a larger pot, green vines sprawling everywhere), and a fast-growing series of objects my art professors did not praise.

What I had were handmade objects that spelled out what was missing. Trees where a family should be. Holes shaped like people, stripped trunks, white like snow, like the sear of a nuclear blast. A bleakness.

For me, like all the art I later made that critics called *harrowing*, it was soothing. My inner world made visible, made real.

———

Cross-legged on the chenille bedspread in the lamp's dim glow, I absently held the hawk bracelet Jon had given me, fondling it like a talisman, turning it over and over in my hands, rubbing my thumbs against its glittering gems, sliding my nails along the edges of its tiny stones, picking at them with a kind of anxious energy.

One of the sapphire eyes flipped up. I gasped and nearly dropped the bracelet, afraid I'd broken it. But no, the sapphire was intact, connected; it had just lifted up on a little flap, like a miniature trapdoor. I held the bracelet close to the bulb of the lamp.

Inside sat a tiny green square embedded with silver dots. Minuscule. The breath slipped out of me, and a strange silence began to throb in my ears.

Quickly, I got my tweezers from the bathroom and hunched near the light. I pried the tracking chip from its niche and laid it on the nightstand. Stared. Thought. Remembered how he'd handed me the red velvet box not long after I'd told him the photo in the locket was me.

So I wasn't the only one with trouble trusting, the only one who felt afraid. Rich men just had a different way (a very different way) of showing it. A way that looked like control.

Not the paranoia, jealousy, hysteria, or nightmare terrors of the sort that plagued me, the desperate, panicked responses of someone with her whole world to lose and no cards worth holding.

Jon's way of handling his fear looked like control, surveillance, ownership. Calm, professional, moneyed. Mine looked like the opposite, the anguished flailing of the powerless. But perhaps they were just two sides of the same sad coin, the fearful undertow that lurks beneath love.

I pulled a tissue from the box and used the tweezers to place the electronic tracking chip in its center. I twisted it carefully and pushed the small white wad deep into the pocket of my expensive barn coat.

———

Who knows what it is, what instinct rises up in some men and says, *She's the one*? What signals to them? The curve of a neck, the soft dark glance of an instant, the way her whole body glides through air?

I have seen the magic other women work—the wrist bent, the way a hush falls when they approach—but have never been able to perceive it in myself, have never known what particular element it was that drove Jon, one late afternoon in Connecticut, to leave people he knew and swallow two glasses of champagne and rush across a field, to leave his shoes and socks scattered among a tree's roots and begin to climb. His handsome face dappled with late sunlight, he didn't pause once as he pulled himself up toward me.

"I don't need saving," I called down, irritated. "I'm not a kitten."

"Agreed." He flashed the steady smile I would come to know so well. "A lioness, more like. Surveying the plains before she hunts."

Despite myself, I laughed.

And just like that, he brought to a close the long string of men I'd chosen—as my mother had—for their brutal strength and the fact that they could not love me.

The Cracked Egg

I woke thick and strange the next morning, my head clotted with frightening dreams I couldn't remember. I groped my way to the bathroom and vomited a watery mess. Showered.

After running a quick iron over my dry dress, I shook it on over my head and slipped into my black pumps, jewelry, my dress coat, my warm black cashmere scarf. It was seven thirty.

Across the street at the Cracked Egg, the warm, close odors of food made me queasy again. I sat at the counter. "Coffee, please," I told Tina. "Dry toast."

I was gingerly crunching into a crisp half slice when a hush fell over the diner. I turned. Heads had swung toward the door, where a Black woman my age had just entered. Close-cropped hair. A steady, open face. Thick-lashed, kind eyes. A calm mouth. She wore a parka the color of mud, her work boots had seen plenty of labor, and her pale jeans hinted at muscled thighs. On the streets of Chicago, she was the kind of woman you'd pass without a second glance.

But here, she was definitely being noticed, and not in any good way. Everyone was still staring. The diner was quiet. She glanced around.

My pulse beat hard in my throat. I needed to do something, but I didn't know what.

A hand shot up at the No-Sanctuary table, and the woman smiled, heading over. The white people greeted her warmly. She took off her parka, and her pale T-shirt clung to her torso. One of the men rummaged in a tote bag and pulled out a black No-Sanctuary sweatshirt. She pulled it over her head.

The diner's glares and silence blistered the whole table for a moment, and then people turned back to their food. Ordinary conversation resumed.

From across the restaurant, I watched the woman covertly. I liked the look of her hands, the length and squareness of them, the short-clipped nails. Her lips were firm, her jaw strong. I felt sad that she was on their side.

She glanced suddenly at me. Caught me staring. I flushed with embarrassment and tried to cover it with a smile. She blinked, nodded, and turned back to her companions.

I drank my coffee and was absently pushing my crusts around the plate when Nic Folio slid onto the next stool.

"Good morning, Isabel."

I turned, nodded. Swallowed.

His eyes scanned my black dress, my heels, my discreet diamond earrings.

"I'm so sorry," he said.

It's what everyone said. There was nothing else to say.

I wrapped both hands around my cup to steady them and swallowed my coffee black, making myself stare at the stainless-steel hot line crowded with plates, the black cat clock with its swinging tail—anything but the sudden semblance of kindness in his face.

When I drained my coffee, Tina materialized in her pink polyester, pouring more, then disappeared. I cleared my throat, but still my voice came out like rust. "I know it's wrong," I said, "but I still miss her."

"A lot of things we feel are wrong. She was your mother. You love who you love." He inspected me. "You okay?"

I looked at him. There were no right ways to answer.

"Anything I can do?" His smile was gentle. "It's a little early to buy you a drink."

"I'll be all right."

He studied me like I was a piece of machinery that had made a strange noise. When Tina came back, he ordered without taking his eyes from me. Under his steady regard, I began to feel uncomfortable.

"What?" I finally said.

"Just funny, is all."

"What's funny?"

"You being here." He glanced pointedly at the rings on my finger. "By yourself." Seconds passed. "If I was your—"

"But you're not," I said quickly. "I wanted to come alone."

Unfazed, he continued to study me. "Like I said. Funny."

I turned away. When his food arrived, he finally opened his newspaper, and I was glad. Outside, old cars and pickups streamed past, their fenders eaten away by street salt and cinders. I finished my coffee and laid my paper napkin on the counter, and Nic tore the blank corner off a page of his newspaper and pulled a pen from the breast pocket of his flannel shirt. "Here's my number," he said, writing. "For later. In case you want that drink."

"I won't."

He took my hand in his and turned it up, placed the ragged triangle of paper in my palm, and folded my fingers over it. His hands were warm and firm.

"Anytime, for any reason," he said. "Just in case. You never know."

———

Out in the street, the sun was high and bright, and the wind blew cold. I pulled my coat tight around me and drew on my gloves. As I walked toward the parking lot, my hand where he'd held it still buzzed.

223

The Grave

I hadn't invited Aunt Della to sit down next to me in the front row at the funeral, but she did, her bulky hip squashed against mine, with Uncle Frank on her other side, and Billy sat on the other side of Uncle Frank. We didn't meet each other's eyes.

The Church of God preacher began to say some words about my mother—*flock, brethren, the welcoming arms of the Lord*—but I couldn't concentrate. My mind drifted. A weird fairy tale—a possible art piece?—occurred to me, its heroine an adolescent girl. Every time she pulled down her pants to pee, she found strange objects in the white crotch of her underwear: pine needles, rose petals, small sparkling gems prized from the secret layers of the earth and sea.

I didn't know what was supposed to happen next, or how it could coalesce into an actual piece. Admittedly, it was weird. Admittedly, it was occurring to me as I sat at my mother's funeral next to an aunt I didn't love, my hands shaking, a grave question mark hovering in my belly. All I could see so far was the girl, her body effortlessly releasing small treasures. All through the funeral service, I turned the image this way and that in my mind, but it remained static, provocative but inert.

Then we were suddenly all on our feet, making our way back down the aisle, and strangers were squeezing my hands and murmuring sympathy. In the parking lot, I was getting into my red rental car and twirling the heater knob all the way to the right, because it turned out I was freezing. And then I was following a hearse up a winding road, down into a valley, and up another hill. A dozen cars wound along behind me with their lights on, like shining segments of a fairly short snake.

The cemetery, as I remembered, was high on a green hillside. The parking lot was gravel, and the heels of my shoes twisted and crunched among rocks. I didn't look down, but I imagined their expensive soft leather nicking and tearing. Then my heels sank into grass, and I was pulling my coat tightly around my body while the wind whipped our faces. We stood together in dark huddles, listening to more words about redemption and forgiveness and God.

At the end, I felt bad that I hadn't thought to bring a rose or lily to drop into the hole. Someone pressed a small spade into my hand—an innocuous thing with a green plastic handle, like a trowel for planting tulips—and I scooped a little pile of black dirt up from the mound and shook it over the coffin. It fell, scattering on the wooden lid, and I thought I would fall, too, but someone grasped my elbow and pulled me back from the edge. I stood there, swaying with waves of nausea, while other people took their turns with the trowel, and then it was over. The grave diggers—two men in heavy Carhartt overalls (black for respect)—stood at the side with their shovels, waiting. The sky was an empty sweep of gray.

I looked next to me at the person who'd pulled me back from my mother's grave, the person whose hand still firmly gripped my elbow. It was Nic Folio, and I did not feel surprised.

People scattered. Car engines rumbled awake. My aunt Della said something about seeing me at her house in a little while, but she didn't wait for an answer before disappearing.

I nodded my thanks at Nic.

He looked at me closely, kindly. "Think you could use that drink?"

I shook my head and pulled my arm from his grasp.

Stumbling a little, I walked toward an older part of the cemetery. It had been twenty-six years since I'd stood there.

———

Small cheap tombstone under an evergreen tree, leaning slightly, its edges soft from years of weather.

My stockinged knees mashed to the frozen earth, my gloved fingers tracing the worn, rough grooves of his name. *Charlie Martin.* The carved years of his birth and death, so close together.

The tears came hot and thick and fast. My forehead pressed to the frigid stone.

I kept wiping my face.

I don't know how much time passed.

When at last I rose, stiff with cold, only three vehicles remained in the parking lot: my red rental car, a small brown sedan, and the large green pickup truck against which Nic Folio leaned, hands in pockets, collar turned up against the bitter wind. On the driver's side door, white block letters read LIBERTY PROTECTION.

I walked slowly to my car, wobbling on the gravel, feeling breakable. The gloves made my hands clumsy as they fumbled with the keys.

From the brown sedan emerged a young man. Pale face, eager eyes, thatch of straight black hair. He was at my side too fast and too close, smelling of cigarettes.

"Ms. Martin, I'm Chris Warner from the Mercer *Daily Star.*" He flipped open a small notebook and clicked the end of his pen. "Sorry for your loss, ma'am, and I'm wondering if you can tell me how this is all feeling for you right now."

I stared. What was it—a slow day? The wind blew cold on my wet face.

"To say good-bye to your mother, the convicted killer of your own brother. How are you feeling? Have you forgiven her?"

I couldn't speak. My tongue had been clipped out.

Then Nic was standing beside me, his tall body between the reporter and me, shielding me from the wind. "The lady needs her privacy," he said. "There's no story here."

The reporter, a full head shorter than Nic, shifted like a fighter in a ring. "But, ma'am, if you'd like to make a comment, our readers want—"

Nic stared down at him. "I don't say things twice."

The reporter's eyes dropped. "Well, ma'am, if you change your mind . . ." He held out his card to me. When I made no move to take it, he shook his head, flipped his notebook shut, and drove off.

Nic hadn't moved from my side. I looked up briefly into his dark eyes. They were full of a kindness I couldn't bear.

Without a word, I got in my car. Gunned the engine. Slammed it into reverse, and pulled out of the lot. Drove fast down the twisted roads.

When I glanced in my rearview mirror, his green truck wasn't there.

Aunt Della's

Back on the outskirts of Mercer, memory steered me up the steep streets. Gray house, gray door, gray vinyl siding to replace old tar paper that had looked like gray bricks, wedged between others just like it on a cramped block. All color had drained out of the world. I parallel parked, got out, and stood for a moment, feeling as empty and bleak as the sky. I didn't want to go inside, to nod at condolences, to taste that mixture of casseroles and grief.

I stared at the porch where Della had waited so long ago, flanked by trash bags full of my things, and walked up the cement path, mounted the steps, and pushed the doorbell, my black-gloved finger hovering overlong in my field of vision like a criminal's in some old noir film.

Uncle Frank opened the door and put his heavy hand on my shoulder. "Come on in, girl, and get you some food."

In the living room, the same old gray drapes sagged like hanged nuns toward the floor, but the space felt small and loud and crammed with people, all the suppressed energy of the funeral spilling out in talk. Uncle Frank ushered me into the dining room, where Aunt Della's table was spread with lace and Corningware. Cut-glass candlesticks stood like sentries, their small flames white in the dim daylight of noon. He put a plate into my hands. "Help yourself," he said, turning away. I surveyed the spread. Biscuits and peppered gravy. Macaroni and cheese dotted with fat yellow kernels of corn. Lima beans in a glass dish, covered in pale scum. Red Jell-O with chunks of fruit trapped inside. Insects in amber. Green Jell-O. Trapped fruit, et cetera. A casserole made of tuna, mushroom soup, and limp green beans, with potato chips crumbled on top. Another casserole. Another casserole. Another casserole.

In the trash can, a pile of soiled paper plates and empty beer cans was already mounting, and I wondered how long I'd knelt by Charlie's grave. I didn't want to learn who all the people were, or whether they'd actually known my mother. People and their memories were too much to consider. Aunt Della bustled through, refilling everyone's coffee cups, whisking around, her cheeks flushed like it was a party. I stood there with my empty paper plate for a long time, and then I put it down.

"Come here, Bel, and say hello to your family." Della's sudden grip on my shoulder made me feel reluctant and faint, like Dante being steered to some fresh circle. I took the cup of coffee she handed me and swayed next to her into the living room, where people were knotted tightly into groups of three or four.

"Now, you'll all remember Bel, but I don't know if she'll remember you—'cause it's sure been a long time, ain't it, Bel?"

I tried to smile at the faces that surrounded me. They were vaguely familiar: distant uncles and second cousins I'd seen a few times in childhood. I shook their various hands and said *Chicago* and *artist* and *doctor* again and again.

"Moved away, did she?" asked one stout woman, her blue cardigan sleeves taut around her crossed arms. They talked about me in the third person, as if I were deaf and mute or just not there at all.

"Oh, that's Bel for you," said Aunt Della. She turned to me—rupturing the fourth wall, as it were. "But you got it all now, don't you, girl? Doctor husband, big-city life. Guess all your big-time plans worked out." Soft snickers rippled around me.

At funerals in movies, families always tell raucous tales of the departed and weep in each other's arms—or else the bereaved people, hollowed by loss and provoked to existential epiphanies, have hot sex in closets with strangers. Here, there was no comfort, no erotic frisson, just unpleasant people eating and talking. No one was even mentioning my mother.

Three middle-aged, heavy-hipped women I barely remembered were still looking at me, their faces full of a kind of quivering, excited dread to see how I'd react to Della's words.

But bait was a thing I'd learned to resist.

"Yes," I said, bland as sliced cucumber, "my life is good. I've been fortunate. I'm very happy."

"Ain't got no kids, though, do you?" said Della.

The flat of my hand flew to my belly. "No."

Della nodded. She let a meaningful pause hang in the air and raised an eyebrow. She nodded again. "Probably for the best." Her smile was aimed at the other women.

I took a deep breath and looked steadily at my aunt. "It doesn't have to be like this," I said, my voice soft. "Between us. It doesn't have to be."

The other women glanced at each other and said nothing.

Della regarded me flatly.

"But it is," she said.

My stout cousin-by-marriage softened. "Let me get you a plate," she said. "You must be like to perish."

But she must have been waylaid on her way to the table, because she never came back with food. Relatives surged toward me in waves, full of sympathy and questions, and I wondered where they'd all been when my mother and I were hungry, when my mother was drunk and using, when I was alone with nowhere to go. *Don't be bitter. Don't be bitter.* Suddenly now, when it was titillating and required nothing, they all cared. I kept making polite faces. Perhaps, when conditions are poor and grim, that's all that family means.

"Bel." Billy stood at my side.

"Go away."

"Come here. Just for a minute. Please." He pulled me back down the hallway to the alcove by the stairs. Little light penetrated the hallway, and the shadows of the banisters coursed around us.

"Bel, I'm sorry," he said.

I nodded and turned away.

"Wait," he said, taking hold of my wrist. "Don't go yet."

I looked at him.

"What can I do to make it up to you? Tell me."

My laugh was bleak.

"Okay. Okay, I hear you. Not make it up, then. Not make up for it. But is there anything I can do? Anything at all?"

His green eyes looked earnest. This was the Billy that Anna had seen, the star-crossed lover—but all grown up now, a hardworking man in his forties. Poor. A single parent.

I pulled my wrist from his grip.

"Just leave me alone," I said. "That's what you can do."

———

I rejoined the crowd in the living room, where Aunt Della waved me over.

"Did you get you some food?" My cousin-by-marriage held out a plate of Ritz crackers daubed with gold Cheez Whiz.

"No, I'm good."

Della took off her glasses, huffed on the lenses, and polished them with a loose fold of her dress. "You give some thought to what you're gonna do with your momma's land?"

Before I could answer, a very old man with a wooden walking stick approached, blinking milk-clouded eyes and tottering a little. His sun-browned face had the collapsed look of the carved-apple dolls that were popular when I was young—a traditional craft, a folk art heavily featured at those wooden forts that serve as tourist attractions, where minimum-wage employees in pioneer garb churn real butter and hammer real iron horseshoes that visitors can take home as souvenirs. What else, after all—besides ski resorts and coal—did West Virginia have to sell? Apple dolls are simple and cheap to make: You peel an apple and carve a face into its soft white flesh. Then you leave it on a windowsill somewhere. All the juice goes out of it. It shrinks and turns brown, like the face of a withered old person.

"And who's this, now? Who's this?" the man warbled.

"Cloyd, this here's Stella's daughter," said Della, her voice overloud. "Bel. Isabella. She left a long time ago. Went off to get a education." The edge of bitterness in her voice, as if I'd turned up my nose and flounced away. "Bel, this here's your great-uncle Cloyd."

The old man smiled. Most of his teeth were gone.

"Why, I knew your momma from a girl," he said. A thin brown dribble of tobacco leaked from the corner of his mouth, and his eyes had the open wonder of a baby's. "Bitty little thing she was. Ornery, too." His smile broadened, and he chuckled. "Wild like the Devil hisself. Purty as a picture, that Stella was." Next to me, Aunt Della stiffened. "Eyes as blue as the flame of a Davy lamp."

I didn't know what he meant, but I smiled back at him.

Wobbling a little, Great-Uncle Cloyd reached his free hand out to me, and I took it. It felt ropy and fragile and warm.

He held my hand and looked into my eyes. He clung on tight, swaying.

It could have just been my imagination, or the trippy, unsteady feeling from too much coffee and grief, but I could have sworn a strange current tingled in the heart of my palm.

"Stella's girl," he said, his clouded eyes wide. He shook his head in wonderment. "Just like her, you are."

The Forest

The old man's words rang in my head as I steered the red rental car down Aunt Della's street, away from her house and everything in it. *Just like her.* My stomach growled.

Back at the hotel, I peeled off my black dress and tights and left them in a little pile on the floor. Socks. Jeans. Boots. The red flannel shirt, the three-hundred-dollar barn coat that had never seen a barn. I got back in the car, let my mind go blank, and swerved out of town.

On the curving mountain roads, enough familiar landmarks remained, like stars to steer by: a feed store, a gas station, an oak tree split long ago by lightning. Urgent and sure as a migrating bird, I accelerated past maples, oaks, buckeyes, black birch, and beech as the elevation climbed. On the radio, loud static crackled between plaintive songs about men and women who'd done each other wrong, and vicious cramps wrung my gut, like rags being twisted inside me. The sky was a cold and cloudless blue, gold afternoon sun poured down, and the weird burden of my mother's box weighted the back of the car. My foot pressed the gas hard, as if speed would let me escape. Maybe I'd open the box back in Chicago. Maybe I'd throw it away. The black road wound emptily through forested hills.

Half an hour later, I crested a ridge and turned down the tree-shadowed gravel road that led into our holler, remembering how, in the summer, the ditches on both sides would be thick with blackberries, honeysuckle, wild roses. White-petaled dogwood trees would glint from the forest. The curved creek ran alongside the road like a strip of gunmetal, and the car rolled fast, tires crunching, until our drive forked off, just two tracks of hard-packed dirt with a long hillock of dead grass between them.

I steered the car uphill between the trees and brush, nosing its way through the overgrowth. My heart pounded.

When the forest cleared and the ground briefly plateaued, I cut the engine at the edge of my mother's land. Our little white house, the only dwelling in sight, stood ringed by a thick, overgrown hedge of forsythia bushes that were just bare woody stalks now, gray with the coming of winter.

I got out and stood beside my red rental car, checking my phone. There was no reception. The air was sharp and crisp with the clean, damp smell of earth and trees. Overhead, the sun had begun to arc downward. A cold wind stirred the scents of the forest: wet earth, moldering leaves, coppery pine needles, moss. A faint animal musk. I pressed my hands to the car's cold roof, trying to quell their faint trembling.

When I'd left so many years before, the night had been scalded red and blue by the lights of squad cars, the forest's peace split by a siren's shriek. An EMT had dashed from the house with Charlie limp in his arms and climbed inside an ambulance. After a minute, its lights and siren had turned off.

A dozen cops had clomped through our little wooden house, and my cuffed mother had been dragged away, sobbing and screaming. A woman in a blue jacket had given me five minutes to gather my things.

Our house was the museum of all that.

I pushed my way through stiff forsythia stalks higher than my head. In the little yard, our three golden rain trees stood stripped and bare, and the crooked brick footpath was nearly buried by moss and grass—I remembered stealing its red bricks, just a few at a time, from falling-down houses and demolition sites, while my mother crouched beside me with a burlap sack outstretched. I was eight or nine. "Hurry up, sister," she'd say, gasping with laughter, "before the staties get here." We lugged the bricks home, sackful by sackful, and together we dug a trench that curved across the yard. We fitted the bricks together like a puzzle. Our own path, made by hand with things we'd stolen ourselves.

The porch sagged, and the steps, each a single wooden board, looked treacherously rotten. On the doorknob, a rusted padlock hung. I had no intention of going inside.

I veered around the house as if it were radioactive, my strides propelled by some weird intensity in my thighs, my breath coming fast, my keys rattling against the phone in my coat pocket. Out behind the house, where deer used to graze, our strip of patchy grass had been plowed up. Tomato cages stabbed the ground at odd angles; Billy should have stored them inside for the winter. I crossed the clods of dark dirt, stumbling. The forest closed over my body, drenching me in all the old familiar scents and shadows.

———

On that summer day in Connecticut, after an hour or so of banter and flirtation, Jon gestured toward the distant, glittering noise on the far edge of the meadow below. Leaves stirred softly around us. Dusk fell in a haze of cerulean and gold.

"What do you think?" he said. "Should we rejoin society?"

"Maybe we should just stay here, hidden," I said, "like the wild, enchanted primates we secretly are."

"Compelling argument." He smiled. "But I promise to make it worth your while."

"Oh really?" I laughed. "And just how do you propose to do that?"

When I said the word *propose*, something flickered in his eyes, and inwardly I shrank. Mistake. Manhattan had taught me which words not to say to men. But Jon's face stayed the same. The flicker hadn't been the stiffening of withdrawal.

"Why don't you find out?" he said, his voice soft.

Wind rushed through me. I looked down at the grass, so far below.

His eyes were warm. I nodded and reached a bare foot down toward a limb.

———

Rough bark against my palms. The crush of dried leaves underfoot. A dark pleasure rippled along my limbs. In the woods, I was home. I could navigate by instinct, without thought. No people, no talk, everything intimate and known. My feet found the old path up the hill. Overhead, bare black branches wove a jagged lace against the sky, and the fallen leaves of oaks and maples lay dry and papery on the forest floor, like thin curling sheets of tanned leather. I stooped and lifted a yellow maple leaf, pressing its skin to my palm like a lover's hand, splaying my fingers to match its five prongs.

Half an hour's steady uphill hike later, I glimpsed the small stone cabin between tree trunks. I stopped and bent, hands on my thighs, breathing hard. A few birdcalls echoed lonely through the late afternoon. More than a quarter of a century had passed since I'd brought Charlie here.

After I'd told him the story of the Lady of the Lake and Excalibur so many times he knew it by heart, he'd wanted to play Sword-in-the-Stone, so I'd fashioned a simple sword from two fallen branches cross-tied with baling twine. On the fieldstone porch of the cabin, he'd pretend to be young Arthur.

I approached the cabin slowly, climbing the broad steps to the uneven fieldstone porch. The air was quiet, cold. Overhead, an arrow of Canada geese passed so low I could hear the flap of their wings.

I spotted the gap between two stones, where I used to slide Charlie's makeshift wooden sword, where I'd pretend to be one knight after the other, swaggering wide-legged with imagined brawn, patting my biceps, bending to grasp the sword's handle, and pretending to struggle with all my might to pull it out. Charlie would laugh as I wiped invisible sweat from my brow and grumbled in mock-frustration and bafflement.

"You're not the king!" he'd say, delighted. Then he'd step forward, his eyes gone all solemn, and slowly draw the wooden sword from the crevice. He'd lift it high, his expression utterly serious. He'd sweep his little arms wide, taking in the whole panorama: the valley far below with its twisting silver creek, the mountains blanketed by deep green forest—even the blue sky. "I rule this kingdom," he would say. "I am king of all you can see."

I'd drop to one knee and make a great show of swearing fealty, and then we'd break character, laugh, and start all over again. It was one of Charlie's favorite make-believe games to play.

By then, I'd known that we were poor, the children of a woman whom other children mocked. Soon Charlie would learn all of it, too. I'd wanted him to have something he could love and be proud of, a legacy to hold on to later, when he learned the sad facts.

My hand crept to my belly. Life had shaped me into a person of intense and singular devotions. Once upon a time, I'd poured all my love and care into Charlie. Then he was gone. For a few years afterward, there was nothing but wasteland, the numb trudge of continuing to exist. Eventually I found art. Later, Jon found me. And that was it, that was my life now: Jon and art.

And lately, not even art.

And maybe soon, not Jon.

I crouched, peering out over the wide dark bowl of the valley, and fingered the rough berms of the separated stones. Far below, the creek glittered white with ice.

When I stood and pushed against the cabin door, prepared to shove my weight hard against long-stuck wood, it swung open with ease, as if oiled by regular use. Stunned, I stopped. From the rafters hung great gray-green bundles of leaves, obscuring everything. I could barely make out the old bare bedstead (its mattress long rotted away), the table, the dresser where mice used to lodge, the wide stone hearth. The air was thick with a sweetish must.

I stood there, my hand on the doorframe, wind rushing at my back. Then a laugh rasped out of me.

Weed. Our cabin, our secret childhood hideaway—my place, Charlie's—was now a drying shed. I noticed that the rotten shingles had been replaced, the fallen mortar patched. No wonder Billy'd been keen to keep my mother's land. For how many years had he been growing on it? How many tens of thousands of untraceable, untaxable dollars did this year's swaying bundles represent? I wondered if Aunt Della knew the true nature of his crop.

I pulled the door closed behind me to keep out the wind. Ducking beneath the sheaves, I crossed to the corner and sat on the old chair. I pulled out my phone: still no texts from Jon. I had four full bars, so I dialed his number.

No one answered.

"Jon," I said to his voicemail. "Hey. I'm good. Everything's good. Kind of weird." I hated the tremor in my voice. "Just getting caught up, taking care of things." I wondered what he was doing. How he was occupying his time. If he'd seen Lily. If he was with her right now—

Under the bedstead, something caught my eye. I hung up.

Beside the bed, I crouched, reaching between the slats toward the small object. It was soft, a handful of crumpled fabric the gray of dark doves. I stood up and shook it. Bits of dirt fell. Leaf fragments, a scattering of squirrel fur. Little sleeves and a torso unfurled.

Charlie's sweatshirt.

And just like that, warm summer light poured in before me. Charlie ran in circles on the bare stone floor, cawing and flapping his arms like a bird. Flecks of dust twirled sunlit in the air, and I was young and laughing, tossing the clean little sweatshirt onto my brother. He was straightening, dropping his arms to his sides.

"Now I am a human prince," he said, his voice high and sweet like a bell. The gold light in the room haloed him. He reached for me. I bent and scooped him up, lifting him tight to my chest. His little fingers touched my face.

"And you can talk again."

The vision faded, and the room went cold and dark and dusty. It was only the empty shirt I clutched. I sank to my knees and pressed the filthy fabric to my face, hoping for a whiff of his scent.

But hunkering there, motionless, all I could smell were the weed and the years and the dirt.

———

At last, hips stiff from the hike and the chill, I pushed to my feet and went out to the porch. Dusk was gathering. The wind rushed through the leaves with the shushing sound a succubus might make. The woods lay dark all around, and the temperature was dropping. I licked my lips with thirst. A shiver twirled up my spine.

Tucking Charlie's gray sweatshirt into the pocket of my barn coat, I hurried down the narrow path in the gloom, stumbling, clutching tree trunks to steady my descent. The wind had turned savage. I focused on the hot shower I'd take when I got back to the hotel, the good dinner I'd eat at Los Norteños. Enchiladas. Guacamole. My empty stomach growled.

The forest was already deep in dusk when I broke out of the woods at the bottom, crossed the plowed dirt, and circled the house. My rental car gleamed red in the darkness, a promise of warmth and escape. Hungry and chilled, I pulled out my keys and beeped the lock open.

But even in the half light, something looked wrong.

Closer, I squinted. Circled the vehicle, peering.

All four of its sturdy round tires had collapsed. They rested flat against the gravel, deflated.

I crouched to finger the cold rubber. Felt the lips of the gashes.

All four tires had been cut.

My Mother's House

I scanned the span of rutted dirt, the trees that lined the dark road. No vehicles' light beams wavered in the distance. No billows of dust hung in the air from a long-passed car. No visible movement. No sounds but the last evening calls of birds returning to their nests. Everything looked peaceful; the woods were lovely, dark and deep. Fear crawled over me. I'd been crazy enough to come back. Maybe I deserved to die here, too.

I pulled out my phone. No bars. No reception at all. Frantically, irrationally, I scrolled to AAA's number and tried to dial anyway. Nothing.

Either someone had slashed my wheels as a random prank—*Teach that city fool a lesson*—or someone wanted to frighten me away. "Billy?" I yelled. "Billy!"

Or worse: someone wanted to strand me here, helpless, to terrify or hurt me. I spread both hands on the car's cold metal to still the quakes that ran through them.

The temperature was dropping. I couldn't climb back up the mountain—not in the dark, not famished and tired—to get a cell phone signal. I was effectively stuck until morning. I opened the car door and grabbed my purse. Everything was intact. No one had tried to break in. The motive wasn't theft.

Crossing the yard, I stumbled on the bricks in the curving path and mounted the front steps. The rotten porch boards sank under my tentative steps to the door. I rattled the padlock. Sharp flakes of rust came off on my fingers.

I ran back and pulled a brick from the path. Gripping it with both hands, I hefted it and smashed it against the lock. With the third blow, the lock broke, and I lifted it away and turned the knob. The door sighed open.

Inside, the dark house smelled tired, like damp old wood and dust, and it felt colder than the air outside. A faint chemical scent—almost like urine—hung in the musty air, and I wondered which animals had made homes inside the walls. I flipped the light switch up and down, but of course the power had been cut off years ago, and the old yellow phone, too, was dead when I lifted the receiver from its cradle. Was someone outside concealed in the trees, watching? I pulled all the curtains shut, coughing at the puffs of dust.

It's funny how the body organizes itself for survival in times of stress, directing one's limbs like automation. Next to the woodstove lay a long box of fireplace matches. I struck one, which flared with a phosphorus hiss, and carried it like a slim torch into the kitchen. Under the sink, boxes of white emergency candles (from when we couldn't pay the electric bill) still sat in the cupboard. I got out a coffee mug, dripped hot wax down into it, and pressed a candle's base into the wax. It made a perfectly acceptable lantern.

I dragged a chair over to the highboy and climbed up. I felt around on its dark top, trying not to think of small creatures with rabies and teeth. My hands closed on the shotgun's cold stock and then on a box of shells. I pulled them down and loaded both barrels, racking the gun as my mother had taught me, and laid it on the kitchen table.

Panting with panic and thirst, I wrenched the faucet with both hands, but it turned easily, and instead of the sputtering brown stream I expected, the water ran immediately clear. I ducked my head and drank directly from the tap, as I often had as a girl. (That taste. Our well. No other water in the world had that taste. Cold, fresh, with the faintest curl of sulfur.) When I straightened, wiped my mouth with the back of my wrist, and looked into the black glass of the window over the sink, I didn't recognize the wild-eyed reflection that stared back at me. I yanked down the brittle vinyl blind.

In the darkest corner of the kitchen stood a huge metal trash can I didn't remember from my childhood. Lined with a black plastic bag, the bin overflowed with empty two-liter pop bottles. I drew closer with the candle, and the strange urine stench intensified. Shreds of labels: Mountain Dew. Farming was thirsty work, for sure, but would Billy really need—

I picked up a bottle and held it up to the light. A brown residue coated its insides.

I set it down fast and stepped away. Opening the kitchen cupboards, I found cans of paint thinner and bottles of white pills. Everything for cooking meth was just there, for anyone to find. Never the sharpest knife in the drawer, Billy. I flipped the back door's dead bolt, which slid smoothly, and the door swung open without a creak. I shut and relocked it. This was the entry he used.

———

I carried the mug-lantern and shotgun into the living room, laid both on the old coffee table, and crouched to open the woodstove's black cast-iron door. I broke kindling from the dusty pile in the basket and propped small chunks of wood into a pyramid. The flame trembled and caught. I waited to be sure, and then shut the metal door. The room would soon be warm.

Hunger. Mug-lamp in hand, steering clear of the trash bin with its explosive fumes, I rummaged through the cabinets, pulling out old groceries, but all the boxes and sacks had gnawed corners. Mice. And even the contents of cans and mason jars were far too old to eat. I cracked the window to let the fumes escape. A shaft of chilled air slid in.

In the living room, I opened my purse and fished through it, betting on my own stress-induced forgetfulness—and indeed, two foil-wrapped nutrition bars, bent and dented, languished at the bottom. Lemon. Apple crisp. I grabbed them and slid down along the woodstove, which was warm but not yet too hot to touch. I sat on the floor, its solidity a comfort. Under my hand rolled the hills and furrows of the braided rag rug where Charlie had once driven his Matchbox cars.

I tore the wrapper open and devoured the lemon bar, crunching its Rice Krispie texture. The sugar and protein began to calm me. My breathing slowed. My wrists and fingers steadied.

I had shelter, water, heat, food, and a double-barreled sawed-off.

I was okay.

I would be okay.

I kept saying it to myself.

Night

And what if it hadn't been random rednecks who'd slashed my tires and driven off laughing? What if it had been Billy? Or someone else? How motivated were they to scare me? I pulled the shotgun onto my knees.

But as time wore on, the room grew warm and nothing ominous occurred—no thumps on the porch, no human howls from the yard. I began to relax a little. To plan. In the morning, I'd climb the mountain again, call AAA. I'd take the gun. I'd hike back down the hill and wait. Four fresh tires and a decent meal. A shower. I'd meet with Conrad Kniseley and his client, sign whatever papers were necessary, and drive back to the airport.

For now, I'd sleep on the sofa. I looked at its sagging plaid cushions, the scratchy nub of its old upholstery. Sheets and blankets would help.

But the linen cupboard was upstairs, built into the wall of the bathroom. The room I'd seen in a thousand dreams, from which I'd jerked awake a thousand times, sweating, my pulse drumming my throat. The room of nightmares. I pushed slowly to my feet.

Mug-lamp in hand, I climbed the steps, my dread mounting with each familiar creak. On the wooden landing at the top, I paused. The space felt small, the ceiling low. I could see the vague pale shapes of beds in the two dark bedrooms.

The white-painted wooden door to the bathroom was closed. I clasped the cold iron doorknob and turned.

Breath rushed fast and shallow in my mouth.

I stepped inside.

———

When I was a girl, my mother brooked no disagreement. Her word was law, and if she'd been drinking or using, Stella Martin's fury was a formidable thing. It was best to be quiet, to stay watchful, to let her rages pass like bad weather. Only once did I talk back.

We were standing in the kitchen, just the two of us. Charlie was playing under the porch out front. Proud, she'd peeled back the bandage from her new tattoo. *Bull.* I'd been unimpressed, and that had pissed her off. She'd taped it up again and was slamming around the kitchen, her lips a thin line. I sat cross-legged and barefoot on the yellow kitchen table ("like a heathen," as Aunt Della would have said), waiting for my mother to calm down.

Late-afternoon light slanted down on the counters and stove, gilding them with a pale buttery glow. It was Indian summer. Warm. A breeze.

Her movements began to slow and soften. She glanced slyly at me. Smiled. She started talking about Bull's friends.

"Baby," she was saying. Her eyes skittered around the room, latching on nothing. "He just wants you to spend a little time with them. He thinks you'd like them, honey." Her hand went to her hip, her scalp. Her hip again. "Just keep them company for a couple hours while we're out tonight, baby. Be sweet to them. Get to know them. See if you like any of them."

I laughed. Not a pretty laugh. "*Like* them? Momma. They're old. With beards." I looked at my mother, her brittle hair, the small scabs on her forehead. She looked old herself. The boys I liked walked down the halls of the high school, smooth and coppery and perfect in cutoff varsity football jerseys that bared their flat and muscled bellies. Bull's friends were legion and interchangeable and left the seat up and yellow spatters when they stomped up our stairs to pee. "They're gross, Momma. They drink beer."

"Baby," she said. "Just do me this one little favor. You'll be getting Charlie his bath and supper anyhow. Once he's in bed, just set down here and watch TV with them. You know I owe Bull money, and he'd be real happy if you could help me out like this. See if there's one you like. Just talk friendly to him for a while till we get back."

Tears welled hot in the rims of my eyes, and I stared hard at the wall clock to make them subside. Quarter to six.

"One I like?" I wanted to hate her. I wanted disgust to be the only feeling inside me. But she was my momma. My momma who loved me. Who meant well. Thirty-two, with a growing daughter and a little son and bills she couldn't pay and drug debts she couldn't even compute, the columns of numbers slipping and sliding inside her mind each time Bull yelled or grabbed her tight and pulled her up against him and cradled her butt in his hand. Cringing anxiously each time he complained about the way she paid attention to Charlie. I could read her plain as the Greek tragedies in Mrs. Brookover's English class. My voice shook. "Are you seriously telling me that you want a bunch of creepy old guys to come here and hang out with me? With your fourteen-year-old daughter? And for me to *like* one of them? Momma. Is that really what you want?"

She rubbed her cheeks with both hands, her eyes dull and distant. A pleading smile curled her mouth. I thought of the nights Bull would clomp up the stairs with her, and then the grunting and panting, and her mewls. Those evenings he was likely to stay, I'd sneak slugs of Wild Turkey in the kitchen while I washed dishes so I'd fall asleep hard and deep and hear nothing. It didn't always work.

"Baby," she said. "Listen. It would really help us out—"

"Help who? Charlie? Me? I don't think so, Momma." I looked her in the eye, and I said out loud—for the first and last time in my life—the words inside my head. "One whore in the house is enough."

She flared back like a cobra; her eyes had narrowed to slits. Her hand swung out, and I heard the thwack of it like a shock in my bones. My left cheek burned, a glowing coal.

"You got no right! No right, goddammit. I'm still your mother, no matter how grown you think you are."

She'd never hit me before. She'd always maintained she didn't believe in beating children. I stood there, my hand to my hot cheek.

"It's time for you to start pitching in, earn your keep around here. You had it good long enough."

"Good?" I waved my arm around the kitchen: the dirty dishes, the shabby house, our whole embarrassing lives. "You call this good?"

Her voice turned to a hiss. She gripped my arm and shook me. "Who do you think you are? You and your books and your bullshit dreams? You ain't going nowhere, sister. Believe you me. Nowhere. You're gonna stay right here and take care of Charlie and do what I say, and one day you'll end up in some little shithole house of your own with your own damn brats to take care of, and then you'll see."

I jerked my arm out of her grip. Her hand swiped the air beside me, but I was younger, faster, with the edge sobriety gives. I spun and slipped away. Out the back door, I flew down the porch stairs in one leap and across the shred of lawn before she made it to the banging screen.

She flung it open. From the top step, she yelled, "You get back here! Get back in here right now! You got to get Charlie his dinner and bath!"

I pivoted at the edge of the forest. Her figure was bony and vulnerable, her hair like bundled straw against the shadowed house behind her. I hesitated.

"You got to." She shook her bandaged arm in the air. "I don't want to—" She broke off, still crackling with anger. "I don't want to—" The look in her eyes turned helpless. It happened sometimes: she just forgot the words she meant to say, as though a fuse in her mind had blown.

"Of course you don't," I yelled, young and pitiless. "You never do."

She found the words. "I don't want to get it wet. The tattoo." Then her grin was sly again, the grin of triumph. "You want me getting infected? Missing more work? You want him going to bed all dirty and hungry?"

I hated her then, and I hated the hold she had over me. For Charlie, I always went back.

"You do it." The force of my yell bent me forward at the waist. My fists clenched at my hips. "He's your kid. Not mine. You're the one who's stuck. You're the one who's going nowhere."

And I spun and bolted into the trees.

———

Later, because I'd looked so hard at the wall clock to keep from crying, I was able to tell the police that I'd been in the forest for precisely two and a half hours. *Doing what?* they wanted to know. Running. Wiping my tears. Crouching to pee. Drinking from a creek. Slapping mosquitoes. Cursing my mother with the worst cusswords I knew. Eventually calming, distracted by the quiet rustling lives around me. Clucking at squirrels, luring them to the lowest branches, where they'd lean down and argue back. Climbing trees to watch deer graze with their fawns in the dusk.

Once my anger wore down, I wandered back toward home. Night had almost fully fallen. My mother, I was sure, would be asleep on the couch with the TV on, and Charlie would be asleep in bed. Stacks of greasy dishes would teeter in the sink, and I'd wash them. Or Bull and his friends would be talking loud and pitching beer cans at the pile in the corner, and my mom would be running around, giddy and nervous.

As I climbed the back steps, I was singing "Let's All Gather at the River," which I'd learned at my grandmother's church. I felt peaceful. I imagined myself telling my mother I was sorry for sassing her. She'd be in a good mood again, her eyes glazed.

Don't worry about it, sugar, she'd say. *I was out of line.* She'd hug me. *You want a beer, baby?*

But inside, the house was dark. There were no smells of hot cooked food. Everything was silent—no dishes clattering, no TV, no talk or yelling—except for a weird keening sound that froze the skin on the back of my neck, and I ran up the stairs, and there they were.

———

Decades later, having gotten as far away as I could in every possible regard, I knew precisely which horror-show images I'd feared would overwhelm me if I ever returned and opened that door. Which visions would shatter my mind and destroy me forever. Charlie, small and naked in the tub, his eyes rolled back, his lips already blue, small purple marks mottling his shoulders where she'd held him under. A green plastic boat, his favorite bath toy, drifting listlessly on water that had grown ice cold. My mother, crouched on the floor like an animal—and how she turned and saw me, her eyes going in and out of focus, screaming that it was my fault, my fault, all my fault, that it never would have happened if I'd just done what I was told.

But the bathtub simply stood there, white and silent and inert. Just an ordinary old claw-foot tub. No child lay dead inside it. No mother knelt, rocking, ripping out clumps of her hair.

Just a room, a sink. At the window hung our thin old curtains, checkered green and white, limp. Linoleum still curled up in the corner behind the commode. My whole body was tremoring, but it was just a room, a space, an empty place where something happened once.

I set the mug-lantern on the lip of the old sink and opened the linen cupboard. Inside lay only harmless stacks of folded quilts, afghans, blankets, sheets, protected all these years from dust and rot and mice. I lifted all I could, grasped the mug's handle, and made my way back down, feeling for the stairs with my feet.

In the living room, I set the candle on the coffee table and listened. Still no sound from outside. I made up the sofa with the linens. A rust-and-peach quilt, sewn by my grandmother from scraps of corduroy and polyester. Old floral sheets, washed and hung on the line a thousand times, soft and light as moth wings. A mustard-gold afghan Aunt Della had passed down. A fuzzy acrylic blanket with a huge tiger's face that one of my mother's boyfriends had bought her at a truck stop.

Warmth and comfort. Those were the essential things.

I sat down. The shotgun lay within easy reach.

I stared down at the braided rug. I wasn't sure how someone could pull herself back together after something like the loss of Charlie, or if I ever really had. For so long, I'd felt like just a simulacrum of a person, my machine parts clanking.

Over the years, the most dangerous times had always been when I imagined what it might have been like, must have been like, to be Charlie in those last moments. One minute to be playing as usual with the green toy boat—and then a sudden lurching backward, the smack of skull against the hard cast iron, the water in my eyes and nose and mouth, and looking up through clear layers of water to see her, Momma, rippling and refracting, seeing the pain in her face at the same time I'm gasping for breath, desperate and confused, choking on thick wetness, my body convulsing as my mind scrambles to comprehend my momma's face, furious and sad, twisted into a monster's face, a horrific not-Momma with pain scrawled all over her, and fear, like my own gasping fear as I struggle to breathe, to get myself upright again, and fail to understand that what's keeping me pinned is the pressure on my upper arms—and then, I do understand. I grasp it as hard and sudden as she's grasping me, and it's in that moment I go limp like a rabbit in a dog's mouth, letting the water enter me, because it's what she wants, what my mother wants, she wants me destroyed, and so it must be right, and so my obliteration is the right thing, the thing that feels most like love, the thing she wants and that therefore I must also want, the thing I need to want, and so the thing I do, finally, in fact, want. The thing to acquiesce to, to slip away to, my mother's desire the only desire to which I can succumb.

And I do. Even as my body keeps thrashing, a machine wired for survival, my mind closes its eyes and knowingly welcomes the dark, and I am gone, simply gone, extinguished, and it feels final and right and somehow like love.

Yes, those were the most dangerous times.

———

Half in love with death I may have often been, Keats. But I never imagined it easeful.

———

I checked the time on my cell phone: only seven o'clock, the sky already inked black. Sleep was nowhere in sight. My mind still spun. I sighed and glanced around. At home in Chicago, I didn't usually go to bed until midnight. What would I do in the intervening hours?

The woodstove had done its work: the little room was warm. I rummaged in my purse for tea bags and found three: Earl Grey, lemon, and chamomile. I saved the caffeine for the morning and, in the kitchen, rinsed an old pot clean. I heated water on top of the woodstove, then set the chamomile to steep.

As its scent suffused the air, I stood, remembering the box that lay in the trunk of my car. My mother's personal effects. I could get everything over with at once.

Shotgun hanging loose at my side, the way I'd seen her carry it, I opened the door and stepped out. The moon glazed the yard silver. The only sound was an owl's faint hoot.

I crossed the grass, pushed through the forsythia stems, opened the trunk, lifted the box, and pressed the hatch down quietly, then made my way fast back across the yard and up onto the porch and into the house, fear rippling like ice water through my spine. The box was even lighter than I remembered, with things shifting inside. I kicked the door shut behind me, breathing fast, flipped the dead bolt, and wedged a chair under the doorknob.

I set the box on the coffee table and sat down on the sofa. Peeling the tape away and pulling the four cardboard flaps open was the easy part. Inside lay a small museum of her life.

A bracelet braided from bits of colored thread. A stack of white envelopes, addressed and stamped. A bicentennial quarter. A stubby pencil, bitten around the metal binding of its pink eraser. A picture, torn from a magazine, of a hot-air balloon rising at dawn.

I picked up the sheaf of envelopes and shuffled through them. They were all addressed to me at Aunt Della's house, like the letters I'd received in high school, but these were far more recent, each one mailed a few days before my birthday for the last five years. The postmarks: October 2, October 1, October 5, and so on.

RETURN TO SENDER, someone had written firmly across each envelope. *ADDRESS UNKNOWN.* The pencil marks dug into the grain of the paper; I could feel the indentations with my fingertip.

I turned them over. The flaps remained sealed, undisturbed. Other than prison censors, my mother had been the last person to see what lay inside.

I slid a tentative finger beneath the paper edge.

October 2

Dear Bel,
It's been a lot of years since I wrote. I hope you're doing
good, Sister.

It's not so bad in here anymore. I'm used to it. I got
friends now. It's not like I'm on the row. The only thing
I got to be afraid of dying from is boredom. And we got
TV, chores, stuff to do. The food could be better, but hey,
it's free.

I figured you give up on me back when you stopped
coming and for a while I was mad. I blamed you. I did.
But then it wore off. I understood. You had to get on with
your life. I know. Sometimes I even think it was better
that way. Clean break.

Wish I could take it all back. Not just what I done
to our Charlie. I already said that about a thousand
times. But all of it. I should of been a better mom. Gone
out with less guys and definitely drank less and never got
started on them pills. Prison gives you one thing for sure,
Sister, a whole lot of time to think.

I remember when you was a little girl. Just the freest
little wild thing. The light that came out of you. You
shined like sun on a creek.

Just had my own problems, I guess. Needs, the
therapist-woman tells us to call them in group. Own your
needs, she says. Tell us about the ways your needs were
not met. Jesus, I say. Where am I supposed to start. Your
intimate relationships, she says. Your family of origin.
How much time you got, I say.

Needs or not, there's a lot of ways I should of been
a better mother. I see that now. It's about to be your

birthday in a few days and I just wanted you to know that. Happy Birthday!
 Love,
 Stella your mom

October 1

Dear Bel,
Hope you are planning something real good for your birthday this year.
 I hope your life is nice. I think of you out there. If you got a man, I hope he treats you right, with respect. People always say that. Truth, I don't really know what it means. Respect. For a man to treat you with it. Better not cheat on me, hit me, or steal my money is all I can say. Anyway I hope your husband is real nice if you got one and you are happy. Or a woman if you got one of those. What the heck. Times are changing.
 I hope this letter gets through. Last year's one came back. I figured Della must know something about how to get ahold of you. I figured she would do that favor for me.
 She's not the kind of sister I would wish on anyone, I tell you. But I hope she will send this on to you.
 Happy Birthday! Like the girls in here say, you're not getting older, you're getting better. We all know it's horses ■ but we say it anyway.
 Love,
 Stella your mom

October 5

Dear Bel,
Sweet girl, there's so much I want to tell you. Don't worry about me in here. Life inside is okay. It's hard, especially on account of I was always one to like my freedom. But it's okay. You follow the rules, it's not so bad. Some folks are nice and some not so much. But that's true outside, too.

One thing I do miss is real good pizza. They got pizza in here, sure, and they make a big deal about it, Pizza Friday, and it ain't cardboard, but you know how a really good pizza tastes coming right out of the oven? Cheese all stretchy, sauce all hot. Them little pepperonis. I'm making myself hungry here, Sister. Probably not such a good idea to write about food. Just makes you want it more, and no hope of that. Life without, Sister. Life without. True in a lot more ways than one.

But you go on and eat me some pizza, you hear? Go on out to some real good Italian place. Get you a deep dish, none of this thin and crispy garbage. You eat that pizza hot and drink some wine and think of me. Okay? You do that for me?

In a way that's a kind of hope, ain't it. Not for me but for you. Hope that Della will send this letter on, hope that you will read it, hope that you smile and think of some of them pizzas we made back home. Hope you go on and do like I said, and when you're chewing on a real good bite, you think of me and feel me in your heart loving you.

Guess that's asking a lot of a pizza. Ha ha. But in here, seems you pin more on the little things. Like everything gets out of proportion. I don't know how to explain that exactly but I hope you understand.

Dreams, for example. Dreams get real big in here, because they're about the only private entertainment you got. In my dreams, I am young. My body moves easy, not like now. Sun shines on the high grass. I hold ripe strawberries in my hand. Boys look at me. I'm always outdoors, moving.

The opposite of here.

Tell you what I do miss, Sister. The smells. Cut hay. Wood smoke. Just about anything baking, pie or cookies or whatnot. Not that I did much baking myself. I should of.

In prison seems like the only smells are bleach, cement, other women's BO, and bad food. The commodes, but I won't go into it.

Used to be, in the early days, the other girls avoided me on account of what I done to Charlie. Not too many of us in prison, turns out. Most go to the psych ward. But seems like if you're in here long enough, your crime kind of falls away. They just take you for who you are, day to day. I'm an old-timer now. Not a lot of lifers here. Most of my friends are in for drugs or killing men that beat them. They only do a few years.

No one comes to visit me. You were the only one, and nobody since then. Not even Della. She ain't laid eyes on me since the day I done it. Didn't even come to the trial. You'd think some of my old friends from the factory would of come, but I get it. Who wants to spend their day off at a prison?

But sometimes I think it is no lonelier here than I used to get back when you kids was little. Hard to imagine maybe but yes, night after night in that house, day after day, you two was fine but just children, needing stuff, tiring me out, not in a bad way, but sometimes a grown person just wants other grown folks to talk to. Sometimes I think that's what all them men were about. Fun, yes, okay, ha ha, but more just someone to talk to. You know. Company. Someone to hold me and say I was pretty. Which I was. Once upon a time.

It's a hard fact, Daughter, but pretend love feels better than no love at all.

Or maybe that's only if you're weak. Which I guess is also what I was. Bel I'm sorry.

Bel I know I wrote you a lot of letters early on and some of them weren't real nice. And some of them were about Jesus. Well, you can pretty much forget about all of them now because I stopped being mad a long time ago. Also I still believe in the Lord but He ain't the solution to everything, unlike what some say. He's part of the solution but He ain't all of it. You still got to clean up whatever mess you made. Praying will only take you so far.

What I'm trying to say to you Baby is I'm at peace. If you hated me or was ashamed of me it's okay. I love you and I know my love wasn't always the best but you always had it. I messed up bad and I will stay sorry forever I guess but the thing is, a person can go on. You can be sorry forever but still have peace in your heart and go on. Took me a while to get to that but it's the truth. We all make mistakes, Baby. I sure did make mine, and they were maybe the worst a person can do. But still we can love each other and keep on going.

Love,

Stella your mom

October 4

Dear Bel,
Well I don't guess it's real likely that you are going to get this, but it's what our therapist calls a LEAP OF FAITH so I am writing it anyways. Happy Birthday!

I guess a mother can't help thinking about her kids on their birthdays. I always do in January, too, but there's no letter can make it to where Charlie is.

I don't have a lot to say this year. I been depressed. The doctor put me on heart meds and that makes you feel kind of old. I hope you eat your vegetables and go jogging or whatever but definitely get some exercise. Watch your cholesterol. I never knew to do that.

Sometimes out in the yard you can see a hawk go over.

It's okay with me if Della don't send this on. I've come to terms, as the therapist says. In a way it comforts me to think of you, reading this, whether you ever really do or not. I make you up in my head like a character. Which is weird, kind of, because you are real. Kind of interesting, huh.

So anyways happy birthday and many happy returns of the day.

Love,
Your mother Stella

Crying, I drew out the last letter from its envelope. In the quiet darkness, logs crackling in the woodstove, the candle's flame beginning to falter, I read my mother's final words to me.

October 6

Dear Bel,
I am tired, Daughter. Tired all the time now. These
new meds ain't working. Dreams come heavy and stay
long, and getting up in the morning is hard. But happy
birthday and many happy returns.

Bel, I want you to know you was never like me.
Make amends, counselor says, but there's no making
amends for some things. Not from in here. But I can
say some stuff. You always took care of Charlie, from the
beginning, and you was always clear and right in your
mind. Did your schoolwork and so on. Think on it. Who
told me it would be better to put Charlie on the formula
if I couldn't quit with the drinking? That was you. And
who sat there on the couch bottle-feeding him? You, girl.
I couldn't sit still to do it.

I don't know why I did the things I done. Counselor
says forgive myself. She says the way I grew up broke me
into little pieces, getting beat all the time and then what
Pap did, which I never talked about until in here. People
didn't talk about that back then. And then after my sweet
husband died I just was trying to find a way to feel good
with the drugs and the men and whatnot. That's what
she says, anyhow, the counselor. It wasn't right but then
the folks that make up the rules about wrong and right
usually didn't go through such hard times. But it was
wrong what I done to Charlie and wrong what I done to
you. My point is, it was not your doing, no matter what
I might of said when I first got put away and was still
detoxing and whatnot. Counselor says you might blame

*yourself. Don't. Don't, girl. Don't ever. It was not your
fault. None of it.*

*You know I can't even remember that day no more?
It's like a blank space in my mind. And that's a blessing.
You won't hear no complaints from me.*

*Just wanted you to know you're a good girl, Bel, you
always were. I love you and Charlie loved you. Charlie
loved you more than anything. You know that. I kind of
hated that but it was true.*

*And I took that away from you. And I am sorry. And
I will never stop being sorry.*

Love,

Your Momma

When I finished reading, it felt like my mind had broken or sprung
loose and was vibrating like a coil of struck metal in the air. I slid the
folded sheets of notebook paper back into their envelope and sat there,
humming a weird tuneless buzz, tapping it like someone afflicted. There
was a charge in the air like static, and I leaned back on the sofa carefully,
feeling like a fragile, hollow thing. A blown-glass egg. My hands were
restless, agitated, quivering with force. I wanted to smoke. I imagined
myself rummaging through every last drawer in my mother's house,
fumbling, desperate for some desiccated pack of Pall Malls. I craved
the touch of flame that would sizzle the ancient tobacco orange and fill
me with chemical calm.

But send the nicotine everywhere inside me.

And suddenly I was curled on my side, sobbing, loud and
unabashed, the way a small child weeps: sobbing for my lost mother,
my lost Charlie, my broken trust in the world. I wept so hard, it was like
long-blocked channels inside me broke open. Weird currents flooded
my body, racking me. I thought I would die of crying.

Eventually it ebbed, like a storm or a tide, leaving me breathless and eased and hiccupping a little. I lay there, my arms wrapped around my ribs, inhaling and exhaling softly, my sinuses scoured clear. I felt limp and tired and grateful, the way you feel when a long fever breaks. Cleansed.

I sat up slowly as an invalid and looked around the room, exhausted, like I'd washed up on the sand somewhere strange. I gazed at the old familiar objects of my childhood, the shabby furniture, the threadbare rug. Colors were brighter, edges clearer. My eyes felt washed clean. Everything glowed with a strange peace. My hands lay still and open on my legs.

My mind a soft and grateful blank, I sat there for a while, and then from my bag I slowly pulled the little linen sack. I spread the fabric on my lap—the small wooden hoop that held it, the bright smooth floss of mustard and black—and laid the packet of needles on the coffee table next to my small antique sewing scissors with brass handles shaped like a bird.

I began to move the needle. Satin stitches, precise and tiny, filled bare space with smooth swathes of color, linking me back across the generations, across centuries. These tools, the soft cloth in my hands. A hundred years ago. A thousand. Sometimes I think I'd like to learn to weave.

I embroidered for an hour or so, hearing my mother's words echo but lulled by the rhythm of stitch after stitch, the monotony, the reassurance of it, the small physical movements. As I sewed, a strange episode with Jon slipped unbidden to my mind—perhaps the strangest of our marriage. Perhaps the strangest of my life. Though my eyes were focused on the bright floss rhythmically sliding through the fabric, I could see it all unwind like a movie.

We'd been married for only a short while, newly moved into our condo high above the lake, and when the election occurred—our first election together!—we watched the results at home on television, eating take-out Thai, cheerful, complacent with the votes we'd cast that afternoon, confident in the long arc of history that bends toward justice.

But my ease had crumbled to confusion, and then melted into horror, like the face of Munch's shriek sliding downward, and I'd been unable to keep putting food between my lips.

"This can't be right," I kept saying, and Jon kept shaking his head and talking about Nate Silver. At some point, my hands started trembling. "There must be some kind of malfunction," I said, robotically. I stared down in despair at the food growing cold and waxy on my plate.

"Look," Jon finally said, putting his arm around me. "There's no sense in staying up," he said. "Let's get some sleep. We'll see in the morning."

In bed, with my cheek pressed to his warm thudding chest, I told myself that surely mistakes had been made, the votes weren't all in yet, that it was all the product of some horrible computer glitch, that we'd wake up and everything would have been put right.

But when we awoke, reaching immediately for our phones, a nightmare of the absurd had come true. Lying there, curled on my side, scrolling through one headline after another, I began to weep. Silently, helplessly, as if the world were collapsing. I kept my face turned away, hidden, and made myself cry without sound. Would Jon say I was overreacting, hysterical, blowing everything out of proportion? It didn't matter. I could not stop. I lay there, paralyzed, hunching my shoulders away from Jon, my body convulsed with uncontrollable sobs. A rich clown who abused women, despised Latinos, hated the poor? I knew what monsters looked like, and now a monster was in charge.

Jon said nothing. He came around to my side and sat down on the bed. He laid his warm hand on my shoulder, and his tenderness made it somehow worse, as if it loosened something. Limp, frozen, my body shivering with some deep, horrible chill of foreboding, I kept crying, overwhelmed by a kind of existential grief, a premonition of disaster. My arms wouldn't work; my legs wouldn't work. Though in some dim region of my brain, I knew I was supposed to hate Jon's seeing me like that—overwhelmed and helpless, the opposite of the glossy silicone wives of his friends (bright smiles in place, always upbeat, serene as Stepford)—I could not care. My fear of what Jon thought of me was there, as always, but it seemed far away and immaterial, drowned by the grief that flooded me. I kept my eyes shut, not wanting to see what he thought of this Isabel.

I felt his hand slide underneath my shoulder and gently lift me upward from the mattress, easing me into a sitting position.

"I can't," I sobbed.

"Yes, you can."

"No." Snot ran down my lip. I knew I was ugly. I knew mine was the Medusa face, desperate, the one we're not supposed to show.

"Come on." Taking my hand, he stood. "Come on, now." And because he was so calm and certain, I stood up with him, and he led me into the gray marble bathroom, where he turned the shower on, and as the water heated, he gently removed my navy silk pajamas, unbuttoning my top and gently pulling it off, untying the drawstring and letting the pants drop to the floor, holding my hands to steady me as I stepped out of them, still sobbing, lifting one foot out and then the other, like a stunned but obedient horse. Steam clouded the bathroom as he pulled off his boxers. There was nothing sexy about it. He steered me into the stream of heat, standing beside me as hot water drenched us both. He put his arms around me and held me, and I cried onto his wet chest until I had nothing left, until my body was done. He washed my hair, soaped my skin, and rinsed the lather away. He thumbed the tears from my cheeks and held my face in his hands and kissed my eyelids softly. When we both were clean, he turned the water off and pulled a towel from the warming rack and wrapped me in it.

I was able to move by myself then: into my day, into the world.

———

At dinner that night, Jon had said nothing about it—my fragility, my sorrow, the resurrection his tenderness had effected. He didn't ask questions or say anything that might make me feel foolish for having lost control so utterly, didn't laud himself for having picked up my pieces when I'd fallen so helplessly apart. Being thanked or praised didn't seem to occur to him. Neither of us said anything about it.

Looking into my eyes, he placed his hand over mine on the table. He nodded, just once, quite firmly, as if something were settled, and I found myself nodding back.

Then we began to eat, looking out over the dark November lake, talking of ordinary things.

Though nothing was ordinary anymore.

———

Later, I'd wondered about that morning after the election when I woke up and couldn't move: that rupture in the normalcy of our interactions, that strange rip in the fabric of who I tried so hard to be. And how Jon didn't turn away. How, instead, he warmed me back to life.

Perhaps he didn't mind a woman who broke down once in a while, a woman with flaws and needs and weakness. Someone who was a bit of a mess. Inside me, something had started to soften.

But then I thought of the immaculate wedding where we'd met, with everyone so effortlessly lovely and groomed, lithe and accomplished and blithe with fine food and Ivy League educations and international travel, curious about the world and sure it was theirs. That was his milieu, and he thought I was part of it. I thought of Helene, and Jon's two sisters, and everyone they knew. Society swans. I thought of his work in Haiti: the satisfaction of jetting in as the white savior, noble and strong.

I wasn't going to be any man's disaster island, a mess to be rescued. There wouldn't be any such breakdowns in the future, I resolved. Even if I had to fake certain things, I'd meet Jon as an equal—on his turf, perhaps, but on my own terms.

And so I'd steeled myself.

————

For the first time, stitching, I thought of what it must have been like: to live with someone made of steel.

————

Vanessa Bell's design was finished. *A Writer's Diary.* I unsnapped the hoop and smoothed the fabric over my knees. Folding the embroidered fabric in half where the bottom crease would go, I imagined furling the edges under and attaching it to the vintage brass frame I'd already harvested from an old minaudière. The only task left was to find some interesting cloth for the lining. In my bureau at home, I had stacks of old saris, a scarf from Seville, some delicate Thai silk shot through with gold thread—

But then it occurred to me, quietly, unbidden. I stood up and groped through the pockets of my coat, slung over the back of a chair, and found the little shirt I'd stuffed there earlier. Charlie's sweatshirt, a soft gray wad in my hands. On the sofa, I sat and smoothed it out across my lap. When I folded the Bell embroidery around it, it just fit. With the sewing scissors, I clipped gently up the sides of Charlie's shirt, opening it. I laid everything out on my lap, matching edge to edge.

If I washed the shirt gently and stitched the two swatches of material together, meshing the artful, educated, careful creation to the cheap, true fabric of my past, it wouldn't be a purse I could ever give to a fancy curator or collector or socialite. I couldn't imagine someone else's little items jostling inside it: her credit cards, condoms, lipstick, keys. It wouldn't be a thing I could give away, and it wouldn't be a conversation piece for art-world parties, with an exotic reveal when I opened it. Its soft interior would hold secrets I wouldn't want to utter. *The shirt of my brother, the Lazarus shirt, back from the dead, come to tell you all.* No. Its story would remain private. The fabric itself was soft, dull, inconspicuous as a sparrow, its provenance unremarkable—some discount mart in West Virginia, many years ago.

I smoothed the embroidery and sweatshirt together in my lap, stroking them. The candle had melted to a pool of wax, and dark shadows cloaked the room. I'd grown tired.

I put everything in my shoulder bag and lay down, pulling the covers over me. Under the quilts and blankets, my limbs grew pleasantly warm, and my mind began to drift, looping nonsensically from one random thought to another. Virginia Woolf's niece, I'd read recently, was apparently out in the world now, publishing her opinions about various things. What a shining gift: to be connected like that, supported. To have a name that provoked immediate curiosity and respect.

My own legacy had always felt like a dirty thing to hide. To escape, if possible. But maybe it was something I could bear, after all, to carry.

The Ridge

One good thing about sleeping on a narrow old couch is that you don't toss and turn. You get uncomfortable, and you stay that way. You fall asleep deep, and you dream hard:

Inside Mercer & Sons Pharmacy, the cashier was plump and middle-aged, with a brown beehive hairdo and a mouth like pink mud. Her eyes swept over Jon and me as she rang up the pregnancy test, and she smiled with approval, liking what she saw.

I couldn't stop smiling, my heart pounding high in my chest like I'd cry. "Do you have a customer restroom?"

"In a hurry, are you?" She raised an eyebrow, chuckled. "Back of the store, on the left."

We thanked her and turned.

"Good luck to you!" she called down the aisle, and we laughed and called thank you again over our shoulders. Between the painkillers and dental hygiene products, our footsteps gathered speed. At the doorway, we pushed between long vertical strips of translucent rubber and found our way down the dirty corridor to the unwashed bathroom.

I ripped open the box and pulled out the small white wand, fragile as a wishbone, from its wrapper. Jon hugged me tight.

And there, among the mildewed mops, we watched the little lines turn pink.

———

Crows woke me, their caws gnawing the corners of my consciousness until sleep crumbled. I lay there stiff in the gray light of dawn, waiting for nausea, which didn't come. The woodstove had kept the living room warm all night, and eventually I sat up, ate my crunchy little bar, and heated water for the Earl Grey. Went upstairs to the bathroom, splashed icy water on my face, and did my best to brush my teeth with my finger and a bent tube of Colgate that had been sitting in the medicine cabinet for decades.

I stopped in the doorway of our old bedroom, now lit with morning sun. There stood our twin beds with their thin coverlets, my dresser (emptied in minutes, so long ago—"Best get everything you need," the woman in blue had said, "'cause you ain't like to come back"), our little bookcase with storybooks on the highest shelf and Charlie's collection strewn across the lowest: rusted springs, old coins, a little red-handled screwdriver one of Momma's men had given him, smooth brown rocks plucked from the creek bed, and his two treasured Matchbox cars, their paint scraped off to dull gray at the points of impact where his little hands had crashed them together a thousand times. Strange diorama of the past. My gaze brushed softly over the objects. I wanted to pick them up, hold them, move them around.

Above Charlie's things was my own shelf, almost empty. Its only object was a lone bird's nest I'd once brought home from the woods. A delicate, small, round thing.

I crouched down and drew a careful finger over the nest's curved and fragile architecture: gray twigs, pale strands of dry grass, brown pine needles. A home to fly home to.

Even back then, I'd known what I wanted most.

———

I headed downstairs to the warm living room, dreading going out into the cold. I bundled up and pulled on my boots and gloves. In the brisk bright light of day, carrying the shotgun felt like overkill, but I took it anyway.

Outside, icy wind speared me. I rounded the house, fumbled my way across the plowed dirt, entered the forest, and began to hike upward. Birds flitted past: cardinals, sparrows, black-capped chickadees. In the distance, white-tailed deer occasionally flashed, startled into arcing leaps.

It took a good half-hour's steady hike uphill to reach the cabin, and my heart was thudding hard when I set the shotgun down on the fieldstone porch and took out my cell phone. It showed no bars, no service. I groaned. Winded, I grabbed the shotgun and headed higher, toward the ridge, my phone held up in front of me like a dowsing wand.

When three bars blinked suddenly to life, I stopped, set down the shotgun, and took off my gloves.

There were no texts from Jon.

I stared up at the crest of the hill, just a stone's throw higher. Clear blue sky showed through the tops of trees, and I remembered from childhood the view that lay beyond the ridge: the whole next valley of pristine forest, as far as the eye could see, unfurling like a vast and beautiful scroll, ringed by higher peaks. Emerald green in summer, a swirl of gold and russet in fall. Now, in early winter, it would ripple black with tree trunks, waiting for snow. I'd sat many times in treetops on that ridge, eating a jelly sandwich and watching hawks soar, listening to the rustle of leaves. It was a view tourists would drive far for, if they knew about it. If there were roads that could take you there. But it had always been only mine.

I scrolled to the AAA number, and when their operator connected me to the local garage, the guy who answered sounded warm and burly; I pictured him in overalls, with a bushy gray beard, in a cement-floored office that smelled of diesel fuel and Folgers. I felt limp with relief. I told him my predicament and gave careful directions, describing the tricky series of winding numbered rural routes through the mountains.

"Yep. Yep. I'm looking at it on a county map right now. Oh yeah, wait a minute," he said. "I know right where you mean. The old Martin place."

I paused, wondering what he knew. "Yes."

"Used to have an uncle lived down the holler from there. Knew Davy Martin, God rest his soul. Good man. Terrible accident, that was."

I murmured agreement.

"Well, I can get out there with a truck in about forty-five minutes, an hour, no problem."

I thanked him, relieved, and explained that I'd lose phone service when I went back down the hill. That I'd be unreachable.

"No problem," he assured me again. "I know right where you're at." We hung up.

I looked up at the ridge. It would take only a few minutes to see the view one last time. I hiked farther uphill. Brown leaves crunched and rustled under my boots, and all around me stood the tall, thick trunks of red spruce and hemlock. The fast-rising sun pearled the sky with gold light.

When I crested the ridge, the vision hit like a gut punch.

Stretching for a mile or more, the scars of surface mining spread and twisted, the earth scabbed dark gray, as if burned. Where soft peaks had once been, flat plateaus stood bare and blasted, like lopped-off breasts. Coal trucks and yellow heavy machinery rumbled along make-shift gravel roads, and green pickup trucks were hiving back and forth. Runoff ponds glowed orange like blisters. Everything smelled putrid.

A different nausea bent me, and I retched my meager breakfast onto the dirt. Wiping my mouth on my coat sleeve, I stared down, shaking, at the scraped, pitted skin of the land.

I'd known strip mines as a girl—grew up wandering the smooth green hillsides where the tailings, as required by law, had been replaced, and the soil had been seeded with grass. Deep-pit mining I knew about, too, in a vague way, as the dangerous game that killed men: fast, in explosions, like my mother's husband, or slowly, like Uncle Frank, with black lung. Boys from my high school who couldn't get into the military went down into the mines, and sometimes they died there. It was the noble old working-class tradition of bravery, labor, sacrifice, and strikes, of colliers and pit ponies in Britain and *Matewan* here at home.

But this vast, barren landscape—this was new. Mountaintop removal: I'd read the words before, signed a few online petitions. But I'd never seen it in real life, had never thought about it much; it was just one more awful thing I'd escaped. I'd never smelled the acrid chemical stench, never spied ponds as lurid as picked sores. I squinted hard at the largest of signs in the distance: SANCTUARY.

Five hundred thousand dollars. This was what someone—Conrad Kniseley's anonymous concern—wanted to do to my land.

I wanted to talk, I wanted to cry, I needed to tell someone. I scrolled down to Jon's number, but he seemed small and far away, tucked into his safe, good world, his black Audi and his parents' summer villa on Lake Geneva, buffered by his computer screen and layers of receptionists and nurses from the actual pain of his patients, earning his marvelous fees. Even Haiti was only a thing he did sometimes, not his home, not who he was. A hard ache gripped me low in the back and belly, and I grabbed a branch. How could I begin, now—with the gulf of differences that divided us, all the secrets that still lay between us, all the history he didn't know—to tell Jon why the torn land mattered? Lily flashed before my eyes. Her shining gold hair, her smile, her ease on stage.

I pulled out the folded number I'd tucked into my coat pocket. *Anytime, for any reason.* I stood in the growing light, looking down at the number Nic Folio had scrawled in a firm, clear hand, and felt an echo of his little finger against my knuckle. The invitation of his dark eyes. The way he'd caught and steadied me at the edge of my mother's grave.

I shifted from foot to foot. The AAA truck was on its way; I needed no practical help. There was no legitimate reason in the world to call Nic Folio. The practical, justifiable thing any good wife would do would be to turn, make my way back down to the house, and wait.

A line from some old country song ran through my head, and I hummed it. *No view so stark as from the highest ridge / No fire so bright as from a burning bridge—*

I pressed each numeral slowly, held my breath, and lifted the phone to my cheek.

The Descent

When Nic answered, everything poured out: the knifed tires, the inability to call for help, the night in my mother's old house with no power, almost no food. At last I came to the end: standing on a mountaintop, shaken and hungry and alone before the sight of the ruined land, which had undone me.

"Hey there. Hey. All right. Here's the plan." His voice was deep, his tone steady and sure, professional, the very sound of logic. "I'll bring you some hot coffee and assess the threat level. Then I'll drive you back to town safe, and we can get you some breakfast, and you can tell me everything."

"The threat level," I repeated numbly. "How serious does it sound?"

A long pause hung in the air. A hawk soared over, its fanned tail feathers lit red by the sun.

"Look," he said. "Not good. I don't want to scare you, but tell you what, Bel: I wouldn't advise anyone I cared about to stick around the property, that's for sure. Not until this gets settled."

Fear spiked in me again, along with a faint flick of something warmer.

"Oh." My voice was small. Scared, touched. *Anyone I cared about.*

"Okay, now. Don't worry. Just sit tight. I'll be there as soon as I can."

"Okay." I could hear the tremor of gratitude and relief. "I just want to get out of here."

"Can do. No worries. I'll be there in half an hour."

I felt the smallest beginnings of a smile.

We hung up, and I looked down at the phone in my hand: a handsome stranger, coming to get me. Far below sprawled the torn, ruined sweep of the land: the reality of what five hundred thousand dollars in my pocket would actually mean. Strange new choices faced me.

Scylla and Charybdis.

The devil and the deep blue sea.

A cold rain began as I hiked downward fast, my boots slipping as clods of frozen earth crumbled and slid beneath me. I grabbed saplings to slow my descent and poked the shotgun's muzzle into the ground to keep from falling. Rushing down the steep trail, I stumbled, gripping a branch to break my fall, and it snapped back, striking me hard across the cheek. A warm trickle salted my lips.

As I veered past the old stone cabin, my passage spooked a flock of wild turkeys into brief, offended flight. A sudden wrenching pain in my belly stabbed me so hard that I gasped and clutched a tree for balance. I stood there panting, waiting for the pain to pass, and then kept hiking downward. Eventually, the gray roof of our house grew visible through the trees below. Dripping with rain, I came to the edge of the forest and crossed the plowed earth now softening to mud. The strip of grass. Circled to the front of the house.

I stood on the sheltered porch as cold rain pelted the roof. My breaths left soft clouds in the air, which smelled of wet moss and earth and wildness. My belly ached and twisted as I stood there, waiting. All around lay the dark woods. The faint growl of a truck engine reached my ears.

The Land

Nic's truck came green and large and fast up the dirt drive. He pulled to a sharp halt and jumped down from the driver's side, lidded paper cup in hand as he pushed his way through the woody stems of the forsythia. His eyes were dark and warm. He held out the cup, and I wrapped my hands around it.

Oh, welcome heat. Oh, small hot sip. And cream, no sugar. He'd noticed how I took it.

A small smile lifted the corner of my lips. "You got here fast." I was trembling again.

He shrugged and smiled. I stood there in my cheap men's flannel shirt and sodden barn coat, my wet hair threaded with fragments of dead leaves.

"I need a shower," I said.

"You need to get warm." His hand settled softly on my shoulder, and he steered me toward his truck. "Get in. The heat's running." His gaze swept the perimeter of the yard. "I'm going to look around."

He opened the door and gave me his hand as I climbed up into the cab. He leaned across my body and turned up the heat.

"Wait here," he said, and shut the door. He began to walk slowly around the edge of the small yard, looking carefully at everything, peering into the woods, up at the roof.

Heat blasted from the vents. My body relaxed. I sipped the coffee and watched his tall, calm muscled figure as he made his way around the house. His steady pace. He disappeared on the far side.

You got here fast, I thought, my own words echoing strangely in my ears. *You got here fast.*

In a green pickup truck.

———

Another wave of trembling swept through me, part panic, part rage.

I'd never given Nic Folio directions to my mother's land.

The cab of the truck tumbled away, the land, the ground beneath me, shattering into shards and falling, as in a child's cartoon. I swayed a little and then felt suddenly small and very distant, as if I'd drifted up like a soap bubble through the truck's roof and was looking down with calm dismay at the silly, unforgivably foolish woman on the seat below. Those deep, efficient cuts in my rented tires: his strong hands could have made those.

I reached for the glove box: locked. I leaned and groped under his driver's seat, and my hand closed on something long and cool and smooth, something that made my heart wince even before I pulled it out and saw the leather sheath, the horn handle. I sat up, unsnapped the leather fob, and drew out a flat blade of heavy tempered steel. In the gray light, it glowed in my lap.

I remembered the devastated mining landscape, the green pickups moving amidst the construction equipment. The flirting at the diner and bar, the kindness at the burial—

What a fool I'd been. What a lonely, desperate fool. How badly I must have wanted to believe that someone was looking out for me, that someone cared.

———

When Nic pushed his way back through the forsythia bushes, I was crouched by the rear tire of my red rental car.

"What are you doing?"

I looked up at him. I drew his blade from where it had so neatly slid into the rubber gash. A perfect fit. I stood up.

He raised his hands in front of him. "Listen," he said.

My pulse raced, but my feet felt solid on the earth for the first time in days.

"Get off my land." I glanced down at the knife in my hand, ran my thumb along its blade. I watched him watch it.

He took a step forward. "Easy now—"

I laughed suddenly, remembering my mother one summer night long ago, cracking her beer bottle down on the front porch railing and chasing some random boyfriend across the dark yard to his truck, the jagged glass throat of the bottle waving in her fist as she yelled, "You want that fat slut Jenny Green, you just go on and fuck her, then!" and his motor gunning, the tires kicking up rocks as he sped away, lurching down the hill at top speed. My mother tossed her bottle to the grass and laughed with her hands on her hips and her head thrown back. "He wants that fat-ass, he can have her," she whooped. "But he better not come round here no more." She howled like a wolf at the sky.

Now the dead grass was flattened by rain.

I gripped the knife hard. "Just get the fuck off my land."

And Nic must have heard something in my voice, because he backed away. He got into his truck, cursing softly, and wheeled away fast down the hill.

As I stood there, trembling, watching his green truck shrink, it occurred to me that I'd called it *my land.*

Not *my mother's land.* Mine.

Well, well, Isabel, I thought.

And then, between my legs, I felt the hot flood start.

Mercer

Bleeding, I climbed the sagging porch steps, pushed open the door, and went upstairs.

In the bathroom, I slid my jeans down. Blood was everywhere, and tiny thickened clots. I peed. More blood came out, but then it thinned and stopped. I cleaned up as best I could, wadded a clean washcloth into the crotch of my underwear, and pulled up my jeans.

In the mirror, I could see the dark-red line that had bloomed across my cheekbone where the branch had thwacked me. Rain had rinsed the cut.

Downstairs, I gathered up my bag and the box of my mother's things and pulled the front door closed behind me. When the AAA man arrived in his red tow truck, I was still standing there on the porch, shivering. He had a comforting drawl and a face like a ruined potato, and he poured me a Styrofoam cup of hot black coffee from his thermos. I climbed up into the warm cab and waited while he set about his business, hooking and chaining the rental car and winching it up onto the truck bed. The rain stopped, the clouds broke, and the cold white sun climbed higher in the sky. I could feel the thin leakage between my legs.

On the drive back to Mercer, I was unaccountably talkative. I chattered about the night in the house, about the sight of the horrible mine, about my life in Chicago. I rambled about yoga classes and Sophia and my mother-in-law, Helene, and the show I'd have in New York and how deeply weird it felt to get fitted for clothes at Marlowe when I'd grown up wearing clothes from Goodwill. I could not shut up. When I leaned over to pour more coffee, my wrist was shaking hard. Dark liquid splashed onto the seat.

The AAA man glanced over at me. "Don't worry about it," he said. He wiped it with a paper napkin from Arby's. "Shock," he said. "Happens all the time after wrecks."

"This wasn't a wreck," I said.

"True," he said. "But getting your tires cut ain't good."

"No," I agreed. "No, it isn't." I kept talking. I talked about art and my mother and Charlie, and I didn't look over to gauge how he reacted; I just kept talking. I talked about cooking Cuban food, and how I'd learned to pick out the right wines to pair with dinner but still couldn't actually taste the difference between cheap and expensive ones, and how I'd never told Magda my name. I talked at him like he was a hairdresser or therapist or bartender. Out the window, trees fizzed past in a hot green-and-black blur.

When we got to the hotel, I pushed open the passenger door and thanked him, but then I couldn't seem to move. I sat there with one foot on the running board. One hand gripped the handle of my open door, while my other seemed unable to break contact with the upholstery.

The AAA man watched my face. The truck idled. "You sure you're going to be all right, ma'am?"

"Yes," I lied. "Yes, absolutely."

He nodded, paused. "Well, you take care now." Nodded again, sheepdog-like, as if nudging me gently on my way.

I got out, closed the door, and let go.

The tow truck drove off, and I stood in the parking lot for a moment, catching my breath. A coal truck ground past. A woman walked by, pushing a cheap plastic stroller, looking tired already, so early in the day.

I headed toward the hotel.

The Cracked Egg

Upstairs in my room at the Mercer Hotel, I stood before the gilt-framed mirror. My hair hung like dark wet snakes on my shoulders, and a long red welt ran down my cheek. My expensive barn coat, streaked with mud, had a small rip where a branch must have snagged it, and the bone handle of Nic's knife protruded from my pocket. I drew it out and laid it on the doilied dresser beside the bracelet with its pried-open eye. Around my mouth hung a gaunt, vulnerable look. A strangled laugh began in my throat. I took a hot shower.

And then I was on my knees in the tub. Sobbing. Scrubbing blood from my jeans with the little white bar of hotel soap.

———

Clean and warmly dressed, with the mud wiped from my coat, I headed to the Cracked Egg.

Voices dropped when I walked in. People turned and stared openly as I crossed to the row of stools. I sat. The local paper lay on the counter.

LOCAL CHILD KILLER LAID TO REST, shrieked the inch-high headline. Below it squatted a full-color photo of the funeral, with me standing there, shell-shocked in black, among my paler relatives. Great-Uncle

Cloyd leaned crookedly on his wooden walking stick. There were Billy, Aunt Della, Uncle Frank, the preacher, a dozen people I couldn't name—and, off to the side, Nic Folio, waiting. Chris Warner's article blurred into a gray mass.

Tina glanced down, then at me. "Hey, hon," she said. She turned my coffee mug over and poured without asking. "What can I get you?"

I looked up at her, mute.

"The usual?"

I nodded. *Child Killer's Daughter Orders the Usual.* Behind me, conversations slowly resumed.

It wasn't the first time the grotesqueries of my family had made the front page. High school rushed back: ignoring the glances and snickers from students, the pitying looks from teachers as the trial spun out in print, day after day. No wonder I'd blocked out so much, drowning myself instead in my crush on Billy.

I thought of Jon's old-money family and their cult of discretion— Sophia said the truly rich never appear in the newspaper except upon the occasions of their births, weddings, and deaths: anything more was vulgar. What would they all say to this hodgepodge hillbilly scandal?

I folded the newspaper and pulled out my phone, scrolling to the last texts Jon had sent. I closed my eyes and thought of the way his throat smelled of cedar when he held me close against him. Jon at our wedding, standing there steady at the end of the courtroom aisle, waiting, his eyes soft and true. The last time he'd come to an exhibition of my work, his obvious glow of pride, and afterward, at the tiny bistro late at night, celebrating with a bottle of their best champagne, and his hands gathering mine over the table, his lips kissing each of my fingertips. The way he pulled me close. The way his hands sought me, even in sleep, and held me warm against his chest, his hip. The way he murmured *My woman* into my hair.

Lily flashed into my mind—onstage, shining, triumphant in her blue gown—and my chest began to crumple. *That imagination will be the death of you,* I heard my mother warn.

With effort, I shoved the image away. Jon was just a fairy tale I'd told myself, and the Isabel he knew was just a fairy tale, too. I stood up. At the No-Sanctuary table, six people sat, talking and eating and making posters with blue markers. I walked over.

"You're not protesting immigration," I said.

The Black woman looked up, her gaze steady. She didn't smile, but her dark eyes were frank and kind. The other activists kept talking.

"Hey, Bel," she said. "I heard you were in town."

I stared.

"Sondra?" I had not recognized her. My face heated with shame.

Her laughter came, abrupt and warm. "We've both changed," she said. "And hell no, we're not protesting immigration. We're protesting the biggest fucking coal-mining conglomerate in the state. Want to help?"

"I don't know," I said. "I'm just an artist." Of course I hated the mines. Uncle Frank's black lung, my mother's husband dying in an underground explosion, children with cancer, polluted creeks. Climate change. Profiteers. The ruined beauty, the threat to my land. "I've never really done that kind of thing."

"No kidding!" She flashed the old shy smile I suddenly remembered. "Me too. I'm an artist, too."

I felt a soft little pop of surprise.

"You're an artist?"

"I paint." She laughed. "But rest assured. Protesting's not rocket science."

"But you live here? In Mercer?"

She nodded. "About three miles north."

"I mean, you work here? As an artist? You make a living?"

She cocked her head, frowning. "Sure. Why not?"

I saw kitschy mountain scenes, autumn sunsets and sparkling spring mornings, the kind of paintings that would fit well on the walls of Conrad Kniseley's law firm. Acrylic landscapes for sale at a booth at the Buckwheat Festival.

"It just seems—I don't know—hard."

She shrugged. "Life's hard. You make it work." She drank the last of her orange juice. "You want to see my studio?"

I hesitated.

"We've got to do our shift out at the railroad tracks," she said. "Blockade. You want to come?"

I shook my head. I could still feel blood seeping into the pad between my legs, and in my chest, I felt a sad, exhausted sinking, the feeling of pushing away the grief I knew was going to hit as soon as I gave myself the time to feel. I didn't think I could stand outside in the cold all day with strangers.

"Well, if you're here at five o'clock, I'll take you up to the studio. Half an hour, there and back. You can see."

"Yes," I said. "Okay."

She put out her hand.

I shook it, unsurprised by her hand's smooth warm strength.

"Thank you," I said.

———

I went back to my stool. When the food came, I chewed mechanically, my phone on the counter next to me. Jon was up by this hour. He was always up by now. But even when my plate was clean and my cup was empty, no texts had arrived. A psychologically healthy, secure wife would have just called him.

I dialed Della.

"What?" Her voice sour.

"I want to see Billy," I said. "Can you have him come over to your house tonight? Around seven o'clock."

"Ready to talk about that land, are you?"

"Yes, I am."

She harrumphed. "It's about time."

"Yes," I said.

———

The sun was lifting like a cold white coin as I walked alone to the middle of the bridge. Overhead, the sky arched crisp blue, and clouds shone peach and gold. Far below, cold water rushed deep and fast and unrelenting. No people were out on the street.

My gloved hands gripped the railing, and I looked down into the swirling dark. *Outsider artist.* How badly it had always stung. How hard I'd scrambled, trying to get in.

But the truth was that I loved to be outside. Outside houses, outside groups—it was the only place I felt alive. Outside structures of all kinds.

All kinds.

I drew the twisted tissue from my pocket, unwrapped the tiny electronic chip, and flicked it down into the gorge, wondering how far south it would be by dusk.

I closed my eyes, remembering how I'd once envisioned shaking a can of gasoline all over my mother's little white house and tossing in a match. I didn't see that anymore. Now I thought of throwing a bottle of rag and flame through the glass wall of Lark Svenson's gallery, of turning a flamethrower on all the galleries and thick, glossy art magazines full of white voices that thought they got to tell us what good was.

I opened my eyes. There was no family waiting for me anywhere. Overhead, dark mountains loomed. No warm Latino community waited to fold me in its embrace; that hadn't been my fate. I'd always been a bastard, and now I was an orphan. No one would miss me if I disappeared.

When I got back to my room, I pulled the curtains, lay on the bed in the dark, and slept all day.

The Studio

When I woke late in the afternoon and opened the curtains, the eerie sky held only an hour's worth of daylight. I stood staring out the window, clutching the curtains, remembering when Jon had first mentioned Lily.

He'd just flown in from Haiti the night before, and we'd gone out for Sunday brunch at Margeaux Brasserie. He was talking enthusiastically about his week at the clinic: the challenges, the crushing moments, the funny things—and he'd mentioned her name with warmth. "Lovely woman," he said. "An obstetrician, very kind, very competent . . ."

He kept talking, but a thin trickle of anxiety slid through my chest, and my mind latched on to her name and began slowly spinning as images flashed in my mind's eye, a montage, quickening: the two of them discussing a case, heads bent close over his laptop's screen, trying to descry some troubling image, and then laughing together when everything turned out to be all right. Sitting on a rooftop terrace in the night wind with the other doctors, clinking their bottles of Prestige to a good day's work well done, locking eyes for just a moment longer than professional camaraderie would warrant. I wondered what he meant when he'd said *lovely*: if that was an assessment of her character, or her beauty. Or both. I could feel my heart thudding hard. The restaurant felt loud and crowded, the clatter of silverware, of voices that swelled around us. I wondered if Lily was one of the local Haitian doctors or someone from Cuba. Teams came regularly from Havana—but I couldn't ask. *Never show fear. Never show weakness*: Saqlain, instructing me on negotiations. *Never show doubt. Never show your hand.* A waiter wheeled past us, laden with high silver domes. I watched the domes speed away, fixing my eyes on their dwindling shine, trying to keep my smile steady. *Trust him. You can trust him. He's your husband. He chose you, married you—*

"Look," said Jon, his face gone stiff, "if I'm boring you—"

"Oh, no, not at all!" Turning toward him, I reached across the table for his hand, but it lay inert beneath mine. "No, I was listening. Really. I'm listening. Go ahead."

"Never mind."

"Oh, please, Jon—"

He shook his head and pulled his hand away. "You know, not right now." He signaled for the check.

"Jon?" I hated the pleading sound in my voice. My hand drew back across the table, retreating, like a beaten dog shrinking into itself. *But you don't understand,* I wanted to say. *I felt afraid. I was trying not to be scared, not to let it show. Not to seem paranoid—*

"Jon," I tried again, but he shook his head again and wouldn't meet my eyes. When the waiter came, he slipped his card into the leather folder, his face all turned to stone.

———

At five o'clock, when Sondra pulled up in a blue Jeep in front of the Cracked Egg, I climbed in. She steered us north out of town and into the hills.

"So," I said. "Working here in Mercer, as a full-time artist." I scratched my knee, hoping I wouldn't have to pretend to like Sondra's art, but I did want to see her studio. "It just seems—I don't know—difficult."

She shrugged. "It's not so bad." We turned onto a narrow county road that twisted skyward. "It's a pretty good gig, actually," she said, cracking her window. The breeze bit sharp and fresh. "I went to Savannah for art school. Got my MFA and was teaching at a little college. Stayed away for fifteen years. It was a good life. Way more Black folks, for sure. But I missed home. I missed the mountains. My mother. When I got back, I had money, so it was great. Peace and quiet, cheap studio space. Wild, wonderful West Virginia and all that—you know the tourist propaganda. But all the shit that's going on here started getting to me. Politically, I mean. The mines and everything. The toxic dumping, the cancer rates, the worker exploitation. Stuff I tried to forget, or maybe just never knew." She glanced over at me. "Growing up, I had other stuff on my mind."

She made a tight left and began tacking up a steep switchback.

"At first," she went on, "I was just picketing with the environmentalists, but I learned pretty fast that we had to follow the miners' lead, because it's not like they don't care. A lot of them really love the land. They're just trying to make a living, feed their kids. You can make sixty thousand a year here working in the mines, or more, even, and that supports whole families—extended families, I mean. Generations. There aren't many other jobs around here that pay half that much. Hell, not many jobs, period."

Cresting a ridge, she took a right turn onto a steep gravel drive, downshifting to keep the Jeep climbing through dense forest.

"I'm sorry about your mom," she said quietly.

I looked out the window. "Thanks." The pine trees blurred.

Her voice turned normal again, but with a softer sound. "Anyway, the miners don't need condemnation—or more sermons, God help us all. They need real options. And their history of struggle is long and tough. I mean, Blair Mountain. Whatever. You name it. What they need is support for what they're already doing." She glanced at me. "Like this railroad blockade we've got going now. Completely stopped shipments. Right now, it's to force Sanctuary to give the miners the back pay they're owed." She flashed me a smile. "But soon, we'll be blocking everything. Coal needs to stay in the ground."

Near the crest of the mountain, the land flattened and flowed smooth. Strip-mining had long ago left a wide meadow that sloped down from the sheer rock face above us. Halfway across the meadow stood a log cabin, ringed by a sheltering stand of new evergreen trees. Across a pavestone terrace stood a massive old barn, its wood worn silver with age, its west wall flush with the edge of the plateau. Below swept a vast valley, a vista of rolling, forested mountains, still pristine.

Sondra swung the Jeep onto the pavestones, cut the motor, and jumped down, heading for the barn. I followed.

"My pride and joy," she said. "I had it relocated here from my daddy's farm after I got the house built."

Beneath the peak of the barn's roof was a small security camera, its dark eye watching us. Sondra unlocked a heavy padlock and slid open the barn's broad door.

Inside, the entire west wall, which overlooked the valley, had been replaced with glass, floor to ceiling. Great waves of trees unfurled below us, their black trunks gilded peach and gold. The sun was dropping over the hilly black horizon, and its last gold rays poured in, filling the whole vaulted space with a blazing light.

All around us stood dozens of huge paintings, leaning on easels and propped against the walls. We stood inside a vast lit church of art.

Massive Virgin Marys and Pietàs surrounded us. All the canvases were magnificent, huge, glorious in their detail, their immaculate conjuring of Renaissance style. Triptychs on wood were done in the flattened perspectival style of medieval icons and illuminated with shimmering gold. I felt as if I were in one of the grand museums of Europe.

But held in the lap of the nurturing mothers—rather than iterations of Jesus—were female infants, dying women. Girl babies were cradled in their mothers' loving arms. Radiant Madonnas looked down at infants who resembled my own baby pictures. Gold disks circled the heads of baby girls and their adoring mothers. Worshipping angels flanked them, blowing slender horns. Dead women's bodies, not men's, were draped across the laps of their grieving mothers.

Everything was motionless. Everything was luminous. We stood together in the vast lit vault of the barn.

"Oh," I kept saying, looking around, my preconceptions shattering. I wasn't sure whether I was most dazzled by the sunlit studio itself, the broad valley below us, or the heretical paintings and what they promised.

Beside me, Sondra laughed. "Talking's not your strong suit?"

I shook my head.

"Eh, that's okay," she said. "It's overrated."

My gaze roved from painting to painting. There were mothers and daughters whose skin and hair and features matched, and mothers and daughters whose didn't: tawny Marys with dark-skinned babies, fair-haired mothers with daughters the color of me, and all manner of permutation. They were as complicated as Mexican casta paintings. The only constant was the radiant love that welded each pair. They shone.

I glanced around, slowly taking in the smaller details of a working studio: the woodstove, the little fridge, the sink. Drop cloths spattered with paint were splayed across the stone floor. Stained paintbrushes of various sizes stood upright in large jars.

In a corner, large packing crates, huge rolls of brown paper, and sheets of foam stood stacked upright. On top of a large new printer sat a stack of adhesive shipping labels.

"You ship your work," I said. "You're based here, but you have a gallery that represents you."

She cocked her head at me and smiled in a puzzled way. "Sure," she said. "New York."

A milk-white Labrador rose from a bed by the woodstove and padded over. I bent to pet her. "Hello, pup," I said. The dog's dark liquid eyes gazed calmly up at me as I scratched her head. I straightened.

"You use egg tempera for the icons?" I asked.

"Yes, and gold leaf. I use traditional methods when I can."

I nodded. My words came even more slowly than usual. "It's a different kind of restoration."

"A corrective," she agreed. "Putting into the image what should always have been there." She stretched her arms over her head and grasped her elbows, cracking her shoulder blades with a sigh. "Think about it. Since forever, the image of women's devoted care for their sons has been stamped with the imprimatur of God. We've all absorbed these images, have seen them as righteous and good, the natural order of things." She picked up a paintbrush and stroked its bristles into a point. "No wonder men expect that kind of devotion as their birthright. Do women ever see images of love like that for *them*? Not in art, in stories, in movies—even when it does happen, if they're lucky, in the privacy of their homes." She laughed. "It did in mine, which is probably why I've got the nerve to make this kind of art. Thanks, Mom." She laughed and rolled her eyes. "Not that she's thrilled about it."

She moved to the glass wall and stood, staring out, running the bristles of the paintbrush between her fingers.

We heard the crunch of tires on gravel, and then a car door slam.

"Ah." She sighed happily. "It's good to have someone who comes home to you." She nodded toward my left hand. "Guess you know."

I didn't answer. I joined her at the glass wall, and we looked out over the valley together. The sky was lit with an unearthly glow.

"But it's just an old story we inherited. A sad, compelling, beautiful story. But we don't need to keep telling it." She waved toward the paintings, and her dark, triumphant eyes held mine. "That's the power of art, of vision. We can re-create the world anew. We can put ourselves in the center of the frame."

I nodded. "Which is maybe why the art world has so many gatekeepers."

Sondra laughed. "Just so."

She crossed to the fridge and pulled out two cold beers. The dog padded behind her as she returned to me. She held out a beer, but my hand hesitated in the air. History welled inside me.

"Sondra," I said. "I'm sorry."

Her eyes widened.

"I don't know if you remember, back in school—"

"Oh, I do." Silence spun around us.

"What I did was wrong."

She nodded.

"I was taught wrong," I said. "But I knew better. Even then, inside, I knew better." I dropped my eyes. Dried splashes of red and gold spattered the cloth beneath me.

"Correct," she said.

Was it agreement or command? Both, maybe.

I lifted my eyes to hers and nodded. "Yeah," I said. "I really am sorry."

"Good."

We looked at each other. She reached down and scratched the dog's head. When she straightened, she was smiling. She held out the beer again.

I took it, and we each opened our bottles at the same time, the cold, fresh hisses escaping together.

"So come on in the house," she said.

———

With the dog padding beside us, we left and locked the barn. The sky had gotten dark. The only sounds as we crossed the pavestones were our footsteps and the wind.

We mounted the porch steps. The cabin still smelled of new logs. Inside, a fire flickered in the stone fireplace, and we heard the shower running as Sondra toured me briefly around. Everything was warm, cozy, and compact, with books neatly shelved and soft crimson rugs on the wooden floors. The dog curled up in front of the fire and sighed.

A door closed somewhere.

"Hey, babe," called Sondra. "We've got company."

A woman walked barefoot into the kitchen in faded jeans and a white tank top, toweling her blonde hair. When she saw me, her face flushed. "Jesus, Sondra," she said. "You could have told me."

I nearly dropped my beer. She rolled her eyes and turned to me.

"Hey, Bel," she said. "You look like shit."

"Anna?"

She lit the flame under a kettle. "Want some tea?"

"Anna," I repeated, stunned.

Anna shrugged. Her tone was matter-of-fact. "I'm ready for change," she said. "One hundred percent. But Mercer's not." She rubbed the rug with her toes. "I need my job. Tommy and the girls know, but they're the only ones." She glanced up. "And now you."

"I won't say anything. It's none of my business."

"Good," she said. "I've got to be careful. People have gone missing for less. Savannah here"—she jerked a shoulder toward Sondra—"doesn't get it. Out and proud—ha. I've got to get my girls through school. Then I can think about what's next. You want that tea?"

I nodded. "Thanks. So you protest the mines?"

She shook her head and put three mugs on the counter. "I can't. Kniseley would fire me in a hot second. But I'm sick of what Sanctuary's done to Tommy, to our friends." She pulled a green canister down from the cupboard. "I mean, we may not be in love anymore, but I care about him. He's a good man. The mine's been chewing him up for years, and it'll spit him out soon, one way or another." She ripped open three tea bags and put them in our mugs. "The mine owners don't care about us. You know where they live?"

I shook my head.

"*England*, Bel. China. It's just a bunch of billionaires. They can afford to treat this place like a garbage dump." She took the kettle off the flame.

"But you work for—" I broke off. "Your boss represents mining interests."

"He represents a paycheck," she said flatly. "But yeah, I know. Of course I know." She poured water over the tea bags. "Look," she said, "I do what I can." She handed me a mug. "Sometimes," she said, "very important documents just—I don't know—go missing." She shrugged, her eyes gone kitten-wide. Fluttering her lashes, she pitched her voice half an octave higher, the way it had sounded in the office: "I am *so* sorry, Mr. Kniseley. I just don't know what could have happened." She shrugged again, and her voice dropped back to normal. "Only for a little while. Just long enough to delay a hearing."

I laughed—at myself, in disbelief. For someone so tired of being underestimated, I could certainly get other women wrong. I dunked the tea bag up and down in my cup.

"She's our stealth bomber," Sondra said. "Our man on the inside." The dog stretched herself before the flames.

"Do you want to stay for dinner?" asked Anna. "I'm making pasta."

"I'd love to," I said, realizing with surprise that it was true. "But I need to be somewhere."

Aunt Della's

At seven o'clock, Sondra dropped me off. The porch light wasn't on. I climbed the dark steps. I could see them sitting inside.

For a moment, I stood alone and silent on the porch, watching the soft clouds of my breath. All my life, I'd willingly made my heart a shrine to Charlie. Like all the Madonnas and Pietàs I'd ever seen—until today—my psyche had remained a bent lap cradling him, the memories of him, shining or horrifying, alive and dead.

It was time to stand up.

I rang the bell.

Della opened the door. She didn't offer coffee. The four of us sat in the gray living room. Uncle Frank wheezed in the corner next to his oxygen tank. Billy glanced up from the sofa and then stared down between his knees at his dangling hands.

"Look, it's simple." My voice was quiet and didn't shake. "You need to clear your operations off the land, Billy." I looked Della in the eye, though I spoke to her son. "It's illegal, and you're going to get in trouble."

"Ain't nothing illegal about farming on empty land," said Della.

"It's not empty. And he's not farming." I turned to him. "Are you going to tell her?"

Billy looked down at his hands.

"Social security ain't much," Della said. "Billy's farming helps us out."

I ignored her. "You need to get rid of all of it," I said. "Tomorrow. The weed, the meth—"

Della's breath sucked quickly in. "You never told me about no meth."

"Oh, good God," muttered Uncle Frank from the corner.

Billy looked up at Della. "You think all that money comes from weed?"

She turned away.

His voice was sullen. "Anyway, I never used it. Just sold it."

"Oh, good God," said Uncle Frank again.

"That stuff explodes, Della," I said. "Unless you want to raise your grandkids by yourself, you'll make him quit."

I felt for Billy. Despite everything, I did. He was my cousin, my beautiful cousin I'd once dreamed about, my cousin who'd grown up under the poverty line and been held back in school and lived in a trailer and sold moonshine, who'd turned himself around and was raising three kids as a single dad and was sorry.

I stood up.

"I don't want to call the cops on my own kin, but if I ever see any sign of you out there again, I will."

I let myself out.

———

Halfway down the dark hill, I was walking fast when sudden footsteps rushed behind me. Billy materialized at my elbow.

"Bel, wait," he said, his voice low and private.

I glanced around. Few lights were on in the windows of houses. Smoke curled from chimneys. No one was near. I kept walking.

"Look," I said, trying to keep my voice calm, "I know it's hard to make a living, and I'm sorry, but—"

"It's not that," he said. "Listen," he said. "I want—I just want to tell you, Bel. I'm sorry."

"You said that."

"I know. I know." His hand swept through his shaggy hair. "I'm just so sorry, Bel. Tell me what to do. Anything. Tell me what you want."

I stopped and looked at him. "Nothing," I said. I picked at the seam inside the pocket of my barn coat. "Nothing would be enough. Nothing could be." I looked at him. "So that's what I want from you. Nothing."

He flinched.

"Bel, just give me a—"

"You know what I'm sorry about, Billy? I'm sorry I had a crush on you. I'm sorry I got in your car. I'm sorry you couldn't be trusted. I'm sorry we can't go back and fix it."

"Me too. That's what I'm saying—"

"No. Listen. For you, it was a mistake you came to regret. Many years later—when you looked at your daughter, maybe, or heard what she had to put up with when she turned into a teenager. You came to regret it."

He nodded. His eyes looked sincere. "I did. I really did. I do."

"Yes. I believe you, Billy. Okay? I believe you." I stared hard at the tar-paper roof of a house, my eyes wide and still to keep from crying. "But for me, it changed the course of my life. Do you see? That's the difference. It shaped everything I did, what I thought of myself, what I thought I was worth."

Why was I talking with him at all? But I felt exhausted past caring, past trying to protect myself with silence.

"I'm sorry, Bel." He rubbed his jaw. "I'm so, so sorry." He looked at me earnestly. "I was just so crazy about you, Bel. I really liked you. Maybe I was even in love with you. But I knew Ma would kill me." He moved closer. "You were so, so beautiful. You're beautiful now." His gaze roamed over me. "Jesus, Bel, it's like you're still twenty or something."

"Stop it. I'm your cousin."

"Yeah, I know. You were my cousin. We weren't supposed to."

"And I was fourteen."

"I know. I'm sorry. I was so stupid." Billy's voice dropped lower. Grew husky. He took my arm, and the light in his eyes pulsed with long-ago intimacy. "But, Bel," he said, leaning closer. "I thought you wanted it, too."

My stomach twisted with guilt, confusion. That night in his car: we'd kissed. I'd craved his arms around me.

But the way I'd struggled. Cried. How I'd gone limp, like prey.

I jerked my arm from his grasp.

"No, you didn't," I said. "You didn't think that."

The Bridge

My pulse beating hard in my throat, I walked fast down the dark hill from Aunt Della's neighborhood into the main part of town, moving from the cold gray pool of one streetlamp's light to another, my breath steaming in small clouds around me, stars bright like salt in the blue-black sky.

On the bridge, I stopped. Far below rushed the river. The night wind blew cold, and I felt free.

I pulled out my phone and scrolled down to Elaine Carter's number. It was seven thirty on a Sunday evening, but she picked up on the first ring.

"Capston Brothers Real Estate!"

I told her my name.

"Oh, am I ever *thrilled* to hear from you!" Her throaty chortling. In the background, voices and laughter. "Yes, ma'am, Ms. Morales. Just thrilled. Just let me turn this thing off."

China clinked against glassware. A sound of bustling, and then silence.

"So," she said. "Right. Okay. You ready to put that property of yours on the market?"

I stared up at the black heavens. "No," I said.

———

Once upon a time in the mountains I come from, there were incursions of settlers and the expulsion and destruction of the people who were there first, and then there was the discovery of the dark shine that burned, and there was the pillaging of land.

But sometimes those settlers and miners wandered lost into the green ravines, into the woods where the black bears still roamed, and they were not seen or heard from ever again. Probably they became meat, washed down with creek water and berries, and it was the bears who told the story to their young. Or maybe they just decided to become Bear, to grow pelts and nuzzle the hives for honey, to fish for trout with their paws. To live more free than any state motto could tout.

Either way, the wild ones told their own story, and they'll keep telling a story.

Just because you haven't heard it doesn't mean it isn't true.

———

Maybe, in the beautiful future, we'll all relinquish the idea of private property, along with the belief that it's fine to sacrifice the wild green world for profit. Maybe we'll stop judging each other based on how much we have. Maybe one day we'll reinstitute the commons, the land that everyone cares for and shares. The water. The air.

One day in that beautiful future, maybe it will feel right and good and safe to bring a child into the world.

But for now, I'd use the leverage I had. I'd sell my jewelry and, with Elaine Carter's help, I'd buy the plot of land adjoining my own. I'd set up an environmental trust.

I'd fight for it all, as long and as hard as I could.

———

I stood there, gripping the frozen iron rail. Far below, cold water rushed black and shining in the deeper blackness of the gorge. Anna, Nic Folio, the No-Sanctuary crowd: I'd misread so many people.

Maybe it was time to stop reading. Maybe *reading* was even the wrong verb, the wrong approach to life: combing every sign, every act for evidence of what I feared or wanted or desired or despised—scanning for proof to confirm some predetermined theory of how the world worked, running everyone's behavior through my own longing, my own fears, which were often just two sides of the same hard coin.

Maybe I was done with trying to read. Maybe it was time simply to see.

And let myself be seen.

The wild black wind rushed through me.

Take Me Home

When I entered the little foyer of the Mercer Hotel, chilled, shaky, and exhilarated, the woman in the gilt-edged mirror stopped me short. She wore no careful eyeliner, and her lips were pale with cold. The torn coat, the clean but bulky flannel shirt, the wind-tangled hair, the bloody welt across my cheek hardening to a brown crust—Anna was right. I looked like shit.

But lean. Strong. Ready to scrap, eyes wide and dark with helter-skelter recklessness. Like the woman I might have grown into if I'd stayed.

I walked into the lobby. Behind the desk, Tim did a double take.

"Ma'am," he said, "are you all right?"

I couldn't answer. I wasn't sure.

He tilted his head and frowned. "Well, there's some guy waiting for you at the bar. He says he's—"

Anger flashed through me. I turned and strode fast across the lobby, squinting into the red bordello gloom, scanning for Billy, for Nic Folio, for that reporter—

My steps faltered when I saw him. Rumpled chestnut curls. The day's newspaper held open in his familiar hands: the blaring headline, that photo of my family at the funeral—his wedding ring.

Jon was alone in the bar. There were no other customers; the bartender was nowhere to be seen. I walked up behind him, beginning to tremble, the rage flaring up like a brush fire inside me.

"What the fuck," I said.

He swiveled on his stool. "Isabel! I've been so—" His eyes widened, taking in my dishevelment. He laid his newspaper on the bar.

"I threw away your stupid chip," I said. "Your tracking chip. Whatever it's called."

He nodded. "The signal cut out."

"You don't own me, Jon." My voice was low and dark. "You do not get to fucking own me."

"I was worried about you."

"Oh, bullshit." My laugh was bitter. "You put me under surveillance. It's just high-end stalking. It's control."

He gazed at me for a moment, and then nodded. "Fair point," he said. "But it's what I know." He gave a rueful smile. "Control is how the Turners show love."

"Yeah, no shit. Your mother. That prenup." I was visibly shaking now. "But I'm no Turner, and I've been under suspicion since day one."

"Not day one." He shook his head. "No. But once things didn't add up, then okay. Yes."

"Bullshit, Jon. She suspected me the moment I couldn't show my pedigree. And you let her."

"Well . . ." He looked me up and down, looked pointedly around the bar. "As it turns out . . ."

"I don't care. You don't get to put me in a fucking cage."

"A cage? Are you nuts? It was never my intention to—that's—" He bit his lip for a moment, as if deciding whether or not to speak. "That's why I gave you all that jewelry."

"What?"

"Those aren't part of any prenup. They're yours. If you want to leave me, you've got—right now, I think—about three years of living expenses. And every year, there'd be more." He took a swallow of his vodka. "I didn't want you to stay with me because of any kind of financial motives. Ever. That sickens me. And to be fair, I think it sickens you."

I bristled. "Of course it fucking does."

"I know. I knew from the beginning that you weren't with me for money. But the longer we lived together, the more I could guess that you had no cushion. That you worried about your finances. You lived on the income from your art—which, okay, good as you are, can be unstable. I didn't want you to ever be tempted to stay with me just out of need. So yes, sure: I gave you those things because you're beautiful and I love you and they look great on you, but also so you'd have independence." He dropped his eyes. "Should you ever want it."

His vodka looked suddenly delicious. I realized how thirsty I was, how shaky, how exhausted. I wondered if I was still bleeding.

"As for the tracking," he went on, his hands spreading in the air between us, "look. I was scared. You weren't honest with me. You know you weren't. I didn't know what it meant. If you had some kind of secret life. If there was someone else. I just knew you were hiding something." He took another drink, frowning. "You've always been hiding something, Isabel."

I shrugged. I looked at the newspaper.

His eyes fell to it. "Yeah, okay. I get it. You're wrong—you're really wrong"—his eyes met mine—"but I get it. But I didn't know what you were hiding, or what it meant. I just wanted to be able to find you, in case—in case everything wasn't okay."

I stared at him.

"Isabel." His voice grew gentle. "Is everything okay?"

"I do not need rescuing." I raked my hands through my hair. "I am not some fucking pity project."

"Who said anything about rescuing?" he said. "Or pity?" He pinched the bridge of his nose. "I'm sorry. I'm sorry about the chip.

It was wrong." He took a breath. "But it's okay to need help once in a while. Help's not the same as pity. I help people I respect."

I looked at him. My heart was pounding.

The bartender with her Gibson-girl hair came out from the back, smiling. "Do you two need—"

Jon held up a hand and shook his head. "Not right now."

"Yes," I said loudly. "I'll take a scotch." I glared at him. "A double. Neat."

"Okay, sure, hon," she said. "We've got Johnnie Walker, Dewar's—"

"House," I snapped. "The house scotch."

She poured it out fast and retreated.

I tossed back the hot scald of the whiskey. I closed my eyes. It was the first time in weeks that alcohol had crossed my lips. Liquid courage. I stared hard at Jon.

"What about Lily?"

"Lily?"

"Don't fuck with me. Lily. The doctor you conveniently forgot to mention lives in our fucking town. The A-list beauty queen who just adores you."

He frowned. "Lily's a colleague."

Staring at him over the rim, I drank half the glass in a series of swallows.

"A great colleague." He shrugged. "A trusted colleague. And a friend."

I set the glass softly, very softly, on the bar. "I don't have time for this shit." I turned and was halfway across the room by the time he called out.

"Look. Okay."

I turned back, waiting. I felt incandescent, incendiary, as if fury would ignite my very flesh.

"For fuck's sake, Isabel. The one thing I ever did to break with my family, besides marrying you, was going down there to Haiti. I love it.

It's so right. It's the right thing to do." His hands reached out in the air toward me, entreating. "I wanted you to come down there with me. It's a good place. The work we do matters. I asked you to come with me. Fuck, Isabel." His eyes were wounded. "I wanted to show it all to you, to have you be part of it. To see. To see that I'm not just some golden boy, not someone who's owned by his mother and her stupid fucking social-ite friends and her bottomless bank account. I thought you would love it there. Everything's so—immediate. Like you are. Intense. Serious. Serious, but joyful. Like, the stakes of every single fucking thing that happens are so high. Life and death. The way I feel when I'm with you. I wanted to show you. I wanted you to see that I could live like that, that I feel like that inside. But you didn't give a shit."

"So you fucked some doctor."

"I did not." His eyes were angry now. "I didn't fuck her. I didn't kiss her. I didn't flirt with her. I don't see her in Chicago. I don't text her. I'm not an idiot, Isabel. I'm not risking my marriage to you for an affair I don't even want. And believe it or not, she's actually not my type. She was the type I was told all my life to want. But I honestly don't. I don't know why I don't—and to tell you the truth, it would be fucking simpler if I did. I'd have exactly the smooth, boring, socially acceptable life and wife I was always taught to want. I wouldn't have to keep taking this endless shit from my mother."

"What?" I walked over to the bar. Finished the last swallow of scotch. "What endless shit?"

"You think my mother drives you crazy? Well, you should listen to the shit she gives me. That she's given me from day one. You think I don't defend you? I do nothing *but* defend you. She's like a fucking bull-dog on speed. I hate it. You think I *like* running interference between my mother and my wife? I gave her an ultimatum, and she still won't quit. I told her she can't say anything about you if she wants to see me. And she will still not shut the fuck up. These little polite digs all the time. I fucking hate it. That fundraiser? That was her first chance in a month. And even then, she blew it."

This was new. I hadn't known.

"But look. Lily was nice. That's all. Someone friendly. Someone to talk to, who listened, who got it. When you so obviously didn't."

"But you never fucked her," I repeated.

"Are you not hearing me? No, I never fucked her. I never even wanted to, Isabel. Do you not get that? I had two decades to sow wild oats. I'm done with that. I was done the minute I met you."

I squinted at him. He held my gaze.

"Haiti's the first time in my life I've deliberately broken with my family, with their expectations, their chronic measuring of me." Jon took another swig and shook his head. "Isabel, my father was a judge. A *judge*. You think my mother's tough? My father was brutal. *Med school* disappointed him, for Christ's sake. He wanted me to be a senator."

I'd never heard any of this.

"Maybe it's easier for women to do something just out of caring," he said. "Society gets that. The way we're all socialized—it computes, somehow. Whereas men are supposed to keep gunning for the top.

"But I don't want the top, whatever that even means. I want Haiti. I love Haiti. I love the people, the brightness, the warmth, the mango trees, the sea, the way everything there *matters*. It's real. It's bare. It's life and death. You know the way they rebelled and then got fucked over for hundreds of years by basically all of Western civilization and then there was the earthquake and today they have not one damn advantage, but they will not give up? *They won't give up?* My God! It's fucking gorgeous. It's the opposite of what I grew up with, all that constant hollow striving for status and display and one-upmanship that drives everyone I ever knew. Wealth and more wealth—for what? I thought medical school would get me closer to the bone—literally, I guess, but you know what I mean—and instead, it all just became more competition, more status-seeking, more bullshit . . ." He shook his head, drained his glass. He looked into my eyes.

"You know why I followed you at that wedding? Why I followed you across a field and climbed a damn tree?"

I shook my head.

"You were beautiful, yes—but look, beautiful women are legion in my world. Big deal. They've all got great nutrition, personal trainers, and the best plastic surgery money can buy. Great genes, if you like the type. No, that wasn't it."

I braced myself. "What, then?"

"I noticed you because you didn't belong. You didn't belong, and you knew it. I could see it in your eyes as you looked around that place, that mansion. Oh, you looked the part well enough." He laughed a little. "No one was going to call security. But your eyes—you didn't *belong*."

I remembered. I'd felt awkward, anxious.

"Isabel, don't you get it? My whole life, I've felt alone. I didn't understand the values of my family, their friends, the slightly wider world we inhabited. I tried to do my best, but I hated it. *I have always felt alone*. And that's what I saw in you. Some kind of aloneness. A deep aloneness."

My hands reached out to adjust the newspaper where it lay on the bar next to Jon's keys. I smoothed the keys into a neat stack, then fanned them out so that each was equidistant from the other, each pointing to one of the people in the photograph. Great-Uncle Cloyd, Aunt Della, me . . .

"And look, all these other rich people say I'm so great for going to Haiti, but I'm no saint. I've got my limits. I know there are so many problems right in Chicago, guns and violence and poverty, but you know how often I've walked around the South Side?"

I shook my head.

"Exactly never. On my own turf, I'm a coward. A fucking chickenshit, okay? And I know it. I know it. There's no excuse, but it's been ingrained in me so deeply that there are just places you don't go. I heard it thousands of times from my parents, their friends, people at school—'not a good neighborhood.' It's coded in my body, in my brain. I know it's fucked up, but it's in me. To stay away from danger zones, which basically means anywhere poor or not white. To keep safe. I'm just being real, Isabel. I'm just telling you how it is.

"But when I go to Haiti, somehow it's different. Fear drops away. I know I could get shot, or hit by a truck, or knifed for my wallet. I sleep on the floor in a compound guarded by some guy with an AK-47, inside walls topped by broken glass. But weirdly, I'm not scared. I feel *right*. Like I'm doing the most I can for people who need it. Like if I die, it's okay."

He smiled and ran a hand through his hair.

"And at dinner, you know what? No one talks about how the damn goat was made, or where the wine came from. We drink water, and we feel lucky to have it. We're exhausted and sweaty and satisfied, and yet it's all wrenching because we couldn't do more that day. There were patients we failed. We fail every single day. There's no self-congratulation. There's no jockeying for position. You feel free."

I nodded, pulling a bar napkin from a stack. I spindled it with my fingers, twisting the ends tight.

"It feels *real*. It feels *right*. None of these bullshit values that mean nothing, the garbage I grew up with. It's close to the bone. Like you, Isabel. The first time I saw you, the hour we spent up that tree—I felt a toughness in you, a goodness."

"A goodness?" My broken laugh. I bent the twisted bar napkin in half, pinching the middle, and arced its wings. A small white bird in flight. I laid it on the corner of the newspaper photograph.

"A kind of goodness that felt real. That felt earned. I felt it from the minute I saw you. A goodness that didn't come from being kept protected and safe. That came from—" He glanced down at the newspaper. His voice dropped and saddened. "From the opposite." He looked back into my eyes. "And I wanted to be with you. Immediately. I sensed it, and I wanted to be with you. I still do."

He signaled the bartender, and she came over.

"Another round, please," he said. "And some water."

She poured and set the glasses down without banter. I nodded my thanks. Jon took a drink of his vodka.

"So that's what Haiti is to me. Why I wanted you to come so much. I wanted you to see Haiti, but what I really wanted, I guess, to be honest, was for you to see that I have that toughness in me, too. That I have goodness. That I can do without all the luxuries. I wanted you to see that. To witness it, to be there with me. To see me that way." He looked away. "But you wanted nothing to do with it all. You didn't even want to hear about it."

I made a soft, explosive sound of protest.

"No, admit it. Things went cold between us. Because you went cold."

I shook my head. "No—"

"Yes, you did. You withdrew. I didn't get it. I didn't know what was going on. I invited you into part of my life, this part I thought you would really get, and you didn't care."

My voice was low. "It's not that I didn't care." I gestured toward the newspaper. "But you get it now. Don't you?"

"I think I might."

I took a drink. Then took another. "I was posing, Jon. Posing, passing—whatever you want to call it. I've been posing for a really long time. I didn't want to get down there and have you see how familiar poverty is to me. I've been covering my tracks my whole life, Jon. I didn't want to get too close to the kinds of situations you kept telling me about. And children . . ." My eyes filled. I drank again. "Children dying. I didn't want to fall apart."

He nodded. "I see that. I do see that." His eyes dropped. "I'm sorry."

"It's okay," I said. "I get it now, too. I get why you wanted me to come."

He took my hands and looked at me. I felt a softening, a melting. We smiled tentatively at each other.

But a sad tension was gathering inside me. My heart thumped slow and hard in my throat. I withdrew my hands, drained the last of the scotch, and set the wet empty glass down on the center of the funeral photograph. Its thick base warped my dark hair, my black dress.

"I can't have a baby," I said.

Puzzlement winged across his brow.

"I mean I won't have a baby." I felt a clogging behind the delicate hyoid bone at the clutch of my throat. "I mean I don't want a baby. I don't want one. Not now. But maybe not ever." I nodded toward the newspaper. "Not because I'm scared I'd be a bad mother, that I'd be dangerous like my mom was. That used to be the reason. But it's not anymore." I cleared my throat. "The reason is . . ." Tears sprang hot. "The reason is I just don't want one."

"Isabel." His smile was soft, his voice gentle, his eyes confused.

"Not that I don't want one." I shook my head. "I mean, I'm not making sense. To be honest, I'd love a family." It was the first time I'd said it, even to myself. A strange hot sadness was rising inside me. "I'd love a baby to hold. I'd love to raise a child with you." I gripped his hand. "But, Jon, it feels wrong. It feels dishonest, it feels irresponsible. It feels like the world is breaking. It feels like the world is winding down, falling apart, like the world needs our help, not another person who's just going to overconsume resources, the way we do, and who's going to suffer when the world gets too hot . . ." A kind of anguish swelled in me. "I mean, how can you love a baby and help it grow up and love it more than anything but then see it have to face—"

He was watching me carefully.

I closed my eyes and spoke. "I was pregnant, Jon."

His hand convulsed around mine.

"I was pregnant," I repeated. "And I lost the pregnancy. Just—just recently. Here." I choked on a sob. "And I'm just so full—"

"Oh, baby."

"So full of grief." Another sob came, but I kept my eyes shut and kept talking. "For this baby we're not having. For the babies I don't want—but that I would want, if the world were okay. But it's not. And I don't. And I'm sorry." Hot tears were streaming down. "I know you want one. I know it's a deal breaker. But I don't. Even though I do, I don't. I can't. And I'm sorry."

I had said it. I opened my eyes.

"Isabel," he said. With his free hand, he stroked hair back from my face. "A baby is not a deal breaker for me."

It was my turn to feel confused.

"You're right about a lot of things, my clever wife. But not that." He gathered both my hands in his, leaned forward, and kissed my forehead. "Not that. I just thought you wanted children." He shrugged. "The women I dated always did. Having kids is another box to check, another thing we're supposed to do to prove something. I would have done it if it mattered to you, and I just assumed it did." He shook his head and laughed softly. "I just—every woman I ever met made a point of how important it was to her to start a family. I guess I just believed you felt that way deep down. I thought you were just worried because you were getting close to forty. I thought I was being encouraging." He smiled. "I mean, I'm not anti-kid or anything. A family would be nice. A family with you would be very nice. If you wanted one. But it's not essential." He squeezed my hands and pulled me slightly, incrementally toward him. "This, this right here, is what's essential."

My eyes closed for a moment. A soft swoon of dark and wordless relief rushed through me, softening my knees. Breath filled my lungs and eased my belly.

"This right here," he repeated. He kissed my forehead again. "I'm sorry about the loss, baby. I'm so sorry." He stroked my cheek.

"But there's more," I said, my eyes still shut. "I belong here. On my land. In my forest." In the darkness behind my eyelids, I saw a sudden vision of my little white house refurbished, made clean and warm and colorful, and the mountain cabin transformed into a studio I could hike to. I saw myself standing on railroad tracks, arms locked with other people, blocking a shipment of coal. "This is who I am." I opened my eyes. "Maybe not all the time. But some."

"Baby," he said slowly. He nodded and ran a hand through his hair again. "Baby, that's not a problem. We can figure that out." He smiled, a little shy. "I'd like to see your forest."

I smiled, too. "It's a pretty great forest."

He pulled me just a little bit closer. His hands were warm around mine, his grip light but steady.

"But no more tracking," I murmured. "Ever. That's just fucked up."

He nodded. "Okay," he said. "Then no more secrets."

I drew away again. "But you could put a chip in my wallet, a tracer on my phone . . . I know it sounds trite, but honestly, how can I ever really trust you again? How can I ever be sure?"

He looked at me askance. "Couldn't I say the same thing?"

I pulled farther back. We stared at each other. Détente.

He hadn't let go of my hands. "Maybe the only real way to find out if we can trust each other," he said, "is just to trust each other."

I stood there. The strange logic of his words sank slowly in.

"But we would need to start over," I said. "From scratch. New rules. Rules we make up as we go." My vision clouded. "Or maybe—"

At the far end of the bar, the bartender reached up and tugged the chain of the ceiling fan. Its blades began to spin, stirring the air in a soft swirl around us. A dizziness came over me, and I closed my eyes. I thought I heard the beating of wings. Time shuddered and slowed.

I opened my eyes. "Or maybe no rules," I said. "No rules at all. No assumptions, no roles, no expectations. Nothing. Just—just being together. Every moment, new. Just seeing what happens."

Jon was studying my face. He nodded and pulled me toward him. I let myself move close, my hips between his knees.

He pressed his face into the hollow of my collarbone, into my tangled hair. When he spoke, his voice was low, almost inaudible.

"Just don't leave," he said. He lifted his naked face and looked at me. "Don't leave me, Isabel. There's no one like you," he said. "Not for me."

I stood there. I looked at him, into him, into his eyes, into the wide dark pupils at their centers, into that open black shine that tunneled inside him. Our chests were rising and falling with breath at the same time.

"Stay," he said. "Stay with me. Fight with me, yell at me, tell me the truth. But stay."

I felt it again. That Red-Sea feeling, that vertigo free fall like fate.

"There's more," I said. "There's more we could do. Together."

He nodded, his eyes bright and soft. "Yes," he said. "Sure." He probably wasn't thinking of flamethrowers, but that was okay. There was time.

I took a deep breath and nodded just once, firmly, as if something were settled.

In the bar, the air returned to normal. Time started to tick in its regular way.

The bartender called, "You two need anything else?"

Jon shook his head. "We're fine," he said. She swept over, laid down the check, and whisked away. He turned to me and rose from the barstool to pull out his wallet. His smile was tired but real. "I'm actually kind of starving."

My hands tightened softly on his.

"I know a place," I said.

We headed out in the cold and quiet night together, our fingers laced. The dark wind rushed around us.

The legacy from my mother is eighteen things, and the last is the capacity to look at life fresh, to not give up.

To tell the truth about our fuckups and our wounds.

To let it hurt.

To change, to let go, to start over—the willingness to *keep* starting over, for as long as we have and as long as it takes.

We stepped onto the icy bridge. Sliding, slipping, we began to laugh, and we clutched each other's arms in the dark. Below us rushed the black shine of the river. In the distance, we could see the restaurant's bright glow.

GRATITUDE

While Isabel feels all alone in the world, *Flight Risk* and I have been very blessed.

To my beloved friend Dr. Kim Coleman, for taking me to Pierre Payen, and to all the patients, doctors, and nurses I met there, especially Roland Poustin and Dr. Jean-Gardy Marius. Thank you for letting me learn from you.

To all the kind staff at the American Academy in Berlin, especially Carol Scherer and Berit Ebert, for welcoming me and making me feel at home when my husband won the Berlin Prize, and to Academy Fellow Azade Seyhan, for the gifts of your warm company and the use of the Walter Benjamin Study, a stunningly beautiful place in which to finish this book.

To the University of Nebraska, where I teach, for all the incredible and inspiring people with whom I get to work in the Institute for Ethnic Studies and the Department of English and for the faculty development leaves that gave me time to write and think.

To Lorraine López, Rhonda Garelick, Lynne Barrett, Timothy Schaffert, and Jennine Capó Crucet, writers and readers extraordinaire, for making this a better book. I'm blessed with the most amazing friends and colleagues.

To my agent Steven Salpeter, for your kind encouragement, persistent vision, and hard work on *Flight Risk*'s behalf; to Ruben Quesada, for including the opening of *Flight Risk* in *[PANK]*'s 2020 Latinx Lit Celebration, and to my editors Jodi Warshaw and Jenna Free, for loving and strengthening this book.

To my dear friends Jeannette Eileen Jones and Alex Vazansky, Julia Keown and Simon Wood, and Emily Hammerl and Roland Végső, for years of talk and wine and dinners. May there be many more.

To my closest friend and most patient reader, Emily Levine: you have both seen through me and seen me through.

To my former foster daughter, Amara, brave and kind and beautiful.

To James, who believed in Isabel from the beginning. Without your steadfast love, support, and faith, none of my books would exist.

To my son, Grey, great gift of my life.

To my brother, Tony, for surviving our childhood with me to become a wonderful man, and to our mother. Peace. Grace.

To Marco: my present that showed up, my partner in crime, the first and final reader of this manuscript. No words suffice.

ABOUT THE AUTHOR

Photo © Shae Sackman

Joy Castro is the award-winning author of the post-Katrina New Orleans literary thrillers *Hell or High Water*, which received the Nebraska Book Award, and *Nearer Home*; the story collection *How Winter Began*; the memoir *The Truth Book*; and the essay collection *Island of Bones*, which received the International Latino Book Award. She is also the editor of the anthology *Family Trouble* and served as the guest judge of *CRAFT*'s first Creative Nonfiction Award. Her work has appeared in the *New York Times Magazine*, *Senses of Cinema*, *Salon*, *Ploughshares*, *Gulf Coast*, *Brevity*, *Afro-Hispanic Review*, and elsewhere. A former writer-in-residence at Vanderbilt University, she is currently the Willa Cather Professor of English and Ethnic Studies at the University of Nebraska-Lincoln.